DECEPTIONS

DECEPTIONS

· A CAINSVILLE NOVEL ·

KELLEY
ARMSTRONG

DUTTON
· est. 1852 ·

DUTTON
— est. 1852 —

An imprint of Penguin Random House LLC
375 Hudson Street
New York, New York 10014

LIBRARY OF CONGRESS CATALOGING-IN-PUBLICATION DATA

Armstrong, Kelley.
Deceptions : a Cainsville novel / Kelley Armstrong.
pages ; cm
ISBN 978-0-525-95306-7 (hardcover)—ISBN 978-0-698-19112-9 (ebook)
I. Title.
PS3551.R4678D43 2015
813'.54—dc23
2015017802

Printed in the United States of America
1 3 5 7 9 10 8 6 4 2

Set in Sabon LT Std

FOR JEFF

DECEPTIONS

CHAPTER ONE

I woke to my ex-fiancé calling. Which was awkward, considering we'd broken up only two months ago and I was in another guy's apartment. Even more awkward when that guy wasn't the one I was currently dating. In my defense, I was on the couch.

My first thought was not *Answer the damned phone, Olivia.* It was of a letter from my father, read right before I went to sleep, which had not been conducive to good dreams and had left me in no mood to talk to James Morgan. I reached for my phone and hit Ignore. A moment later, a shadow loomed over me.

Gabriel picked up my phone. "James. He left a message. I should take it."

"Um, my cell? My ex?"

"Your stalker, too."

I looked up. Gabriel is at least six-four and knows how to use his size to his advantage. Hence the looming.

When I nodded, he listened to the message as I tried very hard to push aside thoughts of James and the roller-coaster ride that began when I found out my real parents were convicted serial killers. The ride had ultimately landed me here, sleeping in the apartment of one of Chicago's most notorious defense attorneys. My lawyer. My boss. And, though I'd never dare say it in front of him, my friend.

Gabriel Walsh doesn't have friends. He has resources: people who can be exploited and used. I'd like to think I'm an exception, but I don't push my luck.

"James heard about last night," Gabriel said after listening to the message.

"The car crash?"

"Yes, but I believe he's more concerned about the crazed killer who caused the crash and held you at gunpoint."

"Oh, that."

"A minor point, but it seems to bother him."

"Unreasonably so."

"Agreed. Coffee?"

I rose and started for the kitchen. "I'll make it. You were in that accident, too, and hurt a lot worse than me. You should be resting."

He moved into my path and waved me back. That wasn't him playing congenial host; it was him telling me to stay the hell out of his kitchen. I suspected last night was the first time he'd brought anyone up here. His apartment. His private domain.

"If you'd rather I didn't stay—" I began.

"I invited you."

"After sustaining a head injury. Which means you aren't responsible for anything you said last night . . . except for the part where you forgave me for wrecking your car."

"You were run off the road."

"I still feel bad. It was a nice car." I paused. "I'm also sorry about almost getting you killed."

"She says, as an afterthought."

"It was a really nice car."

He shook his head and went into the kitchen. I followed as far as the doorway.

"You'll need to let James know you're all right," Gabriel said. "I would suggest a text message. Tell him—"

"I can write my own texts."

"Yes, but this must be handled with care. While I'd prefer you didn't engage him at all, if you don't tell him you're fine, he has an excuse to keep hounding you. Yet if you give any indication you're opening the door to conversation, he has *reason* to keep hounding you."

I had to agree. Gabriel dictated a message. I did tweak his wording—Gabriel's language choices can be very precise, and James couldn't suspect the text had come from him. He seemed to think Gabriel had a Svengali sway over me. Which showed that my former fiancé didn't know me nearly as well as I'd thought he did.

Message sent, we settled in with our coffee, chairs pulled to the living room window, where we could look out over Gabriel's breathtaking view of the city.

"I had a call this morning," he said. "Edgar Chandler wishes to speak to you."

"Chandler?"

"Yes. Elderly gentleman. Currently incarcerated. Formerly involved in CIA experiments. Seems to have unlocked the secret of mind control. Which he used in an attempt to kill us."

"I know who Chandler is."

"It seemed as if a refresher might be required, given the sheer number of people who have tried to kill us lately."

"True. So he'll finally speak to us?"

"Chandler has no interest in me. The invitation is for you. May I presume you'll accept?"

"May I presume you'll come with me?"

His brows shot up. "Of course. Whether he wants me there or not."

Gabriel arranged to see Chandler that afternoon. A half hour later we were in the elevator, taking the fifty-five-story ride down to the underground parking garage.

"So what else are we doing today?" I asked as we exited the elevator. "The only thing on my schedule is working at the diner. Which I'm not." I wasn't sure if I ever could again. I'd told Larry I was unwell—between the accident and the fever that preceded it—and needed some time off, and he'd given me two weeks.

"I require a vehicle," Gabriel said. "Since that is your area of expertise, I'm taking you along to select one. After that, we'll pick up a rental car. Then we'll drop your car back here and—"

"Skip the play-by-play and hit the highlights, please."

"Today will be devoted primarily to cleaning up the mess from yesterday. We need . . ."

An almost imperceptible tightening of his shoulders told me something had caught his attention. Gabriel has an uncanny sense for trouble, which may be because his gene pool, like mine, contains a sprinkling of fairy dust.

"What's up?" I whispered.

He scanned the row of parked cars. "Do you have your gun?"

"Always."

He put his fingers against my back and propelled me forward.

"Any warnings?" he murmured.

"Portents of impending doom?" I said. "Not a one, but honestly? I'm discombobulated enough this morning that I could trip over five dead birds and not notice."

"We're both out of sorts. Which reminds me that I need to stop by the doctor and pick up a prescription for pain—"

When he wheeled, I didn't jump. Nor was I surprised to see a man two paces behind us. Gabriel admitting he needed pain meds had conveyed a warning as clearly as if he'd shouted it.

The man didn't look like the sort who'd be stalking us in an empty parking garage: early forties, decent suit, gray-salted beard. A reporter? I'd had to deal with plenty lately.

"May I help you?" Gabriel rumbled, his deep voice dropping another octave.

"Gabriel Walsh?"

"Yes."

The man held out a thick envelope. "You've been served. This is—"

Gabriel grabbed the guy by the wrist, wrenching his arm up. The guy yelped, but didn't drop the envelope . . . or the semi-automatic pistol he'd tried to conceal in his other hand.

"Give Mr. Walsh your gun," I said.

The man stared in confusion at the gun in my own hand.

"Give it to him now."

He opened his fingers and dropped his pistol. Gabriel grabbed for it with his free hand. Then he stopped sharply. "Oliv—!"

The gun clattered to the pavement. And cold steel pressed into the back of my neck.

"You don't want to do that," Gabriel said, his pale blue eyes fixed on my captor.

A man's chuckle sounded behind me. "I don't believe you're in any position to make that demand, Mr. Walsh."

"Then you are mistaken. Hurt her, and you will regret it."

"Regret it? That's all? I expected 'I'll hunt you down and kill you' at the very least."

"Death is quick. Regret is not."

The gun pressed harder into my neck, as if the man was lean-ing forward. "Clever, Mr. Walsh. I'm sure Ms. Jones is very impressed. Her knight in tarnished armor. Impressionable young women must find that very hard to resist."

"They may," Gabriel said. "Unfortunately, we don't have any here at the moment, so you'll have to trust the threat is for your benefit alone."

"Chivalry *and* flattery. Are your knees weak yet, Ms. Jones? Oh, and do put away the gun. Please."

I hesitated, then lowered it into my bag.

"Now remove your hand *from* your purse, Ms. Jones."

I did.

The man continued, "I'd like to believe modern young women wouldn't fall for Mr. Walsh's act, but the very fact you are with him proves otherwise. We'll have to chat about that later. For now, you'll come with me, Ms. Jones, while Mr. Walsh releases my confederate and then stays where he is until we are out of sight. If he follows, you will pay the price. Understood, Mr. Walsh?"

My assailant dug the gun barrel in hard enough to make me wince. Gabriel punted the other man's gun under the cars and then released him with a shove. My assailant took hold of my arm. When he lowered the gun, I stabbed him in the side, having palmed the switchblade from my purse. He fell back, and I grabbed for his gun arm. I missed. Gabriel didn't.

Gabriel wrenched the man's arm up. His partner crawled after his lost weapon, but when I told him to stop, he saw the gun back in my hand and decided to listen.

Gabriel threw my attacker to the ground. It was another guy in a suit. Bald. Thirties. He immediately started rising, one hand clutched to the knife wound. Gabriel calmly punched him in the side of the head. The guy dropped, unconscious, to the pavement.

"There's blood on your shirt," I said.

Gabriel glanced down and sighed.

"You can put it on my bill," I said.

He shook his head and walked over to the first man, who had started inching toward his gun again. I'd noticed, but at the rate he was moving, he'd be lucky to make it there by lunch. Gabriel grabbed the guy from under the car, flipped him on his back, and put one Ferragamo loafer on his chest.

"I've decided to speak to you instead of your partner," Gabriel said. "Tell me now if I've made the wrong choice."

The man wriggled, as if testing how tightly he was pinned. When Gabriel leaned forward, he gasped and lay still.

"I'll presume that means I did not," Gabriel said. "Prove me wrong, and I'll break every rib in your chest. Is that understood?"

The guy looked offended. Coming after us with guns was fine, but God forbid we should fight back.

"Olivia, could you please keep an eye on the elevator and the entrance lane? It's after rush hour so we're unlikely to be interrupted, but it would be inconvenient."

"Got it."

I moved past the unconscious man and the growing pool of blood at his side. I wondered if I should do something about that, but he seemed to be breathing comfortably.

I took up position about fifteen feet from Gabriel, where I could see anyone driving into the garage or coming off the elevator.

"Who hired you?" he asked our captive.

No answer. Then a gasp, as Gabriel presumably applied pressure—literally.

"We were hired to speak to Ms. Jones," the man said after Gabriel let up a little. "By someone who is extremely concerned about her welfare. She's in a very precarious place right now and—"

"James," Gabriel said, the name a growl.

The man continued, "As my associate said, it's obvious you've positioned yourself as her protector. She's vulnerable and alone. You provided a shoulder to lean on and, in doing so, you've influenced her perception of reality to the point where she can no longer see the truth. It's our job to counter that influence."

"James Morgan hired cult deprogrammers?" It's hard to surprise Gabriel, but his voice rose with incredulity.

"We don't like to use that word. But when undue influence is exerted over the vulnerable, intervention may be required to help the victim see the situation clearly."

"So I'm exerting undue influence. For what purpose?"

"Money, obviously. That's what you always want, isn't it, Walsh?"

"If you are implying that I'm charging Olivia for my time, her account is closed. She did hire me to help investigate the deaths of two of her parents' alleged victims. But we completed that inquiry successfully. In fact, *I'm* paying Olivia now, as a research assistant and investigator."

"My associate said you were clever, Mr. Walsh, and he's correct. Yes, you're paying her . . . to deflect suspicion and to maintain an excuse for ongoing contact, while you continue to pursue the real prize."

"Which would be?"

"A five-million-dollar trust fund. Which comes due when she turns twenty-five. A few months from now."

Gabriel grunted.

After at least five seconds of silence, the man said, "You aren't even going to deny it?"

"To whom? You're hired help. I don't need to convince you of anything. The very thought that anyone—however skilled a manipulator—could persuade Olivia to part with her fortune is ridiculous."

"I offered to pay for the shirt," I called. "But not the car. The car wasn't my fault, and it's insured."

"See?" Gabriel said. "I would also point out that, given how handily she disarmed your colleague, you might be mistaken about her vulnerability. I will forgive you for that, based on your very short acquaintance with her. James Morgan has no such excuse. Beyond the fact that he's an idiot."

The man was silent.

"I have noticed," Gabriel said, "that despite your unwillingness to name him as your client, you haven't denied that he is."

"According to the contract, I cannot identify the man who hired us. There is no provision against acknowledging it, though. He's very concerned about his fiancée—"

"I'm not his fiancée," I called.

"The engagement ended two months ago," Gabriel said.

"Which does not keep him from being concerned."

"Get proof," I called.

"Of his concern?" the man said.

"Of his involvement," Gabriel said. "Prove to me that James Morgan is indeed your client and I will release you."

The man warned Gabriel that he was reaching for his phone. He passed it over. Gabriel read the screen and then waved me over to have a look.

It was an e-mail exchange with James. A little cloak-and-dagger in the wording, but the intent was clear. These men were to take me, by force, and persuade me that Gabriel Walsh was a very, very bad man. I forwarded it to both of us.

Gabriel took his foot off the man's chest. We retrieved the gun from under the car. Or, I should say, I retrieved it. Gabriel wouldn't fit, which I deemed a poor excuse. We left the so-called deprogrammer tending to his partner's wounds.

CHAPTER TWO

Gabriel didn't say a word on the walk back to the elevator, on the ride up, or even once we got through his door. I shot the bolt. At the click, he turned, as if startled, and then nodded.

He changed his shirt, walked to the window and stood there, fingers drumming against his leg. Then he came my way so fast I stepped aside. He unlocked the door and walked out.

He was in the elevator by the time I caught up. The doors were about a hand's breadth from shutting before he stopped them and leaned out.

"You need to come with me," he said.

"I'm trying to."

We returned to the parking garage. Our attackers were gone. Gabriel walked to his space and stood staring at my VW.

"Um, yeah," I said. "Your car was totaled, remember? That's why you need me. Unless you plan to take a cab."

He grunted. Letting someone else drive was a relinquishing of control he couldn't abide with anyone except me and his aunt Rose.

"May I have your keys?" he asked.

"I'm going with you."

"Of course you are. I'm not leaving you alone after that. But I'd like to drive."

I passed them over. We got into my vehicle—an older-model Jetta that I could justify borrowing from my dad's garage, even if it wasn't quite up to my standards for speed and handling.

Gabriel peeled out of the garage. Or he attempted to. It's a diesel, and when he hit the gas, he got a whine from the engine instead of a growl.

"Sorry," I said. "If we were closer to the north end, we could swing by my parents' place and pick up the Maserati."

"If I thought you'd *keep* the Maserati, I would agree to the detour. You insist on depriving yourself—"

He clipped off the rant so hard I wouldn't have been surprised if he had nipped his tongue.

I checked my phone. I had a good-morning text from my boy-friend, Ricky, who was in Miami on business. That business . . . well, I didn't know and didn't ask.

I'd met Ricky through Gabriel, whose main clients are the Satan's Saints. It's a biker gang—sorry, motorcycle club. Ricky's dad runs it, and Ricky is a member. He's also an MBA student at the University of Chicago, not as an escape from the life, but so he'll be better prepared to take over when his father retires. I'd called Ricky last night to give him a heads-up on the accident.

I texted him back and when I looked up, we were in the city core.

"Where are we going?" I said.

"To see James."

"You're going to confront him at his office?" I struggled to keep my tone even.

"Yes."

"That is . . ." I lost the battle and twisted to face him. "Are you out of your mind?"

"No."

"I'm serious."

"So am I."

"I know you're upset—"

"Upset does not begin to cover it." Each word was razor-edged.

"He insulted you," I said. "I get that."

"I could not care less about an insult." His ice-blue eyes swung my way. "This is about sending men to kidnap you at gunpoint."

"If you confront him in public—"

"This requires more than a tersely worded e-mail or an angry phone call, Olivia. If I don't confront him publicly, he will skew the story to paint me as the aggressor. I made that mistake once. I won't do it again."

Last week, Gabriel had confronted James at his house after James had sent me a private investigator's dossier on every illegal and unethical thing Gabriel had ever been accused of doing. Gabriel had taken that dossier and systematically sorted it into "truth, lies, and damn lies." He didn't care; neither did I. What set Gabriel off was the call James made afterward, to inform him that the dossier was only the first strike, and he wouldn't stop harassing me until I came back to him. Gabriel had briefly ended up in jail charged with assault after James's mother had called the cops.

We stopped for a red light. When I looked up, I saw a bird sitting on the signal box.

"Gabriel?"

"Hmm."

"What kind of bird do you see there?" I pointed.

"A robin."

"I see a magpie."

He didn't say there shouldn't be magpies in Chicago. We both knew that, just as we knew there wasn't really one sitting on that box.

"One for sorrow," I said. "That means you're making a mistake."

"Are you sure?"

"If you're implying that I'd make up an omen—"

"I'm saying I don't agree it has anything to do with me visiting James. You've had a hellish twenty-four hours. First you find out that Cainsville is populated by fae. Then you have visions and a fever. Quickly followed by Macy Shaw trying to kill us. An hour ago, you had a gun put to your head." He waved at the bird. "One for sorrow."

He knew that wasn't how it worked. Omens aren't retroactive. Yet he drove through the intersection and refused to spare me even a sidelong glance. He'd made up his mind, and no mere omen would stop him.

Of all the problems that came with the revelation about my notorious birth parents, the most bothersome was the media attention. I'd been a delicious story in a slow news week. And I continued to entertain. *Oh, look, she dumped James Morgan. Oh, look, she's hanging around with Gabriel Walsh. No, wait, she's dating a biker.* I was the Lindsay Lohan of the debutante set.

In the lobby of James's office building, I felt the stares and I heard the whispers. His employees had known me before the media firestorm. To them, I wasn't just the daughter of two convicted killers—I was the stone bitch who'd cut the heart from a really nice guy.

When we got on the elevator and Gabriel said, "Which floor?" I hesitated. He turned to the young man beside him and said, "James Morgan's office?"

The guy pressed the button.

The elevator cleared out before the top floor. As I watched the last numbers pass, I turned to Gabriel.

"Can I handle this?" I asked. "Having you speak for me isn't going to help."

After a moment's thought, Gabriel nodded. Then the elevator doors opened and we stepped off.

CHAPTER THREE

While the top floor is reserved for his company's executives, James likes to maintain a non-corporate feel, with open areas where people can congregate. That's where we found him, standing at the espresso machine, laughing at something one of his employees had said.

When I saw him, I felt as if I'd woken from a nightmare. The encounter with the deprogrammers was so ludicrous it couldn't be anything but a figment of my overworked imagination. *This* was the James I knew, making coffee for himself and those gathered around him. Down-to-earth, easygoing, always helpful and considerate.

When James noticed me, he smiled, eyes crinkling as he turned toward me, as if thinking, *Huh, that deprogramming stuff works fast.* Then he spotted Gabriel, and I saw exactly what Gabriel must—something twisted and ugly simmering behind James's eyes. No, not "something." Obsession.

"I take it Palmer didn't tell you he screwed up," I said.

"Palmer?" James looked from Gabriel to me. "I have no idea what this is about, but we should talk in my office."

"Sorry," I said. "But if we do this in private, this time it might be me who ends up in a jail cell on charges of trespassing and assault. You may know Palmer by another name, but that seems to be the one he used in his e-mail exchange with you." I stepped toward him. "I really don't appreciate being held at gunpoint."

"Gunpoint? Is this about last night? If you think I had anything to do with that—"

"I mean this morning. Yep, it happened again, and this time you had everything to do with it. Palmer confirmed you're his client, James." I took out my phone. "Let me forward you the e-mail where you discussed terms with him in case you've lost it."

"E-mail . . . ? I'm *completely* lost here, Olivia, but if you have an e-mail that appears to come from me, someone has set up a dummy account."

"It's your personal address."

"Then it's been hacked or spoofed. Yes, send it to me, and I'll have my technicians prove that."

"I'm sure they will," Gabriel murmured behind me.

"Is anyone talking to you?" James snapped, and when he did, several employees who'd been wandering off looked over. This didn't sound like their boss; it sounded like a peevish little boy.

"Whatever this is, Walsh," James said, "it's none of your business."

"Anytime you hire someone to put a gun to Olivia's head and kidnap her, I'll make that my business."

James turned to me. "Why the hell would I hire someone to kidnap you?"

"Because, apparently, I'm being brainwashed by . . ." I jerked my thumb toward Gabriel.

"Well, that's the first sensible thing you've said since you got here. I wouldn't call it brainwashing, but it's clearly something, and obviously someone else is as concerned as I am about it."

"And hacked your e-mail to hire people to 'deprogram' me? Who would do that?"

James paused, mental wheels turning. Then he looked straight at Gabriel. "Only one person."

"Yes," Gabriel said dryly. "I hired men to waylay us in my parking garage."

"I'm sure you'd use whatever scenario would allow you to play the white knight."

"Actually, Olivia extricated *herself* from the situation. But your choice of wording is interesting, given that the men who attacked us used a similar phrase."

"We know what you did, James," I said. "We have proof. Back off. Now."

"Or else?" James said.

"I think we're civilized enough to avoid threats."

"But if you'd like one . . ." Gabriel said, his voice a purring rumble. "I'd be happy to oblige."

James stepped in front of Gabriel. When he saw he had to look up, he inched back, seemed to realize that looked bad, too, and stood his ground.

"I have no intention of abandoning Olivia," James said. "So tell me—tell *everyone* here—what you plan to do about that."

"Change your mind."

Gabriel's voice was low, almost soft, but the look in his eyes was bone-chilling. James took another step back and caught himself again.

"You *will* leave her alone," Gabriel said. "One way or another."

"That sounds like a death threat, Walsh."

"Then you lack imagination."

With that, it was time to walk away. I headed for the elevator. Gabriel followed.

I took the driver's seat this time. Gabriel relinquished the keys without a word.

"I'm going to get a restraining order," I said as we drove away. "Yes, having worked in a women's shelter, I know they aren't worth the paper they're written on, but I need to establish a record of harassment."

When he said nothing for two blocks, I asked, "You don't think I should?"

"I agree that a record is wise. I'm just not certain I can help you obtain one."

"No problem. I'll do it myself."

"I don't mean . . ." He cleared his throat. "No matter how you obtain it, your connection with me will . . . I've used restraining orders in the past to establish a record of harassment against a client. Except in those cases . . ."

"Your clients weren't actually being harassed."

"I'll fix this, Olivia."

"It's not really your problem to fix," I said softly.

"Actually, it is. I'm the one who . . . made that deal with him."

"To protect me and get us back together again." Gabriel had accepted money from James, to look after me and help me reconcile with him.

"It wasn't—" Silence. Then, "Whatever my intentions, it's clear that he interpreted our arrangement to mean reconciliation was a strong possibility. You said it was over, and I muddied the waters. I miscalculated."

Two words. Simple enough. *I miscalculated.* But they weren't simple at all. They were an admission of fallibility, and that didn't come easy for Gabriel.

"I'll fix this," he said. "I promise."

As we drove to the dealership, Gabriel got a call. It was Pamela Larsen, my birth mother, phoning from prison. He told me it was her, but he didn't answer.

My relationship with Pamela was strained. When I'd discovered I could see omens, I'd remembered her teaching me all those superstitious ditties as a child. So I'd gone to her for answers. She'd brushed it off as nonsense passed along by a young and foolish mother trying to entertain her baby. I'd refused to see her until she agreed to talk.

She was trying to reach me through Gabriel because he was her lawyer. She'd hired him a few years ago to win her an appeal. He'd failed to do so. As much as she hated him—and hated me having any association with him—she hadn't hesitated to hire him back for her latest appeal. Begging him to be allowed to see me would be difficult for her. I regretted that it had come to that. Yet I didn't regret it enough to visit. If she wasn't going to give me answers, I'd try Todd. Which was turning out to be a lot more complicated—logistically and emotionally—than I could have imagined.

Todd Larsen was a convicted serial killer. A monster. My memories of him should surely be equally monstrous. Except the ones I'd dredged up were bright and warm. By all accounts, I'd adored my father, and he'd adored me. When I'd been unable to get in to see him—we still weren't sure why—he'd sent that letter, and it was everything I could have wanted . . . and everything I didn't want.

I'd had a dad. Arthur Jones. An amazing father I lost to a heart attack a year ago. And now I had Todd, who, from that letter, had been just as good a father. I was struggling to reconcile that. I'd have to face him. I would, when I got the chance. I just hoped I could handle it.

CHAPTER FOUR

A t the car dealership, Gabriel set me loose and said, "Find me something." I tried to get his opinion, but he was having none of that. I don't know if he was too distracted or he honestly didn't give a damn, but he seemed serious, so I had fun.

The new Jag I chose wasn't that different from his old one. The style suited him, and I was loath to change that. I started rhyming off options.

"I usually just pick one from the lot," Gabriel said.

"That's your first mistake."

The salesman cleared his throat. "I can offer a discount on the lot models. We'll be starting the new year soon."

"How much of a discount?"

"I can't say exactly, but if you come inside, we can negotiate—"

"Ballpark it for me," I said.

"Maybe a thousand dollars."

"Not worth it."

Gabriel's lips twitched in amusement. "Whatever she says."

I listed the options I wanted and then said, "Black, inside and out. He'll need it by next week."

"That's not poss—"

"I've picked common options and colors. You'll find one on a lot somewhere. Have it here next week, and in the meantime . . ." I waved at their stock. "He'll borrow one of those."

"We can arrange a loaner, but first we need to settle financing."

"It's a cash sale," Gabriel said.

Despite the cool June morning, the guy began visibly sweating. I'll blame it on the fact that a big guy in a suit wanted to pay cash for a new Jag, suggesting . . . well, it suggested he might not really be a lawyer.

"I know your previous car is a write-off," the salesman said. "But it will take time to get the insurance money."

"It's a cash sale regardless." Gabriel lowered his shades, fixing the man with a cool stare. "Is that a problem?"

"N-no. Of course not. Come inside, and we'll do the paper-work."

The dealership visit lifted Gabriel's mood immensely. I think my handling of the situation amused him. While I'd been following in the career footsteps of my philanthropist mother, I really was Daddy's girl. My father had turned the family business—the Mills & Jones department store—back into the Chicago landmark it'd been in the fifties, and he hadn't done that by letting salespeople tell him he couldn't get stock in until next month.

We had an hour before our appointment with Chandler, so Gabriel decided to swing by the office. It's a Garfield Park greystone, a beautiful building but not exactly the prestigious address you'd expect from a guy who pays cash for a six-figure car. It is relatively close to the Cook County jail. Given Gabriel's clientele, that may be the main attraction.

We parked my car and his rental Jag in the narrow lane between buildings. I was telling him a story as we walked inside.

"My poor mother was on the verge of cardiac arrest," I said. "Here we are, at this thousand-dollar-a-plate dinner, and Dad's wrangling exclusive rights for a line of designer handbags from another guest at our table. He doesn't see the problem because, to him, if you're going to shell out that kind of money, you'd damned well better get the chance to schmooze someone who can give you exclusive rights to his handbag line."

"I would agree," Gabriel said, opening the office door for me.

"So my dad says . . ."

I trailed off as I saw three people in the reception area. One was expected—Lydia, Gabriel's executive assistant, a trim woman in her late sixties who looked as if she had a yoga mat and green-goo health shake behind her desk and could throw a would-be mugger over her shoulder.

In front of her stood an elderly couple. Handsome and well-dressed, but not overly so. They looked like retired professors—perfectly pleasant people. Except they weren't any of that. Not professors. Not elderly. Not particularly pleasant. Not people, either.

Ida and Walter Clark were Tylwyth Teg. Welsh fae. Fairies, though they didn't like that word. With others of their kind, they'd founded Cainsville centuries ago and interbred with select humans. That's how a population survives when the "other" outnumber them. Not everyone in Cainsville had fae blood, but enough did for Tylwyth Teg to work their compulsions and charms and keep us from asking questions. Now I knew better, which is why I'd left Cainsville—and the resident fae—behind.

Lydia rose from her desk. "I was just telling the Clarks here that you weren't expected at the office today, Mr. Walsh. I presume you're just stopping by?"

"I am, but I suspect I'm not the one they came to see."

"Actually, we would like to speak to you as well as Olivia," Ida said. "We won't keep you long."

Gabriel visibly struggled to refuse. It shouldn't have been difficult, all things considered, but we both had fae blood and that inbred compulsion demanded we listen to them.

He glanced at me. I nodded, and he turned to Lydia. "Olivia didn't get her mocha this morning. Could I impose on you . . . ?"

"I'll go grab one." She stood. "When I return, though, there's a case we need to discuss before you leave for your appointment." Which was her way of putting the Clarks on notice that this meeting would indeed be short.

As soon as the door closed behind Lydia, Walter said, "We understand that you're upset, Olivia."

"Mmm, I'm not sure *upset* is the right word." I perched on Lydia's desk. "I mean, I completely understand why you wouldn't tell me what you were. What do you say? 'Hello, I'm a fairy.' Sorry, *fae*, right?"

"Actually, we prefer Tylwyth Teg," Ida said. "You *are* upset."

"No, *upset* is what I'd get from learning that people I trusted aren't what they seem to be. *Pissed off* is what I get when my life is in danger, on account of said people not telling me what the hell is going on. Cainsville welcomes me with open arms and I think, 'Huh, that's really nice,' only to discover the town is run by supernatural beings. The reason they're being so nice to me? Well, I haven't quite figured that all out yet, but I know I sure as hell can't trust any explanation you give, so I'll keep digging. I know my family is connected to Cainsville, on Pamela's side. I know you two had something to do with getting me adopted by the Taylor-Joneses and making me disappear from the system— and from my birth parents. I know that's all somehow connected to my parents' alleged crimes. And I know that, apparently, I'm very, very special."

"You *are* special, Olivia," Ida said.

"I don't want to be. It is, as Gabriel would say, highly inconvenient. I've got you trying to woo me, and the Wild Hunt—sorry, the Cŵn Annwn—trying to woo me, and it's like I'm the top NFL draft pick when I didn't even realize I knew how to play football. I'm being waylaid everywhere—"

"That's the Cŵn Annwn, not us."

"No?" I looked around Gabriel's lobby. "Huh. This certainly feels like waylaying."

Ida stepped toward me. "Olivia, I can assure you that we have your best interests in mind. The Cŵn Annwn do not. Stay away from us if you must, but stay away from them, too."

"And end your association with the Gallagher boy," Walter added.

"Ricky? Seriously? After everything, you still need to bitch about me dating a biker?"

"It's not—" Walter began, but Ida shushed him with a look.

Gabriel cut in. "I believe I know Ricky well enough to vouch for him, but if you have some insight that I don't, anything that would suggest he'd harm Olivia . . ."

With obvious reluctance, Ida said, "Not intentionally. We simply don't think it's wise for her to associate with a known criminal—"

"Ricky Gallagher is not a criminal. He has never even been arrested. He's an MBA student and a member of a motorcycle club. Neither is a crime. Now, if you'll excuse us, Olivia and I have work to do."

Once Lydia returned, we headed off to Cook County for our visit. Edgar Chandler had been a psychologist working on MKULTRA, the CIA's brainwashing experiments in the sixties. MKULTRA was a flop. Yet Chandler had continued working in the pharmaceutical field. With help of the fantastical kind, he'd attained one of MKULTRA's goals: discovering a way to turn innocent people into unwitting assassins.

We couldn't tell the authorities that he'd killed using mind control because, well, rational people don't believe in mind control. Or omens. Or fae. The state attorney's office had settled on charging him with accessory to murder.

"So why didn't Chandler get bail?" I asked as we walked from the parking lot to the prison. "I'm certainly not complaining. It just seems odd, given his age and spotless record. Is it set too high?"

"Edgar Chandler could put up a million-dollar bond as easily as I paid for that car. But he hasn't."

"Which means what?"

"That he's not in any rush to get out."

CHAPTER FIVE

handler looked every month of his eighty-five years. I wouldn't have said I was sorry to see it. Not only had he ordered the deaths of Jan Gunderson and Peter Evans, but he'd used his mind-control drugs to murder Jan's father and a friend of Peter's as a test of his new toy. Two innocent people had died and two equally innocent people were now charged with their murders.

Chandler tottered into the visitors' area on a cane. Not because the weight of his crimes had finally become too much to bear, but because he hadn't recovered from being shot in the leg by Gabriel last month.

When a guard strode over to help him, Chandler peered at him.

"I don't know you," he said to the man.

"Name's Ransom. I was here last week when you talked to your lawyer."

"No you weren't. I've never seen you before."

Ransom rolled his eyes and took Chandler by the arm to help him into his seat.

Chandler shook the man off. "I don't know you."

"Someone's a little paranoid," I whispered to Gabriel.

Chandler turned to us. "Mr. Walsh. I don't believe you were

invited to this tête-à-tête. If Eden feels threatened, I can assure you both I'm quite harmless here."

"Gabriel stays," I said. "So you've decided to speak to me?"

"I have."

"That means you want something from me. Let's get that out of the way first."

"I called you here because I believe we can benefit one another. This was never about hurting you, Eden."

I leaned forward, elbows on the table. "You forget I heard you give Mrs. Evans the order. *Kill the girl.*" He'd brainwashed Peter Evans's wife after having their housekeeper kill Evans.

"Then you misinterpreted, which can happen when you eavesdrop, Olivia."

Reverting to my preferred name suggested he was anxious to show his sincerity, but . . . well, I had the feeling it took someone a lot scarier than me—or even Gabriel—to make Edgar Chandler anxious.

"I offered to protect you from any fallout after Evans's death and to help you better understand your situation," he said. "I tried to work with you."

That wasn't quite how I remembered it, but I said only, "You also warned me about the hounds. You said they'd come to Cainsville and, when they did, I'd regret turning you in. Well, they've showed up there. Hell, they've showed up in a lot of places. But I'm not quite getting the 'regret' part."

"Again, you misunderstood me. I never warned you *against* the hounds. I can promise they're no threat to you."

Bingo. I knew who had Chandler scared shitless.

"The Huntsmen showed you how to perfect your mind control, didn't they?"

"Huntsmen?" He tried for an air of bewilderment.

"Cŵn Annwn," I said. "I think I'm finally pronouncing that right. Welsh. So many letters. So few vowels."

"I realize recent events have been confusing, Eden, but I have no idea what you're talking about."

"No? Huh." I looked at Gabriel. "Is it warm in here?"

"Cool, actually."

"Then why is Edgar breaking into a sweat?"

"It's a fever," Chandler said. "I've been unwell. I'm also under a great deal of strain. You've heard about Anderson's death?"

"We have," Gabriel said. Chandler's former bodyguard had apparently OD'd on morphine in the hospital a couple of weeks earlier. "I presume he was murdered. While you would be the obvious suspect—and mind control the obvious weapon—the fact you contacted us says you are not responsible and, more-over, you fear you're next." He motioned toward the guard. "Hence your paranoia."

Silence dragged on for so long that the guard started walking over, expecting Chandler to declare the visit at an end.

"I need to make amends," Chandler said finally.

"To us?" I said. "Oh, that's sweet."

Chandler looked confused.

I glanced at Gabriel. "Not to us."

"To the Huntsmen, I take it," Gabriel said. "You've outlived your usefulness, and you could be a threat."

"There's someone I need to . . . have removed."

Gabriel's brows shot up. "I provide many services, Mr. Chandler, but that one is outside my area of expertise."

"No, I don't think it is."

"Then you think wrong." A chill crept into Gabriel's voice.

"All right. If not you, then Olivia here. She has the background for it."

"Um, no. I—"

"I'll tell you everything. About the hounds. The Huntsmen. My association with them. Your parents' association with them." An anxious smile as I reacted. "That one intrigues you, doesn't it? I can answer every question you have, for the small price of 'removing' a man who, as you will discover, richly deserves it."

"The name?" Gabriel said.

Chandler turned to him.

"I will require a name."

A genuine smile spread across Chandler's face. "How quickly your ethics change, boy. A word of advice: don't feign outrage next time. It really doesn't suit you."

"The name?"

"Jon Childs."

Gabriel nodded as if making a mental note. Chandler eased back in his chair, chortling to himself, and I realized he wasn't a sociopath at all. That would imply an inability to recognize ethical boundaries. This was a man who recognized such lines and delighted in pulling others over them, because it proved they were no better than him.

I knew Gabriel didn't have any intention of killing Jon Childs. There were a dozen reasons why, starting with the fact that he's not an assassin and ending with the fact that he'd never play one for a guy like Chandler. But with the target's name, we could track the man down and see why Chandler wanted him dead.

I let Chandler enjoy his amoral victory for about ten seconds. Then I leaned across the table. "People who do what you're asking expect a down payment. I want an answer up front."

"Nothing about your parents. I'm not that stupid."

"What exactly did you do to piss off the Cŵn Annwn?"

"I'm in here. They are not impressed."

"Maybe. But you're not a serious threat. You can't unmask

them. That's like Scooby-Doo pulling off Mr. Wikles's face and revealing a monster underneath. No one would believe you. There's more to it. You seriously pissed them off. How?"

When Chandler didn't answer, Gabriel said, "By targeting *you*, Olivia. The Cŵn Annwn are courting you. They certainly don't want you dead. Which explains Mr. Chandler's eagerness to insist he was, in fact, not targeting you at all."

Chandler's hand flexed against the table.

"But there's more," I said. "The whole scheme to keep me from uncovering the truth about Pete's and Jan's deaths. Killing Will Evans and Josh Gray. That was personal, wasn't it? Unsanctioned by the Cŵn Annwn."

"An unsanctioned use of their tool," Gabriel said. "The mind control. You were using it for your own purposes, which is not permitted."

Chandler glowered at us. "Why ask a question if you're going to answer it yourselves?"

"Because it's more fun that way," I said. "All we need is for you to confirm it."

"I'm not going to—"

"Your reaction already did. Not only did you use their drug without authorization, but you attempted to use it against me. No wonder they're pissed."

"We are indeed." The guard—Ransom—had appeared at Chandler's back.

When Chandler tried to scramble up, Ransom put a hand on his shoulder. It seemed a gentle touch, but Chandler's face convulsed in pain.

I started to rise. Gabriel gripped my arm, and his touch may have been as light as the guard's seemed, but the look in his eyes was rock hard. I followed his gaze to see the other guard and the video cameras trained around the room. Gabriel's meaning was clear. *We are in a jail. With armed security. Who will not hesitate to act if we seem to be interfering with a guard.*

Ransom bent to Chandler's ear. "Do you hear the hounds, Edgar?"

Chandler gave a jerky nod. "I—I'm sorry. It was a mistake. I'll make amends. I'm doing that right now."

"He is," I cut in. "Let him make amends. Please."

The guard didn't appear to be more than thirty, but when he turned his gaze on me, I saw someone much older. "I'd be concerned about your sentimentality if I didn't know you were only pleading for his life because it benefits you. Edgar here is a genius. But that does not mean we consider him an ally or that we don't feel the need to bathe in bleach after dealing with him."

Chandler made a noise that might have been a protest but came out as a terrified bleat.

Ransom continued. "He is a self-absorbed, egotistic maniac, Olivia. That means he lies. Consistently and pathologically. He will not tell you the truth. He will tell you whatever version of it best suits his needs. If you want answers, come to us. Only us. As for Chandler . . ." He leaned down to the man's ear again. "You hear them coming, don't you?"

Chandler's head bobbed.

"Good. Then I need say no more." He patted Chandler's shoulder and looked at us. "Visiting time is over."

On the way out, I hit the restroom. I couldn't have been more than five minutes, but from the look Gabriel gave his watch when I exited, you'd think it had been hours. Waiting was one thing. Waiting without doing anything productive was quite another.

"You could have gone out to the car," I said.

"I'm not leaving you alone."

"I'm in a prison. The only danger I face is that they might decide I should stay."

As we passed through security, I recognized the man ahead of us. It was Ransom. When we reached the parking lot, he continued to the streets beyond.

"I'd like to follow," I said. "See where he goes."

CHAPTER SIX

The neighborhoods surrounding the jail were . . . well, pretty much what you'd expect for neighborhoods surrounding a jail. There were good areas in East Garfield Park, but they didn't extend to the doorstep of the nation's biggest prison. Still, it wasn't such a bad neighborhood that we looked out of place. Ransom stuck to the sidewalk, moving at a purposeful stride down one street after another.

"Where the hell is he going?" I muttered. "I've seen them vanish, so why not just walk into the guards' change room and never come out? Do you think he knows we're tailing him?"

"Possibly."

Ransom turned down another street, this one industrial, with a building in the throes of demolition on the left.

"They can't actually disappear, right?" I said. "It must be some kind of Jedi mind trick."

"I believe you are conflating your fantasy worlds."

"You know what I mean. He alters our perception so we no longer see him. Rather than actually vanishing."

"Does it matter?"

"Yes. I want limits, damn it. I'll accept omens and portents and second sight. I'll accept giant black hounds and creepy ravens and magpies. I'm still working out the fae and Wild Hunt thing. But I draw the line at people disappearing into thin air. Don't give me that look, either."

"Look?"

"You're laughing at me."

"I'm quite certain I didn't even smile."

"I can *feel* the laughing."

His lips twitched. That's when Ransom *did* disappear, if only around the side of a coin laundry. I picked up my pace. Gabriel laid his fingers against my back. "Careful, Olivia."

He was right—I'd left my purse in the car, to avoid checking it at security, which meant I was unarmed.

We caught another glimpse of Ransom as he turned into the gap between two buildings. Gabriel stopped me before I could follow. He surveyed the area and then swung his gaze back to that gap, his eyes narrowed. If he were a cat, his fur would have been standing on end.

"Trouble?" I said.

"We've been led up and down these streets. Now our target has vanished into a dark alley. I don't believe it takes an omen to signal we're being led into a trap."

"So we retreat?"

"No, we proceed with extreme caution."

The dark alley was actually a narrow road between buildings. It wasn't all that dark, either, only dim from the shadow of one building stretching across to the other. It was still midday, and we could hear the shouts of men at a construction site a block over. The last dangerous place I'd ventured had been an abandoned psychiatric hospital at 2 A.M. This was nothing.

There was no sign of Ransom. When we got halfway down

the lane, Gabriel pointed to the mouth of an adjoining alley. Which meant that Ransom could have gone that way . . . or be lying in wait there to pounce on us.

"I'm going to check," Gabriel said. "Wait here and stand watch, please."

When he reached the intersection, he peered around it. At a noise behind me, I glanced around to see a plastic bag tumbling my way. I turned back and . . .

No Gabriel.

I was almost ashamed of the sudden impulse to run and see where he'd gone. Um, down the side alley obviously. I waited a minute. Then I walked to the intersection and looked around the corner to see . . .

A dead end.

The alley was only about ten feet long and stopped at a chain-link fence. I couldn't imagine Gabriel hopping that fence. He's too big to be agile, and his dignity stops him from doing anything that could look, well, undignified.

I walked to the fence and peered through. No sign of Gabriel. That's when my heart started pounding in earnest. And when I started cursing us both out for not retrieving our cell phones from the car before we set off to follow a Huntsman.

I returned to the lane and walked along it. When a dark shadow loomed over me, I turned with a greeting on my lips. No one was there. The shadow stayed, though, and I craned my neck to see an owl perched on the roof above.

Owl in daytime. Always a bad sign.

I rubbed the back of my neck.

Across the road at the end of the lane was a block of housing. An old woman stood in a rear yard scrubbing clothing in a basin with a washboard. I crossed the road, pulled by the archaic sight. She had her head down, scrubbing diligently while crooning to herself. I walked right up to the fence and peered over. I could see her long, snarled hair and her reed-thin, wizened arms. When she raised her head, I knew what I'd see. Those blackened, jagged teeth. That long nose and sunken eyes—one black and one gray.

"*Y mae mor salw â Gwrach y Rhibyn*," I whispered.

Her mouth opened. "*Fy mhlentyn, fy mhlentyn bach*," she shrieked. "*Fy mhlentyn, fy mhlentyn bach*."

My child. My little child.

The bean nighe *warns of death.*

As she wailed, I stared at the white shirt in her hand. Gabriel's shirt.

I turned, tripping and stumbling down the road. Then there was no road. I was in a field. I took two staggering steps and felt the soft earth beneath my feet and the long grass whispering against my legs. The field flickered, like a broken recording, and I was on the street again, feeling the pavement and hearing the whine of distant machinery. Two more steps and I was back in the field, a butterfly tickling past, the smell of wildflowers on the breeze.

I stopped and pressed my palms to my eyes.

I have to stay in the real world. Gabriel's there.

I heard the shouts of construction workers and smelled the stink of fresh asphalt, and when I opened my eyes, I was on the street. I searched for a sign.

Nothing. Even the owl was gone. I spun back to Gwrach y Rhibyn, but in her place was an ordinary woman hanging out her laundry.

I raced across the road, ignoring the honk of a passing truck driver. I was almost back to the lane when I heard a *psst*, like a child trying to get my attention. It was indeed a child. A little blond girl, one I'd seen before and one who was as out of place in this world as Gwrach y Rhibyn. Unlike the crone, she *looked* as if she belonged—a girl in a pale green sundress and neon-green jelly sandals. In one hand she carried a stuffed animal, so old I couldn't even tell what it was. Her other fist was clenched, but I knew what it held: black and white stones.

I'd seen her before, in my dreams. I'd *been* her in an earlier vision of Gwrach y Rhibyn. Seeing her here, though, made the ground seem to shift under my feet.

"I have a story," she said. "Do you want to hear it?"

"I want to find Gabriel."

She wrinkled her nose. "Gwynn is fine."

"No, *Gabriel.*"

"I said he's fine. You need to hear my story. It's important."

My heart pounded faster. *It's a trap. She's stalling. Where is he?*

As soon as I thought that, the distant baying of hounds sounded and my breath caught.

"Do you hear that?" I asked.

She smiled. "The hounds. The Hunt. Isn't it wonderful?"

"No, it's—"

The world flickered and suddenly I was in the night forest, and I heard the hounds and felt the ground vibrating under the horses' hooves, and it *was* wonderful. Like the night in the forest with Ricky, when we'd heard them.

Then the scene evaporated, and I was back in the city, dread coursing through me, my face heating now as I started to sweat.

"Back and forth," the girl said as she fingered her stones. "Black and white. This and that. Night and day. Hunt and fae. So it will always be."

"What will always be?"

"Us," she said.

She put out her hand, with just two stones, one black and one white. Then she made a fist. When she opened her hand, there was only one stone, black and white swirling through it.

"There's no escape," she said. "Only balance."

The hounds bayed again, closer, and I stiffened, my heart hammering now.

"They won't hurt you," she said.

"It's Gabriel I'm worried about."

"They won't hurt you," she repeated.

I started down the lane.

"You really should hear my story," she called after me.

"I need to find him."

She sighed, like a gust of wind, and I swear I felt it rush past. Then she was beside me.

"This way," she said.

She headed to the side alley.

"Wait," she said.

A horse neighed. Its scent wafted past on the breeze and sweat dribbled down my cheek as I strained to catch some sign of Gabriel.

"Wait," she said. "He will . . ."

She trailed off, and when I looked, she was gone.

"Olivia?" Gabriel called.

"See?" the little girl's voice whispered in my ear. "I said they wouldn't hurt you."

Gabriel stepped into the intersection of the alley. Relief flickered over his face, quickly swallowed by annoyance.

"I asked you to stay where you were."

My mouth was dry and my heart seemed to short out, as if unable to find a proper rhythm after pounding for so long. "I did," I said. "You . . . you took off."

"Took off?" The annoyance crackled as he came toward me. "I found a dead end, turned around, and you were gone and—"

He stopped short and stared at me. I took a step toward him. My knees wobbled. He grabbed me just as I regained my balance.

"I'm okay," I said.

"No, you're burning up." His hand shot to my forehead, smacking it hard enough to make me wince. "The fever is back."

I pushed his hand away. "I'm fine, just . . ." I took a step and my knees wobbled again. "A little weak."

He tried to put his arm around me, hand braced under my armpit. That was awkward, and not just because of the height difference. Gabriel isn't accustomed to supporting others, physically or otherwise. I took his elbow instead.

"So what happened when you went around the corner?" I asked.

"I didn't *go* around it. I merely *glanced* around it. When I turned back, you were gone. Then I went looking for you."

"Huh. Well, my experience was a little stranger," I said, and then explained.

I don't keep anything from Gabriel, no matter how weird it gets. And no matter how weird it gets, he never so much as quirks an eyebrow. This time we'd both experienced some perception or reality shift, and I don't know if it merely separated us long enough for us to wander our separate ways or if I hadn't been *here* at all. Not in this world or this plane.

Last week I'd been inside the empty Cainsville house that originally belonged to my great-great-grandmother. I'd stepped into an inlaid triskelion of an owl that had triggered a vision of the girl and the *bean nighe*. To have that same thing happen on a city street was disconcerting to say the least.

"I blame the Cŵn Annwn," Gabriel said. "They were close enough to cause it."

He steered me into a dodgy corner store and bought me a Dr Pepper and a bag of ice.

"I'll take the pop," I said. "But I don't really need the—"

"Humor me."

We returned to the car, and I put the ice bag against my forehead, which seemed to be what he expected.

We sat in the parking lot for a while, so I could rest. Gabriel checked his messages and so did I. The curse of modern communications—spend a couple of hours separated from your cell and you'll spend another twenty minutes catching up.

I went to my texts first. Gabriel said, "Ricky?"

My smile must have given it away. "He's coming home early. Which means you won't have to babysit me tonight."

Gabriel gave a grunt that I interpreted as "Good."

"I'll surprise him at the airport," I said. "He can drop me at the office in the morning."

Another grunt. I looked up to see him engrossed in his e-mail. I stopped talking and texted with Ricky. When I finished, Gabriel was sitting with his phone on his leg, his hand engulfing it.

"Everything okay?" I asked.

"Edgar Chandler is dead."

"What?"

"He killed himself shortly after returning to his cell. Cyanide, it seems."

"Ransom must have slipped it to him. He warned Chandler that the hounds were coming and gave him a way out. That's why I heard them. They were coming for Chandler." I exhaled. "Shit."

"There will be an investigation," Gabriel said. "As his final visitors, we'll be questioned. We may also be suspected."

"Of giving him the pill? But we never touched him and the guard can confirm . . . Except the guard wasn't a guard at all."

"There were security cameras. As well as the second guard. I doubt we'd be seriously considered as suspects."

"Okay, so what about Jon Childs? The guy Chandler wanted you to kill."

"I had no intention of actually—"

I cut him off with a look. "I know that. You just wanted to get his name and find out why Chandler wants him dead."

He nodded, pleased that I'd figured it out and relieved that I'd known he wouldn't kill a man—at least, not one who didn't present an immediate lethal threat.

"So let's find Jon Childs," I said.

CHAPTER SEVEN

While neither Jon nor Childs is a particularly uncommon name, when you put the two together you get fewer than twenty adult males in the country. And exactly one in the Greater Chicago area.

The Chicago Jon Childs was a thirty-six-year-old self-employed equities trader. Successful, according to his tax records. Yes, we had access to his tax records. Or Lydia did. Not necessarily legally. She'd spent most of her working life as the executive assistant to Chicago's Field Office Special Agent in Charge. That would be the *CIA* field office.

Before I met Lydia, I'd presumed that husky voice on the phone belonged to some hot young thing. When we did meet, I realized my unforgivable lapse in reasoning. There was no way in hell Gabriel would hire eye candy to manage his office when he could get someone like Lydia for the same salary, given she was past retirement age and just looking for an interesting way to spend her time. Working for Gabriel was nothing if not interesting.

According to Lydia's research, Childs was a graduate of Portland State who'd moved to Chicago ten years ago, immediately opening his own business and attracting a decent clientele.

Never married. No kids. No affiliation with any known political party or other group. In other words, a guy without ties.
Not unlike the man I worked for. A lack of ties meant a lack of
accountability and, well, let's face it, a lack of witnesses.

Childs worked from home, which made it difficult to stake
him out. Problem number two? We could find absolutely no
photographic record of him. No passport. No driver's license.

The only alternative was to call him up, express interest in his
services, and persuade him to meet with me. Except Childs
wasn't home, and he didn't seem to have an admin assistant. I
left a message with my cell number.

Lydia was on the phone as we were walking past her desk. She
flagged me down and covered the receiver.

"I can finally get you in to see Todd," she said.

I froze mid-step. Gabriel turned to me. "You'd rather not?"

"No, I—"

"Let me rephrase that. I *know* you'd rather not. I'm going to
leave this ball in your court, Olivia. If you wish to visit Todd at
some juncture, let Lydia know and—"

"Tuesday."

He hesitated.

"I'll go Tuesday," I said.

"That's tomorrow."

"Oh, right. Maybe . . ." I took a deep breath and turned to
Lydia. "I'd like to go tomorrow if you can make the arrangements, please."

She nodded, and Gabriel led me out the door.

I showered and changed at Gabriel's, and I planned to grab a
taxi, presuming Ricky would have his bike at the airport.
Gabriel was having none of that. He would deliver me to the

doors of the appropriate terminal, where he would watch until I was safely inside. I could say he was overreacting, but given the events of the last few days, he really wasn't.

I stood with the usual crowd of friends and family at the bottom of the baggage claim escalators and tried not to bounce on my toes like an excited kid. As I spotted Ricky at the top, a young woman beside me whispered to her friend, "Who's that?" They began speculating—musician, actor, model . . .

When I first met Ricky, I thought he looked like Hollywood's version of a biker. Six feet, well-built, tousled blond hair to his collar, hazel eyes, and a cleft chin when he shaved. What bolstered the whispering, though, were the two Satan's Saints who stood on the escalator step behind him. To his left was CJ, who looked pretty much exactly like you'd expect from an aging biker. Big guy, late forties, slight paunch, graying beard, stringy ponytail, and shit-kicker boots. The other was Wallace, sergeant-at-arms—Don Gallagher's right-hand man and main enforcer. Wallace is clean-cut and almost as tall as Gabriel, with an extra twenty pounds of muscle. Both men could pass for roadies or bodyguards, and that's what the girls obviously mistook them for.

Ricky was staring straight ahead, lost in his thoughts. Wallace said something and as Ricky looked over, he noticed me and gave a blast of a grin that had the girls beside me twittering. He jogged down the rest of the steps, strode over, and scooped me up in a soldier-on-furlough kiss.

Whispers snaked around us. I'd caught a few earlier, but that kiss made people take a closer look. They recognized me and Ricky from a *Chicago Post* photo a few weeks ago. I heard my name and "biker," and I'm sure Ricky did, too, but he just kept grinning down at me.

"I didn't expect this," he said. "Thank you."

Wallace and CJ walked over.

"Hey, Miz Jones," CJ said.

"Hey, guys." I asked how their flight was as we headed to the baggage carousel. Then I said to Ricky, "I know you thought you'd be clear tonight. Does that still stand? Or does your dad need you?"

Ricky would have texted me if our plans had changed. I was saying this for Wallace and CJ's benefit. My relationship with Ricky didn't thrill Don Gallagher. He seemed to like me well enough. What he didn't like is the Gabriel–me–Ricky dynamic. While Gabriel has made it clear he has no romantic interest in me, Don would rather Ricky kept his distance, just to be safe. Don values Gabriel's legal expertise too much to rock that boat.

"Nope, it's all good," Ricky said. "I checked in with him before I invited you over."

"Ah. Well, in that case . . ." I glanced meaningfully at a sign for the airport Hilton. "It's a long drive back to the city, and I'm sure you had a tiring flight."

His eyes glinted, sending a familiar lick of heat through me.

"Go on," CJ said. "We'll grab your bag."

"Thanks." Ricky put his arm around my shoulders and we walked away.

"Was that okay?" I said when we were out of earshot.

"My girlfriend surprises me at the airport and drags me off to a hotel? I don't think my rep will ever recover. I definitely owe you."

"I'm looking forward to repayment. It was a very long three days."

"Damn straight."

He tugged me around as he backed up. Next thing I knew, we were in a short service hall, partially blocked by a massive cardboard standee. He propelled me to the end and then pulled me into a kiss. If the one at the escalator had started reminding me how much I'd missed him, this one cemented it.

Five seconds later, I had my back to the wall, arms around his neck, hands in his hair, his hands under my ass. By the time I broke the kiss, I wasn't even sure where we were anymore, and I looked around, blinking, before saying, "Hotel, five minutes, that way."

He dropped his lips to my neck as he pressed against me. "So near and yet so far."

I chuckled. "Well, if you don't want to wait . . ."

"Tempting," he said as his lips moved up my throat.

"I *am* wearing a skirt."

"I noticed." His hands slid under it, cupping my ass again.

"Did you notice what I'm *not* wearing?"

His fingers checked, making sure I didn't just have on a thong. Then he groaned, pushing against me. "Now, that is a tease."

"Between that sign blocking the hall, and the fact that no one has come this way since we arrived, I'd put our odds of not getting caught at about eighty percent."

He kissed me so hard it left me gasping. "Tell me you're serious."

"I am always serious," I said. "Even if someone looks in, it'll seem as if we're just making out, very enthusiastically."

"Hell, yeah."

He kissed me again, boosting me up to straddle him, which lowered our odds for discretion, but I wasn't arguing. That's when his phone rang, the tone playing "Big Boss Man." His father. He let out a curse and fumbled to hit Ignore.

"Sorry. I texted him when I got off the plane. He's just saying hello. Lousy timing."

I caught his shirtfront and pulled him back into a kiss. He turned off the ringer and stuffed the phone into his pocket, and within seconds we were where we'd been, my back against the wall, skirt hiked up around my hips. I felt his phone vibrate and let out a snorting laugh.

"Ignore it," he said between kisses. "Please."

More kissing, hotter and deeper now, the bulging crotch of his jeans pushing against me in just the right spot, exquisite teasing as I could feel exactly what I wanted. He reached down for his belt. I beat him to it, and he chuckled. I flipped open his belt and then the button on his jeans and—

A shadow extended from behind the cardboard sign. Ricky turned his head to follow my gaze, his eyes narrowed. Then he caught my chin in one hand, pulling my face back to his, kissing me again, and I could feel the determination there, the lust and the need and the resolve not to let anything get in our way. Except . . . well, while I'm not one to let the words "public place" stop me from having sex, I'm no exhibitionist, either, and neither was Ricky, and even as he kissed me, we'd both slowed, our attention pulled down that hallway.

"I'll get this," he muttered.

He fastened his belt with an angry snap of the leather and strode around the sign. Then, "What the fucking *hell*?"

I smoothed my skirt and hurried after him as CJ said, "I think the hotel is that way."

"No fucking—"

"Your dad called," Wallace cut in as I caught up. They were both standing there, bags at their feet, as if patiently waiting for us to finish.

"I know," Ricky said, his words brittle. "And since when am I not allowed ten fucking minutes to call him back?"

"We weren't interrupting," CJ said. "We were going to give you time—"

"He needs us at the clubhouse," Wallace said. "Something came up. Something urgent."

Ricky's jaw worked until he finally looked Wallace in the eye and said, in a deceptively soft voice, "Is it urgent, Wallace? Is it really?"

"That's what he said, and that's all he said. He called right after you left, so we came after you and saw you duck into the hallway here."

"Oh, to be that young again." CJ thumped Ricky on the shoulder. "We can give you two a few minutes. We'll stand guard."

"No," I murmured. "That's okay. Let's go."

Spontaneous sex in an airport was one thing. An efficient quickie really wasn't the same.

Ricky let CJ and Wallace lead the way.

"I'm sorry," he said when they were out of earshot.

"It's okay."

"No, goddamn it, Liv, it's not. My father needed me to suddenly take his place on a trip to Miami, and I went, even though I knew damned well he was only testing to see if I'd complain about leaving you. Then yesterday, when you were sick, I checked to see if I could catch an earlier flight back and he said no. I didn't argue. Now this? There's no emergency. He's snapping my leash. Yes, he's not just my dad, he's my boss, and I've always respected that. I don't ask for special treatment or shirk my responsibilities—"

"I know that. *He* knows that."

"Then why—" He bit the sentence off with a shake of his head. "You don't need to hear me bitching ten minutes after I get back. I'm sorry."

"Don't be. It's frustrating." A quick smile. "In more ways than one. But Don—and Gabriel—can test us all they like.

Eventually, they'll have to accept that we aren't kids who'll duck our responsibilities to sneak off together. We'll wear them down."

A short laugh, relaxing now. "Yeah." He adjusted his grip on my hand, pulling me closer, our fingers entwined. "About tonight—as much as I would love to say I'll see you in a few hours, that's never worked out before. I don't want you waiting up half the night only to hear that I won't make it. I would like to see you for breakfast, though. Not for sex. Well, I won't argue if we squeeze it in, but mostly just to hang out. I've missed you."

I leaned against him. "Same here. Breakfast tomorrow."

Ricky had recovered his mood by the time we reached the car. Yes, it was a car. Apparently, leaving their Harleys in airport parking would have violated club rules.

CJ joked that it was a big backseat. Ricky good-naturedly flipped him the finger, and we settled in. The plan was to drop me off at Gabriel's condo. I called him at the start of the drive, but he was on the line, the phone going to voice mail, so I left a message.

At the building, Ricky insisted on taking me up, and I didn't argue. If Gabriel had a problem with Ricky coming as far as the front door, he should have replied to my message.

Gabriel had to buzz me in, and he did so without comment, but when he opened the door and I saw his expression, I said, "You didn't get my message, did you?"

He looked befuddled, as if we'd woken him from a nap. He took out his phone.

"Oh," he said.

"Right. So, things came up. Ricky has to go, and I'm here."

"This is the official handoff," Ricky said. "I relinquish her to your custody. I'll pick her up at seven for breakfast." His smile faded as he studied Gabriel. "Unless tonight's a problem . . ."

Gabriel snapped out of it. "No, of course not."

"Then I should run," Ricky said. "The guys are double-parked downstairs." He glanced up at Gabriel. "We need to talk."

Gabriel frowned.

"About that thing? The one we were discussing?"

"Oh, yes. Of course."

"Tomorrow, then?"

Gabriel nodded.

Ricky took off to the still-waiting elevator.

"I don't want to impose," I said to Gabriel. "How about I catch a cab to my parents' place? They have a top-notch security system, and I have my gun."

It seemed to take time for him to process my words, and when he did, he blinked.

"No, of course not." He realized he was blocking the doorway and backed inside.

There were papers spread across the living room table, along with his laptop and what looked like an untouched cup of coffee.

"I'm sorry," I said. "I know this is inconvenient. Why don't I just go into . . ."

I looked around the apartment. Living room. Bathroom. Bedroom. Kitchen and dining room. Closet. That was it. I was sure it was a million-dollar condo, but you were paying for the address and the view, not the square footage. Given how he'd cut me off from venturing into the kitchen this morning, my options for giving him space were limited.

"I could use a bath," I said. "A long one. You keep doing whatever you were doing."

He swept the pages off the table and tucked them into a file. "It was just work. It wasn't going very well."

"If it's anything I can help with . . ." I began.

He shook his head. "It's not."

"Okay, well, let me go take that bath. I know you were expecting an evening of peace and quiet—"

"I'm quite happy to abandon it, given how poorly it was progressing." He closed his laptop with a decisive click, dumped his coffee in the kitchen sink, and when he came back, he was more himself, his movements smoother, words more precise. "If you want a bath, you're quite welcome to one, but given that your evening with Ricky was lost, I'm guessing you haven't had dinner yet."

"No, but—"

"Nor have I. There's a place nearby. We'll walk."

DOWNWARD SPIRAL

Gabriel was six when he learned that other people dreamed at night. He was in first grade, and the teacher had asked them to draw a picture of something from their dreams. While the other children settled in, crayons in hand, bent over their construction paper, he asked the teacher for an explanation. As she gave one, he could tell that she expected him to nod in understanding. He was the best student in reading and spelling and third-best in math. He was not stupid, but he felt like it then, watching her wait for comprehension he didn't feel.

"I don't have those," he finally said.

She smiled and shook her head. "Everyone dreams, Gabriel. You just don't remember them."

"No, I've never had one."

"So you see nothing when you sleep?"

He considered it and then said, "Sometimes I remember things that happened to me."

She patted his shoulder, and he struggled not to tense at her touch. His kindergarten teacher had noticed that he flinched at physical contact, which had led to a talk about abuse. It was a concept he was familiar with, but that was none of his teacher's business. So he let her pat his shoulder and only gritted his teeth against it.

"That's a dream, Gabriel," she said. "Sometimes it's stories we make up in our heads, and sometimes it's memories, good and bad, all jumbled up and strange."

Which was not what he experienced at all. He saw exact replays of memories, as if he was reliving them. And they were never good ones.

As he got older, he hid the fact that he did not dream, as he hid the fact that he'd rather not be touched. Anything that called attention to himself was dangerous. By the time he reached college, he was too old to be put in foster care, too big for anyone to harass. Standing out then was good. It was how you got noticed and got ahead.

So when the topic of dreams arose in a freshmen psych group project, he'd been honest.

"I don't dream."

One of the girls had leaned toward him—too close, and he'd had to brace himself not to pull back. "Come on, Gabriel. *Everyone* dreams."

"I don't."

"Let's look at it another way," she said. "Dreams in general. Hopes and wishes. What do you dream of?"

"Nothing."

They'd gotten annoyed with him then. Clearly he was being an ass, and they'd likely already started drawing that conclusion, which was fine—one could get further being hated than being liked. But in this case, he was telling the truth. Dreams implied wispy, ephemeral things that floated somewhere beyond reach. Gabriel had goals and ambitions.

By now, even the replaying of memories was a rare occurrence. But that night, after he had dinner with Olivia and went to bed, the memories came. Of all the ones from his youth, these were, perhaps, the most terrifying.

His mother—Seanna—had men. They weren't boyfriends. Technically, they weren't clients, either. They were men who came by for sex and gave her something in return—drugs, rent, groceries, goods to pawn. There were men. Suffice it to say that.

The problem began when one of them accused eight-year-old Gabriel of relieving him of the hundred dollars in his wallet. Which was ludicrous. Not that Gabriel was incapable of picking a pocket. He'd inherited his mother's light fingers, and by eight he was an expert. But he knew better than to steal from his mother's friends. That lesson had come from his aunt Rose. The Walshes were a family of con artists and thieves, and so the lesson was as valid as teaching another child to wear a bicycle helmet. Family, friends, and friends of the family are not marks.

Gabriel suspected that the perpetrator was Seanna, who wasn't picky about the rules if they stood between her and a fix. Not that she came to his defense. It had been something of a shock, as he grew up, to realize that other mothers defended and cared for their children. Seanna was like a feral bitch, grudgingly sharing her territory with her half-grown pup, doing whatever it took to ensure her own survival, even if it meant snatching dinner from her offspring's mouth.

Gabriel had denied stealing the money, but the man—Doug— had been determined to teach him a lesson. Thus began a regimen of abuse that lasted three months, until Gabriel scraped up a hundred dollars and gave it to him. That had been almost more painful than the persecution itself. To plead guilty to a crime he hadn't committed? Humiliating. To turn over money— his *own* money—was even worse. But he had, because he'd reached the point where he'd do anything to stop the torment.

In the memory, he was walking to school. He seemed safe,

but about halfway there he realized Doug had simply gone ahead to cut him off. Now Gabriel was flying down alleys and back roads, zipping between cars, running for his life, because that's what Doug had threatened: that he'd kill him. And from what Gabriel had heard, it would not be Doug's first murder.

At last, he'd darted among the debris of a half-demolished building. As he hunkered there, struggling to catch his breath, he burned with blinding rage. But it wasn't true anger, not the sort that would propel him to take action, because he couldn't do anything to Doug without getting hurt worse in return. That's what the rage truly was about: frustration and impotence and self-loathing and disgust, because he couldn't solve this problem, and he could *always* solve his problems. This one loomed like a Titan above him, relentless and all-powerful, and as he crouched there, listening to Doug taunting him, closing in . . .

Gabriel started awake with a gasp. He sat up, then held completely still, mentally listing every weapon in his bedroom—*gun, gun, knife, bat, knife*—his gaze pausing on each hiding spot, as if he could see it in the darkness. Weapons, money, even food— it was stashed throughout his apartment, the security talismans he needed to feel safe. He'd hidden it all well enough that he shouldn't need to worry about Olivia throwing open a kitchen cupboard and saying, "What's up with the twenty cans of stew?" but he still did worry, however irrationally—

Olivia.

The terror of the memory flew back, and he thought of her sleeping in the next room. He scrambled up, crossed the room, threw open the door. He couldn't see her—the back of the couch faced his bedroom door. He couldn't hear her, either, so he jogged over, heart tripping even as he told himself he was being foolish, she was fine, just fine. But the memory lingered, the old threat entwining with new ones.

He rounded the sofa to find her sleeping soundly, lying on her side, blanket pulled up, hands tucked under her cheek, pillow half fallen to the floor. Resisting the urge to push the pillow back in place, he stepped away quickly. Whatever his excuse, he didn't want her waking to find him standing over her. At best, she'd decide she needed to sleep elsewhere. At worst, he'd get a switchblade in his gut.

He double-checked the door locks and alarm. She'd left the curtains open on the floor-to-ceiling window. There was no nearby building tall enough to pose any risk of prying eyes, and if the condo hadn't come with curtains, he'd never have bothered adding them. But he closed them now. Just to be safe.

Before they shut, he gazed down at the city, and that anxiety bubbled again, the memory returning, dragging with it a sense of impotence he hadn't felt in twenty years.

It didn't take a psychology degree to understand where the dream had come from tonight. The situation with James Morgan was growing steadily worse, and for the first time in his adult life, faced with a threat, Gabriel seemed unable to stop it. The fact that the threat was directed at Olivia was inconsequential. It *felt* the same as one directed at himself, and he didn't waste a moment untangling that. All that mattered was that he accepted responsibility for this situation.

When Morgan had approached them outside the restaurant last week, Gabriel had decided to nip this situation in the bud. Couple blackmail with a generous dose of physical intimidation and the idiot would back off. Instead, Morgan had hired a private eye to investigate Gabriel and Ricky. When that failed to bring Olivia running, he'd made it clear to Gabriel that he would get her back by any means possible. Hence Gabriel's visit to Morgan's house, which should have put a clear end to everything. *I'm better at this game and I will break you, James*

Morgan. But Morgan had gotten him arrested and charged, and then sent deprogrammers after Olivia. Every move Gabriel made, Morgan countered . . . and the threat against Olivia rose.

Gabriel finally had to admit the unthinkable. He hadn't merely failed to solve a problem—he was actually making it worse.

Something had snapped in Morgan, and it wouldn't miraculously repair itself. Morgan would continue this downward spiral, and before long Gabriel was sure he'd come after Olivia. Physically.

Gabriel had spent the early part of the evening scouring a dossier that Lydia had compiled on Morgan. He'd been searching for serious wrongdoing. What he had already would smudge Morgan's squeaky-clean image but not soil it. Gabriel needed real leverage—something that, if revealed, would destroy Morgan's chances of ever joining the senatorial race.

Dozens of things could ruin a future politician's chances. Many of them fell into the category Gabriel would deem "no one else's damned business." But Morgan had made it his business. If Gabriel could dig up visits to a dominatrix or a male prostitute, he'd be set. Hard-core drug use would also do the trick. Drug dealing would be even better. Gambling habits were a possibility—that made voters nervous, worried a politician would raid the public coffers to support his habit.

Gabriel would have settled for an interesting fetish or a thousand-dollar tab at a strip club, but there was absolutely nothing. While Morgan might cut corners in business, in his personal life he was as clean as his reputation. The more Gabriel had scoured that dossier, the more agitated and frustrated he'd become—which is when Olivia had returned, providing a welcome distraction.

Gabriel now found himself at the front door, about to go out. When his threat hackles rose, circling the block once or twice

usually settled him. Which made him sound like a dog patrol-
ling his territory, and perhaps there was a little of that, but it was
more about recovering his sense of security. This close to down-
town, he'd see hustlers and dealers and thugs, and even the odd
gangbanger. Not one ever gave him more than a moment's glance.
He wasn't eight or twelve or even fifteen anymore. No one bothered him. No one dared. He was safe.

Olivia would be fine—he had the best security. But as he
touched the deadbolt, she groaned in her sleep, and he turned to
see her, pushing aside the blanket, restless, as if she sensed his
plans.

The blanket slid half to the floor. She was wearing an oversized T-shirt, as she usually did. It had ridden up around her
hips and—

And that was enough of that. He pulled his gaze away, but
the image lingered. He shoved a hand through his hair. None of
that. None of that at all. He valued Olivia and her friendship too
much to let his thoughts wander down that path, which they
seemed to do with increasing frequency, proving that he was
exhausted, less in control than he liked to be, than he needed to
be. Be happy with what they had and do nothing, absolutely
nothing, to endanger it.

He thought of James Morgan, and that cooled him off better
than any stern self-talk. When he glanced at Olivia again, he
only noticed that the blanket had fallen almost completely, and
she was shivering in the air-conditioned chill. He walked over,
tugged it up over her, and returned to bed.

CHAPTER EIGHT

Ricky picked me up at seven, and we rode to a diner he'd scoped out. I presume the food was decent, though I was too caught up in conversation to taste it. Even the possibility that our evening plans would be scuttled again didn't dampen our mood. His father had called him in to deal with an escalating situation. If it couldn't be resolved peacefully today, Ricky would have to help handle it tonight.

"Dad's promised me tomorrow night off. If you're free . . ."

"The cabin?"

He smiled. "That's what I was hoping. Makes me feel like a cheap bastard, though. Promise you a romantic getaway and take you to my family's cabin in Wisconsin. But you did seem okay with it the last time . . ."

"Um, more than 'okay with it,' as I recall. The answer is yes. Absolutely yes."

"Great. It's a date, then. Tomorrow night at the cabin, no matter what other shit comes up. I have his word on that."

As we walked to the bike afterward, Ricky slowed and glanced along the busy road.

"Not really the place for a proper goodbye kiss." His gaze swung behind the diner.

"Yes," I said. "And please."

The back was clear, with only a few half-dead bushes to navigate. I tugged him between the bushes and pulled him into a kiss that took about 0.5 seconds to go from "Good morning" to "God, I've missed you." My hands in his hair, the kiss deep and devouring, me up against the wall, as he pressed between my legs and—

He cut himself short with a groan, and then shifted back to readjust my skirt.

"Sorry," he said. "Wrong time and place. Just . . . skirt."

"It tempts you in spite of yourself?"

"It does. Kind of like a half-open gate."

When I sputtered a laugh, he said, "That didn't sound right, did it?"

"Put it this way. I don't need to wear a skirt for work. If the gate is half open, that's because I left it half open." I ran his hand up my bare thigh to my panties. "See? Only half open. Meaning I am amenable to the possibility, but there are no expectations."

"I'm fine with expectations. Pretty damn good with them, actually."

"That's very sweet."

"Mmm, not really."

I hooked my hands around his neck again. He played with the edge of my panties and then . . . not the edge of my panties. I arched against the wall as his fingers slid into me.

"Very, very sweet," I said.

I gasped, knees threatening to give way. His free hand slid under my rear, bracing me.

"I did debate the skirt," I said. "Because of the motorcycle."

"I thought you said they went together very well."

"Too well. Short skirt. Big bike. Serious vibrations. I have a weakness, as you might have noticed."

"Sure as hell not complaining."

"But as much fun as that is *outside* the city, it could be a bit . . . frustrating inside. I decided, though, that since it would be a short ride, and a slow one, there wouldn't be any grave danger of you pulling into the parking lot and me swinging around on top of you."

His hand stopped moving. "Sorry, got stuck on the mental image there," he murmured, and resumed teasing as he pushed against me, nuzzling my neck. "Damn . . . Can you repeat that?"

I unzipped his jeans and slid my hand inside.

"The part about the short ride?" I said. "Or the long one?"

"Either sounds good," he said, breath picking up speed. "But that last part? Just . . . refresh that image?"

I kissed his chin as I stroked him. "With added detail?"

"Hell, yeah."

I slid my lips over to his ear and told him, in detail, what I'd have liked to do to him in the parking lot. I didn't get very far before my panties were on the ground and I was against the wall and he was inside me, and I don't really remember much after that, just that those few days apart suddenly seemed like months, and I swear I'd forgotten just how good it was with Ricky, like a tidal wave that washed every other thought from my head.

It didn't last long. This was sex against the back wall of a diner. It was release—glorious, fast, hard release, and when it ended, we both stayed there, my legs still wrapped around him, braced against the wall as we panted and kissed and caught our breath between the two.

"Missed you," he said. "Missed you so damn much."

"Missed you, too."

"Oh, that's sweet," said a voice near us. "I'd give you a couple minutes to cuddle, but Liv's not really a cuddler."

Ricky's hands flew to his jeans, getting them done up as he turned to see . . .

James.

"What the fuck?" Ricky snarled.

"That's—" James began.

"No, really, *what the fuck*."

Ricky bore down, and I ran to stop him. I didn't need to. He pulled himself up before he was within striking distance.

"You—" Ricky began.

"I don't think we've met," James said. "It's a little awkward, admittedly, exchanging introductions right after I catch you screwing my fiancée."

"She's not—" Ricky bit it off, knowing it would do no good. "You followed her here."

"No, I was driving by as you walked out of the diner. I pulled in to talk—"

"You *stalked* her." Ricky moved forward now, his body still tense but his temper reined in. "You followed us, and then you waited through our meal to waylay us out here. Do you know what that is? Pathetic. Also? Damned dangerous to your health, because the next time I catch you within twenty yards of Olivia—"

"Enough. Liv's gotten what she needed from you. You can run along now."

"I'm sure it makes you feel better to dismiss me—"

"But I do dismiss you. You're stud service, Gallagher. Nothing more. As you may have noticed, our Liv likes sex. You're certainly not the first guy she's had her back to the wall for."

"Then I should thank them for giving her the practice. It definitely paid off."

It took James a few seconds to regroup. "You can joke, but I bet you still think it makes you special, getting dragged back here."

"It wasn't actually dragging . . ." Ricky said.

"Yeah," I said. "Kinda was."

Ricky chuckled. I wasn't helping matters, but it made Ricky relax, any danger of this coming to blows fading. That was, I presumed, what James wanted—to provoke Ricky into hitting him so he could call the cops.

"Now, as entertaining as this has been," I said, "I need to get to work."

James tried to step in front of me, but Ricky moved into the gap between us.

"Back off," Ricky said. "I've already warned you—"

"And I've already said I'm not concerned, Richard. Or is it Rick? I've heard Ricky, but I'm sure that's a mistake. It's bad enough that Olivia's seeing a college boy almost three years her junior. If you go by a moniker as juvenile as Ricky . . ." The corners of James's mouth twitched. "That'd be almost too good to be true."

"It *is* Ricky. Not Richard. Not Rick. But I'm not expecting you'll have any occasion to use it, because if I see you near Olivia—"

"You're a *boy*." James moved to stand toe-to-toe with him. "A child who fancies himself a biker. You have the jacket and the Harley, but you aren't fooling anyone. You're far too pretty to be dangerous, *Ricky*. The son of a notorious gang leader, and you've never even been arrested. That makes you the worst kind of bad boy. A fake one."

"Maybe. Come after Liv again and we'll test your theory." Ricky put his arm around my waist. "If you'll excuse us, I need to get someone to work or her boss will kill me. He's definitely the real deal." He lowered his voice as we passed. "And right now, he's really kinda pissed with you."

CHAPTER NINE

I am so sorry," I said as we dismounted outside Gabriel's office.
"For what?"
"Umm . . . my crazy ex ambushing us having sex and proceeding to insult you."

Ricky took my helmet and fastened it to the bike. "His craziness has nothing to do with you. Admittedly, I can imagine that a guy would not be pleased if you left him, and I could certainly understand that he'd want to get you back. But that means doing his damnedest to *woo* you back and, if that fails, taking the hint and parting amicably. Stalking you and sending armed deprogrammers doesn't say, 'I love you.' It says, 'I'm a psycho son of a bitch.'"

"He wasn't always like that."

"Obviously, or you'd have left him long ago. It's the leaving that brought out the crazy. There is absolutely no need to apologize. It comes down to this. I have you. He doesn't. He's not going to be complimentary. Insulting my intelligence? My age? My lack of a criminal record? Not exactly wounding me to the core, Liv."

"He also said you were pretty."

"I've been called worse."

We went inside and found Gabriel leaning over Lydia, hands planted on her desk. When I rapped at the open door, he frowned and checked his watch.

"I am exactly on time," I said.

"We need to talk," Ricky said to Gabriel.

Gabriel nodded. "Yes, I know. When are your classes done for the day?"

"I mean now. Same topic, but the situation is deteriorating." He turned to me. "And yeah, I mean James. That's what I meant last night, too. I just didn't want to spoil your mood with the reminder. While you don't want us solving your problems for you, in this case . . . ?"

He was right. I hated sitting back and letting them handle it. But I'd been absolutely clear with James that it was over, and I'd exhausted my know-how for dealing with the situation.

"You're welcome to sit in," Ricky continued. "But again, while I'd never suggest you let us take over . . ."

"I would," Gabriel said. "Strongly."

I wanted to at least listen in, but I wouldn't be able to without squirming and worrying that, whatever they planned, James didn't deserve it. How many women had I met at the shelter, abused by their partners, who refused to call the police? *He's not a bad person. He's under a lot of stress. He doesn't mean it.* I wouldn't be that woman.

"I'll do a coffee run," I said.

The moment the words left my mouth, they both stiffened.

I can't even walk down the street alone to grab a coffee. God-damn it, James. I know I hurt you, but I do not deserve this.

"Why don't we both go," Lydia offered quickly.

Gabriel's gaze dropped to my purse in silent question. I gave him a look and said, "Of course," meaning that I had my gun. He nodded and waved Ricky into the meeting room.

Lydia and I hung out at the coffee shop for almost a half hour. We didn't talk about work, which was a first. It was easier outside the office for conversation to turn to the personal, and I discovered that Lydia was a widowed mother of two, with three grandkids, and was long-distance dating a record label exec from Sacramento who planned to retire to Chicago because, apparently, Lydia herself had no plans to stop working anytime soon.

When Ricky texted me an all-clear, we returned to find him waiting on his bike to say goodbye. I didn't ask him what they'd decided to do about James. Nor did I ask Gabriel when I went inside. I had to trust them.

As Gabriel had warned, the police did want to talk to us about our prison visit to Chandler. We also had to answer more questions about the death of Macy Shaw.

I'm sure someone had connected us to both incidents, but the detective didn't seem particularly suspicious. I was the daughter of convicted serial killers. It was almost as if no one was surprised that I'd morphed into the angel of death. As long as there were no indications that I'd killed anyone myself—and there weren't—well, I was bound to attract some serious crazy.

We visited the station. We gave our statements. That was it.

Next we went to see Jon Childs, who hadn't replied to my initial message, or to the two calls I'd made since.

Childs lived in a corner-unit town house in University Village. Older building. Quiet, tree-lined street. No sign to show that he ran a business out of his place. In this neighborhood they'd frown on that, and given his income, I doubted he needed to advertise for clients.

His condo was dark and the mailbox overflowed with flyers. Gabriel and I were sitting in the car discussing our next move when an older woman marched over from next door and emptied Childs's mailbox.

I arrived at his front step just as the neighbor was coming down.

"Sorry to bother you. My husband"—I waved at the rental Jag—"and I were trying to figure out if Mr. Childs was home. I guess that"—I nodded at her armload of mail and flyers—"answers our question. When do you expect him back?"

"I didn't expect him to be *gone*," she said. "I always tell him, I'm home all day, just let me know when you'll be away and I'll collect the mail. It doesn't look good when it piles up. Attracts the wrong kind of attention." She gestured at a couple of kids across the road—clean-shaven college boys wearing two-hundred-dollar sneakers.

She continued. "But he just takes off and leaves me to collect his mail, and when he comes for it, I barely get a thank-you. He tells me I don't need to bother with it. Well, someone has to care about this neighborhood."

I nodded in sympathy. "I can't say I know Mr. Childs. I'm a friend of his sister, Amy. Have you met her?"

"I never knew he had a sister."

"I'm sorry to hear that. I'd hoped he was close to Amy. She certainly spoke highly of him, and she needs all the help she can get right now. With the . . ." I lowered my voice. "Cancer."

The old woman blinked. "Cancer?"

"They did a mastectomy, but it didn't catch it all and— I'm sorry. I don't mean to get into it. I'm just very concerned about her. With the medical bills . . . Well, she has insurance, but it's never enough, is it?"

The woman harrumphed in agreement.

"Amy had to sell her condo," I said. "Which is right down the road from us. She was going to get in touch once she got settled, but it's been almost a month and I haven't heard from her. I was hoping maybe her brother had." I exhaled. "Sorry for the long story."

"No, not at all." Her voice softened, all traces of annoyance gone. "I completely understand. You're a good friend." A glare at Childs's door. "A better friend than some blood relations, I'll bet. I don't know when he's coming back, but he's never gone for long. I could give you his number . . ."

"I have it," I said with a sigh. "I've called a few times. I guess he's really been busy."

Another glare at her invisible neighbor. "No, he just doesn't have a lick of manners. Tell you what, hon. Give me your number and I'll call you when he gets back."

"Thank you. I'd appreciate that."

OUTCLASSED

Tristan sat at the dining room table, watching Eden climb into the vehicle where Gabriel waited. A rental car apparently, not surprising given what Macy had done to his old one. Tristan was not accustomed to emotions, but at that moment he experienced a surge of what might be called anger. The stupid girl could have killed Eden with that stunt. Even killing Gabriel would have been problematic. He'd have incurred the wrath of the Cainsville Tylwyth Teg for that. One had to be careful playing these old games of power. Particularly if you weren't on either team but, rather, hoping to sneak in from the sidelines and snatch the ball from the field.

Macy had been a poor play. That was the problem with the *boinne-fala*. They were unpredictable, easily swayed by ego and emotion. They didn't understand the meaning of loyalty. He'd offered Macy the one thing she'd wanted most, and she'd betrayed him. Why? Because a small part of the plan hadn't gone exactly as he'd hoped, and she hadn't trusted him on the rest.

He should have foreseen that. Macy was pure human, without a hint of the old blood. When he'd seen how she'd envied Ciara Conway, he should have known she'd turn that envy on Eden, like a child seeing another girl get all the best treats. She'd

70

stomped her feet and wailed, "Why her?" and then aimed all of her small fury at her supposed competitor and . . . been incinerated by it. Which was just as well, because if she'd survived that battle of wits with Eden and Gabriel, Tristan would have had to kill her himself. Not that there'd been much chance of her surviving it. Poor Macy. So terribly outclassed.

He was chuckling to himself when Alis came in the back door. She piled his mail and flyers on the counter and dropped a ripped sheet of notepaper in front of him.

"Her phone number."

"I already have it."

He continued watching through the drawn sheers as the car pulled away.

"She told quite a story," Alis said as she fixed herself a tea. "Did you know you have a sister with cancer?"

"Do I? How tragic. Remind me to send a card."

"She's quite remarkable. Naturally charming and an accomplished liar. Some worried that living with those *boinne-fala* parents would hamper her blood, but she's inherited gifts from both sides."

"As befits Mallt-y-Nos."

Alis walked over to him. She'd shed her "elderly neighbor" glamour and reverted to her usual form. It wasn't her true form—no one used those anymore. Not only dangerous but pointless. Their true form was close enough to human that they were comfortable looking like them.

Alis appeared as a young woman, perhaps a little older than Eden. Dark-haired, slightly built, pretty but not head-turning. A perfectly ordinary form, not unlike his own.

"Do you need me to do anything else?" she asked.

She didn't ask what he had planned next. Like most of their kind, she was content to leave such matters in the hands of one she trusted to see to her interests. He would win the prize and share the rewards, and there was no risk he'd use and discard her. That's what Macy hadn't understood. Of course, as far as Macy knew, she had been dealing with ordinary people. And, if he was being honest, the codes of loyalty that bound him and Alis did not extend to Macy. The *boinne-fala* existed to be manipulated and used, as they always had. The difference was that he'd given his word to Macy.

"Tristan?" Alis prompted when he didn't reply.

"I'm thinking," he said.

Edgar Chandler had set Eden on him, under his Jon Childs alias. The question was: Why? For answers? For help? For revenge? Any of the three was equally possible, but since the Cŵn Annwn had silenced Chandler, he wasn't about to find out. The equally pressing—and more disturbing—question was whether the Huntsmen knew Chandler had set Eden on him. If their hounds came sniffing around, his game was in serious jeopardy.

"Hold on to her number," he said. "I may have you call her. Until then, I can handle things."

CHAPTER TEN

W hat's on the agenda for the rest of the day?" I asked Gabriel as we drove off.

"Nothing until tonight."

My hand gripped the armrest. "Todd."

"I trust that's still all right? We can reschedule for tomorrow, but they have evening visiting hours on Tuesdays, which seemed convenient."

I forced myself to say tonight was fine. He studied me for a moment, then said, "We'll head back to the office. There's work to do, unrelated to Chandler or the Larsen case."

"Real work. That job you have, which I keep distracting you from."

"Don't apologize."

"I wasn't—"

"Not in words, but it was clear from your tone. Apology suggests that you are keeping me from doing what I need to do, which implies I am somehow powerless to do otherwise. It's a choice, Olivia."

"I know."

"Then I would appreciate it, when I mention other cases, that you refrain from experiencing any twinge of guilt."

"How can I refrain from *experiencing* something?"

"You simply need to put your mind to it."

Dinner passed far too quickly, and before I knew it I was back at the office, in the bathroom, staring at my reflection in the mirror.

Will my father recognize me?

It was a silly question. My picture had been in every Illinois paper and plenty beyond. There was no way Todd Larsen hadn't seen it. But that wasn't what I meant.

Will he look at me and see a stranger?

I could tell myself I was going to see my biological father, a man with no more connection to me than DNA. But it was complete and utter bullshit. For twenty-two years of my life, I'd forgotten Todd Larsen. But I hadn't forgotten *him*. My first dad.

I barely swung to the toilet before losing my dinner.

Well, I guess, as similes go, that one was about perfect.

I knelt on the floor, gasping and gagging.

"Olivia?"

"I'm fine."

I gasped and gagged more quietly.

"My hearing is quite functional. Open the door."

"I'm okay."

"If you pass out from fever again—"

"I'm puking, Gabriel. It's not a fever." I struggled to my feet. "Allow me the dignity of cleaning up in private, okay? Go to the car. I'll be there in two minutes."

A long pause. I could still sense him there, looming.

"I really think you should open—"

"Gabriel!" I took a deep breath, gripped the edge of the sink, and stared at my reflection, my eye makeup smudged, giving me a hollow, haunted look. "I am fine," I said slowly. "Just give me a few minutes."

Pause. "All right. But I'm staying right here."

I opened my mouth, then bit my tongue. "Okay."

"There's mouthwash under the sink."

I shook my head and grabbed a washcloth.

I don't chew gum. I suspect that's my mother's influence—she thought it was unladylike. But as I was leaving the office, my gaze fell on a pack of spearmint gum sitting on Lydia's desk.

"Take it," Gabriel said. "We can replace it later."

"No, I—"

"It'll help settle your stomach." He shoved the package into my hand.

The flavor ran out before we left the city, so I spit the piece into a tissue and pulled out another. Chewed it. Spit it out. Took another. The whole way to the jail, I chewed gum, and it had nothing to do with settling my stomach. It was about giving my nerves something to latch on to.

By the time we reached the prison doors, I'd gone through the whole package. When I reached for another and found it empty, Gabriel didn't say a word, but his look made me feel as if I'd stumbled over my own feet. Clumsy and lost, desperate for stability and comfort.

I stopped walking.

"You're this close, Olivia." I caught the faint sigh in his voice, and it cut through me.

"I'm going in. I just . . ." I looked up at him. "I'll do this alone."

"What?"

I straightened, crumpling the empty gum package and pitching it into the trash can.

"I'm going to see him alone," I said. "If you want to come inside, okay. If you'd rather wait in the car, that's fine, too."

When I looked up, his face was impassive. Another five seconds went by before he said, "Why?"

"I think I need to."

He seemed to chew a stick of gum himself, his jaw working. Then, his shades still on, he met my gaze. "Have I done something wrong, Olivia?"

I don't want to break down in front of you. I feel like you're already disappointed in my weakness. You expect better of me. I can't give you better. Not with this. So I'd like you to stay outside.

"I just think I should handle this on my own."

His chin jerked up, lips tightening.

"I'm sorry," I said. "If I'd realized this in Chicago, I'd have caught a cab. I didn't mean to have you chauffeur me out here—"

"I didn't chauffeur you. I wouldn't have let you come on your own. Not until this other matter is settled." He adjusted his cuffs. "I'll escort you in, then, and ensure all the proper arrangements have been made. Is that suitable?"

I could hear the chill in his voice. *Damn it, Gabriel. This is not the time to get your back up.*

"I'm sor—"

"No need. I understand."

He pulled open the door and ushered me through.

CHAPTER ELEVEN

When I went to see Pamela for the first time, I'd been surprised to meet her at a table, with nothing between us. Gabriel had said the authorities would never let me get that close to Todd. He was right. I was sitting on a rickety stool, staring at a battered speaker and scratched Plexiglas, listening to the woman beside me complain to her inmate husband about the neighbors parking in front of their house.

I'd been a fool to ask Gabriel to stay outside. Yes, it would be harder with him here, watching and assessing, but that would give me a reason to be stronger.

I stood and turned toward the door. Should I ask him to come in? I—

"Olivia."

I jerked back. The voice was so familiar, my adopted name so wrong in it.

"If you're leaving, I understand."

His voice was soft, yet still audible over the faint buzz of the speaker.

My knees wobbled, and I think if I could have run without falling flat on my face, I would have, but I couldn't move.

"If you can stay, just back up and sit down. You don't have to turn around. Be careful, though. You don't want to miss the stool."

A soft chuckle. Oh God, I knew that chuckle, just as I knew the quiet voice and the louder raucous one, too. I could hear that voice strumming with laughter as he pushed me on the swing. As he swooped me up, swirling me around. As he put me on his shoulders. As he tossed me onto the couch and whirled me around in a pool. Always playing, always feeding my need to go higher, go faster, to feel the adrenaline rush.

Then his quiet voice, as he bent to fix a scraped knee or whisper in my ear after a bad dream. I had vague images of Pamela as a warm and loving mother. But Todd? The moment I heard him speak, those memories flooded back, sharp and clear, and the tears started. They didn't begin as prickles or even drops. I felt them streaming down my face, soaking my collar, my cheeks wet, my skin red-hot.

"Can you turn around, Olivia?"

He didn't call me Eden. He didn't stumble on my adopted name, as Pamela did. He was being careful, so very careful.

I took a slow step back and bumped the stool.

"There. Now sit down."

The woman sitting next to me stopped complaining about the neighbors and stared at me, her face scrunched up like I was covered in plague boils.

"Ignore her," Todd said, his voice sharper, and he must have glared at the woman, because she turned away quickly. "Ignore everyone else."

I felt myself nodding and settled onto the stool.

I should turn around.

I can't.

This is stupid. I'm making a fool of myself.

"It's okay."

I nodded again.

"You went to Yale, right?"

The question threw me, and I hesitated before saying, "Yes."

"Okay, so tell me what you studied."

I paused again. Of all the things he could ask . . .

"Olivia, I'm not going to talk about the past or what I remember about you or ask what you remember about me. I know how tough this is, so I just want you to talk to me. Tell me something about yourself, about your life."

"I—I have questions."

His voice softened. "I know. You can ask me anything you want, but you don't need to."

"I *should*. I'm supposed to . . ."

I'm supposed to be interrogating you. I came for answers that Pamela won't give, but I don't want to do that. Not now. Not yet.

"You can come back," he said. "Anytime you want, you can come back, and I will answer everything I can."

I started to turn, fists clenched at my sides. And I froze again, heart pounding, breath coming short, a panic attack threatening.

"It's okay," he murmured, his voice so low it was barely audible through the speaker. "This is fine. I'm just glad you came."

I nodded, tears welling again. Then I turned and looked at him. The first thing I thought was, *He looks exactly like I remember.* He didn't, of course. It'd been twenty-two years. The shoulder-length blond hair had been cut, though it was still not short. His face had shallow creases and lines. He seemed smaller than I'd expected, though I chalked that up to a child's perspective. He was maybe five-ten, lean and wiry. His eyes, though? They were exactly what I remembered: green eyes, the mirror image of mine.

Even as I catalogued the differences, those weren't really

what I was looking for. I was assessing, worrying even. *He looks healthy. Fit. No older than I would have expected—maybe even younger. Calm, too. Grounded.* All that came with a rush of relief, that prison hadn't turned him into a wreck of a man or a hardened convict. Then came the guilt, because I hadn't worried about any of that with Pamela.

I took a deep breath. "I majored in Victorian lit. My, um, master's thesis was on Arthur Conan Doyle."

"Sherlock Holmes," he said with a smile. "What's your favorite story?"

I could name *The Hound of the Baskervilles* and swing this conversation exactly where it was supposed to go. *What do you know about the hounds?* I felt the words on my lips, rolled them around, but just couldn't get them out. I didn't want that. Not yet.

"'Silver Blaze,'" I said. "It's one of his later ones."

"About the racehorse."

I nodded, and as I did, a memory sparked, something about a pony ride, me begging for one at a fair, Pamela saying no, I wasn't old enough yet, Todd saying he'd hold on to me, and the two of us running off with Pamela sighing in the background.

He could mention that. *You always loved horses.* Pamela would have. That was how we talked: I'd say something and she'd tie it back to her memories of me. It was a natural inclination, but uncomfortable, that constant reminder, her need to strengthen our connection.

"There was also a dog in 'Silver Blaze,'" Todd said. "The curious incident of the dog in nighttime, right? It's been years since I read any of the Holmes stories. I'll have to check them out again. The ones I remember best are . . ."

And so it continued. We talked, not about our shared past but finding fresh connections. Todd didn't frantically search them out, like on an awkward first date—You like cream in your coffee? So do I!—but allowed them to rise in natural conversation. We didn't get beyond books, and not even far beyond Sherlock Holmes, before our time ended.

When I got up to leave, he sat very still, then asked, "So, do I pass?" He smiled, and that smile, that crooked smile that lit up his eyes, was so exactly what I remembered that the dam burst and the tears streamed down.

The smile vanished and he leaned forward, hands on the Plexiglas. "It's okay, Olivia," he said. "Everything's okay."

I swiped hard at the tears. "Sorry. This isn't . . ." I managed a wry smile. "Not really my style."

"I know."

He could have dredged up a memory there. *You were never a crier* or *You always hated to cry.* Todd only said, "I know." And then, "I'm sorry."

I nodded, but he held my gaze. "I'm so, so sorry. I know that's not enough, and I know this has been hell on you, Olivia."

"It's Liv."

He paused, as if he hadn't heard right, probably because I croaked the words.

"It's usually Liv," I said. "It doesn't have to be. I answer to pretty much anything except Olive, but . . . most people call me Liv."

I could see him struggling not to smile, to keep his expression neutral, not to make a big deal out of this. And it wasn't a big deal . . . except I'd never told Pamela to call me Liv.

"Okay, then. Liv."

The guard came over and stood behind him. The man didn't say anything, actually seemed to be respectfully keeping his distance, but Todd nodded, acknowledging the message.

"Time to go," I said. "I . . . I'll need to come back. If that's okay."

"I'm not sure I can find the time, and it is a terrible imposition, but if you insist . . ."

I choked on a laugh. "Okay. I'll come back. I do have questions."

"I'm sure you do. It was good to see you."

I nodded, stood, and left as he was led away.

CHAPTER TWELVE

The visiting room door opened before I could grab the handle. I looked up at Gabriel.

"Coming to fetch me?" I asked. Then I noticed the window in the door.

He waved me through and shut the door.

"How long were you watching?" I asked.

I waited for him to say he hadn't been, that he'd known my time was up and had come to meet me.

He said nothing.

I let him lead me away, silent as we exited the building.

Had he seen me sitting there with my back to Todd? Seen me crying? Humiliation and anger swirled hot in my gut.

"I asked you—" I began.

"Not to accompany you inside, so I didn't. I waited at the door."

"You *watched* from the door."

A slight narrowing of his eyes before he slapped on his shades. "I knew this would be difficult, and I thought it best if I was nearby, in case you needed counsel."

"What kind of counsel could I possibly—" I swallowed the rest.

If you embarrassed yourself, that's your fault. Don't take it out on him.

I started for the car. It took a moment to realize Gabriel still stood outside the prison door.

"What have I done, Olivia?"

"Nothing. You're right. I just didn't want—"

I bit off the words, shook my head again, and started to turn away.

"Didn't want what?"

"You to see what I did in there, how I reacted."

His head tilted, lips pursing slightly. "Because you were upset?"

"Can we drop it? Please? I'd like to get out of here."

Once we reached the parking lot, he said, "You *asked* me to accompany you. You wanted me there, and then you did not, and I'd like to know what I've done, Olivia, because I cannot figure it out."

"You've done nothing. You've been above-and-beyond helpful, especially in the last few days, and if I haven't let you know how much I appreciate—"

"I want to know what I did to make you change your mind about having me there when you met Todd."

I opened the car door but paused before climbing inside and looked across the roof. "You did absolutely nothing wrong. It was one hundred percent me."

His brows knitted, as if I were a witness deliberately ducking a direct question.

I sighed and then admitted, "I was embarrassed. After the throwing up . . . I was worried it would get even worse when I saw him. And I wasn't wrong. I couldn't face him at first, Gabriel. I literally could not face him."

A pause, so long that my gut twisted. *I overshared. Again.*

Goddamn it, Gabriel, do not ask for answers when you don't want them.

Finally, he said, "I would not judge you for—"

"But you do."

I tried to drop it, just climb into the car and break the conversation, but my hands gripped the roof and the words poured out before I could stop them.

"You do judge me. It's subtle, and it might not be intentional, but I can see it and I can feel it. You have no patience with weakness. You have no patience with emotional outbursts. I might not be what you first expected: a spoiled brat playing at living a real life. But it took me a hell of a long time to prove I wasn't that girl, and I still feel like I'm walking a balance beam, ready at any moment to tumble out of your good graces. To make a stupid decision. To overreact to a problem. To be the useless debutante you expect."

He stood there, blank shades fixed on me, the face below them equally blank.

I exhaled. "And speaking of overreacting . . . I—I didn't mean to do that. I should probably . . ." I caught sight of a taxi dropping off a passenger. "I'll catch a ride back to the city and call Ricky."

I headed for the taxi, picking up speed as it started to pull away. I waved and it stopped, and I was almost at the door before Gabriel intercepted me. He motioned the cab on. The guy sped off without even glancing at me.

"Ricky has club business tonight," Gabriel said.

"I know, but he said if I needed him—"

"You don't." He waved me toward the car. "Don won't appreciate it, not when I'm here and can handle this."

"It's not about watching over me, Gabriel. It's about . . ."

I trailed off as I glanced up at him, seeing that same blank expression. *It's about support. Having someone to talk to. A shoulder to cry on if I need it. Because I might look okay right now, but I'm not. I'm really not. And you don't see that. You're just relieved that I'm not collapsing in tears on the sidewalk.*

"I would like to call Ricky," I said, slowly and firmly.

"I can't stop you, but I don't see the point, unless you're trying to antagonize Don. I have no idea what the Saints are doing—the less I know, the better—but Ricky is very concerned about the situation with James. If he didn't feel he needed to handle this with the club, he'd be with you. You don't *need* to call him, so you shouldn't."

I stared at him. He frowned back.

You don't get it. You can't get it.

I started toward the rental car without another word.

I wished I had more gum. My jaw ached from chewing that entire package, and I think my stomach would have revolted at the merest hint of spearmint, but I desperately wanted something, anything, to do. Also, I wanted a drink. Maybe three. As we stopped at a light, Gabriel caught me glancing longingly at a bar.

"Would you like . . . ?"

I turned away quickly. "No, I'm fine."

He continued driving, and I tried to relax. My fingers itched to pick up my phone and text Ricky, but Gabriel was right. We were going to the cabin tomorrow. I could wait.

When the car stopped, Gabriel's door clicked open and I looked about, but the only open shop I could see was a corner store. When Gabriel indicated I should get out, I shook my head.

"I'll wait," I said. "Oh, but if you could grab gum to replace Lydia's . . ."

He frowned. Then he noticed the corner store. He pointed farther down the road. I could make out flashes of neon and a crowd on the sidewalk. When I put down my window, I caught the thump of music.

"I don't need a drink."

"Yes, but you'd like one. Come on."

I'm partial to small pubs, though I'll make an exception for a good blues bar. Quiet—that's the key. This place had nineties pop music cranked so loud I could feel my fillings quivering.

Gabriel paused at the entrance and peered back down the street, as if expecting other options to miraculously appear.

"This seems . . . loud," he said, and although I had to read his lips to understand him, I swore I could hear the bewilderment in his voice, as if "loud" and "bar" were not words he expected to go together. Other words that didn't go together? Gabriel and alcohol. Gabriel and socializing. Two more I suspected didn't fit? Gabriel and bars.

"This isn't what I had in mind," he said.

"It's fine."

As we walked in, I realized this *was* what I needed—not the alcohol but the bar itself. The anonymity and the darkness and the loud music that saved me from having to talk.

I ordered Scotch, neat. Gabriel got a coffee. And that was the capper on my evening. Gabriel sees alcohol as a crutch. He knows that's why I don't like to drink in front of him. So if I have one, so does he, even if he doesn't finish it. Tonight he brought me to a bar, *his* idea, after I refused twice, and now he was going to drink a goddamn coffee while—

Fuck it. Just fuck it. Let him have his coffee. Let him judge me. I downed my drink and then ordered another, and didn't even glance Gabriel's way. Between drinks, I texted Ricky to let him know everything was fine. He replied that he wanted to talk. I told him I'd call before bed.

I was halfway through my second drink when Gabriel apparently got bored. One minute he was staring at nothing in particular and the next he was on his feet, three paces away before he remembered he wasn't alone. He turned and motioned that he was stepping away. I thought he was heading to the restroom. Instead, he went outside, maybe for fresh air, maybe as a hint for me to drink faster. Didn't know. Didn't care.

Gabriel had been gone about five minutes when a guy waltzed over and swung into his seat.

"Taken," I said, motioning at the empty coffee cup.

He picked up Gabriel's mug and set it on the next table. "Not now."

I looked around, assuring myself that there was, indeed, no shortage of young, attractive women who looked a whole lot more welcoming than I did.

He leaned across the table. "I was walking to the bar, saw you sitting here, and couldn't believe this seat was actually empty."

"Because it wasn't five minutes ago."

"Then I got a good look at you, and I figured it out." A big flash of glowingly white teeth. "I'm guessing there aren't many guys with the balls to sit in this chair, considering who you are."

I looked at him, blank-faced. Then I stood. He grabbed my wrist, pinning it to the table, gripping it so tight I winced. I was about to yank my arm away when a hand grasped his fingers and peeled them off.

The guy looked up at Gabriel. Then he leapt up, swinging. Gabriel caught the blow and threw him onto the dance floor.

Gabriel pointed at my empty glass. "Do you want another?" Behind him, the guy had gotten to his feet. He glowered at Gabriel and then stalked off.

Gabriel asked again. "Would you like another?"

I stared at him. Then I shook my head, threw a twenty on the table, and walked out. Gabriel followed. He didn't say anything. Even when the noise of the bar faded enough to talk, he acted as if nothing had happened. I got in the car and we went back to his place, without a word exchanged.

SEEING RED

icky gripped his cell phone under the table, waiting for the vibration. He sure as hell wouldn't hear a call in this place, the country music cranked too loud for the shitty sound system, every guitar twang raking down his spine. He wasn't even sure he'd feel the phone, considering the whole damned table was vibrating. His untouched beer sloshed in the dirty glass, foam rising like the sea against a storm-tossed ship.

CJ motioned to the beer. Ricky waved for him to take it. CJ grinned and exchanged Ricky's for a glass from his collection of empties.

Don sat in a quieter corner, across from the leader of the Lost Rebels, a club out of Indiana. This bar was neutral territory, the meeting to discuss an issue of non-neutral territory, namely that controlled by the Saints and coveted by the Rebels. While the Rebels had been eyeing the Saints' southern edge for almost a decade, it'd been years since they'd made a direct strike. All that had changed yesterday. And it was, in part, Ricky's fault.

Just over a week ago, Ricky had been helping Wallace confront some morons who fancied themselves a motorcycle gang and decided they'd take a slice of Saints territory. It happened. Usually all the Saints had to do was knock some heads together and the newly formed "club" would decide they should stick to joyriding. Except, in this instance, the leader got more knocking around than he'd bargained for. He'd been released from the hospital two days ago, with a list of injuries that would keep him off his bike for a while. The person who put him there? Ricky.

There were plenty of guys in the club who lived for knocking heads. Ricky wasn't one of them. Of course, he could fight. The Saints had been training him since he was old enough to throw a punch. But that night, Ricky had been on edge, his father starting to suspect he was seeing Liv. When they'd gone to warn the knuckleheads off their turf, the leader had taunted Ricky about the photo of him and Liv in the *Post*. Then he switched to insulting Liv . . . Well, Ricky had heard other guys talk about "seeing red," but he'd never understood what they meant until that night. It was like his temper went from smolder to detonation in two seconds flat, and the next thing he knew, the guys were pulling him off his target, who was lying bloody on the floor.

For a lot of the guys, that fight was the best thing Ricky could have done to show them he was indeed growing into a man they could follow. His father had not been nearly so pleased. Then the guy's "gang" took their complaint to the Rebels and threw in with them. So, in effect, Ricky had caused the current crisis.

When his phone finally buzzed, he scrambled out of his seat. Don looked over and his eyes narrowed, telling Ricky he'd better sit his ass back down. Ricky walked out the door.

No one tried to stop him. CJ even chuckled under his breath. Outright rebellion would be cause for concern—the boss was still the boss. Submission, though, would be just as worrying, supporting what they feared most—that Ricky was a little too easygoing, too laid-back, given too much to thinking and too little to acting.

Subtle *fuck you*s in his father's direction met with equally subtle approval. Ricky didn't give a shit about that. He didn't plan to win the gang over by rebelling against his father's authority or beating the crap out of rival leaders. It would be at least a decade before his father stepped down, and that was ten years to prove that Ricky was the man they wanted in charge, and to do it his way.

Right now, though, he didn't give a shit what Don thought, either. He'd told his father that Liv was going to visit Todd in prison for the first time, and he'd explained how difficult that would be for her, and asked if there was any chance he could bail on part of tonight. Maybe leave early? Or arrive late?

No. That'd been Don's answer. No discussion. No room for negotiation. If Olivia had a problem with it, then Ricky should cut her loose now.

Cut her loose? Sure, because *she* was the one who pursued *him* and, really, it wasn't like he cared about her. Oh, wait.

Ricky let the bar door slam. Don refused to understand how important Liv was to him, and what made it all the worse was that it was, quite possibly, the first time in Ricky's life that his father *hadn't* understood him.

He pushed that thought aside and answered the phone with, "Hey, thanks for calling me back."

He could barely hear Gabriel's reply over the booming beats of Madonna's "Vogue."

"Damn, it's louder there than it is here. Where are you?"

"At a bar."

Ricky tried to picture that and failed. When the Saints had first hired Gabriel, Don had made the mistake of suggesting they meet at a strip club. Their last lawyer had expected that. Hey, that was the advantage of representing bikers, right? Hanging out in dive bars and strip clubs, associating with gun-toting thugs, surrounded by barely clad young women. Which had proven the lawyer didn't know much about the Saints. Don had accommodated him . . . until they replaced him with Gabriel, who'd gotten as far as the door of the strip club, turned his cool gaze on Don, and suggested that it might not be the most conducive environment for business.

"Is Liv still with you?" Ricky asked.

"Of course," came the frosty reply, as if Gabriel was offended Ricky would suggest otherwise. "If she hasn't contacted you—"

"She texted to say she was fine."

"Then she is." Impatient now.

"Just because she *said* she's fine doesn't mean she *is*, Gabriel."

Silence. Ricky could imagine him struggling to process the possibility. There were guys in the gang who joked that Don had hired a cyborg who did a remarkably lifelike impersonation of an actual human. Gabriel wasn't robotic. He just wasn't exactly personable. Or emotionally literate.

"I'm worried about her," Ricky said.

"I'm watching out for Olivia. I've seen no sign of Morgan—"

"I'm not worried about her *safety*, Gabriel. She just saw her birth father for the first time since she was *two*."

"And she's fine. She's having a drink."

Ricky relaxed a little. "So she talked you into a bar?"

"No, I thought she might need it, so I insisted."

Ricky leaned against the tavern wall. Okay, maybe Gabriel wasn't as emotionally illiterate as he seemed. At least not with Liv. Maybe that should worry Ricky. Hell, the whole Olivia–Gabriel situation should worry him. It didn't. Gabriel had been perfectly clear that he had absolutely no romantic interest in her. Which was bullshit. But he'd given Gabriel the chance to step up, and he hadn't, which meant it was only a passing interest. If Gabriel wanted something, he'd never let someone snatch it from under his nose.

"Okay, so you guys are having a drink—"

"Olivia is. I'm having coffee. Under the circumstances, I need to remain alert."

"Macarena" began in the background, loud enough that he had to raise his voice another notch. "Did you choose the bar?"

"I found it, yes."

"Not to question your taste, but Liv might prefer something . . . uh, quieter. She probably wants to talk about seeing Todd and . . . well, not much talking is happening in that place, I'm guessing."

Silence.

"I know you can handle this, Gabriel. I'm not questioning that. I'm just worried. I could blow off this meeting and—"

"No need. Don wants you there."

"Forget my dad, Gabriel. If you have any reason to think Liv needs me, say the word and I'm on my way."

"She's fine."

"Okay, then. I trust you to make that call." Not exactly true. He didn't trust that Gabriel would necessarily be able to tell, but he did trust that Gabriel would tell him if Liv had given any indication she wanted Ricky there.

"She's fine," Gabriel said again. "You're seeing her for breakfast, aren't you?"

"I am."

"You can speak to her then."

"I know. Sorry to be a pain. I'll let you go. And thanks. I appreciate you being there for her tonight."

What the Saints lacked in numbers, they made up for in cash flow. The Rebels left the meeting salivating at the possibility of a minor trade alliance, declaring the borders fine where they were. Whether the alliance came about depended entirely on the profit analysis Ricky would run after delving deeper into the Rebels' finances, but in the meantime, the Rebels were getting off Saints territory as fast as they could, lest it damage their prospects.

Don, Ricky, and Wallace met briefly back at the clubhouse. After Wallace and CJ left, Ricky grabbed the Rebels file from the back office. He was coming out when his father said, "We need to talk."

"Nope," Ricky said. "Pretty sure we don't."

Don was in his path before he reached the door. "It's becoming a problem."

Ricky stopped dead. "What?"

"You and Olivia."

"I was there tonight for all but five minutes, when I stepped out to talk to *Gabriel*."

"You're getting too serious about this girl."

Ricky rubbed the back of his neck, struggling to control his temper. "Yes, I am. I'm a helluva lot more serious than I've been about a girl since . . . well, ever, I guess. But it has no impact on my commitment to the club or to school. I went to Miami, without complaint, despite the problem she's having with her ex—"

"You don't want to get mixed up in that."

"Get mixed up—?" He bit his tongue. *Keep it calm. Reasonable.*

"You said she's with Gabriel tonight. We can't afford to lose him, Ricky."

"And he can't afford to lose us. This isn't about Gabriel, so don't use him as an excuse. It's not about Liv, either, because you like her just fine. So what *is* the problem?"

"I just don't think this is wise—"

"That's not good enough. I need a reason. A real one."

"You don't belong with her."

"What the fuck does that mean?"

When Don pulled his gaze away, Ricky sidestepped to catch it again.

"No, seriously," Ricky said. "What does that mean?"

"I have a bad feeling . . ."

"A bad feeling? You want me to dump a girl that I'm crazy about because you have a bad *feeling*?"

Don's jaw set. "I don't like this relationship. Does that work better? I just don't like it, and I want you to end it."

"Is that an order?"

His father gave ground as Ricky tried to close the gap between them.

"No, really," Ricky said. "You're the boss. You can give me the ultimatum: end it or walk away from the club. Is that what you're doing?"

"I'm asking—"

"Quit pissing around, Dad. You're always telling me I need to be decisive. So make up your mind. Are you *telling* me?"

Don met his gaze. "Yes, I am."

"All right, then." Ricky shucked his jacket and held it out to him. "Here's my answer."

When his dad didn't take the jacket, he dropped it at Don's feet and walked out.

Ricky climbed off his bike, then sat there, one foot on the curb, as he shivered. The night wasn't cold, but without his jacket he felt . . . Well, he felt a lot of things.

He rubbed the goose bumps on his arms and looked at Gabriel's condo tower. Liv was up there. All he had to do was park the bike, walk into the lobby, and buzz.

Where's your jacket? That's the first thing she'd say, and then he'd tell her, and her eyes would widen in alarm. *Are you crazy?*

Yes, maybe.

You don't want to do this, she'd say.

I know . . .

Has he called?

He'd nod and tell her yes, a half-dozen calls and texts from his father, none of which he'd read, let alone answered.

Call him and tell him if he wants to talk, he can meet at your place. Now. I mean it. You don't want to run back to him, but you need to talk about this. You need to fix this.

I know.

She'd hug him and he'd feel her heart pounding, worried for him, and that would calm his own racing heart, reassure him that this could be fixed, that she'd make sure he fixed it.

He knew exactly what she'd say and what she'd do. All the right things.

His father wanted him to give that up? Because he had a bad feeling?

Goddamn it! Ricky knocked the kickstand out hard and swung from his bike. He looked up at the apartment. Then he yanked off his helmet and started for the door. Knowing what Liv would say was one thing, but right now he really needed to hear it.

He strode into the silent lobby. Apartment 5512. He checked his watch. It wasn't ridiculously late yet, but admittedly, if he pushed that button at this hour, he might piss off Gabriel, which he really didn't need. He should text Liv first and make sure she was still up.

He pulled out his phone. He had five voice-mail messages. Four were from Don, but the last was from Liv herself. He hit Play.

"Hey, it's me. Really hoped to catch you before I went to bed." She paused. "Which sounds whiny, doesn't it? Sorry. Long night. I know you're busy. I'll see you in the morning."

He checked the time stamp. It'd come right after he'd stomped out of the clubhouse, ignoring all calls, thinking they were his father.

Liv had had a hellish evening, and she'd gone to bed to get some rest. How could he wake her up and dump his own problems on her? How the fuck had he even considered that? *Hey, I know you were reunited with your father in a prison visiting room tonight, but I've got some dad issues, too, so let's talk about mine.*

Ricky ran his hand through his hair and exhaled, shaking his head. *What the hell was I thinking?*

I wasn't thinking. I was reacting. It's all shot to hell and the only good thing left is fifty-five stories up, out of reach. But I'm going to do the right thing and let her sleep.

He pushed open the lobby doors and walked out. As he did, he caught sight of a Volvo parked across the road. The car was running, a man in the driver's seat, the window down as he watched the building. Seeing Ricky, the driver quickly put the window up, but not before Ricky got a look at a familiar face.

Morgan? Are you fucking kidding me?

The car pulled into the street. Ricky strode to his bike and hopped on.

You picked the worst possible night to pull this shit, Morgan. And you're about to find out why.

A REASONABLE MAN

G abriel paced the living room, checking the locks and the security system, looking out the window, then sitting on the edge of the couch, hoping to settle in for the night, only to be compelled to get up again.

He'd given Olivia the bedroom. He felt better being between her and the front door. The chances of Morgan breaking in were as infinitesimal as the chances that Gabriel had somehow failed to engage the locks or arm the security system, but taking the couch helped dull the edges of his gnawing anxiety.

He should feel better about the situation. He and Ricky had come up with a rational plan for dealing with James Morgan. The problem was that Gabriel was becoming increasingly convinced they were not dealing with a rational man.

He'd had two e-mails from Morgan today. The first had come late morning. A photograph with the subject line "Thought you might want to see this." Which had told Gabriel he almost certainly did not. He'd cautiously opened it on his phone, getting the smallest possible preview before realizing what it was, deleting it, and going into his trash and removing it from there, too, on the off chance he might somehow stumble over it later.

It'd been a picture of Ricky and Olivia. Ricky had told him

Morgan had interrupted him and Olivia kissing behind the diner. While Gabriel hadn't seen much before he deleted the picture, he was quite certain "kissing" didn't quite cover the situation. That was not an image he wanted anywhere in his brain.

But it raised the question: What kind of man purposely walks in on his ex-fiancée with another man and takes a photo of them? And sends the picture to someone else? The levels of incomprehensible behavior were too much for Gabriel to even process.

He was looking out the window when he caught a noise from the bedroom. He walked to the closed door and listened, and then reached for the knob. He stopped himself. Yes, there was a bedroom window—fifty-five stories up without even a balcony to climb on. Most likely, Olivia was using the bathroom. His brain whirred through everything she could find in there. The most damning items—the weapons and the money—were gone, though. He'd removed them earlier that day. With Chandler's death, the defense attorney in Gabriel had finally overruled the little boy who needed his security blankets, and he'd stashed them in an untraceable storage locker he kept.

Still, he shouldn't have insisted Olivia take the bedroom. It wasn't about putting her in a safer spot, he realized. It was about giving her a better place to sleep as a way of saying, "I'm sorry for how monumentally I fucked up tonight."

When she'd insisted he stay out of the prison visiting room, he'd racked his brain for what he'd done to deserve the rejection. Whatever the cause, he hadn't taken the snub well. Not until he'd stood at that visiting room door, seen the tears streaming down her face, and all he could think was, *Thank God I'm not in there.*

It wasn't that he didn't want to deal with her emotional breakdown. He wanted to fix it. To make her feel better. And he didn't know how.

Olivia knew whom to turn to for comfort. She'd wanted Ricky. And he'd talked her out of it. He'd been hurt and, yes, jealous, unwilling to acknowledge that someone else could help her when he could not. So how had he handled the situation? By making it worse.

His intentions had been good. He could tell she wanted a drink, so he'd taken her to a bar where they could talk about the visit. Except he'd inadvertently chosen a place where they couldn't talk about anything. When she said that was fine, again he'd felt relief. He could get her a drink and be spared the necessity of conversation, which would save him from failing to make the correct response.

He'd watched her mood drop ever lower, and he'd known he'd made a mistake. Then Ricky had called, and he'd had the chance to repair the damage. Admit Olivia was not fine and Ricky would be there within the hour. Problem solved. *Olivia's* problem solved. By someone else. Which meant there was no way he could bring himself to say, "She's not fine." Three simple words. One crushing admission.

"If you have any reason to think Liv needs me, say the word and I'm on the way."

"She's fine."

"Okay, then. I trust you to make that call."

Another sound from inside the bedroom. He rapped softly enough that it wouldn't wake her, but when she didn't answer, his anxiety grew.

He eased the door open. The room was pitch-dark, Olivia having pulled the blackout blind. He pushed the door so that the living room light shone through, and then he scoured the familiar room for anything unfamiliar. Nothing.

Olivia was still asleep, tossing restlessly, making the bed creak. He eased the door farther open, light illuminating the bed. That's when he saw her, really saw her. She lay on her side, head on his pillow, her nightshirt riding up around her waist, her legs bare . . . *more* than her legs bare.

Olivia. In his bed.

The image was as unwelcome as the one Morgan had sent to his phone, but he didn't delete this one. No, he stood, and he watched, and he thought, considered, imagined—

He closed his eyes, but it didn't do any good. He could still see her there, in his bed . . .

Where she should not be. Not in his bed. Not in his apartment. What the hell had he been thinking? What was he doing, not just bringing her here, but any of it, all of it?

I'm sorry, Olivia. I understand you're going through a difficult time, and if you need my help as your lawyer, I'm quite happy to give it, but otherwise . . .

Otherwise . . .

Otherwise, he should extricate himself from the situation. Completely and thoroughly. He'd been wrong to make this his problem, to get wrapped up in the madness, to get wrapped up in her.

He thought of leaving and felt pain. Physical pain in his gut, as if someone had sucker punched him and left him gasping.

I don't want to leave. I don't want her to leave.

But you need to. Leave before she does, because you know she will. You'll drive her away. You'll do something or you'll fail to do something, and she'll give up on you.

Olivia whimpered in her sleep, and when he looked, she'd doubled over, her head down, legs drawn up as if she was the one in pain.

I can't help her.

Yes, I can. Maybe not with what happened tonight, but there is something I can fix.

He took out his phone and flipped to the second message from Morgan.

We need to talk. I'll be home all night and the house will be otherwise empty, so we can discuss this in private and, I hope, come to an understanding. You're a reasonable man, Walsh. I think we can reason this out.

A reasonable man. By that, Morgan meant that Gabriel could be bought off. The spark of indignation lasted only a second before cold reality snuffed it out. He *had* been bought by Morgan once, and there was no reason for the man to suspect it wouldn't work again. That would not happen, of course. Whatever impulse Gabriel had to extricate himself from this situation had been crushed by the determination to prove he could fix this, he could help her, he could be what she needed.

Gabriel dropped his phone into his pocket, eased from the room, and headed out of the apartment, arming the system as he went.

CHAPTER THIRTEEN

Ricky picked me up for breakfast. When we reached his bike, I noticed the bulging saddlebags and the smell of bacon.

"Are you up for a picnic breakfast?" he said. "If you don't want to eat outside, we could commandeer the meeting room table at Gabriel's office."

"No, a picnic is great. Eating out means dining with strangers, and I wasn't really feeling up to that today."

"I figured you might want some privacy."

"I do." I kissed his cheek before I pulled on my helmet. "Thanks."

He drove us to the Lincoln Park lily pool. One of my favorite spots. I'd mentioned that to him *once*. In passing.

The park had just opened for the day, and there was no one else around. Ricky still led me to an out-of-the-way corner, where we could enjoy a view of the pond and the ducks without much danger of interruption.

We were settling in on the rocks when I noticed scrapes and bruises on his knuckles. I caught his hand as he reached into the bag of food.

"Trouble last night?" I asked.

"Mmm, yeah. Minor resistance."

He busied himself pulling out breakfast sandwiches and a cardboard carton of coffee.

"Did it go okay?" I asked. "You seem quiet."

"It went fine." He paused, holding the coffee carton in one hand, the cardboard cups in the other. "Well, the negotiations did. After that . . . I kinda quit the club."

"What?" My gaze shot to his leather jacket, set on a rock beside us.

"It was temporary. I stormed off, cooled down, went back, and talked to my father. We worked it out. No big deal."

"Um, yeah." I took the coffee from him and set it aside. "You *quit* the *club*. Even if it didn't last an hour, that's an hour too much. I know what the Saints mean to you and what your dad means to you."

I rubbed my fingers over his shoulder, where he had the Saints patch tattooed on the back.

"Some people will bluff and bluster to get their way," I said. "Threaten to end a relationship. To quit a job. To drop out of a group. That's not you."

He dipped his chin, gaze sliding away from me. I snagged it back. "I'm wrong, right? You were bluffing. Showing Don how angry you were."

Ricky exhaled. Then he shook his head. "I wanted to show him I was serious, but I wasn't bluffing. I wouldn't do that. I was ready to walk away."

"Wh-what?"

"Shit." Ricky grabbed my hands and tugged me onto his lap. "This isn't what I wanted to talk about. Hell, I wasn't even going to tell you. I planned to come out here and talk about what happened yesterday. To *you*."

I twisted to look at him. "If you were seriously ready to quit the club because of our relationship, then we have a problem."

"The situation just kept escalating, Liv. It's like putting out tiny fires and, somehow, you're fanning the flames instead. By not resisting my dad's interference, I was proving that you weren't important to me. When I did resist, he gave me an ultimatum. Choosing you was the only way I could say, 'I'm serious,' and if that cost me my patch . . ." He went quiet. "I just really hoped it wouldn't."

I turned in his lap, arms going around his neck, my kiss telling him everything I couldn't put into words—how much that near-miss worried me, how badly I didn't want to come between him and the club, or him and his father, but how badly I didn't want to lose him, either.

I said all that in the kiss, and when it deepened, urgency and hunger and fear igniting as he pulled me down onto the rocks, I showed him exactly how much he meant to me, and how glad I was to have him.

I lay under Ricky as he caught his breath, his eyes threatening to close. When I made a move to slide from under him, he put one hand between my shoulder blades, the other on my rear, and flipped onto his back with me atop him. Then he pulled me down in a slow kiss. When it broke, I tried to back away again. His arms tightened.

"Eager to escape this morning, aren't you?"

"No. Just thinking I should probably pour us some coffee before we drift off to sleep, half naked, in a public park."

A languid grin. "Anyone spots us, they'll steer clear."

He pulled me back down into a kiss, and I started thinking maybe he had a point. The sun was bright and warm, and it felt so quiet and peaceful. Right up until we heard the distant sound of voices. Kids' voices. He rolled me over onto my back, saying, "I'll get that coffee."

"No," I said. "I'll get it . . . along with my jeans."

While I pulled on my clothes, he propped himself up to watch. I had my own view to enjoy. As fine as Ricky Gallagher looks in clothes, he's even better without them. He had his jeans still on, pulled up now but unbuttoned, his shirt off as he reclined on his elbows, his sweaty chest glistening in the sunlight.

He smiled. "You keep staring at me like that and I'll put you on the bike and spirit you off to the cabin early."

"Spirit away," I said, bringing back two cups of coffee. "I have the day off."

He buttoned his jeans. "Seriously?"

"Seriously. A gift from Gabriel, though I suspect he wants me out of his hair so he can get some actual work done. If you have things to do, you can drop me at the office and Lydia will play bodyguard until—"

"My day's plan was killing time until you're free."

"So you want to head up early?"

"Hell, yeah."

"Anytime you're ready, then."

"Not so fast." He caught my arm as I began to get up. "I want to hear about last night first."

He sat, and I leaned against his shoulder.

"When I first went to visit Pamela, I prepared myself to see a killer. Someone who'd done terrible things . . . and who'd given birth to me and raised me and was a part of my life while she did those terrible things. I knew that would be difficult to reconcile, but I think my greater fear was that I'd walk into that room and be unable to see a killer. That I'd remember my mother and I'd think, 'No, she didn't do it.'"

"And?"

"I tried to hold her crimes in my head, like a barrier. It took effort to keep that wall up, but I managed it, and I came to accept that she could have been a good mother *and* a murderer. When I found out she wasn't responsible for the deaths of Jan and Peter, it was . . ." I trailed off, trying to find the right words. "It was a relief," I said after a moment. "A sign that maybe she could be innocent. But I also knew that I had to steel myself against the possibility that if Gabriel and I keep digging, I'll find out she killed six people." I looked at him. "I can't do that with Todd."

"Can't do what?" he asked, his voice soft.

"Keep the wall up. I can't . . . Damn it." Tears pricked my eyes. "I can't *find* that wall, Ricky. I couldn't even look at him right away. When he walked in, I was ready to flee, and then I heard his voice and there was no doubt. Everything in me said, 'This is my father. And my father is not a killer.'"

"You don't want to think that way."

"No, I don't. It makes me feel like a gullible fool. But when I walked out of that visiting room yesterday, all I could think was that we've got to move faster on this case, forget everything else and focus on proving them innocent."

"What did Gabriel say about that?"

"I never told him. The rest of the evening was . . . not exactly conducive to conversation."

"The bar."

I looked over.

"I texted him," he said. "I know you said you were fine, but I wanted to be sure. I asked him to give me a call and when he did, I could hear the music. Not a chance of talking in that place."

"You spoke to him?"

"Sure. He insisted you were fine, which I suspected you weren't, but . . . he thought you were doing okay, and I didn't feel right running over if you'd rather I didn't."

Gabriel had told Ricky he shouldn't come? After I had made it clear—*very* clear—that I wanted to see him?

"Liv?"

I pushed down the rising anger. "Sorry, just . . . Goddamn it, Gabriel!"

Ricky chuckled. "I'm guessing he missed a few cues that you weren't fine."

"Just a few."

"I'm also guessing that's why you didn't talk to him about Todd. It's one thing if Todd gave you proof he was innocent, but it would be hard to say to Gabriel that you *feel* he's innocent. He won't understand."

"And he'd think I was being foolish."

Ricky made a face. "I wouldn't go that far. He just won't get it. Either way, maybe you *should* push harder on your parents' case—"

The jangle of "Big Boss Man" cut him short. In the past, when that ring tone sounded, Ricky would roll his eyes, but when he answered there was always a warmth in his voice that belied the grumbling. I'm sure I used to do the same when my dad called—no matter how inconvenient the timing, I was always happy to hear from him. Now Ricky tensed, like a deer spotting a shotgun.

"You should answer it," I said softly.

"I know." He did, saying, "Hey." His face stayed tight as he listened and then said, "Actually, we were heading up to the cabin early. Liv has the day off." As Don replied, Ricky relaxed. "Okay, sure." A soft laugh. "Yeah, I know. I set out a few traps when we were up the last time."

I walked to the pond to give him privacy while I checked my own phone. No texts. No messages. A few e-mails, the last from

Gabriel. Changing his mind about giving me two days off? God, I hoped not.

I opened Gabriel's e-mail so I could shoot back a quick response before we hit the road. Then I read his message.

I've tried calling, but you aren't answering your phone. Something urgent has come up. I need you to meet me as soon as possible. It's in regards to the Larsen case and not something I wish to put in an e-mail. I'll be at the address below. I'll expect you there within the hour. This is important, Olivia.

I checked the call log. While it was not impossible that I could have been too, um, preoccupied to hear my phone ring, there weren't any missed calls. But my cell service fluttered, the bars rising and falling.

I called Gabriel. It went straight to voice mail. I hung up and walked back to Ricky, who was on his feet, tugging on his T-shirt.

"Everything okay?" I asked.

"Yep. I suspect something came up and he was hoping I could get to it before I headed out. When I said we were leaving right away, he just wished us a good trip and asked if I'd pop into town to check messages tonight and tomorrow morning, in case he needs to contact me. Which is protocol anyway."

"So situation normal?"

"For now. Let's hope it stays that way." He looked down at the cell still in my hand.

"Gabriel," I said.

He swore. I passed over the phone with the message on the screen. As he read it, he swore some more, but said, "You *do* want to move on your parents' case. We'll get this over with and then take off."

CHAPTER FOURTEEN

t was not a short drive. Fifty-five minutes, in fact. Luckily, the route was easy enough—straight up the shore of Lake Michigan. We arrived on a quiet country lane. I spotted the rental Jag pulled over ahead, Gabriel standing at the roadside. I swore I could feel his impatience strumming from a hundred yards away.

Ricky pulled over and lifted his helmet visor. "He doesn't look happy."

"Does he ever?"

Ricky chuckled. "I'll go hang out in town. Call me when you're done. No rush."

I swung off the bike and headed toward Gabriel.

"Yes, it's been more than my allotted hour," I said. "But given how long it took to get here, I think you could have given me more time. Also, I didn't ignore your call. I never got it. We were out for a picnic breakfast and cell service sucked."

Gabriel stared at me as if I were speaking in tongues.

"I said I didn't get—"

"I heard what you said," Gabriel said. "I'm trying to figure out what you're talking about *and* what we're doing here. I don't mean to be rude, Olivia, but I did have a full day planned."

I held up my phone. "You summoned me here. On urgent business."

As he read the message, the furrow between his eyes deepened. Then he passed me his phone, with an e-mail displayed.

Hey, I hate to do this to you, because I know you're busy today, but I just got a huge lead on the Larsen case. Tried calling, but it keeps going to v-mail. Can you meet me? Sorry to be cryptic, but I don't want to put this in an e-mail. I'll be at the address below in an hour. I'll owe you. You can even bill me if you want. :)

I checked the address, expecting to see it was spoofed. It wasn't. I could hear James telling me he hadn't hired those deprogrammers, and my mocking reply.

"Get in the car," he said.

We got in, but Gabriel didn't start the engine. He peered out. When I caught a glimpse of something moving outside, I twisted to peer awkwardly through the back window as a raven settled onto a dead oak.

"Cŵn Annwn," I murmured.

Gabriel adjusted the mirror to look. "A hound?"

"No, raven. They're with the Huntsmen, owls with the fae. That's my theory anyway. There was a raven in Cainsville shortly after I arrived. It attacked TC. Veronica helped me scare it off. She said ravens weren't supposed to be there. I thought she meant in the region, which is true, but I think she meant the town. I remember laughing when the raven avoided the gargoyles, like it thought they were alive. That night, when I came out of work, I found it dead, killed by a couple of owls."

"So the Huntsmen send the ravens to watch you?"

"And, more rarely, the fae send owls. I've even seen both birds in the same place. At the abandoned psych hospital and in the gully after our car crash."

"Did they attack each other?"

"No. They just watched me."

I looked around again. Then I spotted something through the trees.

"Shit," I said. "Do you know where we are?"

"The middle of nowhere?"

I smiled. He'd been in a bad mood when I left this morning. Cool and distant, bordering on impatient. I'd practically been hovering at the door, overnight bag in hand, when Ricky arrived, like a kid waiting for parent #2 to pick her up for the weekend because parent #1 had had quite enough of her, thank you very much.

Now we'd been summoned to a deserted country road, for unknown and almost certainly nefarious reasons, and he had relaxed, was even joking. Because, let's face it, a dangerous and potentially deadly situation was so much easier to handle than an emotionally distraught houseguest.

"We're at Villa Tuscana."

His look said that didn't help.

"It's an estate," I said. "Built by Nathaniel Mills for his wife, Letitia Roosevelt, at the turn of the century. She was his second wife, a third his age, and a distant relative of the presidential Roosevelts. The rumor was that he married her for that political connection. To prove otherwise, he built her this house, modeled after one where they first met in Tuscany. It's said he built it from memory, because he remembered every moment of that night."

A terribly romantic story, and when I paused for effect, Gabriel motioned for me to get to the point.

"She never spent a night in it," I said. "He threw a ball to welcome her, and as the guests were leaving, they realized no one had seen her for a while. They found her in the lily pond, drowned. Accident, suicide, murder . . . no one ever knew, but

Mills walked out the front door that night and never returned. He let the house fall to ruins. Which is how it still stands."

After I finished, there were about ten seconds of thoughtful silence where I thought Gabriel was actually experiencing some emotional reaction. Then he said, "Mills? Any relation to . . . ?"

"James Mills Morgan? Yes. Nathaniel was a distant cousin."

"Which is how you know the story."

"Um, no. Plenty of locals know the story. You've seriously never heard it?"

He shook his head. "If this house is connected to James, then the obvious answer is that he lured us here. The e-mails would be easy enough to fake with his technical skills."

"His *team's* skills. James himself isn't much of a techie. But yes, he could have convinced someone to do it. He doesn't have any direct connection to the property, though. I'm thinking of someone else who lured me to an abandoned building under false pretenses."

"Tristan."

I looked at the weed-choked lane leading to the ruins. "We should take a look."

The proper response at this point would be: *Are you kidding?* Or, *Are you fucking shitting me?* Gabriel would never be so profane, but the sentiment held. We'd been lured to an abandoned estate, and I wanted to go check it out? Clearly madness. But Gabriel only sat there, gazing down that lane, considering.

"I have my gun and my switchblade," I said. "Which I suspect wouldn't stop Tristan, but if he wanted me dead, he'd have done it at the psych hospital."

"He doesn't want you dead. None of them do. But that doesn't mean they don't pose a serious threat."

"So . . . no?"

He opened his door and got out. I followed.

CHAPTER FIFTEEN

I t was said that the driveway to Villa Tuscana had once been topped with crushed marble, imported from Italy. I don't know how likely that is, but there was no sign of it now. The lane passed between rows of giant hemlocks and was choked with ivy and wild roses, so thick that we couldn't see beyond the tangle.

I knew what was there, though: one of the most haunting and beautiful places I'd ever seen. My dad had brought me there, twelve years ago, after I heard about it at a party with the Morgans and I'd begged to go see it. We hadn't told my mother, of course. It was trespassing. Also, we'd get dirty.

My dad had been almost as enamored of the Villa as I was, but in a very different way. I'd seen spectacular architectural beauty reclaimed by nature. Even now, I could feel the pull of it, an intimate, primal mingling of the civilized and the wild that called to me.

To Dad, Villa Tuscana had been a lesson. No matter what you accumulated in life, it meant nothing if no one cared enough to continue your vision. Now, being here and thinking of him, my mind turned to the department store, his life's work. Yet as soon as I felt guilty for abandoning it, I could hear his voice.

You've got a world of choices, Livy. Don't let anyone make you feel like you're supposed to do anything you don't want to do.

I cleared my throat and pointed at the house, now just visible ahead. "Villa Tuscana is considered one of the finest examples of Italian landscape design in America."

"I . . . see."

"My dad used to bring me here," I said. "Lots of memories. That means you have two options: either you let me play tour guide or I collapse in a blubbering blob."

"Blubbering blob?"

"I could say that I'll collapse like a grief-stricken Victorian lady, sobbing silently on your loafers, but I'm not a pretty crier, as you may have noticed. Tour guide, then?"

I didn't wait for him to answer.

"When my dad first brought me here, I was already into architecture, so he got me a book on Italianate and we spent the day, me snapping pics on my new digital camera and him pointing out structures and details for me to identify. Like a reverse scavenger hunt."

"What's that?" He pointed at a structure almost hidden on our left.

"Tea house," I said. "It's an open pavilion at the end of a promenade terrace. While tea houses are generally considered British architecture, this one was done in Italian style. And thank you for playing."

We continued the game until we'd crossed the vast lawn to the front of the house.

"It's very . . ."

"Plain?" I said.

"I was going to say large, but yes, I suppose I would have expected something more ornate."

"Italianate style in nineteenth-century America was a reaction to the more ornate Gothic Revival and Victorian that you see in Cainsville. Personally, I like ornate. But I can see the appeal of the smooth lines and simple arches. I will point out, though, this grande dame's face is on the other side, overlooking the lake. And it is *amazing*." I inhaled. "Which is not why we're here at all."

Gabriel shrugged. "There's no reason not to enjoy the setting."

"A point of view I share, which likely means we have been in dangerous situations far too often. Summoned to an abandoned house? Huh, well, let's do some sightseeing first before all that life-and-death nonsense crops up."

He smiled, a real and unmistakable one. "A perfectly valid way to look at things."

"Agreed. But we should at least pretend to be figuring out *why* we were summoned."

Gabriel walked along the side of the house. I climbed the steps and poked my head through a hole in the boarded-up door. Inside, it was too dark to see more than walls and shadowy piles of debris.

"Anything amiss?" I asked.

"Nothing I can see."

"Me neither."

I hopped onto the thick marble railing as Gabriel murmured, "Careful." I balanced there and surveyed the grounds, seeing only weeds and rubble.

"Nothing at *all*?" Gabriel said as I jumped down.

"If you mean omens, no, there isn't a helpful trail of magpies."

"Keep looking."

"It's not like that. I can't conjure them up—"

"Then don't look. Observe."

"What the hell is that supposed to mean?"

He shrugged. When my gaze moved left, he said, "That way, then."

"I don't *see* anything that way."

"But you feel as if you should." He strode around the side of the house. "*You see, but you do not observe. The distinction is clear.*"

"I hate it when you do that."

"No, I don't think you do."

We rounded the side of the house to see a collection of small buildings.

"And this is . . . ?" Gabriel asked.

"The service court. Stables over there and there." I pointed to the crumbling buildings. "Servants' quarters around back."

"And that?" He nodded toward a long narrow building lined with copper doors. "They look like garages."

"They are. Twenty of them, built in a day when few people could afford cars. An obscene luxury . . . though admittedly, one I can appreciate."

We walked to the garages. Most of the windows in those fancy copper doors had been smashed and some of the doors themselves were ripped open, revealing only debris inside.

"Not terribly exciting," I said. "And I'm not picking up so much as a twinge to tell me where to go next. Any more Holmes quotes for me?"

His brows arched. "Is that who I was quoting?"

"You know damned well you were. Not for the first time."

"It is entirely accidental."

"Right, so you've never read Sherlock Holmes? Or seen any of the endless movies and TV shows?"

His brows shot higher. "That would imply I have time for such frivolities. I don't watch television or movies, and while I read a fair bit, fiction would hardly advance my education. *Data, data, data. I cannot make bricks without clay.*"

I crossed my arms and glowered up at him. "Obviously, you've made an exception."

"I never make exceptions. *An exception disproves the rule.*"

"I hate you so much right now."

He laughed, and it was a glorious thing to hear, and I wanted . . . I wanted more. I wanted to capture this mood and hold on to it. Abandon any purpose for being here, grab his hand and race around to the lake side, show him the best place to climb up and gaze out over the water, to explore the ruins and not care why we'd come. Seize this playful mood of his and see how far I could take it. To be immature and, yes, childish.

The moment I thought that, I heard a child's giggle. I spun around.

"Olivia?" Gabriel said.

He stepped closer, shades off as he looked about, frowning slightly, but the good humor lingering in his eyes, along with a warmth and an openness I hadn't seen there before.

The giggle came again. I wanted to ignore it. *Go away and let me have my moment. It might never come again and—*

A small figure slipped from the shadows of the garages. It was the blond girl from my dreams and visions. She wore Mary Jane shoes and an organdy party dress covered in roses.

I spun to check on Gabriel.

"Don't worry," she said. "He's still there."

He followed my gaze, and his frown deepened.

"He doesn't see me." She tilted her head, her eyes fixed on him. "Not really. But he senses I'm here."

I remembered the alley, how we'd been separated and I'd seen Gwrach y Rhibyn washing what seemed to be his shirt. I glanced back at him. "Stay close, okay?"

Another lift of his brows, as if to say, *Of course.*

"He will," the girl said. "For as long as you let him. And you must let him. Both of them. It's when you choose that you are doomed. All of you. All of us."

"I'm not good with riddles," I said.

"Olivia . . . ?" Gabriel's voice was low, as if to avoid frightening away whatever he could not see.

"It's the girl," I said.

"The girl?" She scrunched up her nose. "I have a name. Many of them."

"And they are . . . ?"

"You already know a few. Matilda. Eden. Olivia. I have more, but the others aren't as important."

"So you're . . . me? Some memory of myself?"

"I am you, and I'm not you. I'm all of you. All of them. They are you, and they are not you."

"More riddles. Great."

Her nose scrunched again. "They aren't riddles. They're facts. You just don't understand them. I need to tell you the story."

"Is that why we were summoned here?"

She hesitated. Then she gave a sly smile. "Yes, that's exactly why—"

"How'd you do it?"

"Summon you? I . . ."

"You didn't. Someone else did, for some other purpose."

"Yes, but it's not important."

"It is to me."

"It shouldn't be. In the larger scheme of things, it's inconsequential. This is important." She held out her handful of black and white stones. "The rest?" She scooped up sand from around her feet and let it run through her fingers. "The rest is not. What you find here will be terrible. But, in the end, it is but a distraction luring you from the path."

"So you know what I'm supposed to find here?"

"Yes."

"Will you lead me to it?"

"No. I will tell you a story, and then you should leave. What lies here is best not found. Not by you. Not by anyone, if that were possible. It will only interfere. Ashes to ashes, dust to dust."

"And if I disagree?"

"Then you'll have to find it yourself. I'll not bring you pain."

I turned to Gabriel. "There's something here I'm supposed to find, but she won't help me. She wants to tell me a story."

I thought his answer would be quick. *Forget that and get to work. Find what we were brought here for.*

"Hear the story," he said. "This is the second time she's tried to tell you. You should listen."

I glanced at her. "Fine. Go on."

"Another day."

"What? Look, if you have something to tell me—"

"I do. A different story. You aren't ready for the other yet. You don't understand enough. I see that now." She spun, her dress belling out, face raised to the sun. "You like it here. Do you know why?"

"I appreciate fine architecture and—"

"Don't be silly. There are old buildings everywhere. But you're drawn to this one. As he is." She darted to the nearest wall and ran her hand over an ivy-filled crack. "It tells a story of our past. Of our revenge."

"Our . . . ?"

She pointed at Gabriel. "His. Ours. Fae. Our memories. We can hear the laughter here, feel the joy, smell the fire, touch the pain, see the mighty hand of nature taking vengeance for us."

She fingered the ivy, creeping ever deeper into the stone, those tiny green vines slowly but relentlessly ripping the stone building in two.

"Do you hear them?" she asked.

"No—"

"Because you aren't listening. Close your eyes."

I sighed, shut them, and crossed my arms. Gabriel murmured, "Olivia . . ." and I knew what he meant. *I know this makes you uncomfortable, but we aren't getting any answers as long as you resist.*

I like my mysteries clear and real, with facts and clues that I can follow. Ego, I suppose. I wanted to solve the mystery myself, not stand before a ruined house talking to a child no one else could see.

I uncrossed my arms and let my mind clear, as I did when I was looking for omens. Shifted to that other state, where the smells and sounds of the real world faded and—

Laughter. Voices, too, speaking in a tongue I didn't recognize. It didn't sound like Welsh, though it had similar notes. I caught the strains of strange music, unlike any I'd heard, and I started toward it—

Gabriel caught my arm, and I jolted from that other place.

"Tell him what's happening," the girl said. "He's trying hard to be patient, but he isn't very good at it. He needs information." Her voice rose to a singsong. "Data, data, data."

"That was a quote," I said.

"Perhaps, but it's also him. Tell him what's happening."

I did. Before I finished, the girl took off, racing around the garages.

"Hey!" I said.

"The next part is over here," she said. "Hurry or you'll miss it!"

CHAPTER SIXTEEN

I ran after the little girl. There was a tumble of ruins past the garage, some building not strong enough to withstand the crushing hand of nature. I picked my way around it and through a tangle of bushes and—

Three men stood there. I stopped short, backing up into Gabriel, who caught me. I glanced over at him. He was scanning the landscape—the field and trees, the lake just visible behind them. He gave no sign of seeing the men, and when I looked again, I realized why. The one closest to me was dressed in an old-fashioned hunting jacket and boots, his hair slicked back, with massive sideburns.

Men from a different era. Ghosts or visions. One leaned on a shovel. Another held a gun. The third was dapper, wearing gloves and a bowler hat. When I turned, the Villa and all its buildings were gone, and I saw only field and trees and holes. Construction had just begun.

"I'm telling you, there's something here," said the man leaning on the shovel. The foreman, I guessed. He had a thick Scottish accent.

"And I'm not denying it," said the man with the hunting rifle.

"We've got squatters, Mr. Mills. That's what happens when you build on land long empty. Folks consider it theirs."

The foreman shook his head. "If it's squatters, then where are the huts? The tents? Whatever's here, it's not natural."

"It's perfectly natural," the hunter said. "We've seen them and we've heard them. They're canny, always flitting about, hiding on us. But you're making a fool of yourself, Campbell, filling Mr. Mills's ear with your old-world nonsense."

"Mr. Napier?" The dapper man—Nathaniel Mills—spoke to the hunter. "I believe you have work to do. I want those fox holes cleared out today."

"I'd rather be clearing the squatters," Napier said. "Begging your pardon, sir, but I believe they're a greater nuisance than a few foxes."

Mills dismissed the hunter, and the man stalked off, grumbling under his breath. When he was gone, Mills turned to the foreman.

"Whatever's out there isn't *canny* at all," Mills said. "It's *uncanny*. Unnatural. I've heard laughing when no one's there. I've seen figures that disappear in broad daylight. The other night, when I was walking the grounds with my dogs, I heard music and my hounds wouldn't take another step. They tore back to the motorcar and cowered there. Napier might think me a fool for saying so, but I'll believe what I see and what I hear. My granny used to tell me stories . . ." He peered across the wild yard. "Something's out there, and I'll not bring Letitia here until it's safe."

"You're a wise man, Mr. Mills. Folks like Napier don't understand. They think every danger can be fought with a good hunting rifle."

"This one cannot." Mills looked at the foreman. "I trust you know how it *can* be handled?"

"Not myself, sir, but I know folks that do. The question is how you'll want it dealt with. Like those foxes, we can smoke them out and hope they'll relocate. That's what I'd advise myself."

Mills shook his head briskly. "No. I told Napier I don't have time for that with the foxes, and the same goes for these . . . whatever they are. I want them gone. Permanently. Get them gone and call in a priest to bless the land. I want a good Christian home for my wife and our children."

The foreman looked uneasy. "These aren't foxes, sir. They're—"

"—a far more dangerous sort of vermin. Get them gone. If you can't, I'll find someone who can."

Mills strode off, disappearing as he walked. I turned back to the foreman. He'd vanished, too. The ruins reappeared, and the little girl, who stood watching me, waiting.

"There were fae here," I said. "But they weren't the sort that are in Cainsville."

"They were and they weren't. When the woodlands began to vanish in the Old World, some fae came to the new one and founded towns like Cainsville."

"Where they could control their environment. Keep to themselves and maintain the boundaries. Mingle with humans only as much as they cared to mingle."

"Yes. As those safe havens grew, some of the wilder fae found homes there. But in the early days, they took refuge where they could. In places like this. Today, wherever they might live, the Tylwyth Teg and the Cŵn Annwn are kept safe by human ignorance. One cannot fear what one doesn't believe exists. In the early days, though, there were more believers, and sometimes it ended like this . . ."

The sun flashed, blinding bright, forcing my eyes shut, and I reopened them to a moonless night. Men carried torches at the perimeter of the main property. A dozen men with torches and bags. They dumped something from the burlap sacks in a ring around the grounds.

"What is this?" one man called. "It looks like . . . metal shavings."

Iron. They're sowing iron.

I shivered in spite of myself and rubbed my arms. I glanced around, but Gabriel and the little girl were gone. It was just me, alone in the yard, watching the men work. At a whisper, I saw a shadow slip behind a tree.

"Cad atá ar siúl?"

I turned toward the voice. A woman stood beside me. Or it looked like a woman—I struggled to focus on her, as if she were behind old glass, her form and features shifting and blurring. She was my height, with dark hair and sky-blue eyes. Those eyes were fixed on the men.

"Cad atá ar siúl?"

What's happening? That's what she was asking. I knew it, though I couldn't place the language.

They're sowing iron filings, I wanted to say. But what came out was, *"Níl fhios agam."*

I don't know.

The men finished the circle, a huge one that wrapped around us and the land that would one day hold Villa Tuscana. Then the torches went out. I stood there, with the woman, unable to speak or move, as voices whispered all around me. *What's happening? What's going on? What should we do?*

We don't understand.

The torches leapt to life again, but the flames . . . the flames were blue, and I caught a whiff of something both unfamiliar and terrifying, something that chilled my very core. That's when the screams began.

"Run!" I shouted, wheeling to the woman beside me. "Run!"

I heard my voice, my English words, and saw her stare in fear and incomprehension, and I struggled for the right words, any that would help, but I knew none would. Nothing could help.

The men threw the torches, and the blue fire ripped through the dry field, devouring it at an impossible speed. The woman ran. Others ran, too, shadows and forms in the night, all racing for safety . . . and stopping when they reached the perimeter the men had drawn. The ground sown with iron.

They cannot cross. They're trapped.

The fire caught a shimmering figure in the field, a blond man. It caught him . . . and it rolled over him, consuming him, leaving screams long after he'd vanished. Terrible, unearthly, impossible screams, as if the very ground continued to shriek after he'd disappeared.

I could see the iron filings on the ground. I raced over and reached down. They burned my fingers. I lifted a handful to throw aside, to clear an opening for the others, those whose blood ran true, who could not cross. But the filings fell through my fingers. I frantically tried to scoop them, then to kick them aside, to no avail. The field was aflame and all I could hear were the screams of the dying, trapped within the circle.

Then I saw another figure. One of flesh and bone, no shimmering phantasm, no blurred and shadowed being. Gabriel, standing where I'd left him, the blue flames swirling around him.

I raced back, shouting his name, but the screams drowned me out. He just stood there, impassive, his shades still on as he stared out into the blazing field. When I drew close, he turned to me.

"I smell fire," he said. "And I hear . . ." He trailed off, brows knit in confusion.

The flames licked at his feet, and I grabbed for him, but I stumbled and it was like falling face-first through a portal. I was in darkness, and then I wasn't, and I was still stumbling, still falling. Gabriel caught my arm and pulled me upright.

"Did I startle you?" he said. "I was only saying that I—"

"—smelled fire and heard something."

"Yes." He looked out at the ruins. "It's gone now."

"It was . . ." I gulped for breath, and it felt like inhaling that terrible fire, as it scorched my lungs. Gabriel took my arm again, keeping me upright.

"Before the construction, they trapped the fae in a circle of iron and lit the field with some kind of blue fire. I don't know what it was, but it was . . ." I shivered. "Awful. The smell and the sound and the screaming. They died. They all died, horribly."

Still gripping my arm, Gabriel turned. I glanced back to see the girl there. He yanked off his shades with his free hand, staring in her direction.

"Is this really necessary?" he said. Then he shook his head sharply. "No, let me rephrase that. This is *not* necessary. There is no possible reason she needs to see a hundred-year-old massacre."

I expected her to smile and answer with some riddle. Or perhaps to solemnly say that it *was* necessary. Instead, she walked to him and reached out to touch the hand hovering there, holding his sunglasses. The moment her fingers made contact, he yanked his hand back and then covered the reaction with a scowl.

"What have they done to you, Gwynn ap Nudd?" she said.

"Leave Gabriel out of this," I said.

She smiled at me, wistful. "You protect him as he protects you. And the other, too. The three of you, in a circle of support, as it should be, as it was once, before the circle was torn asunder and the darkness came."

"The *other*. What *other*? I have no idea what—or who—you mean."

"You know exactly who I mean. Matilda, Gwynn, Arawn. Over and over, until the damage is fixed. Until the two sides"— she held up her hand, a black and a white stone on her palm; she closed her fist, and when she opened it again, there was one stone, two colors swirling through it—"are one again."

"You realize I have no idea what you're talking—"

"You will."

"But this Matilda . . . am I her? Reincarnated or something?"

"Or something." She pursed her lips as if in thought. "Reimagined. Not reborn, but born anew. As he"—she motioned at Gabriel—"is not Gwynn ap Nudd, nor the other Arawn. You are, and you are not. You are destined to play the roles again. To give us another chance. But when two sides have been at war so long, neither cares for peace. Only victory."

"Two sides," I said. "You mean the Tylwyth Teg and the Cŵn Annwn, right?"

"There's more to this story," she said. "Follow me."

CHAPTER SEVENTEEN

The girl tore off. When I started after her, Gabriel caught my shoulder.

"We're done here," he said.

He still had his shades off and was looking toward the house, his gaze distant.

"Gabriel?"

"We want answers, but not at the expense of showing you horrors you can do nothing to stop. It's pointless and cruel."

"It's data."

His eyes narrowed as if I were mocking him. I took his hand from my shoulder. When I touched it, I expected him to pull back. He gave no sign he even noticed, still watching me with that wary look. I lowered his hand but didn't release it.

"It's information," I said softly. "You need it. I need it. And this is the only trustworthy source."

I thought he'd say there were no trustworthy sources. He only gazed in the direction the girl had run, that cautious look easing but not evaporating.

I squeezed his hand. He still didn't pull away. He looked as if he wanted to retreat behind his wall, snap at me not to be foolish, to leave this place. Yet he couldn't. He looked at me, and I felt so much. Too much.

I dropped his hand and turned in the girl's direction. She was long gone.

"I need to see this through," I said, and took off.

Gabriel ran after me. I heard a grunt and turned to see him pulling off his suit coat. He caught me looking and scowled as he laid the jacket over his arm.

"Next time you plan to take us climbing through ruins, I would appreciate advance notice, so I may dress appropriately."

"Do you even own anything appropriate?"

Another scowl, as if this wasn't the point.

"Tell you what, the next time you get a fake message telling you to meet me at some remote location, just hit a Target on your way."

I took off again, hearing him growl in annoyance as he came after me. As his mood darkened, it lightened mine. This wasn't Gabriel truly angry—it was pique and ego and mild discomfort. It was a Gabriel I knew well, and it chased off the last shadows of my vision.

We came around the side terrace, picking through rubble and brambles until . . .

"This," I said, waving my arm toward the lake. "This is what I want."

He didn't even look. He was too busy loosening his tie and undoing the top button of his shirt. But when I walked across the ruined patio and climbed onto the railing, he noticed. "Get down from there."

"I'm looking for the little girl. Also, it's an amazing view." I stepped to the side and motioned at the railing. "Hop on up."

He didn't dignify that with a response, just gingerly laid his jacket over the railing after inspecting the level of filth.

"You obviously don't see her, so get down from there, Olivia. It's not safe and if you fall, let's hope you're still able to dial 911, because I won't do it for you."

"Grumpy."

"No, *cautious*. One of us has to be. Down. Now."

"Yes, sir."

I hopped down—the other way. I heard a sharp intake of breath, and then he scrambled down the steps . . . to see me standing on an intact planter below, grinning at him.

He crossed his arms, pinned me with a look, and then shook his head. "I suppose I should be glad you bounce back from trauma so quickly."

"I have to, don't I?" I said as I hopped off the planter. "Given how quickly the traumas come these days. It's that or assume the fetal position and wait for the white coats."

I looked out toward the lake again. As he turned, he blinked, and then stared at the gorgeous ruined terraces, green-choked fountains and pools, an endless cascade of gardens and patios and water features leading down to the shore of Lake Michigan.

"Did I say it was amazing?" I said. "I'm serious, too. I want one of these."

"With a five-million-dollar trust fund? You'd be lucky to get a house on the lake at all."

"Your pragmatism will not deter me. I don't want a house, anyway. I just want this." I waved at the terraces. "I'll find my own ruins, where I can hide away with a book and a bottle of wine and contemplate the impermanence of empires."

"*Look on my works, ye Mighty, and despair?*"

"*Nothing beside remains. Round the decay of that colossal wreck, boundless and bare the lone and level sands stretch far away.*" I gazed out at the sands below. "Fitting, don't you think? And deservedly so." After what happened here, I meant. The girl was right. The beauty I saw here was the revenge of nature, destroying the claims of interlopers and murderers.

"You could possibly buy the property with your trust," he said. "I suspect there would be significant back taxes, but the trick would be to first secure the right to sever the property and obtain development permits and then divide it and sell most of the land for vacation condos. If done right, you could even turn a profit."

I smiled at him. "Very practical. And not the nature of fancies at all, Gabriel. I wouldn't buy it, and I'd certainly never sell it for development. I'll just bring my book and my wine and trespass like ordinary folk."

He nodded and looked out at the view. "If the girl is gone . . ."

"I'm pretty sure she didn't send those e-mails."

"Though it sounded as if she gave you some idea what you were brought here for."

I hesitated.

"Olivia . . ." He moved in front of me, blocking both the sunlight and the view.

I started down the marble steps. "To your left and to your right, you'll see what appear to be matching horse fountains, though I don't know why horses are leaping out of water."

"They're kelpies. Look at the hooves."

Long feathers of hair covered their lower legs and hooves, like the spats on a Clydesdale. When I looked closer, though, the hair was seaweed, and under it the "hooves" were actually frog-like feet.

"I remember a story about kelpies," I said. "They lure children to the water, and when the kids climb on their backs, they can't get off again. The kelpies ride out to sea and the children are drowned. The story I heard was about ten children. Nine climb on. The tenth refuses, but he makes the mistake of reaching to touch the horse's nose. His hand gets stuck, and he hacks it off to escape just as the kelpie leaps back into the sea."

"That's a charming bedtime tale."

"Did I mention I was raised by serial killers?"

"Alleged serial killers."

I smiled. "Right. Sorry. And honestly, I don't think Pamela is responsible for the more gruesome tales of my youth. Definitely *not* Todd."

"Why definitely?"

I shrugged and continued down the steps. "I'm pretty sure I found the stories on my own." I turned to head out across the next terrace. "Ahead, you'll see the lily pond—" I stopped. "Shit. Lily pond. Ricky."

"Interesting word association."

Hopefully, I didn't blush. I busied myself pulling out my cell phone and typing in a text, and then . . .

"No signal," I said. "Do you . . . ?"

He checked. "The same. Did he have classes today?"

"No, he's free. I guess he'll just be well-caffeinated by the time we're done." I stuffed my phone back into my pocket. "Okay, as I was saying, the next stop on the tour is the lily pond, which is completely overgrown. If you look beyond the sunken gardens, you'll see vandalized statues. The historical records call them herms, which is technically inaccurate. A herm is a column with a head and, well, Hermes is a fertility god, so you can guess what else they had. These ones were clothed, much to my twelve-year-old self's bitter disappointment."

He shook his head as he followed me down more steps.

"The swimming pool is way down here," I said. "Right at the beach side."

"The girl said you were here to find something. What?" When I sighed, he said, "Did you really think I'd be distracted?"

"Hoped."

"The fact that you are reluctant to tell me indicates the message was not a positive one. There's some sort of danger, isn't there, if you go looking?"

"She said that I'll be hurt, but not physically."

"Doesn't *that* matter?"

I walked down the last few steps to the beach.

Gabriel continued. "Seeing something that leaves a mental or emotional mark is no different from tripping and breaking your ankle on the way to see it. In fact, I'd suggest it's worse."

I turned to look at him.

"Yes?" he said.

Did you really just suggest that emotional pain is worse than physical?

He repeated, "Yes?" with a touch of impatience.

I said, "Nothing," and continued toward the pool.

"Am I arguing with myself, Olivia? What *exactly* did the girl . . ."

He trailed off. When I looked back, he was gone.

CHAPTER EIGHTEEN

G abriel?"

The sun flashed, as it had done earlier, and I was again plunged into night. This time there were lights everywhere, the Villa glowing with them. Music poured from the open windows. Not ethereal fae music, but the sounds of a string quartet. I could hear chatter and laughter, too, human in origin. The house was whole and new, sparkling in the moonlight. Figures walked down the curving steps.

"Oh my," a girlish voice said. "Thank goodness Nathaniel installed an elevator. I only wish it was working already."

Two other feminine voices laughed with her. They turned a curve into the moonlight. None looked older than me. All three were wearing gorgeous Empire-waisted dresses. The one in the middle was no more than twenty, with finger-curled blond hair. She'd referred to Nathaniel Mills by his given name, which left little doubt who this was. His bride, Letitia Roosevelt.

But if my history was right, Letitia had never spent a night in this house. She . . .

I looked up at the Villa again, the lights blazing, music and laughter pouring out.

It's Letitia's grand welcoming party. The first time she saw

the house her husband built. And the last time she sees it,
because . . .

I wheeled and stared at the swimming pool. Then I turned
back to the three girls.

"No," I said. "You can't—"

They stepped right through me, still chattering and giggling.

"Aren't you glad we pulled you away from that dull party?"
said one of Letitia's companions—a dark-haired beauty with
perfect skin and bright blue eyes.

"I know *we're* glad to meet you," the other said. "The social
life here is as dull as that party. I'm sure the three of us can liven
it up." She was light-haired and green-eyed, as strikingly beautiful as her friend. "Oh! Is that the pool?"

"It is," Letitia said. "There's a bathhouse over there."

"Are there any suits?" the brunette asked.

The light-haired girl giggled. "Do we need them?"

Letitia turned bright red. The other two giggled, and she
tried to shake off her embarrassment. Whatever the time period,
no girl wants to seem uncool in front of her new friends.

"Don't listen to her," the brunette said. "We'd never do anything so shocking." She grinned. "Not when there's a house full
of people close by." She walked to the pool, lifted her skirt, and
lowered herself beside the water. Then she dangled her fingers
and let out an exclamation. "It's warm! What magic has your
handsome groom wrought to accomplish that?"

"There's a heating system of some sort," Letitia said. "I don't
quite understand it."

"Who cares?" said the light-haired girl. "If it makes swimming water warm at night, it is the best kind of magic." She
tugged off pointy, low-heeled shoes and then reached under her
skirt. She paused and looked at Letitia. "You won't be shocked
if I remove my stockings, will you?"

"Not if that's all you remove," the brunette said with a laugh. There was something about that laugh . . . a tinkling music almost too low for the ear to detect.

They're fae.

"No," I said.

I hurried over to the two girls, the light-haired one now sitting on the edge of the pool, dangling her feet in. The brunette swished her hand back and forth in the water, and under the surface, seaweed swirled about her hand, like the spats on a horse.

"Come here, Letty," the light-haired girl called. "Sit with us."

"Look at the water," her companion said. "Isn't it marvelous."

They reached out their hands as Letitia walked over.

"No!" I said, jumping between them. I turned to the brunette. "Don't do this. She's not responsible. *He* is."

I knew it was pointless. These were only phantasms, memories. But the brunette met my gaze, and she smiled, a terrible and beautiful smile.

"We know who is responsible. And this is how we repay him. Take from him as he took from us. That is our way. Death is quick. Regret is not."

I remembered Gabriel saying almost the same thing, first to the men in the parking garage, then to James. Letitia walked through me and took the young women's hands.

"Shall we go for a swim?" the light-haired one said.

"What?" Letitia forced a ragged laugh and pulled back. "You are really quite amusing, but I ought to go—" When the women didn't release her, she said, "This isn't funny. Please let me go."

They opened their hands, but her fingers remained stuck to theirs.

"Wh-what?" she said, backpedaling uselessly.

"We're taking you for a swim, pretty Letty. A swim in your new pool."

They wrapped their arms around her and leapt, and as they did, their gowns puddled at their feet and their hair tumbled from its pins, cascading over their bare backs, pitch-black now on one, glowing white on the other. The brunette's skin darkened, too, turning as black as her hair. Their bodies thickened, necks lengthening, as they transformed.

I raced to the pool edge. It didn't matter that it would do no good. I shouted at the kelpies to stop.

They dove into the water with Letitia trapped between them, flailing wildly. Even after the water closed over them, I still heard her screaming. Down they went, so fast and so deep that I was certain the pool bottom was a mirage, that it somehow opened into the lake itself. Otherwise—

The kelpies hit the bottom and they kept going, right through it, vanishing. But Letitia did not. Instead, her body jolted and a red flume of blood swirled up, suffusing the water, spreading out in crimson tendrils.

She floated to the top, her pale blue dress billowing around her. Blood kept pumping from her crushed skull, an impossible amount of blood, the water darkening with it. She floated there, her hair and dress swirling around her. Then she dropped out of sight into the bloody depths.

"I'm sorry," I whispered.

"Why?" said a voice beside me. I looked over to see the little girl. "This is how we repay death. We know no other way. We have no understanding of mercy."

"I do."

She cocked her head. "I misspoke, then. *They* have no understanding of mercy. We may . . . and yet we would do the same. It is in our blood. We answer fire with fire. Blood with blood. In our hearts, there is no other way. Protect those we hold dear. The rest can fall to ash and dust."

"I'm still sorry," I said. "For her."

"But are you sorry for him?"

She waved at the house. Nathaniel Mills was leaning over the top railing, scanning the garden for his missing wife. I looked at him, and it was as the girl said. I understood that I should feel pity. And I did not. He'd earned this fate the day he ordered those fires.

"How does one fight fire?" whispered a voice beside me. I turned to see the dark-haired kelpie, in human form now. She reached out and traced a dripping-wet finger across my cheek. "With water. Fitting, don't you think?"

I wanted to retreat from her touch, but I found myself transfixed by her eyes. I saw the blue fire ripping through this field, and other fields and forests, iron circles and dying fae.

"They scream in pain, but they never scream for mercy," the kelpie said. "They know it does no good. The fae learned that lesson from humans, and this is how we pay it back."

She dove into the pool. Except there was no blood in it. Little water, even, only a foot or two in the bottom, filthy and bloated with dead leaves.

"Is it over?" Gabriel asked.

I nodded.

"What did you see?"

"They killed her. Letitia Roosevelt. Kelpies did."

My gaze lifted to the fountains on the hill. Nathaniel Mills had murdered fae and yet he'd had them carved in stone to decorate his home. They'd had their revenge. Killed his wife, drove him away, let the house fall to ruin, reclaimed by nature.

"Hopefully, that means the visions are over, and we can finally do what we came here to do."

"You mean what we were *brought* here to do," Gabriel said.

I started back up the stairs. "Yes, someone brought us here, and from what the girl says, it's not for tea and crumpets, but it's not to hurt us, either."

"Yes, I believe that's exactly what she said. Whatever you find here will hurt—"

"*Me*. Just me. Which means it's my choice, right?"

"And my opinion on the matter carries no weight."

With every word, his voice chilled ten degrees.

"You know it does," I said as I continued climbing. "Hell, sometimes yours carries more than my own. But when it comes to matters of personal safety, you can be . . ."

I trailed off, and we made it all the way to the top terrace before he said, as if through clenched teeth, "Overprotective?"

"We've both been through a lot," I said carefully as I turned to face him. "I think that might lead us to overestimate the threat level—"

"Really?" His shades were off, ice-cold eyes boring into mine. "After all this, you think it's possible to *overestimate the threat level?*"

You're pushing him away. Don't do this.

I took a deep breath. "I can't leave not knowing what I was supposed to find."

"Yes, you can. You can return to the car and wait there while I search the house."

"And what in God's name has ever led you to believe that I'd go hide in the car while you do this for me? I am not some—"

I cut myself short and turned away, my arms crossing as I fought to regain my temper. I didn't want to fight about this. I really didn't.

So what do I want?

To have him agree I should search and accompany me into that house.

Isn't that as unreasonable as what he wants?

There was no middle ground here. I wanted what I wanted, and damn him if he didn't give it to me.

I exhaled, let my arms fall to my sides, and turned. "I'm sorry. I—"

Gabriel wasn't there.

I looked about, expecting to see the scenery changed, the house new again, some sign of a vision . . .

Then I spotted his back, as he walked into the house.

"Damn you, Gabriel," I muttered, and took off after him.

CHAPTER NINETEEN

I knew what every structure on the Villa's grounds had been, no matter what its condition. Inside the house? Inside I found only endless empty rooms, with the occasional rotting chair or moldering carpet.

Legend had it that when Mills discovered his bride's body in the pool, he'd walked up the stairs, through the house, out the front door . . . and never returned. He'd ordered everything to stay exactly as it was, allowing priceless antiques to rot. My father had told me a different version. He'd heard that Mills had ordered his men to sneak in and spirit off the most valuable of the furnishings, so he could maintain the romantic fiction while recouping the most significant losses.

Judging by the wall of broken windows, I'd just entered the conservatory. Brisk lake air blasted through. I jogged to the next room, but I could see no sign of Gabriel. I called, "Gabriel? I'm apologizing, okay? I was being bullheaded, and while I don't think I'm the only one, I want to talk about this."

No answer. As I walked to the far doorway, I made tracks in the dust on the floor. One set crossing the room. None at the doorway, meaning Gabriel hadn't come this way.

Was there another exit from the conservatory? I took three

steps back the way I'd come and then heard an impatient, "Olivia," from the opposite direction. I hurried into a long, narrow room with two fireplaces . . . and a half-dozen doors.

"Shit," I said.

"Where am I?" a voice demanded. "What the hell is going on?"

The voice seemed to come from all corners, booming, oddly distorted, like speakers turned up too loud. Not Gabriel. Yet it seemed familiar.

"I know you're here," the voice continued. "Damn you, come out and face me."

I turned and there was Nathaniel Mills. He was older, bloated and unkempt, a flask in one hand as he staggered toward me.

"Do you think I can't hear you?" he shouted at the empty room. "Whispering, laughing, taunting? Do you think I don't know what you did, you ungodly sons of bitches? Come out and face me!"

He stormed around the room, kicking at invisible debris, shoving aside invisible furniture. Then he stopped dead. He seemed to move around something, carefully, and then let out a cry as he dropped to his knees.

"Letty! It can't be. You're wet. So wet. And your poor face. Your beautiful face. What have they—?"

He stopped abruptly again and staggered up. "No, you're not real. You're dead and buried." He wheeled, shouting, "Damn you all back to the hell you came from. You—"

His gaze lit on me. "You."

I took a slow step back.

"Do you think I can't see you?" His figure pulsed, shimmering as he moved, and then it wasn't Mills coming at me. It was James. He stopped short and wavered there, his eyes wide. "Liv? What's going on? Where am I?"

"James?"

I reached for him, but he vanished. The little girl's voice whispered at my ear, "Gabriel was right. You need to go."

"But Gabriel's here," I said.

As if on cue, I heard his voice, snapping with impatience.

"Olivia? I do not have time for this."

I took one step his way and then stopped.

That's not Gabriel.

It sounded like his impatience, his diction. But if Gabriel thought I was in danger, would he really storm off? *I* might lose my temper and do such a thing. Gabriel was ice, exact and calculated. He'd freeze me out, but he would never walk away if he thought I was in trouble.

That's why I hadn't seen his footprints. Because he hadn't really gone into the house. It was like that alley near the prison when we tried to follow the Huntsman. I'd turned my back and then stumbled into a vision that I mistook for reality.

I jogged back the way I'd come and ended up in an unfamiliar room. I retreated, and tried the door to the left of it, then the one on the right. Neither returned me to anyplace vaguely familiar.

Okay, I'm hallucinating. No big deal.

I sputtered a laugh at that. I suppose it was a sign of progress that the thought I was going crazy didn't even cross my mind.

The question was: *Which* was the hallucination? The house now, as I tried to get out, or earlier, as I was coming in? Either way, there were plenty of exits—both doors and broken windows.

In the next room, I found the younger Nathaniel Mills, at a desk, telling his foreman his plans for burning out the fae.

They both looked up as I stepped in.

"Yes?" Mills snapped. "What do you want?"

"Nothing. Sorry."

I backed away . . . and tripped over Letitia, lying in her

soaked party dress, tributaries of bloody water creeping across the floor. When I retreated, she lifted her head. Her face was crushed—nose smashed flat, blood streaming from her mouth, one eye bulging, the other a dark pit.

"You didn't save me," she rasped through broken teeth.

"I couldn't."

"You can't save anyone. You ruin everything you touch. Mallt-y-Nos?" She spat blood and broken teeth. "They should have left you as you were. Crippled and useless."

Her cold hand wrapped around my ankle. I broke free and raced through the next doorway. It was a library.

"Liv?"

James stood at a shelf, fingering the moldering books. When he saw me, his face lit up. He started my way and then faltered, his smile evaporating in a look of despair.

"I—I don't know what happened, Liv," he said. "All I wanted was to get you back. He said he'd help and then . . . it went wrong, and I don't understand how. I know I hurt you, frightened you, and I don't understand that, either. It seemed so simple. You were in danger, and I had to save you, and nothing else mattered."

"It's okay," I said.

Another smile, this one wry and sad. "No, it's not. I can see that. It's clear now. Everything's clear." He looked at me. "I never meant to hurt you."

"I'm fine. I'm—" I inhaled deeply. *I'm lost in a house of visions, and I'm talking to one of you, which is not fine at all.*

He looked over his shoulder. "I need to go. I just . . . I saw you and I wanted to say I'm sorry. I'm so, so sorry."

"It's all right."

"It isn't." That wry smile again. "But do you forgive me anyway?"

"Of course. And I'm sorry that I—"

He put his hands behind my head and I felt them, just the barest whisper brushing aside my hair, and then his lips against mine. My eyes closed, and when they opened, I was alone in the room.

"James?"

I felt stupid calling for him, but he'd given me what I wanted—an explanation—and I couldn't help wishing that we really could say our apologies and part with a kiss, hanging on to those memories of something that had been good, once upon a time.

But I knew James was in Chicago, at work. So what did seeing him here mean? That these weren't visions at all, but figments of my imagination? Overactive daydreams—things I imagined and things I wished for?

I needed to get out of here.

I stepped through the next doorway into an absolutely empty room. I breathed a sigh of relief and strode forward—

The wallpaper rippled. I pushed myself to continue, but I couldn't look away from that bubbling wallpaper. Then a line of blue fire ripped through it, curling and smoldering and blackening it in its wake. The fire flashed out, leaving burned words.

There is no freedom from the prison of the mind.

I'd seen the same message at the abandoned psych hospital, when Tristan set me up to "rescue" Macy Shaw. And I understood it no better now than I had then.

I turned away quickly, only to see another message burned on the opposite wall.

We are imprisoned by the truth we dare not see.

We are imprisoned by the questions we dare not ask.

"I'm asking!" I shouted. "I'm asking and asking and asking, and all I get are riddles and useless visions. What else do you want me to do?"

The answer came in a flash of blue fire that spelled out one word in foot-high block letters clear across one wall: *Understand.*

Then, in a blink, it all vanished, and I was left staring at moldy and tattered wallpaper.

I ran through the next doorway, then stumbled over something. I looked down to see an arm on the floor.

Not real, not real, not real. None of it is real.

I tore across the room . . . to find myself facing three blank walls. There was no other way out. I turned, keeping my eyes away from the body on the floor.

Not real, not real.

But I'd caught a flash of the arm. An arm wearing a watch.

I know that watch.

No, I don't. It cannot possibly be the watch I think it is, because that watch is on the wrist of—

I looked down.

There it was: that watch.

"It was my dad's," I'd told James when I'd given it to him.

"I know."

"I don't expect you to wear it. It's just a keepsake. Something to say thanks. For getting me through . . ." My voice caught, the grief surging fresh.

His arms wrapped around me, and when I pulled back, the watch was on his wrist. And from then on, it was always on his wrist.

Now I was seeing my father's watch . . . on a bare arm, lying on the floor of an abandoned house, blood congealed in a pool—

No, not him.

You know it is. You know that arm. Look.

No, I won't. I—

I looked.

It was James. Lying on his stomach, head turned to one side, his back bloodied, his face and shoulders battered, his lips split, his eye black. His eye . . . open. Staring. Empty. Dead.

CHAPTER TWENTY

I fell to my knees and doubled over, screaming until my throat was raw, every muscle shaking as I crouched there.

I heard Gabriel shout my name and footsteps pounding toward me. I staggered up and stumbled into the library as he came through the door, breathing hard.

"I was looking for you," he said. "I heard you scream. What—?"

"Nothing," I said, grabbing his sleeve and tugging him across the room. "A vision. I just had a vision."

"Of what?"

I shook my head and kept pulling him, desperate to get him out of there, to get *us* out of there.

He stopped me. "What did you see, Olivia?"

"Lots of things. Mills. Letitia. Writing on the wall. Let's just go—"

"What made you scream?"

"I—" I took a deep breath. "I imagined I saw James . . . James's body."

"What?"

I pulled out of his grasp. "It was a vision. Or a hallucination. Like Letitia. I just want to get out of here. Now. Please."

I ran for the opposite doorway. When I reached it, I realized he wasn't with me and turned to see him walking in the opposite direction.

"No!" I said. "Don't you take another step, Gabriel Walsh."

He turned, slowly, and the look on his face . . . I wanted to see doubt and confusion and disbelief and skepticism. Even a look that said he thought I'd lost my mind. But that's not what I saw.

"Stay where you are," he said. "I'm going to—"

"He's not there," I said, my voice barely above a whisper. I wrapped my arms tight around my chest, but my legs were still shaking. "It's not really him."

Gabriel didn't say a word, just turned and went through the doorway. I followed him.

James still lay on the floor. I'd seen the bruises on his shoulders and face. Now I noticed them around his neck. He'd been strangled. His back wasn't covered in blood as I'd thought. It was a single swath up the middle, a perfectly excised strip of skin. I'd seen the photos of my parents' alleged crime scenes and the bodies had looked exactly like this.

Strangled. Half dressed. Skin stripped from his back.

That proved it wasn't real.

I looked up to find Gabriel watching me.

"You don't see him, do you?" I said.

Silence.

"Tell me you don't see him." I looked up at him, his face swimming behind my tears. "Please tell me you don't see James."

His jaw worked. The tears streamed down my face, hot and fast. I took a half step toward Gabriel before catching myself. I teetered there and then started to step back, but he reached for me and pulled me against him.

I won't say it was a hug. I won't even say it was an embrace.

It felt like falling against a statue. He held himself so tight and still that I swore I heard his teeth clench as his arms went around me. It was awkward and strange, and he hated it. Yet he did it. He gave me what I needed.

After a long moment, I stepped away from Gabriel and turned to James. I knelt beside him.

"I'm sorry," Gabriel said.

I nodded, and I knelt there, looking at James.

I hated you. I didn't think that was even possible, and if someone had accused me of it, I'd have denied it. But in these last few days, I came to hate you. I wanted you to let me go, and you wouldn't, and now I'm kneeling beside your body, and I don't feel hate. Certainly not relief.

No matter what you did, you didn't deserve this. It's my fault. I don't know what happened, but I know that much: it's my fault.

Tears threatened again.

"We're going to walk back to the car," Gabriel said, his voice rock-steady. "I'll call the police and Ricky. You can sit with him while I bring the police here. I'll take care of everything. All you need to do right now is walk out to the car with me."

That was Gabriel's real embrace. *I'll fix this for you.*

I nodded and started to rise. Then I paused to stare again at that missing strip of skin. I moved around the body, crouched, and reached for James's shoulder.

Gabriel rocked forward. "You can't touch—"

"I need to know."

He didn't ask what I meant, just caught my hand. "The police will check. I'll be here to verify."

I shook my head. "I need to see."

He hesitated and then bent down to James.

"No," I said. "I should—"

It was too late. He'd already eased the body up. James's chest was discolored, either from bruising or from the blood settling. But what I was looking for was there. A symbol painted in blue on his stomach. He'd definitely been strangled. And beaten, too—the blood around his head seemed to have come from his mouth.

"The symbol is the same," Gabriel said. "I don't want to open his mouth or check his thigh, but I'm presuming the stone is there and the other symbols."

"And the bruising?" I pointed at his face and upper body. "Someone beat him. Badly. I don't remember that with the other murder victims."

"No, they weren't. This is clearly a copycat—" He cleared his throat. "We'll discuss that later. Will you leave now?"

I closed my eyes. Then I felt his hand on my shoulder, squeezing gently, and I let him guide me away from James.

CHAPTER TWENTY-ONE

O n the walk back to the car, Gabriel dialed 911 over and over until he finally got through. He gave his name and said he'd discovered a body at Villa Tuscana and would be waiting out front for the police. The dispatcher tried to get him to stay on the line. He repeated that he'd be waiting by the roadside, hung up, and texted Ricky.

I kept thinking about how we'd tramped all through the grounds and the house. Sightseeing, trading quips and quotes, wandering about, while James lay murdered a hundred feet away.

"How will we explain that?" I said. "Our footprints everywhere."

"We were summoned here by duplicitous means. We were trying to figure out why." After a few steps in silence, he said, "Which is exactly what we were doing, Olivia."

I said nothing.

"You were having visions. We weren't enjoying a picnic by the beach."

I heard the distant police cruisers. The first car crested a rise, lights spinning. Then another engine roared and a motorcycle screamed past the cruiser, the driver hunched over, blond hair whipping back.

"Ricky," I said sharply to Gabriel. "What did you tell—"

"Nothing. I just said we were done and asked him to come get you."

Ricky skidded to a stop in front of me. His hazel eyes were dark with panic, the collar of his jacket tucked half in, his helmet still attached to the seat.

"I saw the cops," he said, catching his breath as if he'd run the whole way. "I'd just gotten Gabriel's text, and I tried calling, and then they whipped by—" He took a deep breath. "Are you okay?"

I nodded.

He swung off his bike, leaving it in the middle of the road. "You don't look okay, Liv."

"I—I am. I mean, I wasn't hurt. It's—"

"I'll tell him," Gabriel said.

"Tell me what?" Fresh panic lit Ricky's eyes.

"I'm fine," I said. "I can—"

"No."

Gabriel waved Ricky away from me with a look that forbade argument. As he talked, Ricky stiffened and looked toward me, but Gabriel moved in front of him.

Ricky didn't need a full rundown—not with the police climbing out of their cars—but Gabriel seemed determined to give one. Finally, Ricky turned away, his hands going up, fending off further commentary. Gabriel stepped into his path again and said something, and Ricky nodded, and I heard him say, "Okay, thanks, right, I get it," obviously intent on escape. Gabriel finally let him go and headed for the police.

Ricky ran his hand through his hair; he looked stunned and a little sick. Then he saw me watching. He caught me in a hug, pulling me tight against him as he whispered, "I'm so sorry."

I buried my face against him. I didn't cry. That was done for now. I just rested against him and—

Someone cleared his throat beside us. Ricky caught my hand and entwined his fingers with mine. Then he turned to face three uniformed officers. Behind them, Gabriel was talking intently to two detectives.

Two of the officers weren't much older than me, the third maybe forty. All three looked from me to Ricky—or, rather, to Ricky's jacket. From their expressions, you'd think they'd just stumbled on an Uzi-toting, cigar-chomping Colombian drug lord. Their reaction to me wasn't much better, though clearly to them I was more Hannibal Lecter than drug lord.

"You're the Larsen kid," the youngest said.

"No," Ricky said, his voice iron-firm. "She is Olivia Taylor-Jones. Preferably Ms. Jones, but Olivia is fine."

They gaped at him, as if an ape had spoken English with a Harvard accent.

"And you're . . . ?" the oldest said.

Ricky passed over his driver's license. As the cop read it, the youngest officer stepped behind Ricky, who reacted like the guy had pulled a knife on him. Obviously, the kid didn't have a lot of experience dealing with bikers. You don't walk up behind them. You just don't.

Ricky let go of my hand long enough to take off his jacket. He held it out with the patch toward the officer.

"Is that what you wanted to see?"

"Satan's Saints?" the young cop said. "That's a stupid name."

"True, but changing it would be a bitch. You'd need to buy all new jackets, and then hold a media awareness campaign to let everyone know. Plus there's the issue of tattoo reconstruction."

The officer's eyes narrowed.

Ricky sighed, tossed his jacket into Gabriel's car, and took my hand again. "I know you'll need to speak to Olivia, but—"

"We need to talk to you, too," the oldest one said. "Seeing as how you're obviously involved in this."

"He just got here," I said. "You couldn't have missed him, whipping past you on the road."

"Right," the youngest said. "Which means he was speeding."

"Oh, for fuck's sake," Ricky muttered under his breath.

Gabriel came over. "These are my clients, officers. If you wish to speak to them, I have to ask that you include me."

"They're *both* your clients?"

"I represent Ms. Jones, as well as her birth mother, Pamela Larsen. I also represent Mr. Gallagher and his father, Donald Gallagher, president of the Saints motorcycle club. Now, I suggest you allow me to lead you and the detectives to the body"— he checked himself—"to Mr. Morgan."

"You know the dead guy?"

Gabriel's voice chilled. "The deceased is James Mills Morgan. Ms. Jones was formerly engaged to him."

The confusion on the young man's face looked painful. "I don't get it."

"I'm relaying facts which may or may not become important to your investigation. I hope you're taking notes. The house— Villa Tuscana—was owned by Nathaniel Mills, a distant relative of Mr. Morgan."

"His maternal great-grandfather's cousin," I said.

Gabriel nodded. "Ms. Jones's family has been close to Mr. Morgan's for several generations. Connected through the joint enterprise of the Mills and Jones department store, as I'm sure you already figured out."

From the cops' expressions, they were a million miles from

figuring it out. In short, Gabriel was screwing with them. By the time he led them toward the Villa, they followed him as docilely as lobotomized lambs.

Ricky boosted me onto the hood of Gabriel's car. When I stiffened in horror, he chuckled and held me there.

"One, it's a rental. Two, there's nothing metal on your butt to scratch the paint. Three, even if there was, Gabriel wouldn't give a shit and you know it."

As I eased onto the hood, I spotted an owl perched in an elm tree. Ricky followed my gaze to the bird.

"An owl? In daytime? Didn't you say . . ."

"It's bad luck. An omen of a shitty day, which means it's several hours late." I raised my voice. "Did you hear that?"

The owl ruffled its feathers and continued staring at me.

"Owls in daytime. Creepy and unnatural," Ricky said. "Which, as I mentioned, I believe applies to owls in general."

He'd said that when we'd spotted one in the woods near the abandoned psych hospital. He didn't like the birds—too many stories from his youth. I'd thought it was cute, my biker boyfriend casting nervous glances at an owl.

I thought of the cabin, and when we'd seen the hounds and horses. The Cŵn Annwn—I was certain of it. Ricky had brushed it off as a regular hunt, but I'd seen the way his eyes glittered when he heard it. I remembered what he'd told me, about going out at night searching for something in those woods.

"I'd wake up, and I couldn't sleep. I'd go out and spend the whole night out here, looking."

"Looking for what?"

He shrugged. "I don't know."

After we'd heard the Hunt, he'd tried to explain the phenomenon.

"*It was riders from the stable. A midnight hunt. Logically, I know that. But when I was a kid, sometimes I'd hear the horses and the hounds, and I'd tell myself it was the Hunt.*"

"The *Hunt?*"

"*My nana used to tell me stories. She's Irish, and she grew up with all that. I liked her stories of fairy traps and enchantments. And the Wild Hunt. Have you heard of it?*"

Then I'd seen the Huntsman, another time, watching Ricky sleep.

There are two things you'd best keep close, for protection: the boar's tusk and the boy there. They'll look after you.

Walter and Ida, at Gabriel's office the other day.

End your association with the boy.

The little girl just an hour or so ago, speaking of Gabriel and . . . someone else.

"*You protect him as he protects you. And the other, too. The three of you.*"

"*The* other. *What* other? *I have no idea what—or who—you mean.*"

"*You know exactly who I mean.*"

My gut clenched.

It's not true. I won't let it be. Take the rest of my life and twist it into madness, but leave me this one normal, perfect thing.

"Liv?"

Ricky looked concerned, and I wanted to kiss that worry away. But I could see Gabriel approaching, with the detectives in tow, and I wasn't going to be caught making out with my boyfriend at the scene of my ex-fiancé's murder.

I nudged Ricky aside and hopped off the car.

"The detectives need to speak with both of you," Gabriel said. "I've asked them to begin with Ricky, as his should be a very short interview."

———

My interview wasn't nearly as brief as Ricky's. I got the impression that they thought Gabriel and I had sent each other the messages as some kind of alibi. As for why we'd want to be the ones to discover James's body if we'd killed him, well, maybe that was part of our defense strategy. Which was preposterous. At last Gabriel suggested that a proper interview should be conducted later, at the station, and the detectives agreed.

As Gabriel led me back to the car, Ricky came over.

"I'd like to get Liv out of here."

Gabriel nodded. "If you could take her to my office, I would appreciate that."

"I'd rather—" Ricky began.

"We have things to go over, and it's best done there. It won't take long."

"That's fine," I said. "I'll pick up some work, since it looks like no cabin for us—I'll be stuck in Chicago."

"That doesn't mean you need to work—"

"It'll help. I'll see you there."

As we neared the office, Ricky hit the brakes, his free hand going to my knee, bracing and warning me. A TV van rounded the corner ahead.

Ricky continued to the next intersection and took the back route. There were three cars and two news vans outside the office. Seeing that, Ricky pulled a U-turn and idled at the curb. We both checked our phones. Ricky lifted his to show me a call and a text from Gabriel. I had three of the first and two of the second, plus one of each from Lydia. The upshot was the same: don't go back to the office.

I texted Gabriel and Lydia both a quick *Got it. Thanks!* Then I typed in another message and held the phone up for Ricky to read.

How the hell did the media hear about it already?

"Scanner," he said, raising his helmet shield. "We'll go—"
When he stopped, I followed his gaze to a car turning the corner.
He lowered his shield.

The car reached us and then veered, a guy in the passenger
seat jumping out even before it stopped. A camera flew up, snapping shots.

"Eden!" I saw the cameraman mouth. "Rick!"

We were already tearing away from the curb, but the fool
tried to jump in front of us. Ricky steered around the reporter
and roared off, one hand raised in a middle-finger salute.

When he kept his hand raised, I figured out what he was
really doing—making it impossible for them to get a photo they
could use.

We rode to Ricky's place. He detoured around the back of the
student-housing complex. Sure enough, the car we'd dodged
was arriving from the other direction, and there was already a
TV van waiting.

As we pulled over, Ricky took out his phone and typed a
message for me: *They won't dare come to the clubhouse. And I
suspect they can't easily find Gabriel's home address.*

There was a third option. I sent a text to Gabriel: *Media at
Ricky's. Need your advice.*

He texted back immediately: *There's only one safe option
here, Olivia.*

I replied, *Cainsville.*

Yes, I'll meet you somewhere and drive you in.

Ricky, who was reading over my shoulder, shook his head
and motioned that he wanted to stick close.

I nodded and replied that Ricky would drive me.

All right. I'll see you both at Rose's.

CHAPTER TWENTY-TWO

Cainsville is a cloistered little town, physically cut off from the rest of the world. The highway passes close by, but you have to circle back twenty minutes on a narrow thirty-mile-an-hour road to get there. There is no industry, no tourism, and the housing market is tightly controlled. In short, unless you have good reason to visit Cainsville, you wouldn't.

As we rode in, I kept my arms around Ricky, my eyes on the back of his jacket. He turned onto Rowan and stopped in front of Rose's. It wasn't hard to find, given the "Rosalyn Z. Razvan, Take Charge of Your Future" sign in the window. And it was across the road from my apartment.

I glanced over at the three-story, yellow-gray Renaissance Revival walk-up that had been my home for the past couple of months. My landlord, Grace, sat on the front stoop, perched like one of the town's many gargoyles, the most forbidding of them all. She made no secret of the fact she was watching me, her sunken dark eyes glued on the motorcycle the entire way from the corner.

After a moment's hesitation, I pulled off my helmet and said, "I'm going to speak to Grace."

He nodded and lifted a hand to her in greeting. She acknowledged him with a dour nod.

I crossed the road and climbed the steps. "So," I said. "You're a bogart, right?"

"Is that how you're going to start conversations now?"

"Just in Cainsville."

She snorted.

"Hey, it's the only way I'm likely to find out."

"You bringing him here?" She pointed at Ricky.

"Is that a problem?"

"Not for me."

I sat on the stone railing. "I'd like to know what the elders have against him. It isn't because he's a biker, is it?"

Another snort. "He could be a banker and they'd feel the same. Though, if he was a banker, I might mind. Worse than *aufhockers*. I'd rather invest my money with bikers. Probably get a better rate of return."

"*Why* don't they like him, Grace?"

Her eyes met mine. "Oh, you know, girl. You can pretend you don't, but you do."

I fought to keep my expression even. "Humor me. Explain."

She eased back in her chair. "I believe the modern slang is cock-blocking."

"Excuse me?"

"What? You don't think I understand the lingo, girl? I've got the Internet."

"I know the term. I just don't get how it applies . . ." I trailed off as I figured it out. "No . . ."

"Your frisky racehorse there is in the way of their prize stallion, and their fondest breeding hopes."

"They—? No— Is that really—? No, just . . . no, and if that's what they're hoping for, then they've got a world of disappointment coming. If you think—"

"Oh, I don't give a damn who shares your bed. But you asked what their problem is, so I told you."

So the only reason the elders disliked Ricky was that they saw him as an obstacle to me getting together with Gabriel. Which meant that all my earlier fears had indeed been my overactive imagination, making connections where none existed.

"All right, then," I said. "Next time I see them, I'll set them straight on their wedding dreams."

She pursed her lips. "I don't think they much care whether there's a wedding involved, just as long as you two are—"

"Not happening. There are no babies coming, not from this girl and *any* guy."

"They'll go on hoping for what they hope for, whatever you say. The one you need to worry about is me. I don't like having that apartment sitting empty."

"It's paid up. And I suspect half the rooms in this building are empty—and unpaid."

"Doesn't matter. It's an empty *occupied* apartment that's a problem. If someone breaks in, you'll blame me."

"I won't. You have my word."

Grace peered up at me. "You should stay. Forget their bullshit. You belong here. You're safe here."

"And Ricky? How badly do they want that path cleared?"

"Not that badly. Which isn't to say they aren't capable of it. They are, and you'd best never forget that. But killing your boy would drive you off, and they'd never do that. He won't get a warm welcome in Cainsville, but no one's going to interfere."

Rose's place looked like a Victorian dollhouse. Not much more than a thousand square feet, it's a narrow two-and-a-half-story house with a tower, balconies, and plenty of gingerbread. It's not in the best shape—I suspect Rose figures as long as it's structurally sound, it's good enough. The yard is another matter. It's a perfect English garden with a manicured lawn and flowers in blossom that shouldn't be out for weeks yet.

The front door opened before we even climbed the steps. Rose may not sit on her porch like Grace, but she knows just as much about what's going on outside her door.

She filled the doorway nearly as well as her great-nephew. She's in her late fifties, a few inches taller than me, buxom and sturdy. She's a karate brown belt, but I wouldn't have tangled with her even before I knew that. She shares her nephew's dark hair—hers laced with gray—and his blue eyes, hers light but not as startlingly so.

Ricky extended a hand. "Rick Gallagher."

"Isn't it Ricky?"

He smiled. "Yes, thanks, though I learned to stop introducing myself that way when I passed my twelfth birthday. Thanks for giving Liv a place to hang out for a while."

"She's welcome anytime." Rose turned to me. "I'm sorry to hear about James, Olivia. More sorry you were the one to find him."

I nodded and was about to reply when I caught a movement behind her. A black cat had stopped halfway down the stairs. Rose stepped aside, and we went inside.

"Hey, TC," I said. "I'm back."

His tail twitched once, as if to say, *Oh, it's just her*, and he headed back up.

"Good to see you, too!" I called after him. "We'll catch up later."

"He missed you," Rose said.

"I'd be shocked if he realized I was gone."

"He did. Now, take Ricky into the parlor and I'll make tea. Gabriel should be here momentarily."

The parlor doubled as Rose's office, and it was my favorite room in the house. It's like a museum of folklore and spiritualism, filled with antique tools of the trade. There's a wall of books, too, with a shelf of British and Celtic lore, and as I looked at it, I made a mental note of everything I'd been wanting to ask about since I'd seen her a few days ago.

"I have no idea what most of this stuff is," Ricky said, looking around. "But . . . wow."

"Yep," I said. "It's an amazing collection of occult paraphernalia. Over there is—" I stopped myself. "Sorry. Get me started and I won't stop."

"Did I mention my nana and her stories? I might not be able to identify anything except that Ouija board, but I'm definitely interested."

"Well, first, that's not a Ouija board. It is a planchette, which is similar. Ouija is a brand name. Not that I knew that, either, until Rose told me. . . ."

NOT EVIL

ose could hear Olivia and Ricky in the parlor. Yes, she was
thinking of her as Olivia now. She'd been calling her Eden,
if only to herself, but had come to accept that the possibility of "slipping" made it inadvisable. She liked and respected
the girl, which meant she shouldn't call her something she
clearly didn't wish to be called.

Speaking of names . . . When she'd heard that Rick Gallagher went by Ricky, she'd dismissed him. He was younger than
Olivia, and his choice of diminutive only seemed to emphasize
his youth. He'd be cocky and brash, immature and insubstantial, a pretty plaything for a young woman in desperate need of
distraction.

As she eavesdropped on them in the parlor, she realized that
Ricky was indeed distracting Olivia, but intentionally, guiding
her attention away from shock and grief, immersing her in a subject she enjoyed. He listened to her explanations, made insightful
remarks, asked intelligent questions, and coaxed out laughs along
the way. Neither immature nor insubstantial.

Damn him.

Rose had slipped her deck of tarot cards out of the parlor
before they arrived, and now, as she fixed the tea, she consulted

them, hoping they'd tell her that Ricky Gallagher was a duplicitous bastard and the sooner Rose squashed this dalliance, the
better off Olivia would be.

The cards said no such thing. They did tell her there was
trouble. She'd known that from the moment she'd woken this
morning from a sleep plagued by swirling nightmares. Tragedy,
danger, darkness, grief, circling Gabriel and Olivia—and some
shadowy third party. As soon as she'd seen Ricky Gallagher,
she'd known who that third party was, and it had been easy to
pounce on the conclusion that he was the cause of the rest. But
the cards said no. He was intricately involved, and there was
blame here, but it was through impulsiveness, not evil intent.

Olivia and Ricky laughed, and Rose slapped two cards on the
counter. The Queen of Swords and the Knight of Wands. She
swore under her breath. She shuffled, focused on the young
couple, and tried again. The Queen of Swords and the King of
Wands. Even worse.

The Queen of Swords was Olivia's card. Bright, perceptive,
intuitive, independent—it fit her perfectly. As did the reverse
position, the more negative qualities that could slide to the
fore in the wrong situation—cold-hearted, critical, cynical. The
Knight of Wands was Ricky Gallagher. Energy, passion, action,
adventure—those were the traits that guided the knight, and from
what she'd seen, the card fit Ricky. Reversed, it meant he had a
tendency to be easily frustrated, to act in haste. As for the *King* of
Wands, that suggested a process of evolution—that Ricky was
becoming a leader, someone with vision and honor, the reverse
retaining that impulsiveness and adding a streak of ruthlessness.

She should seize on that last one. Ruthlessness. A sign of evil,
was it not? Sadly, no. There was nothing wrong with ruthlessness. It was a trait she admired, and the only way for a young
man like Ricky to come into his own.

Good cards, both of them. Excellent, in fact. Which was the problem. She wanted something minor for Ricky, something forgettable, a sign that he himself was inconsequential. But a knight evolving into a king? Not inconsequential at all.

Rose put the King of Wands aside, flipped over so she wouldn't have to look at it. Then she cut through the deck until she found the card she wanted. The King of Pentacles, symbolizing control, power, security, and discipline. Reversed, it suggested a tendency to be controlling, authoritative, domineering. Gabriel's card.

She smiled at the austere and foreboding figure on the front. She laid it beside the Queen of Swords with a snap of satisfaction, stepped back, and . . .

Her grandmother's voice sounded at her shoulder. *You can't do that, Rosie. It doesn't work that way.*

But this is what I want.

I know, but you can't force the cards to come. You can put them there, but what do you feel when you look at them?

Rose looked at the two cards on the counter. They *did* work together. Her gut said they did. But her gaze kept drifting to that discarded King of Wands.

Damn it.

If fifty years with the sight had taught her anything, it was exactly this. She could use her gift to manipulate circumstances and guide people down a path, but ultimately, they made their own choices.

At the creak of a floorboard, she glanced into the hall to see that Gabriel had arrived. He was standing outside the open parlor door, tucked back into the shadows as he watched Olivia with Ricky. His face was impassive, but she could see the turmoil in his eyes, the hesitation in his stance, as if he wanted to back up and walk away. Run away.

Goddamn it!

She wanted to march into the parlor and tell Ricky Gallagher to get the hell out of her house. To turn on Olivia and tell her to smarten up or she could get out, too. She needed to see what she was doing to Gabriel and tell Ricky it was over.

None of that was fair, of course. Ricky was doing nothing wrong. Nor was Olivia. If there was blame here, it fell on . . .

Her gaze slid to her nephew, and she stifled a pang of guilt. It wasn't his fault. Not really. The problem could be traced back to everything that had gone into making Gabriel the way he was today: his mother's neglect, his father's negligence, and, yes, Rose not doing enough to mitigate the damage.

She had told herself he was fine, and he was, in so many ways. Brilliant, driven, successful, as capable and competent as a man twice his age. And completely, utterly incapable of forming anything remotely resembling a normal human relationship. Until Olivia.

Rose didn't have a romantic bone in her body, but she wanted it for Gabriel. With Olivia, he could have that perfect bond between two people who are both partners *and* lovers. Ultimately, though, what mattered was having *a* bond. For Gabriel to have someone he cared for, who cared for him in return. Someone who made him happy. A few months ago, she'd have said that was impossible. Now she'd seen it wasn't. He had Olivia. And Olivia had Ricky.

Gabriel turned toward the kitchen, as if to come look for Rose instead. Olivia noticed him there. She said, "Just a sec," to Ricky, came out into the hall and retreated with Gabriel to the front door. Rose watched Olivia's face for any sign of distance, proof that her bond with Gabriel was thinning. There was none. She was relaxed and comfortable with him, her gaze as warm as ever, her regard as strong as ever.

And Gabriel? He answered her questions about the police

investigation concisely but sincerely, no impatience or sign that he'd rather be anyplace else, doing anything else.

Good. Now, ask her how she's doing. How she's holding up.

"Everything is under control," he said. "You have nothing to worry about."

"Thank you. I'm sorry I couldn't stick around and answer more questions—"

"There was no need. That's what I'm for, as your lawyer."

Damn it, Gabriel. No. Not as her lawyer. As her friend. She just found someone she cared about murdered. If you can't express some sympathy, at least let her know you're thinking of what she's going through.

"Right," Olivia said. "Anyway, billable hours or not, I appreciate it."

Her tone was steady and her thanks sincere, but Rose didn't miss the rueful twist to the words "billable hours."

Goddamn it, Gabriel. You have no intention of adding a single dollar to her bill. Clarify that. It's a gift, not a service. Make sure she knows—

"Is Rose around?" Gabriel asked.

"In the kitchen, making tea."

"Would you mind giving her a hand? I need to speak to Ricky."

"Sure."

Rose slid the cards into her pocket and opened the cupboard.

CHAPTER TWENTY-THREE

Ricky and I escaped to my apartment after tea. That wasn't the plan, but I decided I really needed to grab a few things as soon as possible . . . escaping the most awkward tea party ever.

Gabriel had spent the entire time on his phone, typing e-mails and checking messages. I kept telling him I was fine and he could go back to the office, but he stayed—and kept working, without so much as a grunted answer when a question came directly his way.

I finished my tea. "Okay, we should get over to my place—" I looked into Ricky's cup. "Oh, sorry."

He drained his cup in one gulp. "Done."

I got to my feet and turned to Gabriel. "Go back to Chicago. I promise to stay in Cainsville and behave myself until further notice. Okay?"

His jaw twitched. "Are you saying you want me to leave?"

"No," Rose snapped. "She's saying you've been on that goddamned phone since you got here, and you're making her feel like she's imposing."

He looked at me, startled. "I've been working."

"Right," I said. "Exactly my point. You don't need to babysit me. Especially if I'm paying you by the hour."

Ricky turned on Gabriel. "You're *billing* her?"

"Of course he isn't," Rose said.

Gabriel addressed me. "If I left that impression, I apologize. Basic legal services are covered, as a benefit, under your employee contract."

"Can I speak to you, Gabriel?" Rose said. "In the kitchen, please?"

"It's okay," I said. "We're going."

We hurried into the hall. TC was on the stairs. Before he could escape, Ricky scooped him up and stroked his head. TC flattened his ears and glowered at me as if to say, *Fix this.*

"He, um, doesn't like being picked up," I said.

"He's just not accustomed to it. I'm going to change that."

He lifted TC toward me. The cat kept his ears flattened, and slitted his eyes, looking like a grumpy little old man. I stifled a laugh, shook my head, and reached for the doorknob. My phone buzzed with a text. It was Gabriel.

We need to speak to Rose.

I replied, *I know. But not while Ricky's here.*

Tell him to stay at your apartment.

I gritted my teeth, sent back, *He's not a dog*, and stuffed the phone in my pocket.

"Gabriel's texting you from the parlor?" Ricky said. When I looked surprised, he said, "I can tell who it is by the way you replied. Like you were poking someone with a sharp stick."

I shrugged and grumbled under my breath. We walked out and down the front steps.

"Want to know the trick to dealing with Gabriel?" Ricky said. "Three words. *Don't take offense.* No matter what he does or what he says. He probably doesn't mean it the way it sounds, and even if he does, he intends no actual offense. You'd know if he did. Now, let's get a coffee."

"We just had tea."

"Which we both gulped so fast we burned holes in our esophagi. What you need is a mocha. Come on."

Ricky started down the sidewalk, TC still in his arms.

"Um, cat?" I said.

"A field trip. He'll love it. We'll get him a saucer of cream."

After coffee, we hung out at my apartment for a few hours. At seven that evening, Ricky walked me over to Rose's and handed me and TC off. He'd come by later, and we'd go back to my place for the night.

Gabriel had retreated to one of the upstairs bedrooms to work.

"Run up and get him," Rose said.

I followed her into the kitchen and lowered my voice.

"Um, I'd rather speak to you alone for—"

She cut me off. "I know you're annoyed with him, Olivia."

"I'm not."

"He handled that billing discussion badly."

"If I let things like that bother me, I'd be permanently pissed off with him. I've learned what to expect, and not to expect anything more. We're fine."

It seemed a good way to put it, balancing honesty with diplomacy, but I could tell by her expression that it wasn't what she wanted to hear. It can be hard knowing how to discuss Gabriel with Rose. She's the first to acknowledge his flaws, but the first to defend him, too. Something in what I'd said rubbed her the wrong way.

So I continued. "He's been great to me these last few days. I know he's put his life on hold to help me, and maybe I haven't been grateful enough about that."

"If you make a big deal out of it, you'll only make him uncomfortable. But he'll want to be here when we discuss anything fae-related."

"It's something else. A vision, I think."

My hands started to shake, and I stuffed them into my pockets.

"Olivia . . . ?"

"Ghosts," I blurted. "Have you ever seen them? Do you believe in them?"

She stepped closer, her voice dropping. "What happened?"

"Before I found James, I . . . I saw him. In the Villa. Twice. The first time, it was just a moment. He was . . . confused. He didn't know where he was. And then I saw him again, and he was still confused, but he tried to explain things to me. He—"

I broke off with a "Shit," and moved to the back door, looking out over the yard.

"Sorry," I said after I'd regained my composure. "It's still . . . raw. We'll discuss this another time. Or maybe not. It was almost certainly just a vision or whatever in which I imagined him saying what I wanted to hear."

"Was he wearing whatever you found him in? No, that's not a question. It's a fact, because otherwise, you'd already have dismissed it as a hallucination."

"I—"

"You want it to be real, and you *don't* want it to be real."

Cold sweat beaded across my forehead and trickled between my shoulder blades. She was right. I didn't want it to be real, because it only made it harder, made the guilt more unbearable.

All I wanted was to get you back. He said he'd help and then . . . it went wrong, and I don't understand how. I know

I hurt you, frightened you, and I don't understand that, either. It seemed so simple. You were in danger, and I had to save you, and nothing else mattered.

I'd wanted an explanation, so badly. And here it was.

What had I done?

You got him involved. You pulled him into something he didn't understand, couldn't understand. You pulled him in, and then you abandoned him.

"Olivia?"

My head snapped up. Rose was right there, but she hadn't spoken. That was Gabriel, standing in the doorway, those pale blue eyes fixed on me.

I took a deep breath, tugged from Rose's grip, and ran my hand through my hair.

"I just . . . I need a minute." I forced a wan smile that felt more like a grimace.

"Gabriel?" Rose said. "Could you give *us* a minute? Olivia and I were talking—"

"It's okay," I said. "We're done. I'm just . . . I'm going to take a walk. I won't be long. Just . . . around the block. Get some air."

I hurried out the back door.

CHAPTER TWENTY-FOUR

I took Rowan at a near jog and turned left onto Cherry. The moment I slowed, I heard the thump of footsteps behind me.

"It's only me," Gabriel called after me. "I'll stay back here."

I stopped and waited for him to catch up.

"I didn't mean to interfere with your walk," he said. "While the situation has changed and you no longer require protection, this is Cainsville, and you may be safe from outsiders, but some here wish to speak to you. You wanted a quiet walk. I'm ensuring you get that. I won't bother you."

"You never bother me, Gabriel," I said, managing a smile. "Walk with me. Please."

He nodded, and we continued in silence. When we reached the corner of Beechwood and I started to turn onto it, he cleared his throat.

"Maybe we shouldn't go that way."

I looked down the street. The sun was still out, people cutting lawns and tending gardens, enjoying the warm June evening. I couldn't see the house, hidden behind the towering maples, but I could spot the fence, wrought-iron with chimeras. The Carew house, where I'd first had the visions, one of Matilda that had spiraled me into a dangerous fever.

"I just want—" I began.

"Quickly," he said.

I started walking, faster now, pulled toward that house. When we reached the gate, I unlatched it and stepped through. He stayed on the sidewalk.

"We aren't going inside," he said.

"I'm not. I'm just . . ." I trailed off, looking at the house.

"We aren't going inside." Anger edged his words. "I know you want answers, but this isn't how you'll get them. I won't do that again."

"I didn't take off on you at the Villa. I—"

A middle-aged couple walking on the opposite side of the road slowed to watch us.

"Can we go around back?" I said. "Into the gardens. I won't step inside the house. I just don't want to stand out here."

Seconds ticked by as he considered.

"Please," I said. "I need a few moments of . . . of peace. I'll find it in the garden. Five minutes, and we can leave. I swear."

He nodded abruptly.

We went around the house. It was a Queen Anne, with a rounded porch, columns, and huge bay windows. The gardens were classic Victorian. No grass here. Only cobblestone walks, empty flower beds, and a fishpond with a fountain. I walked over to a statue in the corner. It was of a young woman, naked, raking her fingers through tousled, wet hair. At her feet was what looked like a fur rug, until I got closer and saw it was a sealskin. She was a selkie.

There were at least a dozen other statues, perhaps more small ones hidden under ivy. When I'd first come here, I'd paid little attention to the ones that seemed human, my attention instead drawn to the fantastical—the water dragons and trolls. Now I realized the humans weren't human at all.

I glanced at the house. Had Glenys Carew known what Cainsville was? Or had she, like Rose, only sensed it, and become captivated with images of the fair folk, like Rose was fascinated by their folklore?

Gabriel stood in front of a bench but gave no sign of wanting to sit. Silently waiting. On guard, too, against me breaking my word.

I joined him. "At the Villa, when you didn't want me going inside, I really wasn't ignoring you. I saw you go inside, so I followed. Like in the alley. I was only trying to find you."

He dipped his chin, acknowledging me, but he stayed rigid, his eyes hidden behind his shades.

"I can be stubborn," I said. "But you know it's more than that. I want to face whatever's out there. It'd be too easy to hide. Too tempting. Just pull the covers over my head until it all goes away. But today? You were right. I didn't need to see . . ." I swallowed. "I really didn't need to see James like that."

"True, but encountering his ghost may help in the long term."

"You heard me tell Rose I saw that?"

"I wasn't supposed to? I'm sorry for not realizing it was a private conversation. But you mentioned that he apologized and I'm glad you had that opportunity, even if I'd have preferred you could have avoided seeing his body."

He said it so matter-of-factly, just like he treated omens, fae, and visions. The question of what I'd seen was not a question at all. Clearly, I'd seen a ghost.

James's ghost.

My breath hitched, and I turned around fast, before the tears came.

"Sorry," I said. "Just give me a moment." Did I actually just say that? All the times I'd given him shit for saying *take a moment*, the very phrase bristling with impatience. I wanted to

make a joke about that, but when I opened my mouth, a hiccup-
ing sob escaped. I pressed my palms to my eyes.

*Get it together. You can break down later. Don't dump this
on him.*

"I'm sorry," I said. "It's just that it's still sinking in."

"I wish you wouldn't . . ." He trailed off.

"You wish I wouldn't keep breaking down."

A long moment of silence. Then, "That wasn't what I was going
to say, Olivia."

He cleared his throat, as if struggling to find words, and I
swore I heard a soft growl of frustration.

"It's okay," I said. "Whatever you meant, I—"

"I meant that I wish you wouldn't apologize for your reactions.
I wish that you didn't feel the need to apologize. But I understand
why you do. You are correct. I have little patience with emotional
outbursts. Yet sometimes I may convey the impression of impatience when I'm simply frustrated by the awareness that I am . . .
not responding . . . in a way . . ."

I felt sparks of friction, of discomfort, as if I were forcing his
hand into a tank of electric eels.

I wanted to turn to him, but I was afraid if I did, he'd mistake my smile for mockery. I squeezed my eyes shut, finding the
right expression, and—

Gabriel's hands slid around my waist, pulling me against
him, his chest warm and solid, his chin lowering to rest on my
head as his arms tightened around me. As I leaned back into
him, I kept my eyes closed because I knew if I opened them, I
wouldn't see the garden. I wouldn't see Gabriel's arms around
me. I'd fallen into a vision.

The arms tightened again, hands finding mine and holding
them, calming me. I tried to tell myself it *could* be Gabriel, that

in the right moment, the right environment, the awkwardness and discomfort could fall away and Gabriel could hug me like this.

I still didn't open my eyes. Not even a crack. Because I knew, in my gut, it wasn't him.

The arms loosened then, hands still holding mine, tugging me around to face him. Then the hands went around me, sliding up my back, into my hair, his mouth coming down to mine in a perfect kiss, so sweet and warm and all-consuming it pushed everything else from my mind. And if there was any doubt, any at all, it vanished, and I knew this was not Gabriel.

And if it was?

I jumped at the thought, disentangling fast, eyes snapping open to see . . .

The man from my vision, the night of the fever.

CHAPTER TWENTY-FIVE

Tall, golden-haired, impossibly handsome. His skin seemed to glow as bright as the sun over his shoulder. We were in a field, long grass swaying in the breeze, a blue butterfly winging past, the distant burble of a stream mingling with soft birdcalls. A perfect summer's day in a perfect summer's meadow, and all I could think was, *Where's Gabriel?* I heard the words coming from my lips, "Where is he?"

The man stiffened, and in that movement I saw something familiar, but it vanished in a blink. As he opened his mouth to answer, I said, "I need to get back to him."

"No, you do not."

"Yes, I—"

"You chose me, Matilda. You said it was me. Always me."

While I heard anger in his voice, all I saw in his eyes was worry and fear, bordering on panic.

Yes, it's you. It's always been you. It will always be you. But we need to speak to him. He must know. That's only right. He's important. To both of us. You cannot do this to him. We cannot.

I felt the words inside, waiting to be spoken, and he paused for them, like an actor patiently waiting for his cue. In the other vision, it had felt as if I was a spectator, watching from inside the body of another, unable to control her words or deeds. This time, I felt the words, but they simply swirled there, awaiting release.

"Who are you?" I asked instead.

A flicker of confusion. "Who am I?"

"Yes. Who are you?"

His lips lifted in a slow smile. "Making a point, *l'annwylyd*? All right, then. I'll play along. I am Gwynn ap Nudd."

The breeze chilled, sun slipping behind a cloud, and I remembered the little girl, reaching for Gabriel's hand, and how he'd seemed to sense it and had pulled back with a scowl.

What have they done to you, Gwynn ap Nudd?

I shivered. The man's hand gripped my elbow, his touch as warm and welcome as the sun in winter.

"Matilda?"

I looked at him, and I remembered the little girl again.

Not reincarnated. Reimagined. Not reborn, but born anew. As he is not Gwynn ap Nudd nor the other Arawn. You are and you are not. You are born to play the roles again.

"I don't understand," I said.

The man sighed, his arms going around me. "I know. You're angry with me for not wanting to tell Arawn. But it is only because I don't want to distract him from his duties. We'll tell him soon and he'll be happy for us, and he'll dance at our wedding."

His hands went to the back of my head again, pulling me into a kiss, but I broke free.

"No," I said. "I won't do this. I promised."

His face clouded. "Arawn? You promised—?"

I stepped back, squeezing my eyes shut. "No, I promised I wouldn't try to find answers. Not tonight." I took a deep breath. "Gabriel?"

A hand closed on my elbow, and even before I opened my eyes, I knew it still wasn't him.

"Matilda?"

I looked up at Gwynn and tried to *see* Gabriel instead, but I couldn't.

Not reborn. Not reincarnated.

And I was glad of it. One less thing for my overloaded brain to deal with, one less complication—

"Matilda?" He tilted his head, and when he did, something in the angle of his jaw . . .

"No!" I snarled the word and squeezed my eyes shut. "Gab-ri-el!"

The force of the shift hit me like a sandbag in the gut. I toppled backward. Hands grabbed me. Too hard. Too tight. Yanking me upright before I fell. Holding me there, still too tight, like a parent restraining a wayward child. Gabriel. There was absolutely no doubt that it was him, even before he said, "Olivia?" his voice tight with annoyance. My eyes were open, but everything was blurred by a red-tinged fog. He gripped me by both wrists, his fingers digging in.

"Olivia?"

The fog cleared, and I saw those ice-cold, pale blue eyes boring into mine. I felt his rough grip and heard his snapped words, and I didn't wish for anything else. This was the Gabriel I knew, and that was more comforting than any kind words or gentle embraces.

"I'm okay," I said.

"No, you are not." His hand went to my forehead, a near slap that made me flinch. He didn't seem to notice, just pressed his cool fingers there, then muttered, "Goddamn it!" I wasn't sure what startled me more, the curse or the venom in it. He released one of my wrists but tightened his grip on the other and started half dragging me. When I resisted, he turned sharply and said, "Can you walk?"

"Yes, but—"

He pulled me to the bench and propelled me down, then crouched in front of me, his eyes level with mine. In them, I saw rage seething like a winter's storm.

"I—" I began.

His hand slapped to my forehead again. "You have a fever." He held up one hand. "How many fingers do you see?"

"I didn't hit my head, Gabriel. I—"

"Given that you were shouting for me and I was right there, trying to shake you out of it, I'll ask whatever I damned well want. How many fingers?"

"Two. I—"

"This has to stop."

"If I'd known it would happen when I came here—"

"The location doesn't matter. Not anymore. At this house, at that Villa, on the street, in a field. One minute you're here, and then you aren't. It has to stop."

"If I had any idea how to do that, do you think I wouldn't? If it's such a goddamn inconvenience, Gabriel, then walk away. If I zone out? If I wander off? Walk away."

He got to his feet. "Have I *ever* said it's an inconvenience? That *anything* you do is an inconvenience? I'm trying to help, Olivia."

"Then stop yelling at me."

His gaze went so cold I shivered in spite of the lingering fever. "I have not raised my voice—" he began.

"Stop snapping at me. Stop snarling and glowering and making me *feel* like I'm inconveniencing you."

He put his shades back on. When he spoke again, his words

were formal. "I cannot help how I make you feel, Olivia. If you misinterpret—"

"How the hell else am I supposed to interpret it, Gabriel? You're giving me shit for—" I got to my feet and walked to the back of the garden, trying to get my temper back under control.

"What do you want?" Gabriel said.

"The same thing you do," I said. "For these damned visions—"

"Not you. *Them.* What the hell do *you* want?"

I turned to see Ida and Walter at the gate. Between the tone, the glare, and the profanity, Gabriel had stopped them in their tracks.

"Is everything all right?" Ida said.

There was a moment when he seemed almost ready to snarl and say, *What the fuck does it look like? Yes, everything's just fucking wonderful.* Instead, he rubbed a hand over his face, and when he lowered it, that winter's storm was gone and the cold front was back, freezing the Clarks with a stare.

"I would like you to leave now," he said.

Walter looked at Ida, and Ida stepped back and started to close the gate.

Gabriel strode forward, so abruptly he startled them. "No," he said. "Actually, I don't want you to leave. I want you to fix this."

"Fix what?" Ida asked.

He waved at me.

When they looked perplexed, I said, "He means me. Apparently, I'm broken, and it's annoying him."

Now I got the cold glower. I met it with one of my own. He turned back to the Clarks.

"Olivia is having visions, and—"

"Visions?" Ida worked hard to affix a proper expression of sympathy on her face, but she looked like a starving coyote spotting roadkill. "What kind of visions?"

Gabriel moved between us. She looked up at him. "What kind of visions, Gabriel? I can't help her if I don't know."

He met her gaze and said nothing. After five seconds of silence, he replied with, "She is having visions. You will fix them or tell her how to fix them. Now."

"The visions are important for—"

"For you, I'm sure. For Olivia, they're dangerous. She spiked a hundred-and-four-degree fever after one last week. I understand that you might not be well versed in human physiology, so let me explain. At a hundred and five degrees, brain damage can occur and the fever becomes life-threatening. If you suspect me of exaggerating, please speak to Dr. Webster."

A hundred-and-four-degree fever? No wonder he worried every time my temperature rose.

"I'm sorry—" Ida began.

"No, you're not."

Her lips tightened and a warning flashed in her eyes. "Yes, Gabriel, I am. You're upset, so I'm tolerating your disrespect—"

"You will tolerate my disrespect even when I'm not upset, Ida. Or you can ask me to leave Cainsville. If I was respectful in the past, it was due to compulsion. I don't give a damn what your plans are. I care that Olivia is being forced to watch visions of people and fae dying, horribly, for no apparent purpose—"

"There is a purpose, Gabriel. Anything she's seeing is for a reason."

"She's having dangerous fevers and falling into visions in the street, ones that could have her stumbling into the path of a car. If anything happens to her, Ida, I will hold you responsible."

"We would never hurt—" Ida began.

"Then fix this."

Ida locked glares with Gabriel. "If Olivia is seeing visions, Gabriel, it's because she needs to see them. We can't stop them. As angry as you are right now, I know you understand how important Olivia is to us and that we'd do nothing to harm her."

"Can I control them?" I asked. All three looked at me as if one of the statues had begun speaking. "Is there some way of letting them play out, fully and safely, and getting it over with?"

The silence that followed told me the answer was no, but after a moment Ida said, "If you tell us exactly what you're seeing—all of it—we might be able to figure out some—"

"Nice try," I said. "Let's do it the other way. Tell me when you figure out how I can have these visions safely, and if it works, I'll share what I see. Deal?"

Gabriel nodded, agreeing with my suggestion. Then he put his hand to my back and steered me past them to the gate.

"We'd still like to speak to you, Olivia," Walter said. "Not about this. About other things. We're glad you're back."

"Temporarily."

"Still, we're glad you're back."

"Even if you didn't come alone," Ida added. "But we're pleased you sent him away."

"Olivia didn't send Ricky away," Gabriel said. "He will return tonight. I trust that won't be a problem."

"We would rather—" Walter began.

"I trust that won't be a problem," Gabriel said, enunciating slowly.

The Clarks looked at each other, undoubtedly seeing their fae-baby dreams pop like soap bubbles.

When they didn't respond, Gabriel continued. "If Olivia chooses to come to Cainsville, she may bring whomever she likes. If she cannot invite whomever she likes, then she'll need to find a home where she can, and I will help her do that. Is that clear?"

After a long pause, Ida spoke, so grudgingly the words seemed to be dragged out with an industrial winch. "Yes, that's clear, Gabriel. We'll respect your wishes."

"They're Olivia's wishes."

A glimmer lit her eyes. "That's why you're insisting, then. Not because you agree about him, but because it pleases Olivia—"

"They're *our* wishes," he said. "Ricky Gallagher is an associate of mine and I do not appreciate hearing him maligned."

Something like alarm passed behind Ida's gaze. "Because he's your client? Or your friend?"

Gabriel rocked back, as if flinching from the word.

I cut in. "This isn't about friendship or a lack of it."

"Actually, yes, it is." Ida looked at Gabriel. "Do you consider Richard Gallagher a friend?"

"I don't see how that's important," I said.

"It's very important."

I shook my head, said, "We're done here," and let Gabriel steer me past them and out the garden gate.

CHAPTER TWENTY-SIX

"Are we okay?" I asked Gabriel as we walked back to Rose's.

Dusk was deepening to night, but he still had his shades on. "What do you mean?" he asked.

"We've had a rough couple of days," I said. "The visions, Macy, Todd, James. It's been a roller coaster. Between us, too. We're fine and then . . . we're not. I know that's because of everything that's happening. Stress and tension. But I feel as if I'm the one instigating it—"

He removed his sunglasses and tucked them into his pocket. "You aren't. It is, as you said, fallout from the situation. For both of us."

"Then what I'm trying to say is that I understand if you need a break. From the strain. From the angst. From me."

That wall behind his eyes shot up. "If you mean that you need a break—"

"If I needed one, I'd say so."

"If I want one, I will take one."

"Sorry. I'm just feeling a little frazzled."

"And I'm not helping."

"Sometimes . . . ?" I shrugged. "But ninety-five percent of the time? I don't know what I'd do without you."

"You'd manage," he said.

"Maybe," I said. "But I wouldn't want to."

"You won't need to," he said, and we finished the walk in silence.

Since I'd last spoken to Rose, I'd had at least three episodes—if I counted all the visions at the Villa as a single one. So, lots to talk about, right? Not really. They didn't boil down to much that needed her folklore expertise.

We discussed the fae massacre at Villa Tuscana and the result: the kelpies murdering Letitia. Rose confirmed that they were indeed kelpies. As for the blue fire used to slaughter the fae, she had no idea what it was. Some metal salts could turn fire blue. The only metal she knew that was supposed to affect fae was iron, and while I'd seen the men sowing iron filings to trap them, we were all a little confused about exactly how that worked. It seemed simple in the vision: the fae couldn't come in contact with iron. But there had to be plenty of iron in Cainsville, and no one made any apparent effort to avoid it. Which suggested the issue was more complicated than that.

What I really wanted to discuss was Mallt-y-Nos, Gwynn ap Nudd, and Arawn—who they were and what they had to do with us. I couldn't tell her about the Gabriel connection in front of him. I had to figure that out before I brought him into it.

"Arawn is from the Mallt-y-Nos folklore," she said when I finished describing what I'd experienced. "But Gwynn ap Nudd . . . ? There is a connection, but to Arawn, not Matilda." She got up from her desk. "The vision you had before the fever was a version of the Mallt-y-Nos legend," she said as she perused her bookshelves.

"Right," I said. "A young woman—Matilda—is about to get married. She loves to hunt, but has promised her future husband she'll give it up for him. But she wants one last hunt on the eve of their wedding. He says it's past midnight, and she made a vow. She thinks she still has time and leaves in spite of his protests. She loses him and is cursed to hunt forever as Mallt-y-Nos. Matilda the Crone. Very flattering. Except in my vision, she ran back to her betrothed and the palace was gone, and she fell into flames and perished."

"Or so it seemed. The hunt is *the* Hunt. We know that." Rose took down a book. "The Wild Hunt. Cŵn Annwn. In your vision, it's represented by the man Matilda runs to meet. That would be Arawn. Lord of the Otherworld. Leader of the Wild Hunt."

"Which makes sense. But in the stories, the fiancé she leaves behind is just some random nobleman. In my vision, he's definitely otherworldly. Blond guy, all sunshine and daylight and gold. Fae, I'm guessing."

"Gwynn ap Nudd."

"Right. He said that he was Gwynn and I was Matilda. We were getting married, and Matilda wanted Arawn to know, but Gwynn didn't want to tell him."

"A love triangle, then."

"I never got that impression. Matilda said she was friends with Arawn, but that he and Gwynn were also friends. When she went to meet Arawn that night, there was no sense that she was running off with a lover or reconsidering the marriage to Gwynn. She'd made her choice. It really was about the joy of the hunt—and sharing it with a good friend. Gwynn couldn't accept that."

"Jealousy."

"I guess, but it still boils down to the basic question: What the hell does this have to do with me?"

Gabriel had been silent until now, listening. He shifted, folding his hands on the table. "An answer I don't think we're going to get until you have the full story."

"Until I see the full vision."

He shook his head. "If Rose can figure it out, then there should be no need of the visions."

"Except *Rose* can't figure it out," his aunt said as she lowered herself back into her seat, book in hand. "It's only following the folklore to an extent. Matilda and Mallt-y-Nos? Yes. Olivia's vision is similar enough to a version of Matilda's story. Arawn fits, too. But Gwynn?"

She opened the book to an entry on Gwynn ap Nudd.

"Arthurian legend?" I said. "Please tell me I'm reading that wrong."

"It's one variation. Gwynn was said to be a member of King Arthur's court who annually fought another member over the most beautiful woman in the land. Who was also his sister."

"And he was fighting to protect her honor, right? Pure brotherly love."

"Depends on the version you're looking at. In some—"

"Let's stick with brotherly love."

"So there's that version, a reshaping of local folklore, like most Arthurian legends. In older accounts, Gwynn is the king of the Tylwyth Teg, which seems closer to what you've seen. But there's confusion there, too. Sometimes he's Welsh fae. Other times he's more closely associated with the Cŵn Annwn and merges with Arawn. Even the etymology of his name is confusing. Ap Nudd just means 'son of Nudd.' Gwynn means 'bright or shining,' but he's usually described as dark—a great warrior with a blackened face. He's linked to woodland, again like the Cŵn Annwn. And to owls, which would seem the arena of the Cŵn Annwn, too, but . . ."

"They aren't," I said. "Ravens are Cŵn Annwn and owls are Tylwyth Teg." I asked her to hand me the book and I skimmed the entry, seeing the same mess of contradictions that Rose described. I put the book down. "None of this helps."

"Because the answer isn't here," she said, tapping the cover. "Your visions reveal the truth *behind* the folklore."

Which did not help me one bit. More questions than answers, with no idea what difference those answers made to my life.

I'd planned to stay up, working with Gabriel, until Ricky returned. But while it was barely past ten, I was exhausted, and I think "someone" texted to tell Ricky I was falling asleep on my laptop, because at 10:15 I got a message from Ricky telling me he'd be another hour at least, and I should go to sleep. Rose was leaving the front door unlocked so he could take the sofa without disturbing anyone.

I texted back to say I wanted him to wake me when he got there. His response wasn't exactly a refusal, but when I woke after midnight, I was alone in Rose's guest room.

I found Ricky in the parlor, sitting on the sofa, lost in thought. Troubled thoughts, his face pensive and half shadowed. The breeze from the open front window ruffled his hair, a tendril tickling his cheek. Normally he'd brush it back, but he just sat there, his gaze fixed on the window, a haunted look in his eyes.

Gabriel and I weren't the only ones stuck on this roller coaster. Ricky was just better at hiding it and more comfortable being the guy in charge of cheering everyone else up. As I stepped into the room, the floor creaked, and he was on his feet, ready for trouble. Then he saw me.

"Tonight didn't go so well?"

He frowned, as if not sure what I meant. Then he shook

his head. "Nah, it was fine. Routine shit. How are you holding up?"

"Managing. I'm more worried about you right now. You were a long way away when I came down, and it looked like you'd settled in for a night of that."

He made a face. "Just thinking about some stuff."

He came to me and one hand went around my waist, the other to the back of my neck. He pulled me in for a sweet and gentle kiss. When it broke, he stayed there, his hand against the back of my neck, his face an inch from mine. His eyes closed and he gave a shuddering sigh. Then he kissed me again, something else there this time, a caution that spoke as much of uncertainty as tenderness.

"What's wrong?" I said when the kiss ended.

He hesitated, then took my hand and tugged me over to the sofa. We settled in together, me on his lap, turned to face him.

He cupped my chin, pulling me in for another slow kiss. Then he held me there, so close I could see nothing except his eyes.

"You know I'd never do anything to hurt you," he said. "*Never.*"

"Okay . . ."

"I've made a mistake, Liv. A huge one. At the time . . . At the time, it seemed like exactly the right thing to do. The *only* thing to do. I was so worried about you, and all I wanted was for you to be safe."

"What happened?"

"I was . . ." He inhaled. "It was after—"

A throat clearing cut him short. Gabriel stood in the doorway, still in his dress shirt, tie off, pen in hand.

"I didn't hear you come in," he said. "I was working in the kitchen hoping to speak to you."

"We're going back to my place," I said. "You two can talk in the morning."

"It can't wait," Gabriel said. "Ricky?"

I started to protest, but Ricky cut me short with a squeeze of my hand.

"He's right," he said. "Go on back to bed."

"But—"

"You're tired. I'm out of sorts and keeping you up. We'll talk later."

"You'll come get me?"

"I will."

CHAPTER TWENTY-SEVEN

About twenty minutes later, Ricky slipped into the bed-room. I started to rise. He held out a hand to stop me.

"Gabriel wants us to stay here," he whispered. "Something about an encounter you had earlier? Is there a problem?"

"No, he's just being cautious. I'd prefer to go to my place."

"So would I." He rolled his eyes toward the door. "But I'd rather not piss him off when he's sticking close to help."

Ricky peeled off his shirt. I tried not to watch—I hate window-shopping, and there was no chance of a purchase tonight. When he got to the jean-shucking, though, my resolve buckled.

"Keep looking at me like that . . ." he murmured as he folded his clothing onto a chair.

"I know." I sighed. "Just too damned tempting."

He chuckled as he climbed into bed. "While I'm perfectly willing to satisfy that temptation . . ."

"It's not the time or the place," I said. "I know."

He pulled me against him. "About earlier. What I was trying to say is that I feel like shit about . . . well, about . . ."

"James?"

He exhaled, air hissing through his teeth. "Yeah. Definitely not what you want to talk about."

"I'd rather talk about it than lie awake worrying about what's bothering you."

He nodded. "It's just that I feel bad. I was so pissed off at him. For good reason, considering how he was treating you. But whatever James did, it was hard for you hearing me talk about your ex like he was some dirtbag psycho. That obviously wasn't the guy you got engaged to. I mishandled the situation, and I hurt you. I'm sorry."

"You didn't hurt me or mishandle it. Yes, it was tough. I felt like it reflected badly on me, plus it might scare you off. I'm just sorry that it happened. That all of it happened."

I was about to pull back, a fresh wave of grief rising, but he took my face in his hands and pulled me down into a kiss. When it broke, he held me there.

"You could never scare me away, Liv. I hope you know that."

I nodded, and he tugged me into an embrace. When at last I shifted to settle in for sleep, he looked up—way up. I followed his gaze to see TC perched on the headboard.

"That's a little unsettling," he said.

"TC? Down."

He did jump down—onto Ricky, who let out an *oomph*. I went to scoop up TC, but he gave me a baleful glare and lay down on Ricky's chest and curled up.

"Congratulations," I said. "You now own a cat. Don't forget to take him when you go."

"Didn't I just say I'm not going anywhere?"

"Damn. Well, at least he likes someone."

"Oh, he likes you just fine. This is a warning. If I try to jump you in the night, he'll rip my heart out."

I laughed softly and he pulled me against his side. I closed my eyes, and before I knew it, I was asleep.

———

I was in the kitchen the next morning, helping Rose with break-fast. Gabriel was at the table, busy on his laptop. Ricky had taken over the parlor desk to work on an assignment for school. As I washed berries, I said to Rose, "So, do you feel like you're running a boardinghouse?"

"Starting to," she said, putting a tin of muffins into the oven. "I might charge rent. And impose curfews. Seemed like doors were opening and closing half the night."

"Sorry," I said. "Ricky and I planned to go back to my place, but—"

"No," Gabriel said, without looking up from his computer.

"I don't see why—"

"Would you like a list? Let's start with the fact that you seem to be sliding into visions randomly and end with the one where at least two very powerful fae really would prefer your boy-friend went home. As long as—"

My phone rang. "Saved by the bell," I said, then looked down at the incoming call and blinked. "Oh, hell. Shit, shit, shit."

"If that's a reporter—" Gabriel began, his hand extended for the phone.

"No, it's my mother. I completely forgot, she's coming home this weekend."

It'd been weeks since I'd spoken to her directly. Lena hadn't taken the media onslaught very well. She'd fled to Europe to hide under the wings of protective friends. When I wouldn't do the same . . . well, I'd like to say she was angry because she thought that was best for me, but I suspect it was because it would have made things easier for her. Everyone has people like my mother in their lives. They're frustrating and flawed, and there are things both in them and in our relationships with them that we'd like to change, but ultimately we have to accept who they are.

I answered the phone with, "Hey, Mum."

"Olivia. I heard the news. I'm so sorry."

Shit! Of course.

"I should have called you," I said. "I just . . . I'm the one who found him, and I haven't been thinking clearly. I'm sorry."

"I wasn't blaming you for not calling. Despite what happened between you two, I know how much you cared for him."

I exhaled and lowered myself into the chair across from Gabriel. "Thanks. Yes, the situation makes it awkward. I'm holed up avoiding reporters. I don't know what I'll do about the funeral and . . . Maybe we can talk about that. How to handle it. When are you getting in?"

"I'm not coming home, Olivia."

"What?"

"Given what's happened, this would hardly be the time."

"But the funeral—he was . . . he was almost your son-in-law, and you've known his family forever."

"I can hardly go to the funeral of a man my daughter left at the altar."

I gripped the phone. "I did not—"

"James stuck by you, Olivia."

"Um, no, he—"

"He got over the shock of your parentage and tried to make amends, and you wouldn't let him. You had your reasons, but to outsiders, it does not reflect well on our family."

Gabriel pushed his chair back, a hard look in his eyes. Eavesdropping and making no secret of it.

"I understand you wanted to tough it out," Mum went on. "My concern is . . . You're twenty-four, Olivia. In a few months you'll be old enough for your trust fund, reaching the age where your father and I agreed you'd be mature enough to handle the responsibility. But in recent weeks you broke off an engagement to a wonderful man, and began investigating your birth parents' crimes with a man that our family lawyer has nothing good to say about. Now James is dead—murdered—and you're dating a member of a motorcycle gang. All I can hope is that last is some misguided publicity stunt to divert attention from your birth situation."

"No, I—"

"He's a biker, Olivia. And according to the papers, he's two years younger than you." She said it as if that was as bad as dating a criminal.

"Whatever's happening to me has nothing to do with attending James's funeral. We need to pay our respects—"

"*We?*" Her voice rose. "I certainly hope you don't intend to go."

"I was engaged to him, Mum. I'd never march up and stand at his graveside, but that doesn't mean I can't go, discreetly, and pay my respects."

"After you . . . ?" She trailed off.

"After I what?" I said, my voice thick with warning. "What exactly did I do that strips me of the right to mourn James?"

You killed him. Maybe you didn't wrap your hands around his neck and squeeze the life from him, but you caused this. You know you did.

I didn't catch what my mother said; I only heard the accusation in my head. I lowered the phone. Gabriel reached over to take it, but I lifted it again to discover my mother had hung up.

"I know it's important to you to go to the funeral," Ricky said as he peeled off his muffin wrapper. The four of us were at the kitchen table. "You could do it exactly as you suggested. Go to the graveside service, where you can hang back—"

"There's no reason for her to hang back," Gabriel said. "She's done nothing wrong."

"It's about propriety and respect," I said. "I'd hardly honor his memory by turning his funeral into a prime-time news event."

"Obviously, I'd like to go with you," Ricky said. "But *that* would extend a big middle finger to his family. I'll be nearby, in case you need me. Someone, though, should escort—"

"I will," Gabriel said.

"Actually, I was going to ask Rose. James had you charged with assault and his mother was the one who called the police."

"His mother won't see either of us. For anyone who does spot us, my presence would merely signal that Olivia should not attend without accompaniment."

We debated it some more, but Gabriel had made up his mind. If I was going, so was he.

CHAPTER TWENTY-EIGHT

The next day, Gabriel got a message that Pamela wanted to see me. I'd refused to visit her until she told me what she knew about omens. Now she was ready and, despite the bad timing, I had to go before she changed her mind.

We sat in the visiting room, which was almost a jail cell itself, so small and empty even our lowered voices echoed. Then the door opened, and a guard escorted my birth mother in.

I'd been told I look like her. While I didn't see it, I could logically break down the component parts. My hair color came from Todd. Hers is dark, laced with gray. She's only forty-five, but I now realized she looked older than he did, as if prison had taken more of a toll on her. Old pictures showed we shared a body type—tall and slender. She'd put on weight since and her looks had faded. When she saw me, though, her face lit up, and sparked memories of me looking up at her and thinking she was the most beautiful woman in the world, and how I wanted to grow up to look just like her.

Then she saw Gabriel, and that glow evaporated.

"I told you I wanted to see my daughter alone."

"He knows about the hounds," I said. "About the Huntsmen, the omens, everything I was asking you about."

From the look on her face, you'd have thought I'd promised Gabriel my eternal soul. Or slept with him. For Pamela, either would be equally horrifying.

I met her gaze with a hard look. "I told you I needed help. You refused. Gabriel didn't."

"Of course he didn't. He'd do whatever it takes to get into your bank account. You can't trust him, Olivia." She stared at Gabriel for two long seconds before saying, "You aren't even going to dispute that, are you?"

"Whether I've earned Olivia's trust is for her to say. I know I've lost it more than once. I'll freely admit that. As should you."

"You can't even feign respect, can you, Gabriel?"

"Respect, like trust, is earned. Also reciprocal."

She turned to me. "Why do you tolerate him?"

"Because I like him. Also because I respect him. Trust . . . ? Mmm, that's a tough one. But I'll bite the bullet and say yes, I trust him. And as fun as it is to dance this waltz again, I'm really going to ask that we talk instead."

"Not with him here."

Gabriel murmured to me that he'd wait in the hall, and got up and left us.

"You should ask yourself why he didn't just do that in the first place," Pamela said as he left. "He wanted to make an issue of it. If I ask him to leave and you defend him, then he wins."

"I didn't come here to fight about Gabriel," I said. "Let's talk about hounds."

"That's not—"

"Not what you called me here for? It damned well better be."

I expected her to take offense, but she only smiled and shook her head.

"You look like your father when you put your foot down like that."

"About the hounds . . ."

"We will discuss that, Olivia. First, though, I heard about James." She reached out and squeezed my hand, quickly, before the guard noticed. "I heard you were the one who found him. You and Gabriel. The news said something about bizarre circumstances leading you two to James's body. It hinted you were lured there."

I didn't tell her what had been done to James's body. That wasn't part of the media coverage. If I told Pamela about the way his corpse had been mutilated, she'd seize on the possibility that whoever killed James was the real Valentine Killer. That wasn't where I wanted my focus right now. James deserved better.

"It's no random murder," I said. "Gabriel and I were summoned there."

"Are you sure *both* of you were?"

"Um, yes. I got a message, and I saw his."

"And he absolutely couldn't have sent yours?"

I stared at her. "Oh, no. Don't you dare even suggest—"

"If you know what I'm going to suggest, that's because you already suspect it."

"No, it's because I can follow a trail of leading questions."

"I had a visitor who told me that Gabriel Walsh murdered your fiancé. Beyond any doubt."

"Then your visitor has an agenda—"

"He also has proof."

"I don't give a damn, because you could show me a video of Gabriel murdering James and I still wouldn't believe it."

"James came to see me last week."

"What?"

"He was desperate to figure out what hold Gabriel had over you. He thought, since I've worked with the man, I might know. We discussed our mutual concerns. Now, having someone tell me that Gabriel murdered James—"

"He did not. Which I know because I was in his condo that night. All night. And no, not in the same bed. I was there because James had tried to have me kidnapped."

"Gabriel convinced you that James was a threat and persuaded you to stay in his apartment?"

"Didn't you hear me? James *was* a threat. Look, I'm not getting into this—"

"You *need* to get into this, Olivia. You need to take a cold hard look at Gabriel's behavior. He keeps you from your family. He turns you against James. I hear he even took you away from your job so you could work for him. Now you're staying in his apartment? Don't you see how he's controlling you?"

I wanted to laugh, but her expression was dead serious.

I pushed my chair back. "This isn't about James's murder. It's about distracting me from asking questions, while planting seeds of doubt about Gabriel, for whatever ridiculous reason—"

"For whatever *ridiculous* reason?" Pamela gripped the edge of the table. "To protect you, Eden. You may not like being called that, but to me you are Eden Larsen, my daughter, and I will do whatever it takes to protect you. I know you want answers, and you think I'm holding back. I'm *protecting* you. Nothing could make me happier than if you'd lived your life without ever knowing any of this."

"Maybe, but it has nothing to do with Gabriel."

"It has *everything* to do with Gabriel. Everything you want to ask me about? He's part of it. James was a threat, so he murdered him. If your new boyfriend becomes a threat, he'll do the same to him. If you don't toe the line and give Cainsville what it wants, Gabriel will turn on you. They'll *make* him turn on you."

"If the Cŵn Annwn are telling you this—"

"They don't need to." She leaned forward, her hands still on the table. "I can't help you from in here, baby. All I can do is give you the most sincere piece of advice possible. Run. Get someplace they can't find you."

I got up and walked out.

Gabriel was waiting in the hall. As I came out, he caught my expression and said, "She told you something?"

"Yes. You're evil."

His brows shot up. "That's news?"

I smiled as he fell in step beside me. "Sadly, that was the gist of the entire conversation. She wouldn't talk about the hounds and the omens, because it was far more important to warn me against you."

I'd decided I wouldn't mention the ridiculous murder accusation, because even to put it into words seemed as if I gave it some credence.

I continued. "Pamela's bloodline might be fae, but she has a connection with the Huntsmen. They seem to be warning her about you, just like they warned me. The question now is the nature of that connection. Edgar Chandler was involved in the murders of Peter Evans and Jan Gunderson *and* he was involved with the Cŵn Annwn. Does that mean the rest of the murders could have been connected, too?"

We walked through a set of doors.

"Then there's the significance of what was done to James," I said. "We haven't discussed that."

"That's what I was thinking about while I waited. Some aspects of the earlier crimes weren't released to the general public. The court records are open, which means anyone could duplicate the crimes, but the way he was murdered does open a strategy for freeing Pamela."

"Even if she hates your guts?"

"If I failed to give my best defense to every client who hated me, I'd have a very poor record indeed."

CHAPTER TWENTY-NINE

The rest of Friday was quiet. Ricky and I went to a movie in the city. Big, loud, and action-packed, it was the perfect mental vacation. Afterward, I had to visit the police station with Gabriel for a follow-up on James's case. The case was now being handled by the CPD. Gabriel explained why, but . . . let's just say that as soon as I had a moment to relax with a book, I'd be eschewing novels for a few basic legal and law enforcement texts.

Saturday morning, Ricky gave me a lift to my parents' house so I could find something appropriate to wear to the funeral. Gabriel picked me up at the house. He had his new car now, having retrieved it that morning. About five minutes before we arrived, Ricky texted that he'd found a shaded spot for us to stand, a couple of hundred feet from the grave site.

Grave site.

James's grave.

James was dead.

Even after three days, the reminder hit with the force to nearly double me over. When my father died, I'd had warning. He'd suffered a series of heart attacks, so I'd had time to say everything I wanted. I had never realized how important that was until now.

I'd loved James. More than that, I'd cared for him. Love was about what *I* felt. Caring was about James—the life I wanted for him, whether I shared it or not.

I had pictured another future for James and me, one where he'd come to accept our separation, and gone on to meet the perfect woman and become senator, and then we'd meet on the street, years later, him with a little girl holding his hand and a boy on his shoulders and I'd tell him how good it was to see him, how happy I was for him, and I *would* be happy. I would look at him, with everything he'd wanted from life, and I'd be so pleased that he had it.

And now there was none of that. His life—his future—gone. Because of me.

Gabriel parked where Ricky had suggested, far enough away that we could walk through the trees, in hopes few would notice us.

"I realize this is inconsiderate of me to mention, but . . . James won't know you're here, Olivia," Gabriel said, studying my face before we got out. "Do you really want to go through with this? You had your goodbye. I firmly believe you did. And you did absolutely nothing to cause his death."

"Maybe not directly, but—"

"While I realize it is wrong to speak ill of the dead, the fact remains that if he was targeted due to your association, then that happened because he would not dissociate himself from you, despite your insistence that he do so."

I turned to gaze out the car window. "What if he was compelled to pursue me? Fae compulsion."

"Is that what you think?"

I shrugged.

His voice softened. "There is a limit to such compulsions. If there was not, neither the Tylwyth Teg nor the Cŵn Annwn would need to persuade you to speak to them. The desire and the will must be there or the compulsion doesn't work. You did nothing wrong. If you still wish to watch the service—"

"I do."

"We should go, then. I will ask one thing of you, though."

"What's that?"

"That you do not feel the need to restrain yourself. This is the funeral of someone you cared about. I don't expect stoicism."

I found a smile for him. "Thank you," I said, and we got out of the car.

It was a hot June day, humidity creeping in, as it is wont to do in Chicago. I remembered being at a garden party with James just last summer, both of us choking in the heat, me lamenting my decision to wear makeup, which was dripping onto my white sundress. He'd said that come February, when I was trudging through three feet of snow, cheeks raw from the subzero winds, I'd be dreaming of such weather. He was right. Complaining about the weather is an official pastime in Chicago, but the truth is that I'd never consider giving up those mercurial changes. I love the crazy weather. Just as I love my city, almost as much as James did.

The city is what had brought us together, at another party. Someone had been commenting on the wind that day, howling off the lake like a wild beast, and another guest had joked that's what you expect from the Windy City. I mentioned that Chicago got that name from its politicians, historically known for their bluster, a situation that hasn't changed. James had chimed in, and we went off on a riff about the weather and the politicians, entertaining our fellow guests, and it was the first time I'd seen him as someone other than the son of a family friend, someone I'd paid no more mind than the furniture.

When our group had broken up to mingle, he'd steered me into a corner to talk Chicago history, which sounds like an inauspicious start to a relationship, but when James spoke about his city, there was a passion—a spark and a light and a humor—that made me say, "Wow, he's not what I expected at all."

Now I stood at his funeral, watching them prepare to lower his casket into the ground, as I sweated in my dress and thought about that party and looked out past the treetops at the city sky-line, and I remembered him, all the best of him, because there was so much that had been good. And I cried. I cried and I cried.

Gabriel was careful that day. He stood at my shoulder, but slightly behind me, so even if I turned, I couldn't see him or—more important—check how he was reacting to my tears. Yet he stayed close enough that I could feel him brushing against my back and hear the whisper of his breath.

Gabriel may not have been able to provide a shoulder to cry on or a warm embrace to fall into, but he did everything he could to make up for that.

The crowd was huge. Hundreds of people, from colleagues to college friends, from those who'd supported his father as sena-tor to those who'd hoped to see James in that seat. We were a hundred yards from the grave site, too far to catch more than snatches of the service. Also too far to catch anyone's eye, but as it was winding down, someone said, "Oh, excuse me. Didn't see you there," and I started to turn, but Gabriel's hand moved to my shoulder, keeping me still.

"Mr. Walsh," the man said. "Ms. Jones. Sorry. I didn't know it was—"

"Yes, you did," Gabriel said, his voice a deep rumble. "And if that phone rises another inch, I will take it from you. I will not take it gently. Nor will I return it in one piece."

"I'm not trying to—"

Gabriel moved so fast I stumbled as the bracing wall of him disappeared. I turned to see a young man, maybe thirty. Though he wore a suit, he wasn't a mourner—his tie was loose, the top button undone, his cheeks unshaven.

Gabriel took his phone. As he'd warned, he did not do it gently, yet the reporter was still caught off guard and jerked back in surprise as the cell vanished from his hand.

"You can't—"

"I did."

Gabriel flipped through the pictures. The reporter had been snapping shots from a distance, slowly closing in. Gabriel removed the sim card, again so quickly that the reporter could do no more than yelp in protest.

"Jesus!" The man leapt forward. "You can't—"

"I did." Gabriel tucked the sim card into his pocket. Then he forced a factory reset on the phone and handed it back. "Now leave. This is a funeral, and I won't allow you to cause a scene."

"Me? You just—"

"I *avoided* a scene, one where you invaded a mourner's privacy and I was forced to take more serious action to stop you. Now turn around and leave."

He did, grumbling and cursing Gabriel.

"Thank you," I said when the reporter was gone.

"I'm simply relieved it didn't escalate to violence given . . ." He nodded toward the crowd of mourners.

"Witnesses," I said.

A twist of a smile. "I meant because it's a funeral."

"That, too."

He gave my shoulder a light squeeze before turning me back toward the service, letting me lean against him once more.

As soon as it ended, I said, "We should go before anyone else notices us."

"Hmm."

I followed the angle of his shades to see a cameraman and reporter heading our way, another crew following behind.

We moved at Gabriel's long-legged march until he realized that I had to jog to keep up. He slowed before we called more attention to ourselves. But the moment we'd set out with a half-dozen reporters in tow, it was like the wake behind a power-boat, spreading behind us, alerting every reporter nearby. Some of *them* had no compunctions about running. As they closed in, Gabriel's hand went to my back and his other lifted, ready to warn off anyone who came too close. No one did. That hand was enough.

I kept my face lowered, slipped on sunglasses plucked from my purse, moving quickly as cameras snapped and reporters called questions from all sides. Gabriel didn't acknowledge them. We just kept going until . . .

Until we saw the new Jag . . . with police cruisers parked in front of and behind it.

Despite Gabriel's shades, I swore I saw him aiming blast rays at those cars, his jaw tight enough to snap teeth.

Two officers were heading straight for us.

"Gabriel Walsh?" one said as he drew near.

"Yes," Gabriel said.

The other stepped into his path. "Gabriel Walsh, you're under arrest for the murder of James Morgan."

CHAPTER THIRTY

I n that moment, I failed Gabriel. The officer announced he was under arrest and all I could think was, *Oh my God, Pamela* . . . She'd accused him of murder and now he was being arrested, and that had to be her fault. I froze in horror and dismay, and when Gabriel looked at me, *that's* what he saw. As if I thought he might actually have done it.

He turned away, his shoulders straightening. His hand dropped from my back. He walked toward the police cruiser, his chin high as one officer read his Miranda rights and the second told him to put his hands behind his back. They were going to cuff him—with news cameras on every side.

I jumped forward then, saying that wasn't necessary, that he wasn't resisting. But Gabriel said, "Enough, Olivia," and put his hands behind his back as the cameras snapped.

I didn't say, *I know you're innocent*, because there was no question, and I would not act as if there was. Instead, I said, "Tell me what to do."

"I'm fine," he said.

"Please. Tell me what to do."

He kept walking. I caught his coat sleeve, ignoring the warning grunt of the officer.

"Gabriel, please. Tell me what I *can* do."

He glanced at me then, and my panic must have shown, because a little of that stiffness went out of his shoulders. He started rattling off instructions. Notify Lydia. Have her lock down the office pending a search. Do not go into the office until it had been searched. Same with his apartment.

"Do you need a lawyer?" I said.

"I'll handle it."

"You can still call me, right?" I said. "One phone call? To let me know if there's anything more I can do?"

He lowered his voice, turning to look at me as we reached the police car. "I'll be all right, Olivia."

The officer opened the door and guided him in. As I hovered there, the officer gave me a surprisingly sympathetic look and said, "You'll have to step back, Miss Jones."

I did.

Gabriel ducked his head to look at me out the cruiser window. "May I have a brief word with Ms. Jones? Please?"

The officer hesitated. I suspect he wasn't as willing to be nice to Gabriel, but the request was worded so politely, the tone downright deferential, that he told his partner to hold up. Gabriel motioned me closer, and the officer stepped away. As I bent to listen, I could see the tightness in his face, the anxiety. He might be acting calm, but he'd just been arrested for murder.

I opened my mouth to speak, but he beat me to it. "I didn't do this, Olivia. Whatever you may hear, whatever you may think—"

"I know you didn't," I said.

I squeezed his arm, fast, the briefest touch, not giving him time to flinch.

"I'll fix this," I said. "You've said that to me many times. Now it's my turn. I'll fix this."

"Take my car." Gabriel struggled for a wan smile as he

nodded for me to take his keys from his jacket pocket. "Just be careful with it."

The cops tried to intervene, but Gabriel told them he'd only picked up the vehicle that morning, so it wasn't evidence. The bill of sale was in the glove compartment.

As soon as the patrol car pulled away, the reporters swarmed.

I had every intention of making a calm statement. Admittedly, my past record for this had not been good, but I wasn't going to walk away without supporting Gabriel. Except it was like trying to kneel and pray in the middle of a rugby mob. When I opened my mouth, I got shouted down. When I tried to step back, I got jostled and blocked. Just as I was ready to give up, the crowd began to part, and I heard a familiar "Hey!" and "Move!" When they saw who it was, they stepped aside, much like a herd of ravenous swine makes way for the guy carrying the fresh bucket of slop.

Ricky elbowed through to me.

"Gabriel—" I began.

"I heard," he said, his face grim. He took my arm and turned to the guy nearest us. "Move!"

Getting me out of that crowd wasn't as easy as getting himself in. But he managed, while also keeping his middle finger raised in front of me.

The crowd wasn't as big as it seemed, maybe a dozen reporters and beyond them a layer of curious mourners, which pissed me off more than the journalists. The media was just doing its job, but the others were supposed to be there to honor James.

I whispered to Ricky, "I need to make a statement." He could have said, *What the hell?* He'd rescued me from the mob and now I wanted to engage it? But he only nodded and led me to Gabriel's car, where he positioned us with our backs to the vehicle, blocking anyone from coming up behind us, while also securing an escape route.

"Listen up!" Ricky said, his voice ringing over the shouted questions. "Ms. Jones is going to give a statement, and if you want to hear it, you're going to shut the fuck up. Got that?"

A murmur of outrage from the mourners. Obviously, joining a mob at a funeral was fine, but God forbid someone should swear.

"She's going to do this once," Ricky said. "If you don't let her finish, she'll get in this car and you'll have nothing, because she's not answering your questions or—" He spun on a young woman, slipping up beside him with her recorder. "You! Get the hell back *now*."

She scrambled away so fast you'd think he'd pulled a gun. Which is probably what they expected for the encore.

"Anyone else gets that close?" Ricky said. "We leave." He turned to me, his voice lowered. "Go on."

I gave my statement. Gabriel had been arrested for James's murder. It was obviously a trumped-up charge, stemming from ongoing animosity between Gabriel and the police. The fact that they felt the need to dramatically arrest him at the funeral proved it. I felt guilty saying that after the officers had been relatively decent about how they carried out their orders, but it was the slant Gabriel would put on it.

I went on to express my dismay and anger at the fact that James's service had been disrupted. I was appalled by the way the police—and media—had disrespected his memory. I made it absolutely clear that I supported Gabriel and that I had no doubt he'd be released quickly.

When I finished, Ricky said, "We'll take Gabriel's car. Do you want to drive?"

I shook my head. He reached for the passenger-door handle.

"Olivia!"

When I heard that voice, I froze.

"Go on," Ricky murmured, the door open. "Get in and we'll take off."

I wanted to. But if I'd come to pay my respects to James, there was no way I could turn my back on the woman making her way toward me through the crowd.

Even before I started dating her son, Maura Morgan had barely tolerated me at family gatherings. "Poor Lena," I'd heard her whisper when I was twelve. "That girl of hers is . . . well, she's a little odd, don't you think? Too headstrong by far. It's her father's influence. Arthur's a smart businessman, but his manners leave something to be desired."

When James and I got together, you would have thought he'd taken up with the town whore. Give it a few months, she must have thought, and he'd be done with his fling and settle down. When he decided to settle down *with* the unsuitable girl, Maura decided I wasn't a whore after all. I was a gold digger.

I'd never let her drag me into a fight, but I had always stood up to her. Nothing she could do or say would change how James felt about me, and I'd reminded myself that, after her divorce, her son was all she had left. I was a threat to that relationship. So I felt sorry for her, which was particularly satisfying, knowing how much she'd loathe my pity.

But now, when I saw her, I froze like the proverbial headlight-stricken doe. On the outside I might be holding up, but inside I was a seething mass of panic, anxiety, and confusion over Gabriel's arrest.

My mouth opened, no words coming out until she was right in front of me and I managed to squeak, "Maura."

Her hand flew up and I flinched, bracing for the blow. Instead, I heard a soft gasp and opened my eyes to see Ricky holding her wrist.

"No," he said, locking eyes with her.

"Who are . . . ?" she sputtered, trailing off as her gaze traveled up him, taking in the boots, the worn jeans, the leather jacket, and finally his face. Then she recognized him, and yanked her hand away fast.

"Maura," I said. "I—"

"You brought your—?" She stared at Ricky, struggling to speak. "You brought a—? To my son's—?"

"No," Ricky said, his voice calm. He waved at his clothes. "Obviously, she did not bring me here. She came with Gabriel, to pay her respects. I was on the other side of the cemetery, in case some people"—a slow glower around the crowd—"didn't let the fact it's a funeral stop them from pursuing her. But I would like to offer my condolences—"

"Don't you dare." She enunciated each word like spitting glass.

"I offer them anyway, and I apologize for grabbing your wrist. You're understandably distraught, and I wanted to prevent you from providing a photo op that I don't think your son would have appreciated."

Despite all the times I've stood up to Maura, I've never been able to render her speechless. Ricky did. All around us, cameras snapped, recording the spectacle of the society grande dame having her manners shown up by a biker a third her age.

Ricky was right. This *was* a photo op that James would not have appreciated. So I didn't relish the moment. I reached over and embraced her—too quick to be thrown off—and I said, "I'm so sorry." I know maybe having *that* picture in the papers would be worse for her, but it's the one James would have wanted. I let her go; then I turned and climbed into the car.

CHAPTER THIRTY-ONE

W̶e were leaving the cemetery when I said, "You need to go back for your bike."

"I will."

"I know the club rules. You can't leave it there. I'd prefer you got it now, so you don't need to take off when we reach the police station."

I dropped him off, and he caught up before I reached the station. As we walked in, he went over how the process differed from the assault charge, where bail was set automatically. Gabriel would be kept in a holding cell for up to forty-eight hours, pending the arraignment, where the charges would be read and a plea entered. Bail would be set at that hearing.

"Everything will be okay. I'll handle this." He struggled for a smile. "Yeah, handling homicide charges is not my usual gig. Last time we had a member charged with murder, I was in high school. I'll call my dad and see what we need to do. Gabriel will handle the legal stuff, though. I'm just saying . . ." He paused and met my gaze. "Gabriel didn't do this."

"I know."

"I'm sure you don't *suspect* he did, but I absolutely *know* he did not. Beyond any doubt. I guarantee this will be resolved."

He couldn't guarantee that at all, and part of me wished he wouldn't say that. It felt like patting me on the head during a tornado and telling me everything would be all right. But when I looked at him, I didn't see a hint of condescension. Just resolve plastered over panic.

I hugged him, and we headed inside.

Ricky had warned I wouldn't be able to speak to Gabriel. I still tried. Tried damn hard, with Ricky beside me, both of us arguing with as much determination and eloquence—and as little animosity—as possible. I think the desk sergeant was impressed in spite of herself. That didn't mean we were getting a visit, though. So I parked my ass in the visitors' room, where I'd sit for as long as it took, either until I got to see him or until he was arraigned.

Gabriel had managed to send me further instructions from the back of the police car. He asked that Lydia be present for his office search and Ricky for his condo, because both were familiar enough with the process to stop the police from digging beyond the scope of the warrant. If Gabriel was concerned about having his office and condo searched, he gave no sign of it. I still fretted. Ricky reassured me that Gabriel was a defense attorney. If he had a nosebleed, he probably incinerated his shirt that night, just to be safe.

At around seven, I got word that the arraignment was set for noon the next day. I thanked the officer and told him I'd wait.

Ricky returned with dinner. After we ate, he started getting calls from his father. There was a club meeting that night, and I knew that, short of illness or imprisonment, Ricky was supposed to attend. He joked that he was *near* a prison. I made him go anyway.

Rose showed up shortly after Ricky left, likely after a call from him. She brought tea and cookies. We talked. I sent her home when the clock ticked near eleven.

Once Rose left, the night shift desk clerk came in to inform me that I absolutely could not stay. I pointed out that the station was open all night. If they wanted to make an issue of it, they could toss me in an empty cell on charges of being a pain in the ass. The clerk shook his head and left me alone.

At 11:45, my phone rang. I didn't recognize the number and held off answering until it was just about to switch to voice mail. Then I picked up.

"Olivia, you are not spending the night in the police station waiting room." It was Gabriel. "Ricky has my apartment keys. You can both stay there for the night. Arm the alarm and lock the doors. I'm not convinced his apartment is secure. My arraignment is at nine tomorrow—"

"I thought it was noon."

"They moved it up, which may have something to do with you being camped out in their waiting room. I appreciate that, but you should go now. There's no way we can meet before the arraignment."

"Pamela," I blurted. "When I was there yesterday morning, she said she knew you'd killed James. Someone had told her— one of the Cŵn Annwn, I think."

"Whatever Pamela said, I did not—"

"I know. But that's why I froze up when they arrested you. Because I hadn't warned you about what she'd said."

"Ah."

"I know you don't have much time, so if you have anything important you need to say, cut me off, but I want to say that I'm really, really sorry. I didn't tell you because I didn't want to give it any credence. If I'd thought, for one second, that you might actually be arrested—"

"It's all right. It helps to know where to begin looking for answers. The only important thing I have to say is 'go home.'"

"You'll be okay?"

"Of course." He sounded mildly offended that I'd ask. But I wasn't really asking. I was diverting him from realizing that I hadn't agreed to leave. He fell for it, and went on to tell me to bring him fresh clothing, along with a comb and a razor.

Ricky arrived a few minutes after we hung up. He brought a pillow, blanket, and hot chocolate.

"You don't have to stay," I said as he settled in, pulling the blanket over our legs.

"It's like a sit-in," he said. "I missed all that fun in my undergrad years. Not really my scene. But a protest against trumped-up criminal charges? I can get behind that. Now drink your cocoa. It's like a mocha with less caffeine."

"You could have gotten a decaf."

"That's just wrong."

I smiled and leaned against his shoulder.

I did get some sleep, partly because Ricky kept haranguing me until I closed my eyes, and once I did, I drifted off. I'd been propped against him, his arm around me. At some point I fussed enough to end up lying across the chairs, and he'd put the pillow under my head and draped the blanket over me, and when I woke, I was alone. I sat up quickly to find him still there, pacing.

"Go home," I said. "Seriously. It's a police station. I'm safe."

I was teasing, but when he turned, the smile fell from my face. He looked like he'd been awake for three nights straight.

"What's wrong?"

"Nothing. I'm—" He sat beside me. "Sorry, you don't need my shit right now. I know that. I just can't . . . I can't keep . . ."

"Ricky . . . ?"

"We need to talk, and I know this isn't the time, and I've been trying to push this off, but I can't."

"Do you want to step outside?" I asked.

He nodded.

"We'll tease the desk officer," I said. "Make him think we've actually given up our vigil."

I smiled, but his expression stayed dead serious. My heart started to thump.

When we were in the parking lot, I said again, "What's wrong?"

He glanced back toward the police station. "I shouldn't do this now. It's just . . . I managed all day, but then night comes, and what I can put off during the day . . . I can't anymore."

"Let me guess," I said. "It's over."

"What?"

"You and me. You were looking for easy and comfortable, and that's not what you're getting. Between your father and James, and now this . . ."

"Hell, no. I do not want that. At all."

"Well, it's obviously something you'd rather wait to tell me, and that's the only thing that came to mind."

"I don't want to lose you, Liv," he said. "I really, really do not, and I'm afraid . . ." He exhaled hard. "I just want you to know that I thought I was doing the right thing. Obviously, my solution was the wrong one—the worst possible one—and if I could go back and change it, I would. In a heartbeat."

"Okay, now you're freaking me out."

He exhaled again, and I could see the fear in his eyes, and I wanted to slap my hand over his mouth and say, No, don't tell me. Whatever it is, if you're this afraid to say it, don't, because I don't want to mess this up. I really do not want to mess this up. Instead, I took his hands, pulled him in front of me, and said, "Tell me."

"It's James. His death. I think—I think it might have been me."

CHAPTER THIRTY-TWO

I was still asleep. I had to be.

I had no doubt Ricky was capable of violence. He'd put a man in the hospital two weeks ago. Like Gabriel, he'd grown up in a world where that was a reasonable way to solve your problems and, indeed, sometimes it was the only way.

My mother taught me that there was never any excuse for violence. I remember her horror when my private school principal called after I slugged a fellow third-grader because he tripped me on purpose. And I remember my father taking the phone and saying he sure as hell hoped the boy's parents had gotten the first call, and that if someone lashed out at me, I had the right to hit back. Guess whose words I took to heart?

But now Ricky stood there saying he thought he'd killed James, and I was one hundred percent certain I was still asleep in the police station. Whatever Ricky was capable of, it didn't include murdering James. It just didn't.

I squeezed my eyes shut and waited to drift out of this nightmare.

"Liv?" Ricky's voice at my ear. "Can I explain? I know there's no excuse, but just hear me out. Then you can go. I won't stop you."

I was still holding his hands, which were trembling now. When I looked, he was right there, his hazel eyes bright with panic, and I knew this wasn't a dream.

I ran my fingertips over his knuckles and felt the scabs there. Scabs from the scrapes I'd seen Wednesday morning. After James died. They were still there, his knuckles rough.

James had been beaten. I hadn't more than briefly noted that, because what mattered were those bruises around his neck and the symbols carved into . . .

My head jerked up. "He'd been strangled—like the other victims. And he had the marks. The ones my parents—"

"No," he said emphatically. "Absolutely not. I didn't do any of that."

"But the beating," I said. "That was you?"

He nodded and shifted his weight. "After the blowout with my dad, I went to Gabriel's place to see you, and James was there. I just . . . I'd had enough. He was still stalking you, and I decided I was going to show him why that was a very bad idea."

"So you called him out?"

A short, humorless laugh. "You don't call out guys like James Morgan. They'll walk away and phone the cops. He drove off. I followed. I decided I'd wait until he got someplace quiet, cut him off, and confront him. Except I didn't need to. He drove to an empty building and went inside. The place was up for demolition and reconstruction. Something to do with tech, so I figured it was his project."

"You followed him inside."

"Followed him. Confronted him. Told him that if I caught him within five hundred feet of you, his hospital stay would be a lot longer than it had been when he mixed it up with Gabriel. He came at me. I knocked him around a little. That's all I planned. But he . . ."

Ricky exhaled, hissing through his teeth, shifting his weight again. "I'm not used to guys who don't fight back, Liv. I know that's no excuse. And, yeah, he started it, but he had no idea what he was doing. What he did do, though, was talk. About you. Insulting you. Saying he was getting you back no matter what. Saying . . ." He shook his head. "I won't repeat what he said, because words are no excuse for what I did. I'll just say that he threatened you. And I saw red, like I did with that other guy. Except there wasn't anyone to pull me off this time. I kept hitting him until he was out cold on the floor."

He stepped back, lifting our hands so I could pull away without resistance. He looked down at his bruised and scabbed knuckles. "I hit him until he shut up."

"And then?"

"I left him there, in that empty building, on the floor."

"Did you strangle him?"

He shook his head. "But I don't think he woke up after I knocked him out. He'd obviously been summoned there by his killer, who came in after me . . . and finished it. He never had the chance to fight. Which means even if I didn't stop his heart from beating, I still killed him."

I could argue, but Ricky didn't want excuses. He had done something that led to James's death, and he took responsibility.

I wanted to reach out for him. Hug him. Tell him I didn't care. That no matter how horrible I felt over James's death, whatever role Ricky played in it, I understood his intention had been only to stop whatever mad and hell-bent course James had been on.

But he wasn't looking for absolution. He just wanted me to know what had happened.

"You've talked to Gabriel about this, haven't you?" I said. "If you know the legal cause of death . . ."

He nodded. "I told Gabriel that night. I realized I'd fucked up, and I figured James would call the cops. So I drove back to the condo, and I was a block away when I saw Gabriel."

"*Saw* him?"

Ricky nodded. "I think that's one of the reasons he's been charged. The condo security tapes must have caught him leaving the building."

I remembered Pamela asking if I knew for certain Gabriel had been inside all night. Whoever had accused him knew he hadn't been.

"He'd gone out for a walk," Ricky continued. "I didn't ask why. I was just relieved to see him. We walked and talked. I left over an hour later. Which puts it past the time of death, meaning I'm Gabriel's alibi. I can testify, beyond a doubt, that he couldn't have killed James. That's what I'll do, if these charges aren't dropped. I can prove he's innocent."

"By admitting you're the one who beat James."

"What's the alternative, Liv? Let him go to jail?"

I felt as if someone had nailed me in the gut. If it was anyone else, I would not want Ricky turning himself in. But this wasn't anyone else. This was Gabriel.

My stomach heaved.

"It's okay," he said, pulling me into a hug. "I shouldn't have mentioned it."

I pushed him away. "You *absolutely* should have mentioned it."

"I mean planning to confess. I know I had to tell you what I did to James, as much as Gabriel didn't want me to."

"And I mean planning to turn yourself in. You need to talk to Gabriel first. We need to see how serious this is, how big the risk is, before you do anything."

"I know. I wasn't planning to walk in there and confess tonight, Liv. I'm not that selfless, or that stupid. It comes down to this: I won't let him go to jail. If it looks like that's going to happen, then I'll do whatever I have to."

I reached over and pulled him into a kiss. He went slow at first, as if braced for me to pull away. I only kissed him harder, held him tighter, and the kiss turned hungry, rough, with an edge of desperation.

"We're okay?" he said, as if he had to check, no matter how clear that seemed.

"I'm just sorry," I said. "I'm so damned sorry—"

He cut me off with a hard kiss, then said, "You have nothing to be sorry for."

Nothing to be sorry for. But I did, didn't I? As inadvertent as our roles were, we still felt the weight of them, the guilt of them, and anything we could do to divert our thoughts from that, if only for a few minutes, we seized on it, losing ourselves in the moment, banishing the rest into the night.

CHAPTER THIRTY-THREE

The next morning, Gabriel was arraigned on charges of second-degree murder. While I'd held out some hope that wouldn't happen, the arraignment was simply a formality, a chance for Gabriel to enter his official plea. Not guilty, of course. That's all he got to say.

Next came the bail hearing. That's where I got nervous. Gabriel wasn't exactly a popular lawyer. In court, he could be an arrogant, condescending asshole. But Ricky reminded me that he was careful never to be arrogant or condescending or asshole enough to turn judges against him, because that's like intentionally pissing off the referee. Gabriel balanced his belligerence with perfect self-control and a dead-on grasp of the law.

While the state's attorney tried arguing against granting bail, that was difficult when they'd decided on second-degree instead of first. Gabriel put forward his case for bail clearly and succinctly. No previous record. No passport. Established and successful local businessman with ties to the community.

Bail was set at one million. By noon, Gabriel was free.

"Your car is in the lot," I said as we walked out, jogging to keep up with Gabriel's long strides. "I'll drive you back to your place.

I'm sure you want a shower and a nap. Hell, I'm sure you want to spend the rest of the day holed up by yourself."

"I've had quite enough solitary confinement, thank you."

"You know what I mean. That couldn't have been a restful night—"

"I convinced them to give me my own holding cell by suggesting I might otherwise give my fellow inmates free legal advice. While it was not quite the accommodations I'm accustomed to, I've had worse."

He said it offhandedly, but with him it didn't mean the bed in his college dorm had been lumpy. He'd slept on the streets.

"Well, you'll want a shower at least," I said.

"Stop fussing, Olivia."

"I'm just—"

He looked down at me. "Stop fussing."

There was no annoyance in his words. But I still fell back. Ricky took my hand, squeezing it and mouthing, "It's all right." After a few steps he called up to Gabriel, "We'll let you do your thing, then. If you need us today, just call."

Gabriel glanced over, and then I *did* see annoyance, irritation that we weren't beside him.

"I need to speak to Olivia about all this," he said. "You and I need to speak, too. I would rather have both conversations at my apartment, for privacy." He turned to me. "With Ricky, it's a business matter. Confidential. I'll have you stop by the office for a few files while we—"

"I told her everything," Ricky said.

Now that hard look turned on Ricky.

"I know you advised me not to," Ricky said.

"Strongly and unequivocally advised—"

"It was still advice. Which I was free to take or ignore." Ricky kept his tone casual, but steel crept in. "I agreed with that advice before you were arrested, because I'd only be confessing to unburden myself, which wasn't fair to Liv. But with all this, she had to know. Now she does."

Gabriel glanced down at my hand, which was still holding Ricky's, and he resumed walking.

"You'll both come back to my apartment, then," he said. "Olivia, ride with me. We'll stop to pick up those files."

"I'll grab lunch," Ricky said.

We returned to Gabriel's condo. I could tell he didn't like having Ricky there. For a moment, I thought he was going to start hyperventilating. But Ricky had been up during the police search. The bridge had been crossed, and there was no sense retreating now.

We got comfortable—or Ricky and I did—and the three of us started to talk. Gabriel would learn the nature of the evidence against him shortly. From his brief talks with the police and assistant SA, Gabriel had figured out his apparent motive. They knew his recent history with James, of course, given those outstanding assault charges. They would argue that on the night of James's murder, Gabriel had gone after James again, following their public disagreement in James's office the day before. They believed Gabriel had intended only to frighten James into withdrawing charges—hence second-degree murder instead of first—but the beating had gotten out of hand. When James died, Gabriel had seen an opportunity. He could stage the body to look like one of the Larsens' victims, and then use it as further proof that Pamela and Todd were innocent.

I think Gabriel was more offended by the stupidity of that scenario than by the actual charge of murder.

The security tapes from his condo building showed him leaving and returning over an hour later. He would say that was proof he hadn't gone out with criminal intent—he knew the cameras were there and how to avoid them. Besides, the ones in the garage showed his rental car had never left. Even if he'd found an alternate vehicle, an hour wasn't enough time to kill James, take his body to the Villa, and return home.

"This is where I come in," Ricky said. "Because I know where you were during that hour and what you were doing."

"Which remains between the three of us."

"Unless it looks as if you're in danger of—"

"I won't be. Even if I was, I hardly see the point in being set free only to have your father kill me for getting *you* locked up in my place."

Ricky's lips twitched in a smile. "Then you'd need to give me a really good defense."

"I'll give it to myself and save the trouble. The point is, the charges against me are false, and I can prove that." He met Ricky's gaze. "Even if I have difficulty, which I do not expect, no confession will be forthcoming. Under any circumstances. Is that clear?"

"It is."

Which only meant that Ricky understood Gabriel's stance on the issue, not that he planned to go along with it.

"What were you doing out that night?" I asked Gabriel.

"Walking."

He seemed prepared to leave it at that, but when I kept watching him, he said, "I rearmed the security system and locked the doors, and I didn't intend to be gone as long as I was—"

"I'm not asking why you left me alone, Gabriel. So you went for a walk. That's it?"

"Yes."

"While I understand that simple answers are best on the witness stand, if you say you randomly decided to go out for a walk at one A.M.—"

"I do that," he said abruptly, as if blurting out some embarrassing confession. "If I can't sleep, I walk. That night, I was going to speak to James, but decided a walk was safer."

"So you've walked like that before?"

Gabriel turned a cool look on me. "I wasn't aware I was on the stand *now*."

"More than once a month?"

"Yes."

"Good, then the security cameras will show it's an established pattern. There's nothing unusual about getting fresh air and exercise when you can't sleep. If you can get access to any street cameras to prove—"

"—that I was indeed walking . . . with Ricky?"

"Right. Okay. Well, the building cameras should do, then, establishing that you regularly walk at night."

"Thank you, counselor. Anything more?"

"You had motive and opportunity. The third part is means. You're big enough to overpower James, and you only needed your hands to strangle him. Finding the knife used to inflict the postmortem wounds isn't necessary, is it?"

"No," Ricky said. "But *some* form of evidence is. That's the wild card."

As they continued talking, I withdrew into my thoughts. I'd still hoped this was just a trumped-up case that would shatter on impact. But this wasn't some small town where the sheriff could throw you in the drunk tank for being a smart-ass. This was Chicago, and the guy being charged was a crackerjack defense attorney. The SA's office would never have accused him without concrete evidence. Which meant someone was framing Gabriel.

I now believed that James had been compelled to stalk me. Compulsion meant Tylwyth Teg or Cŵn Annwn. In other words, whoever set James on Gabriel was very much determined to separate us . . . and might have the ability to conjure up evidence.

No matter how determined I might be to stay away from the fae and the Huntsmen, others were equally determined to pull me in. At any cost. Including getting rid of anyone who stood in their way. In the end, maybe all that would really protect them was to do exactly what Pamela said.

"Maybe if I go somewhere, this will stop," I said.

Gabriel turned those cool blue eyes on me and said, "It's a little late for that."

I blanched.

"He doesn't mean—" Ricky began.

"Of course I do," Gabriel said. "What good would it do her to leave now? This isn't a civil suit. The charges can't be withdrawn."

"I—I'm going to step out," I said, getting to my feet. "I need some air."

"I'll go with you," Ricky said.

"No. Please. I'll just be a few minutes."

Gabriel said, "You shouldn't be wandering about on your own."

"Why not?" I said. "No one's stalking me now. James is dead."

I shoved my chair aside and made my escape.

I sat in the coffee shop with an untouched black coffee, lost in my thoughts.

"You said a few minutes. I gave you twenty." Ricky leaned forward to look in my mug as he sat. "They don't have mocha?"

"I didn't feel like one."

He nodded and left and returned with a coffee and a cookie. He put the cookie in the middle of the table. "For whenever you do feel like it."

I looked at him, at the smile on his lips belying the worry in his eyes, and I thought, *How did I get so lucky?* Also, *How the hell can I keep screwing up the life of a guy like this?*

"Your dad was right to be worried," I said. "He thought I'd be trouble for you, and I am. I should go away for a while. The situation keeps getting worse—"

"I pursued you, knowing your life isn't exactly sunshine and roses right now. I wasn't coerced or seduced, and I'm insulted at the insinuation I'm not mature enough to make my own choices. No one made me go after James that night. I'm responsible for what happened. Fucking harsh lesson, but it's still mine to learn."

"I—"

"Yeah, you don't need this shit when you're already kicking yourself. But that's exactly why you need it. Reassurances aren't helping. So I'll be a dick and say that if you run off to protect me, we're through. Also, I love you."

"Wh-what?"

"Yes, I know, it *seems* like a completely inappropriate time to say it. But if I say it before sex or after sex or, worse, during sex, then it could seem like I'm caught up in the moment. Endorphins and all that shit. If I say it now, when I'm pissed off, obviously I mean it."

"Unless you're saying it so I'd feel even worse if I did leave."

"There's that, too."

I laughed. He pulled his chair in so that our knees touched as he leaned across the table.

"Both Gabriel and I are grown men, capable of making our own choices. Plus, Gabriel is an asshole."

I choked on another laugh.

"He isn't accustomed to considering how his words sound," Ricky said. "Or giving a shit. What he said back there was exactly what you're afraid of: that he's stuck and he blames you.

I told him so, and he had no idea what I was talking about because he never *said* that. He only meant there's no point in you leaving now. As for the part about him not *wanting* you to leave, that should go without saying." Ricky leaned back. "And he needs your help with his case. Our help. I want in."

I went still.

"I may not be a PI," he continued. "But I have killer research skills plus extensive criminal contacts. I'll work for free, and I'm highly motivated: if we don't discover who killed James, I could go to jail."

"The help would be wonderful. But . . . there are . . ." *Damn it, how do I word this?* "There have been things going on, inter-twined with this and linked to my parents—to the Larsens—that I haven't told you about."

"Ah. Confidentiality issues. That could be tricky. Do you want me to talk to Gabriel?"

"No, I will."

CURTAINS

abriel stood in Rose's parlor, looking out the front window at Olivia's apartment. Inside, she was telling Ricky everything. He'd spent the last twenty minutes thinking of nothing except what was happening in that apartment, and yet each time he let it coalesce into a clear thought, his jaw clenched tight enough to set it aching.

"I need to tell him," she'd said. "It's gone too far, and he's too involved. Not knowing exactly what's going on puts him in danger."

"So you're going to tell him that you can read omens . . . and the town of Cainsville is populated by fairies."

He won't believe you. He'll think we're both mad and get as far away as possible.

"You're right," he'd said. "You should tell him."

Even as the words came out, he'd felt a stab of guilt. As unfamiliar an emotion as the jealousy that roiled in his gut, thinking of her sharing their secrets with Ricky.

But they're ours. Damn it, they're ours.

Their secrets. The part of her life Ricky didn't share. As long as Gabriel knew about the omens and Cainsville, and Ricky did not, Olivia would stay with Gabriel. He had a purpose.

Now he would not.

Unless, in telling Ricky, she lost him.

Which Gabriel should not want.

He's good for her. Good to her. He makes her happy.

But why *him*?

Because it's always been him.

Gabriel rubbed his temples. It'd been two days since he'd started hearing that internal dialogue. It wasn't the proverbial "voice in his head." He'd handled cases where his clients claimed that's what compelled them to commit crimes. They were lying, of course. But he'd researched the phenomenon enough to counsel them on how to present their symptoms in a believable fashion.

Gabriel knew he was hearing his own unbidden thoughts. Yet they made no sense.

"You're hoping it doesn't go well."

That voice came from right behind him. Rose.

"You're hoping he won't be able to handle it, and he'll leave her."

Ice seeped into his voice. "I realize you may not think much of my ability to empathize with others, but I would never wish to see Olivia hurt like that."

"Good. Because the only acceptable reason for hoping *that* is if you planned to take advantage of the situation and offer yourself as a replacement, which I doubt."

"That would be correct."

"Then stop staring out that damn window, hoping you'll see Ricky Gallagher storm out of her life."

He fixed his aunt with a look known to make even expert witnesses quail. She didn't flinch.

"You want her all to yourself," she said. "Her time and her attention. If you wish to speak to her, she'd better be there to take your call. If you wish to see her, she'd better be available. And she sure as *hell* better not be sleeping with another guy, even if you can't bring yourself to cross that threshold yourself. That's not fair, Gabriel. You might be accustomed to getting what you want, but you aren't going to lock Olivia up on your terms. You just aren't."

"I have never expected—"

"Then step away from the window. Because if it doesn't go well with Ricky tonight, she'll find someone else. Someone you'll like and respect a whole lot less than him. Someone who will be a hell of a lot less understanding about how much time she spends with you. Olivia appreciates men. Unlike some people, she's not going to be content to bury herself in her work."

"I'm well aware of that, too."

"Then, as I said, the only reason you should be at that window is if you plan to offer up yourself as a replacement."

"Olivia is an employee and a friend. My feelings for her don't extend beyond that."

"Save the bullshit for a jury, Gabriel. Your feelings extend well beyond that. You just won't do a damn thing about them, because you're terrified of trying."

"Terrified?" He gave a short laugh. "While your choice of words is highly dramatic—"

"—my sentiment is dead-on?"

"Hardly. I have no interest—"

"You have every interest, and it's driving you crazy. Would it change anything if you knew she'd reciprocate?"

"No."

"So it's not fear of rejection. It's fear that it won't work. That you'll drive her off. That in trying for more, you'll lose her completely."

I always do.

He rubbed his temples again.

"Gabriel . . . ?" Concern in her voice now as she stepped forward.

He moved away from her. "As entertaining as it might be to try extending your powers to mind reading, I find the need to continually defend myself against groundless accusations irritating."

She kept her voice low. "I only want you to be happy."

"Then allow me to continue this vigil in peace, because what I'm doing, had you asked, is waiting until they finish their conversation so I can return to the task of making sure I don't go to jail for murder. *That* would make me happy."

"No, that would just be a relief. What makes you happy is her."

She walked away before he could reply. He turned back to the window.

She was right, of course. Not about all of it. Any sexual attraction was an unavoidable matter of biology. He was spending his days in the company of an attractive young woman and it had . . . been a while.

Sex was a problem for someone uncomfortable with physical intimacy. When he'd been a teenager or a college student, the drive overrode the revulsion. As he got older, the edge wore off that drive, and the anonymity he needed became much harder to come by when he made a conscious effort to get as much public exposure as possible. Women might pretend to have no idea who he was, but afterward he'd often get a "Remember me?" call at the office. The last one had actually shown up there. That had been almost a year ago. Which explained the "issues" with Olivia. He could solve them by breaking his dry spell but he recoiled at the thought. And he had a feeling it wouldn't be more than a very temporary solution. Because, if he was being honest, there was more to his attraction than biology. That didn't matter, though. Having such a relationship with Olivia introduced far too many uncontrollable variables into the equation.

She won't stay. She never does.

The other night, when he'd insisted Ricky join Olivia in her room upstairs, it had been, admittedly, an effort to prove their relationship didn't bother him. Of course, as soon as Ricky had climbed the stairs, and Gabriel realized how quiet the house was, and that he'd hear them if they engaged in anything, he'd felt very differently about the situation. Sure enough, the sounds from their room did drive him out of the house. But they weren't "that" sort of sound at all, simply them whispering and laughing, their voices too low for him even to make out what they were saying. That was enough, those whispers and laughs pounding through his skull like red-hot spikes.

That was exactly what he wanted from Olivia. That casual intimacy. That connection. They would go to dinner, and they'd relax and talk, share a bottle of wine, and it wouldn't matter if they were surrounded by people—it felt like just the two of them, wrapped up in the meal and the conversation. Or they'd be someplace together, talk turning light, teasing, and he'd see that glow in her eyes, feel the warmth of it. Then circumstances would intervene and the mood would evaporate, and he'd have no idea how to get it back again.

Ricky did. Effortlessly. In the midst of the worst situation, Ricky could engage Olivia as easily as flicking a switch. Change her mood. Make her smile. Win a laugh. He made it seem so easy.

It was not easy. Not at all.

But she'd spent the night in the police station for Gabriel. The officers occasionally came by his holding cell to tell him his "girlfriend" was still hanging around. He told them Olivia wasn't his girlfriend. Finally, one had said, "Well, then someone should tell her that, because she sure as hell acts like it." To have someone do that for him . . . it was confounding and almost unfathomable. He kept trying to tell himself that she had to have a reason beyond not wanting to abandon him. But she hadn't. She'd stuck by his side simply to say she was standing by him.

Gabriel checked his phone in case Olivia had texted, perhaps to say things were going poorly and she needed his help, his advice. He had messages. None from her. As he put his phone back, he noticed Ricky crossing the street, moving fast. Walking away from Olivia's building. Away from Olivia.

Ricky pulled on his helmet, climbed on his bike, and drove off without a backward glance.

Gabriel got as far as the front door before Rose made a noise behind him.

"I'm just going over—" he began.

"I heard the motorcycle."

"Yes, Ricky has left, which means Olivia is free. We have work to do."

Rose shook her head, looking very tired. "If there is anything worse than racing over because you're hoping she's been dumped, it's racing over to tell her to get back to work right *after* she got dumped. How about this: you're going over there to support her because she'll be upset, and she should have someone to talk to about it?"

Gabriel paused. Then he said, "Exactly."

Rose shook her head again. "Go on."

Gabriel tried to check his pace as he crossed the road. When he reached the apartment building, Grace called from the stoop, "Barely even waited until he got around the corner, did you?"

Gabriel ignored her. When he reached for the door, she said, "Presuming you want the girl, you're going the wrong way."

Gabriel followed her finger to see Olivia heading up Rowan. He calculated time and distance, trying to determine whether she might have left first—walking out after a fight. No, Ricky had, leaving Olivia upset, wanting to walk it off and . . .

And she was heading in the direction of the Carew house.

Gabriel took off at a slow lope, with Grace calling, "You're welcome!" behind him.

Ricky must not have believed what Olivia had told him about the omens and visions, and that had set her own doubts swirling again. She was wondering if she was imagining things. Heading to the Carew house for proof that she wasn't.

Olivia didn't need this. Ricky hadn't been there, not for any of it. He had no right to judge, goddamn him.

At the corner, Olivia stopped. Her head swiveled in the direction of the Carew house. Then she turned around and started heading back. It took a few steps for her to notice him. When she did, he tried to read her expression, but the sun was just beginning to drop, and long oak-tree shadows hid her face.

As she came close, he saw a tired, almost wry smile on her lips.

"Hey," she said. Before he could speak, she lifted a hand to stop him. "Yes, I was going to the house. Now I'm not."

"What happened?"

"I realized it was a very stupid idea."

He fell in step beside her. "Telling Ricky?"

"Hmm?" She looked over. "Oh, right. No. That's fine."

"You're all right with him taking off?"

Another vague look, as if her mind was elsewhere.

"I saw him leave," Gabriel said. "Clearly, he didn't take the news well and—"

"Oh, that. No. He's fine. He just went to grab dinner."

"Dinner?"

"Pizza, I think. Can't find that in Cainsville. I'm sure he'll bring plenty, so you're welcome to join us if you want some."

There were many things Gabriel wanted. Pizza was not one of them.

He cleared his throat. "So you told him everything and . . ."

"Not everything. Just about the omens and Cainsville. The omens part was fine. He's struggling a little more with the fae. As one would. I think he offered to go get pizza to take time to process everything. But he's not questioning it. He's more like you that way. I may have grown up with those superstitions in my head, but that was my only exposure to anything preternatural. You have Rose and her second sight. Ricky grew up with the stories, including the Wild Hunt."

"What?"

Olivia slowed as they neared her apartment. "When I was out at his cabin, we went . . . for a walk at night. We heard the Hunt. The Cŵn Annwn. He joked about it being the Wild Hunt—he knew the stories from his grandmother. Of course, he rationalized it away—just nighttime hunters—but I think he said that for my benefit, that deep down he suspected what it really was."

Of course he did.

He squeezed his eyes shut, forcing the voice to be quiet.

"Gabriel?" Olivia said.

"A slight headache," he said.

"I'm not surprised, given the last forty-eight hours. If you want to rest, I promise I won't go to the Carew house. I might go for a run, though. Or we could walk, if you need fresh air more than a rest." She grinned at him. "I know better than to suggest you join me in a run."

"I would, but my sweats are at home."

Her grin grew, as if she thought he was joking. Then she saw that he wasn't.

"You run?"

He shrugged. "Not much lately."

"And you never mentioned it?" A short pause, then a wry smile. "You were afraid I might ask to join you, right?"

He didn't know how to answer that. He would happily run with her. He just never wanted to presume. There was, too, always the possibility that he overthought these things. It was foreign ground to him. He did recall a couple of tentative childhood friendships. There'd been a girl before he was old enough for school. She lived down the hall. That lasted until his mother took advantage of his access to their apartment to steal everything that wasn't nailed down. Then there'd been a boy in first grade. That ended when his mother slept with the boy's father.

Thus began the slow process of learning to avoid anything that could be taken as an overture to friendship. It hadn't bothered him, really. He wasn't sociable by nature, and to be honest, his "friendships" had been more "playing in the same room as an equally unsociable child." Learning what might constitute an overture had been profitable later in life, as a way to manipulate marks into thinking they'd earned his friendship. The result, though, was that he was, perhaps, a little hyperaware of his interactions with others. Even Olivia. No, *especially* Olivia.

"Don't worry," she said. "I'll never pester you to run with me."

"I—"

"I get it," she said, that wry smile touched with something like sadness.

And thus an opportunity evaporated again, as it often did, and he was left stuck between cursing himself for losing it and telling himself it was for the best.

"But the walk?" she said. "Are you up for that?"

He motioned for her to carry on past the apartment building. "We'll walk."

She smiled then, a real one. Someone else did, too—Grace, on her stoop, watching them with a smug look.

CHAPTER THIRTY-FOUR

As we walked, I kept glancing at Gabriel. The quieter he was—and the faster he walked—the more I suspected he really would rather be resting at Rose's.

"We can go back," I said.

"I'm fine."

We reached the park. It was empty, the swings twisting in the breeze. We both stopped near the fence, as if each was waiting to see if the other planned to go in or continue on. I broke the impasse by opening the gate and walking through.

We sat on the bench in silence. I wanted to explain *why* I'd been going to the Carew house. In talking to Ricky, I'd realized that I needed to get these damned visions over with. To see whatever I was supposed to see. Otherwise, we wouldn't know enough context to figure out what had happened to James.

The problem was that the visions came with a price, and if I mentioned my plan to Gabriel, he'd snap and snarl and insist that I really didn't need them, that I could just ask the elders or Patrick. I couldn't, because everyone had an agenda and they'd slant the story to their advantage. So I was stuck.

I need these answers. I can't help him without them.

The thought flitted through my mind . . . and then I was

standing in a field. A perfect midsummer field, the grass long and sweet-smelling, tickling me in the breeze. A dragonfly landed on a stalk in front of me, its jeweled body glittering in the sun. I could hear the distant trill of a bird and the burble of a brook.

I knew what lay beyond that brook. The forest. Dark and shadowed, yet in its way as wonderful as the sunlit meadow— peaceful, shady, and cool. Two halves of the whole.

"Two halves of your whole," said a voice beside me.

The little girl reached for the dragonfly, laughing as it zipped away. This is where I'd first seen the *bean nighe*, down by that stream. I'd been the girl, walking through the meadow to the forest. When I lifted my hand now, though, it was clearly mine.

I turned quickly. "Gabriel . . ."

"He's fine. Would you rather try to talk him into returning to your house?"

"My house?"

The girl smiled. "Of course. It was built for you, long before you were born."

I shook off the illogic of that. "But Gabriel—"

"You want the rest of the story. You can't convince him to let you see it, and you wisely won't attempt to without him, so this is the best answer. A blameless way to get what you want."

"Except it's not blameless, is it? You're in my head. Meaning I called you up to get the rest of the story. Which is also in my head. Locked away."

She grinned like a teacher with a slow pupil who has finally learned to read. "Clever girl. Yes, you have the memories. We all do. Now, do you want to finish Matilda's story?"

Guilt flickered, but my answer came quickly. "Yes."

"Good. You've seen how it ends, in fire and death. Now see how it begins."

———

She pointed to a rise about twenty feet away. A boy shouted beyond it. Then a girl laughed. I crested the rise and saw them below. A girl with long, light brown hair sailing behind her as she ran from a blond boy. They were both no more than eight or nine. They tore through the meadow, the girl laughing as the boy tried to catch her. Then a blur shot from the forest. Another boy, dark-haired, riding a black horse. He raced up alongside the girl, leaned over so far I thought he'd fall, grabbed her arm, and swung her onto the horse. Then he tore off, laughing as the blond boy stopped and stared after them.

The girl clung to the horse, her hair whipping behind her, eyes narrowed in rapture as the horse galloped ever faster. They leapt over the stream, and the girl shrieked with delight. In the meadow, the sun itself seemed to dim as the fair-haired boy stood abandoned. Then they shot from the forest and tore back. The dark-haired rider launched from his horse and tackled the blond boy. The girl swung off, too, and moments later they were all walking through the forest, running, laughing, and playing.

"Matilda, Gwynn, and Arawn," I said.

"This is how it begins. With two boys and a girl, back before Romans set their filthy boots on our shores. The Tylwyth Teg and the Cŵn Annwn are the two sides of fae—light and dark. Light is not good nor dark evil."

"Just two sides of the same coin. Or stone."

She smiled. "Yes. Light and dark. Day and night. Meadow and forest. The living and the dead. The ties between the two were strong, and the ruling families were close. So, too, then, were the children of those kings. Gwynn and Arawn grew up together, along with a girl from the most respected family of *dyn hysbys* and *dynes hysbys*. Cunning men and women."

"Which means witches and seers. That's what Matilda was."

"She was also Tylwyth Teg and Cŵn Annwn. Half of each. Both sides claimed her. She grew up with Gwynn and Arawn, separately in their lands, and together as three friends. Which is fine for children, but when a woman comes of age, things change . . ."

I heard a shout, but it was deeper, Matilda's answering laugh more musical. Three horses shot from the forest, a coal-black stallion and a dappled mare leaping over the stream, their riders Arawn and Matilda, no longer children but perhaps seventeen, eighteen. They raced into the field.

Gwynn crossed the stream behind them on a white stallion. Then he climbed off and walked back to crouch and peer into the water. Matilda circled around. She swung off and went to kneel beside him. He pointed out something in the stream, and they talked, serious and intense, until he reached into the water, took out something, and laid it in her palm. Her hand closed over it, and when she looked at him, it was not the look a child gives a friend.

It's you. It's always been you.

Arawn rode back. Before he reached them, they climbed onto their horses, and the three took off across the meadow.

"And so there was a dilemma," the little girl said. "One girl, two boys. The young men knew that if they vied for her hand, their friendship might not survive, and the ties between their kingdoms could weaken, as the boys turned to men and warriors, on the path to inheriting their respective crowns. So they made a pact that they would remain friends—all three of them. Neither would court Matilda. What the men forgot was that there was a third party in this arrangement, one they did not tell of it."

I heard the shout again, and the laugh, and once more it was Gwynn and Matilda, in the meadow. They were older now, early twenties. Matilda had a basket, Gwynn a blanket. He laid it down and she set out a meal: cheese and bread and wine. She was leaning to pour his wine when he moved forward to take a piece of cheese, and they nearly collided. Matilda leaned forward, her face a few inches from his. Then she darted in and kissed him on the mouth before pulling back quickly, blushing. He froze there, touching his lips. Then, after a long, careful look around, he pulled her to him and kissed her again.

CHAPTER THIRTY-FIVE

A nd so Matilda made her choice," the girl said. "And Gwynn broke his promise. He'd only agreed to it because he was certain he was no competition for the charming prince of the Cŵn Annwn. The moment Matilda showed him otherwise, he forgot the pact. He courted her in secret and made her swear not to tell Arawn. The Cŵn Annwn prince was busy with fractious matters of state, he said. They ought not to disturb or distract him. The truth was that Gwynn was convinced she also loved Arawn, that he'd only won her because Arawn had played by the rules."

"Which wasn't true," I said. "She chose Gwynn. She loved Arawn as a friend."

"Gwynn never could—never would—believe it. He kept their engagement a secret until two nights before the wedding."

The sun went out, pitching the field into darkness. I heard voices, angry voices, speaking Welsh. Arawn and Gwynn, the venom in their words growing stronger with each exchange.

The girl said, "They were young—Arawn hot-tempered and impulsive, Gwynn intense and unbending. That night, both said things they didn't mean. Eventually, they came to an agreement. A terrible agreement. One they didn't—again—share with Matilda. She would get one last chance to choose. On the eve of her wedding, if she stayed with Gwynn, then she was his and the land of the Cŵn Annwn was closed to her forever."

"And if she went to Arawn, she was his and the land of the Tylwyth Teg would close."

As soon as I said it, the dark field erupted in flame, and I quickly turned away, wrapping my arms around myself and trying not to remember what it felt like to be immersed by that flame, plunging into it, trying to return to Gwynn. I could hear Arawn shouting, so loud his voice cracked.

"He couldn't save her," the little girl said. "Neither of them could, each on his side. In trying to return to Gwynn, Matilda plunged into the fiery abyss and was lost. They never forgave themselves . . . or each other. Those flames of rage and guilt burned through every tie between the Tylwyth Teg and the Cŵn Annwn. Late in life, the two kings came to fully understand the damage they'd done to their peoples, and they reconciled. While they managed to bring an uneasy peace to their lands, it was not the same. It would never be the same."

"And now they're enemies again? The two sides?"

She pursed her lips. "Not enemies. They have been known to help one another, but it is not so much kindness as survival. There are other groups of fae. Some are allies, others are not. The Tylwyth Teg and the Cŵn Annwn will help one another to stand against them, but their ultimate goal is freedom from that obligation—to stand strong enough that they do not require the other's help."

"And I play a role in that because I'm the new Mallt-y-Nos. The new Matilda. Or something like that."

She smiled. "Yes, something like that. The cycle repeats. New Matildas are born. Not often. Not at all often. She must share the blood of the original, and she must be, like the original, of both sides."

"Half . . . ? If Pamela is Tylwyth Teg, then Todd is . . . ?"

"Cŵn Annwn. That is, they have the blood. Strong blood, mingled many times, from many sources, one path linking back to the family of the original Matilda."

"Okay, so a new Matilda is born, and she meets the new Gwynn, presumably from the same bloodline as the original . . ."

"She may not meet him. I never did."

"But the *goal* is for her to meet the new Gwynn?"

"Or the new Arawn, preferably one or the other, the choice dependent on the side."

I shook my head. "Okay, you lost me."

"For the Tylwyth Teg, the goal is for a new Matilda to meet her Gwynn, but not her Arawn, because that restarts the original scenario. Likewise for the Cŵn Annwn."

"So she meets one and . . . There are babies involved here, aren't there?"

She laughed. "Only if you want them, which I think you do not. No, the only requirement is the bond. Of course, the stronger the bond, the more likely they can woo the girl to their side, so they would not object to babies."

"Well, they aren't getting them. If Gabriel is the new Gwynn, and we're friends, that's it, then, right? The bond is there. My mission accomplished."

"There's more to it than that—the fate that awaits the Tylwyth Teg if you don't actually choose them."

She settled onto the ground as the sun rose again. I sat in front of her.

"Fate?"

"Extinction."

"You mean . . . wiped out?"

"For this settlement, yes. It happens. Nothing lasts forever. There are other Tylwyth Teg and Cŵn Annwn, other groups. Fewer and fewer. Our time is past, yet we are stubborn. But what keeps fae alive is limited, and it dwindles as the world is consumed by what passes for progress."

"And what keeps fae alive? Wait. Ley lines, correct? Cainsville is built on a ley line."

She laughed, the sound tinkling. "Ley lines are a human invention. What sustains us are three of the four elements. Air, water, earth. The other—fire—kills. But the first three keep us alive, so long as they are pure and untainted. Tell me, what is a ley line?"

"A geographical alignment. Streams combining with mountain ridges and such."

"In broader terms, then, it is a mixing of elements, such as water and rock. Humans had an inkling of the truth there, though they overcomplicated the matter. For fae, the ideal habitat is one that combines as many elements of nature as possible. Rock, rich earth, water, forest, meadow . . ."

"Like Cainsville," I said. "Bounded on one side by river, another by marsh, the third by rocky ground. Surrounded by field and forest. The Cŵn Annwn use that forest, other forests, too. They're more nomadic. Less bound to territory. Still, both govern land valuable to other fae. And as remaining woodlands are developed, Cainsville becomes *more* valuable, and threats emerge."

"They do. Even as we speak. Those others grow bolder, knowing you're here. Yet even here, the land dies. It cannot avoid contamination—air, earth, and water. You can cleanse and renew it, and give them the power to resist those threats."

"Hopefully not with my blood, scattered over the land."

"Nothing so drastic. You cleanse the land of Cainsville by

living on it. You would cleanse the lands of the Cŵn Annwn by riding with them."

"How about the Persephone solution? Not that I'm volunteering . . ."

"Neither will accept that, because it dilutes your power and they both want it all. They will insist you choose."

"Framing Gabriel for James's murder is part of this, isn't it?"

"Presumably, yes, but do not ask me to name the murderer or the motive. I know only what you do."

"I'm guessing it was the Cŵn Annwn. Moving the Tylwyth Teg's champion off the field to make room for their own. To ensure I meet Arawn—his representative, right?"

A giggle rocked her whole body. "That is a silly question, and you know it. The cycle is already repeating, and the longer you pretend you don't know who Arawn is . . ."

"Ricky." I forced his name out on a sudden exhalation of breath, as if I might not let it escape otherwise. "It's Ricky, isn't it? The Hunt. That's why he hears it. Why he's drawn to it. He's . . ."

"Cŵn Annwn. Motorcycles instead of steeds. The joy of the ride, of the hunt. You feel it, too."

Fast cars. Fast bikes. The way I craved speed, that unbelievable adrenaline rush.

I always had.

"He doesn't know," I said. "He can't know. And his father . . . his father isn't a Huntsman. Is it his mother? Is that possible? No." The answer came quickly. "It's Don Gallagher's father. He was never in the picture, and that's why. Don is the son of a Huntsman. Ricky is a grandson."

I took shallow breaths, struggling to orient myself. The girl stayed silent, watching me with a look between sympathy and pity.

I'd known. Somehow, deep inside, I'd known.

Known and feared.

I don't want this. I don't want him touched by this. It's not fair.

Not fair to him, to be sure. But also, if I admitted it, not fair to me. Ricky was my one good and pure thing right now. Even telling him about Cainsville and the omens had been difficult, as if it tainted what we had with the madness that was my life these days.

Matilda. Gwynn. Arawn. The cycle repeating.

"Is it fated, then?" I asked. "Us?"

"You mean does Ricky love you because he has to? No. It's not fated that you'll meet. It's not fated that you'll feel the same. You aren't truly Matilda. They aren't truly Arawn and Gwynn. The cycle isn't set. It shifts and it changes. You could choose Arawn this time. You could choose Gwynn again. You could choose . . . and they might not reciprocate. Nothing is decided."

"And which is the best solution?"

She lifted her thin shoulders. "Who knows? It's never happened. Now, you need to go."

"I have more—"

"You aren't worried about *him* anymore?" I followed her gaze. The meadow faded into the Cainsville park. I saw myself on the bench, sweat pouring down my face, soaking my shirt as I stared glassy-eyed. Gabriel crouched in front of me, his hands on my shoulders.

When I squeezed my eyes shut, I could hear his voice, feel his touch.

"Olivia. Damn it, *Olivia*."

My eyes snapped open.

CHAPTER THIRTY-SIX

Gabriel was right there, his face taut. He moved away, releasing me fast.

"I couldn't get you back," he said, as if in explanation.

"I know. I was just sitting here and . . ." I inhaled. "It's over now. I got the whole story."

"I couldn't get you back," he said again, and there was a different note in his voice now, almost angry. "You would not come back. Your temperature kept rising, and you were gone."

"I'm sorry," I said. "I—"

"I'm not accusing you of anything, Olivia," he said as he stood, snapping his shades back on. "I'm telling you that I could not bring you back. It keeps getting worse, and I don't know . . . I couldn't get to you—" He bit off the sentence, and I remembered the fire, the terrible fire between the worlds, Arawn shouting, Gwynn shouting, trapped on their opposite sides, Matilda lost in the middle, screaming, as she burned.

They couldn't save her. Couldn't get to her.

Gwynn . . .

I closed my eyes. Gabriel wasn't Gwynn. Thrust into the role, but not the same person, not bound to the same fate, not feeling the same emotions, the same bonds. I had to remember that.

Otherwise . . . well, otherwise, I thought I'd go mad, trying to reconcile it, Matilda and Gwynn, me and Gabriel.

"I think it's over now," I said. "I've seen it all."

"And you'll tell me."

I hesitated.

"*Olivia*."

"Of course." *As much as I can, as much as I dare.* "Not here, though. We should go someplace. Maybe . . . Shit! Ricky." I checked my watch.

"I heard his bike a few minutes ago."

"He'll be wondering where I went. Did you text him?"

A cool look. "At the time, I was a little more concerned with snapping you out of a trance state before fever short-circuited your brain."

I texted, telling Ricky I was out for a walk with Gabriel and heading back now. Then I rose, my knees shaky as I started for the gate.

"We aren't discussing it, then?" he said.

"Not while Ricky's waiting with pizza."

"I should think this is more important than pizza."

Now I was the one giving him a look. "It is, but he just rode twenty miles to get it for me, and you want me to say I'm too busy to eat it? Or that I'm busy talking to you about things that I can't tell him . . . when he thinks I've told him everything? Unless you *want* me to tell him everything."

"Fine. But I expect to speak to you tonight about this."

I nodded and headed out the gate. We'd just reached the walkway beside my building when I heard Ricky's voice along with another I recognized.

"Patrick," Gabriel murmured.

Patrick was, technically I guess, one of the Cainsville elders, though the form he took didn't look much older than me. That was even more disconcerting, given that he was Gabriel's father. Not that Gabriel knew that. Rose did, and we'd agreed that was one secret we were keeping for now.

Patrick was a *bòcan*. A hobgoblin, which didn't mean some kind of troll-like creature. The best-known example of a hobgoblin is Puck from *A Midsummer Night's Dream*, which about sums up Patrick.

I hurried down the lane. Ricky kept glancing over Patrick's shoulder, clearly eager to be gone but not wanting to be rude.

When he caught sight of me, he grinned, pleasure mixed with relief.

"Hello, Liv. Gabriel," Patrick said. "We were discussing motorcycles. I might buy one. They look like fun."

"Isn't there some kind of rule against that?" I said. "Crossing into enemy territory?"

There was, for one split second, the most wonderful look of surprise on Patrick's face before he covered it with a breezy grin.

I turned to Ricky. "Gabriel's joining us for pizza."

"Actually," Gabriel began, "Olivia and I need—"

"Can you take it over to Rose's?" I asked Ricky. "I'll meet you both there. I'd like to speak to Patrick."

I waited until they were gone, and then I said to Patrick, "Leave him alone."

"Which *him*? You have so many."

"One fewer now."

His lips pursed. "I wasn't going to say that. It seemed rude."

"I'm making a point. James's death had something to do with this Mallt-y-Nos nonsense."

"Nonsense?"

"Oh, I know, it's life or death to you. But to me? It's a whole other kind of life or death. The kind that is getting people I care about killed. And other people I care about charged with murder."

"That is unfortunate."

"*Unfortunate?*" I choked with sudden rage. "He's your *son*. I know that doesn't mean fuck-all to you, but could you at least have the decency to acknowledge he's in trouble?"

Patrick had abandoned Gabriel. No, not abandoned him, because he'd always been in Cainsville, like an old family friend—and that somehow made it worse, made it colder. He'd seen the hell that had been Gabriel's young life, and he'd stood back and watched, then dared to claim it was for Gabriel's own good. Tempering steel, he'd said.

"Take a deep breath," Patrick said.

My fists clenched.

"You can hit me if it'll make you feel better. I promise not to hold it against you. It won't do any lasting damage."

"Then why would I bother?"

The son of a bitch smiled.

I forced myself to continue. "I would appreciate it if you could see fit to at least acknowledge what is happening with Gabriel the next time you see him. At least say you're sure it will all be fine."

"But he will be fine. He obviously didn't kill the man, and he's an excellent lawyer. He'll fix this."

"And if not, well, hey, what better way to toughen him up than twelve years in maximum security?"

"I'll acknowledge the situation and express my certainty that it will resolve itself."

"On second thought, don't bother. You'll only screw up that, too."

He met my gaze with a cool look, one of the few times I could see a resemblance to his son. "I might suggest you moderate your tone with me, Olivia."

"You don't like it, *bòcan*? Then curdle the cream and get me fired. Oh, wait, no . . . I have another job." I headed for Rose's. "And stay away from Ricky."

"I was simply talking to him," he called after me. "I have no issue with him being here. In fact, I find it an intriguing set of circumstances."

"No, you find it an *amusing* set of circumstances. You love seeing the elders squirm, and what's better than this? They've pinned all their hopes on me, certain I'll hook up with their golden boy and save them from extinction, and instead, the competition is sharing my bed, in their own town, and there's not a damn thing they can do about it."

His lips quirked. "It is rather amusing."

"For you. Not so much for me. Or Gabriel. Or James. Or any of us caught up in this mess. I'd think you'd be less amused, given the ending if I ride off with Ricky. I hear it would be your ending, too."

"Hardly. They'll go down with the ship. I'll bail. I've done it before."

"Like a rat."

"An apt comparison."

"Then none of this concerns you, so unless you can help, stay the hell away from Ricky. From both of them, in fact. And speaking of helping, if you know anything that can assist Gabriel's defense—anything at all—you'd better—"

"I would let you know. You don't need to threaten me. In fact, I daresay you'd better not."

"And again, I don't give a flying fuck."

"You're angry with the elders, but you're furious with me. They lie to you. They deceive you. They'll use you if they can. But my crime is greater because you believe I've wronged *him*."

I followed his gaze to see Gabriel at the end of the passageway, standing back on the sidewalk, out of earshot, but waiting and watching.

"Can I leave now? I have pizza waiting."

He smiled. "Pizza. That's very important. You can leave any- time you want. But you aren't foolish enough to turn your back on me. Remember this, *bychan*. I'm no threat to you. Or to him. I can be an ally, if you can put aside your anger long enough to ask for help. If not for your sake, then for . . ."

He nodded toward Gabriel, and fresh rage whipped through me.

"Yes, I'm exploiting your weakness," he said. "I'm not above that. In fact, as you might imagine, I'm extremely pleased by it. Gabriel doesn't need my help or my support. He has more than enough of yours."

I glared at him.

"You think I mock you," he said. "I don't. You might not be sleeping with my son, but sex is only sex. If a choice were to be made, I have no doubt who it would be. It's the Cŵn Annwn who should be worried."

"No, it's both sides that should be worried, because I'm not playing your little game."

"I'm afraid you don't have that option, *bychan*."

"Oh, I think I do."

I turned and strode back to Gabriel.

CHAPTER THIRTY-SEVEN

Ricky and I were back from Rose's, lying in bed after sex. TC was perched on the foot of it, staring at us. Ricky was on his back, eyes half closed, arm around me as I traced the Celtic crown tattoo on his upper arm.

"That one is for my dad," he said. "Since you'll never ask me to explain. The triskele is for my nana and the asklepian for my mom. Obviously, the patch is for the Saints." His gaze shifted to my hip, his fingers tracing the dip of my waist. "I want to get one for us, like we discussed. But I don't want to without . . ." He frowned. "Your permission? Does that sound right? Sure, it's my body, but if you get a tattoo because of a girl and she doesn't want you to, then it's kind of awkward. And a little creepy."

"A big 'Property Of' sign would be fine with me."

He laughed, so loud it startled the cat. "I'm tempted to do that, with a Sharpie, just to see the look of horror on your face." He sobered. "Is that a yes? Or are you kidding in hopes of changing the subject?"

I leaned in to kiss him. "No games, remember? I would be honored to have a permanent place on your body. And, yes, I know the tattoo isn't about *expecting* anything permanent. It's memorializing me."

He sputtered a laugh. "That makes it sound as if you're dead. It's like the rest of my tattoos—marking someone or something significant in my life."

"I want one, too." I rolled half onto his chest, looking down at him. "Like we discussed."

"You don't have to, Liv."

"I want to."

He studied my face, then gave a slow smile. "Okay. But I'm going to insist you get a small design, something easily hidden. I have an idea, too."

He reached down for my jeans and pulled something from the pocket. It was the boar's tusk given to me by one of the Cŵn Annwn.

He'd first seen it the night we'd heard the Wild Hunt, and I remembered the fascination glittering in his eyes as he'd turned it over in his hand. A gut-level recognition that this was signifi- cant somehow. Like his grandmother's stories of the Hunt.

I should have known what he was.

The girl was right. I *had* known. Deep down.

He pointed to a symbol on the tusk—a Celtic-style sun and moon, intertwined. "For my tattoo, I'd like this. It reminds me of you. Don't ask me why. It just does."

The sun and the moon. Tylwyth Teg and Cŵn Annwn. Two halves of my whole.

I ran my fingers over the engravings of the moon. The symbol of the Cŵn Annwn. Ricky's symbol. It fit him. It always had, and maybe it wasn't what I wanted for him, but it *was* him. There was no changing that. For Ricky, then, I chose this design. When I said that, I thought he'd ask why, but he only nodded, looking pleased.

I put the tusk aside. "Okay, so we have the design. Where should I put it?"

His grin was devilish now as he rolled me onto my back. "Well, that's going to take some exploration. If the spot's too hard, it'll hurt too much. Too soft, and it's really not going to look as good in thirty years."

I stretched out, hands behind my head, covers kicked off. "Explore away. I trust your judgment."

I woke to the buzz heralding a text message. As I reached for my phone, I glanced out the window. It was pitch-black . . . except for a faint glow from Rose's house. Shit.

Sure enough, I had three texts from Gabriel. They grew increasingly terse as I failed to reply. The last was simply: *Are you coming?*

I looked out the window at that light. I could feel the pull of it. *Go talk to Gabriel. He's waiting for you.*

I glanced at Ricky, soundly sleeping, his leg over mine, his hand on my hip.

Patrick said that if I was forced to choose between Ricky and Gabriel, he had no doubt whom it would be. I remembered the smug smile on his lips, the conviction in his eyes.

I cared about Gabriel. Deeply. But we weren't Gwynn and Matilda, no more than Ricky and I were Arawn and Matilda.

I sent back a message. *Talk tomorrow.* And the light across the road went out.

I woke to a message that Gabriel had headed home the night before, so I needed to drive myself to the office. I arrived expecting to talk to him about my vision, only to discover he'd retreated with his door closed. He'd left work for me in the meeting room. Lydia buzzed to tell him I was there. He didn't come out.

Gabriel had left me Pamela's file. The note on top gave me instructions. Or I think they were instructions. It was exactly two words: *Inconsistencies. Motive.* Motive was underlined twice.

If there were inconsistencies in the Larsens' case, he'd have found them by now. As for motive—seriously? No one had figured out my parents' motive during their trial. How the hell was I supposed to?

More information would help. Hell, actual sentences would help. But I dug in.

When a client arrived, I gathered my work and went into the reception area. The client—a guy wearing an expensive but ill-fitting suit—glared as if I'd cut him off in traffic. Gabriel ushered him into the meeting room without a glance my way.

It was not a long session. It consisted of a lot of angry words from the client, followed by the only two that counted: *You're fired*.

The man stormed out. Then his shoes squeaked as he pulled up in front of me.

"Let me give you a word of advice, girlie," he said. "Unless you want your boyfriend defending traffic violations, you'd better back the hell off and let him do his job."

Gabriel beat me to a reply, saying, "Ms. Jones is my employee and my client."

"Really?" The man snorted. "If you aren't at least getting some pussy out of the deal, then you really are an idiot. You want some advice, boy? A couple hundred bucks will buy you better and won't cost you clients."

The man stomped out. Gabriel glanced at Lydia. "Please move Mr. Harris's file to the drawer for former clients and prepare his final bill. How many is that so far?"

"Three, but you've—"

"That's all I asked." He turned his gaze my way, just for a second, empty eyes meeting mine; then he returned to his office.

I slid my chair up to Lydia's desk. "He's lost three clients because of me?"

"Three *minor* clients, with *minor* cases. Since Edgar Chandler's confession, I'm fielding a half-dozen calls from potential clients a day. He's not mentioning that part because he's fuming about something. I take it you two had a falling-out?"

"Actually, no. There's a reason he might be annoyed with me, but this is beyond annoyance."

"Then it's stress. It'll pass."

Maybe, but if he *was* that upset with me, working it out might decrease his stress.

I rapped on his door. When he didn't answer, I turned the handle.

"Yes?" he said, voice crackling with such irritation you'd think I'd pranced in ahead of a marching band.

"Can we talk?"

He waved a hand across his desk, covered in files.

I closed the door behind me. "I wanted to apologize."

"I'm busy, Olivia." An emphatic gesture at his desk.

"If you're upset about last night . . ."

"Why would I be?" He lifted those empty blue eyes to mine. "First I had to stop you from going to the Carew house—"

"No, I was coming back on my own. I realized I was doing something stupid—"

"Then you went and had a vision anyway, knowing how I felt about it."

"I was *sitting* on a *bench*. The vision came—"

"I do not have time for this, Olivia. You can see the state of my business . . . in addition to the murder charge I now face."

"After weeks of telling me that you're helping because you want to—and because it'll further your career—you've suddenly decided I'm ruining that career?"

"I did not say—"

"Bullshit." I strode over and put my hands on his desk. "You are in a pissy, pissy mood. Lydia says you're stressed. Completely understandable. But do not take it out on me. Yes, maybe I didn't handle last night as well as I should have. I apologize for that."

"I have work to do, Olivia." His eyes were ice-cold. "And if you intend to keep your job, I might suggest you do as well."

The temptation to quit then and there was almost overwhelming. Instead, I straightened, said, "Yes, sir," and walked out.

CHAPTER THIRTY-EIGHT

I pored over Pamela's file for a while longer before deciding to do some legwork. Traffic was good, and in thirty minutes I made it to my destination: the home of Jon Childs, the man Chandler had wanted us to kill.

I hopped out of the car and cut across the lawn, because whoever set up the underground sprinkler system apparently thought the walkway needed water instead. That's when I kicked a sparrow.

A dead bird in your path is a sign to turn your ass around. There are few superstitions surrounding sparrows specifically, though, meaning the warning wasn't exactly a red flag. Maybe burnt orange. I decided it meant there was something worth investigating here.

I knocked on Childs's door. There were no flyers in the box now, but the town house was dark and no one answered. I rapped again . . .

"He's out."

The neighbor had a trowel in her hand and wore knee guards.

"He's back from wherever he went," she said. "But he just stepped out."

"Oh. I . . ." I checked my watch.

"He'll probably be home at any moment. Why don't I fix you a coffee while you wait. I could use a break from the war of the weeds."

"And I'd love to take you up on that, but I was just popping by on my way past. Thank you, though."

My cell buzzed with an incoming text. I ignored it, and thanked the woman again before heading back to my car.

"I spoke to him about you," she called after me.

Shit.

"He said his sister has taken a turn for the worse, and she's in care. He appreciated your concern and said if you stopped by, I was to ask for your number again. He's misplaced it."

So Childs knew my story was bullshit. Huh. I scrawled my number on a scrap of notepaper. As I handed it to her, my cell buzzed with another text.

"I really do need to run," I said, "but please give him that and thank you for all your help."

When I got to my car, I checked my phone. It was Gabriel. First message: *Where are you?* Second message: *Olivia . . .*

I replied with one word: *Working.*

He responded immediately. *Where are you?*

Out. Working.

Where?

Chicago.

His response took a moment. I imagined him starting to seethe, possibly hitting a wrong key or two, cursing me as he fixed it.

Olivia . . .

Gabriel . . .

I didn't wait for a reply, just quick-typed: *I'm working on the case, as requested.*

I didn't tell you to leave.

Am I not allowed to leave?

Pause. Pause. Pause. Thinking through an answer. Well, no, I'm sure he didn't need to think about it. His answer would be that I should be right where he left me just in case he needed me. However, being a smart man, he did not say that.

Where exactly are you?

In my car.

Five seconds. My phone rang.

I sent one last text. *Working the case. No time to chat. Talk later.*

I turned off the ringer and left the phone vibrating in my bag as I pulled from the curb.

I drove to a little bungalow in Brighton Park. A ten-year-old van sat in the drive. I pulled in behind it, walked up to the stoop, and knocked. When the door opened, I was ready to stick my foot in the gap to keep it from slamming shut. I've seen Gabriel pull that trick many times. I suspect it works better with a size-twelve loafer.

Luckily, I didn't need to risk bodily injury. The man took one look at me and said, "I wondered when you'd show up." Then his gaze went to my Jetta. "Walsh isn't with you, I take it."

"He's not."

"Did they deny his bail?"

I shook my head. "He's out. Just busy working on staying that way."

The man nodded. "Strange business. But it always was." He moved back. "Come on in."

He backed his wheelchair into the kitchen. Detective Chris Pemberton. Retired a year ago, having spent eight years behind a desk after getting in the middle of a gang dispute and catching a bullet in the spine. Twelve years before that, he'd been the secondary detective on a career-making case. Ending a spree of horrific murders and putting the perpetrators behind bars. The Valentine Killers. My parents.

"Wife's out," he said. "I'm going to text and tell her to stay away for a while. She doesn't like it when I talk about the case. I always wondered what happened to you. Adopted by the Mills and Jones department store guy." He shook his head. "I'd say I was glad to hear it—you deserved something good after all that—but it seems things haven't been too easy for you lately."

"I'm doing okay."

"Looks like it." He pulled up to the kitchen counter. "Coffee? Tea?"

I said I'd take either, and he started fixing coffee as I settled in at the kitchen table. I'd presumed a detective who'd helped make the case would want nothing to do with me, which is why I'd come over unannounced. This wasn't what I expected, and I couldn't help bracing for trouble.

"I was there when they arrested your parents," he said, getting cups from a low cupboard. "World-class fuckup, pardon my French. It should never have gone down that way. We were told you and your mom were away, and that Todd had guns. I never forgot the look on your face when the team broke in."

"All I remember is that it was my half birthday," I said. "We were going for a pony ride."

When I saw his expression, I wished I hadn't said that. He felt bad enough.

"It's okay," I added. "I forgot all about it until recently."

"Maybe, but you never really forget. Any shrink would tell you that. Cream and sugar?"

"Cream, please."

He poured it. I got up to retrieve my cup from the counter,

but he waved me down. "I've got it. Nine years in this thing, and I'm a pro."

He brought both coffees to the table. I thanked him and sipped mine.

"You have questions," he said. "And since my partner has passed on, it's down to me. What do you want to know?"

"Why they did it."

He winced. "Ah, hon, of all the questions . . ."

"It's the only one I need answered. The most important."

"You think they're guilty, then?"

I looked up, startled. "Don't you?"

He took a long sip of his coffee before answering. "All the evidence pointed that way. I didn't want to believe it. None of us did. We'd been to your house once, on a tip."

"Where you pretended to be warning people about a rash of break-ins."

"Yeah. We talked to your parents, and you were there, and we walked out thinking we were wrong, that it couldn't have been your folks, and we were glad of it. No one wants to think that about a nice young couple with a cute kid. They were good parents. Whatever else they are, remember that. Anyone could see they loved you very much."

"Thank you."

"So did I believe they did it once the evidence piled up? I guess so. There wasn't much of a choice. But when you and Walsh found that Chandler guy, I'll be perfectly honest, I . . . I didn't know what to think. There's always been a part of me that hated that case. Hated what happened. That's why my wife doesn't like me talking about it. Too many sleepless nights, wondering if we'd put the right people in jail. Now that there's doubt, I should be happy, right? It's not like I'll catch any fall-out. I'm retired, and this"—he banged the chair's side—"makes me a goddamn hero. No one's saying I screwed up. They don't dare."

"But you aren't happy we've raised that doubt."

"I . . . I don't know." He paused. "You won't want to hear this, but where there's smoke, there's fire. I cannot believe the system locked up two completely innocent people."

"Which is why Gabriel Walsh and I are still investigating. Let's say they did it. Why? I know motive is the prosecution's concern, but you must have had theories."

He sighed. "No, I didn't. That was the toughest part. Why would they do it? It wasn't about sex or thrills. I've seen my share of both. The prevailing theory, as you well know, was witchcraft."

"You don't believe that?"

He fingered his half-empty cup. "I always thought it was the best answer. The only sane answer, as insane as it was. But it still takes you back to the original question, doesn't it? Why?"

I looked at him.

"Why conduct such a ritual?" he said. "No one seemed interested in answering that. I suppose, if they tried, they'd just list the usual reasons people commit regular old murder all the time. Money, power, revenge . . . But none of that fits your parents. Anyone who spent five minutes with them knew they weren't interested in that. They only cared about each other. And of course—"

His gaze went to mine and he stopped himself, as he realized what he was about to say, to imply. That there were only two reasons the Larsens would commit murder. For each other. And for *me*.

CHAPTER THIRTY-NINE

f Gabriel was seething before, he'd hit a roiling boil when I refused to answer my phone. I wasn't trying to piss him off, but the angrier he got, the more annoyed I got.

I texted him. *I really am working. I'm a big girl, Gabriel. I can handle this. Talk later.*

I arrived at my next destination: lunch. I had one final stop on my schedule, and I needed sustenance for that one. I was eating a sandwich when my phone rang.

"Gabriel called you, didn't he?" I said as I answered the phone.

"Yeah," Ricky replied. "I'd say you must have seen an omen, but with Gabriel, you don't need them. Apparently, you took off and can't be trusted to survive alone in the big city."

I answered that with a few choice words, then said, "I left to do some legwork, and apparently I forgot to ask permission and deliver my minute-by-minute itinerary. I'm not making a statement—I'm just trying to get some damned work done. I'll text him."

I sighed as I approached the prison's front doors. "The point of texting to tell you where I was going was to assure you I was fine. It wasn't an invitation to join me."

Gabriel didn't say a word, just bore down on me with a look that made me consider an end run around him. There were guards with guns inside. Surely they'd protect me.

"Stop right there," I said, putting up my hand. "If you've come to give me hell, head back to your car and save it for morning."

"Are you *coming* to work in the morning?" he asked.

"Of course. Why wouldn't . . ." I trailed off. "You thought I quit?"

"I suggested you weren't doing your job properly, and you walked out."

"To *do* my job properly. I went out to speak to someone about the case. I told Lydia. I told you. And you thought what? That I'd swanned out, and I was sitting in a coffee shop, sipping a mocha, chortling to myself as I texted you pretending to work? How old do you think I am? Twelve?"

"I—"

"Don't answer that. Here's what I was up to: First, I tried to speak to Jon Childs. He wasn't home, so I visited Chris Pemberton, following up on your question about motive. I hoped maybe he might have some insight. Then I came here to see Todd and get the answers that Pamela won't give. It's work, Gabriel. It's *all* work."

I strode past him. He followed. Sadly, the prison doors moved too slowly for me to slam them in his face.

"Does it help if I apologize?" he asked.

"Let me give you a tip," I said as I turned. "If you feel an apology might work, you don't ask if it will. That defeats the purpose."

I started to walk away, but he swung into my path. He pulled off his shades.

"I'm sorry, Olivia. You were correct. I was under a great deal of pressure, but that was no reason to take it out on you. I apologize."

When I hesitated, his eyes widened, as if frantically trying to figure out where he'd gone wrong. Shades off, check. Eye contact, check. Sincere tone, check. Clear and unambiguous wording, check.

"I mean it," he said finally. "I *am* sorry."

"Okay. I'll see you in the morning—"

"We haven't spoken about your vision."

"I thought I'd speak to Rose about it first."

I wanted to tell Rose about Gabriel's connection to Gwynn and get her opinion on how to tell him. I wasn't punishing him. But his expression said that's what he felt.

"I thought maybe you didn't need the distraction," I said.

"It's not a distraction. It's essential information for understanding the situation. We'll discuss it over dinner. But first, you need to speak to Todd. I'd like to meet him as well."

"Um . . ."

"Is that a problem?" His gaze met mine, that wall ready to fly back up.

I exhaled. "I guess not."

It wasn't the most enthusiastic response, but he pocketed his sunglasses and steered me down the hall.

Gabriel agreed to give me ten minutes alone with Todd. When they brought my father in and he saw me, he grinned, and when he did, I remembered what the little girl said: that he was Cŵn Annwn. Of their blood. Like Ricky. When Todd grinned, I saw it. Not a physical resemblance, but something in the way his grin sparked, easy and genuine.

When my smile faded, his grin vanished. He quickened his

pace to the window and leaned forward to murmur, "You don't have to do this, Liv."

"I'm fine. How are *you* doing?"

Todd tried to hide a smile, and I relaxed in a laugh. "Okay. Dumb question. Sorry. I'm not very good at this."

"I'm fine," he said as he sat. "I'd say that I was rereading a Sherlock Holmes collection, but that might sound like I'm trying too hard. So I won't mention it."

"You just did."

"True, but I worded it in a way that I'm hoping will help me avoid looking like I'm trying too hard, while still giving us something to talk about. I read *His Last Bow*. It's horrible."

I laughed again. "It is not horrible. Maybe not his best—"

"Horrible. He should have quit while he was ahead. Yes, I know, the fans wouldn't let him, and he felt he had to bring Holmes back after Reichenbach Falls, but let's face it, it was about money, and it showed."

"Okay, to some degree yes, but . . ."

We chatted comfortably about the later Holmes works until Todd glanced over my shoulder and then got to his feet.

"Mr. Walsh," he said. "Good to finally meet you."

I made a show of gesturing at my watch, to say it hadn't been ten minutes, but Gabriel wasn't looking at me. He was staring at Todd, his head slightly tilted. Was he recognizing the fae blood? Or was it what I'd felt on my first visit, that Todd simply wasn't what he'd expected?

"I've heard a lot about you," Todd said.

Gabriel recovered then, pulling over a chair from the next window. "I'm sure you have," he said in a tone that made Todd laugh.

"Yes," Todd said. "Not all of it good, but what counts is that you've gotten closer than anyone to getting Pamela out of prison. Thank you for that. And for looking after Olivia."

Gabriel tensed, as if expecting a trap.

"I know about the arrest," Todd said. "Obviously you're out, which is good. While I'm hoping that means charges were dropped . . ."

"They weren't."

"But it was obviously a setup," Todd said. "Someone trying to make it look as if you were pinning James Morgan's murder on the real Valentine Killer. Maybe connected to this man who admitted to killing the Evans and Gunderson kids? The one who took his own life last week."

"Edgar Chandler. We're working various angles, including that one."

"Have you talked to . . . to my mother?" I asked.

"Not since I saw you. We speak a couple of times a month. After twenty years, there's not much to say beyond 'How are you doing?' and, as you might imagine, the answer to that doesn't change."

"One reason I'm asking . . . I should warn you, before you speak to her again, she's convinced Gabriel killed James."

"What?"

"He didn't," I said quickly. "He wouldn't. And he had an alibi. But even before he was arrested, Pam—my mother—"

"You can call her Pamela, Liv."

I exhaled. "Sorry. It's just—"

"You've had other parents for most of your life. I understand that. So before Gabriel was arrested, Pamela . . ."

"She told me he did it. Someone convinced her."

He frowned. "Who?"

"She won't say, but I'm sure it was a Huntsman. One of the Cŵn Annwn."

He hesitated, and that hesitation told me he knew exactly what I was talking about. That was one thing he didn't have in common with Ricky—the ability to pull a charming smile and say, convincingly, *I don't know what you mean.* Todd didn't even try.

"Okay," he said, exhaling. "So you know . . ."

"Cainsville, the hounds, the ravens, the owls, Tylwyth Teg, Cŵn Annwn, Mallt-y-Nos, Matilda of the Night." I met his gaze. "I don't know everything, but I'm figuring it out. I know what you are. Cŵn Annwn. The blood, anyway."

He nodded slowly. "My father, apparently. I found out— Well, it doesn't matter how I found out."

"Maybe it does."

He shook his head. "It might, sweetheart, but I can't talk about it. Your mother . . ."

"But you're like them. The Huntsmen. They hunt and kill, and their prey isn't foxes and rabbits. Is that why you did it?"

There was genuine shock in his eyes. "What?"

"The thrill of the hunt. The need to hunt."

"No. Absolutely not. I don't— If there is any of that—any at all—I don't feel it. I would never— I wouldn't."

"Tell me more, then. How did you find out about yourself, about me? What—"

"No, Liv." He met my gaze. "If I know anything that will help Gabriel fight his charge, I won't hold back. But my primary concern is protecting you. It always has been."

"Is that why you did it? To protect me?"

I expected the same reaction. Shock, with the emphatic and immediate denials. Instead, he hesitated again, and my stomach clenched so hard I had to clamp my jaw shut before I hurled my lunch on the floor. When his denial came, I was already on my feet, staggering toward the door.

CHAPTER FORTY

Gabriel called after me, not raising his voice, just sharpening it, as if I were a puppy who'd escaped her harness.

I kept jogging. He finally surrendered to indignity and ran in front to cut me off.

"If you want me to call Ricky, I can do that for you. I would argue, however, that I'm better equipped to deal with this. I understand the situation, and if—"

"They did it. They *actually* did it."

"My car is over here."

"And mine"—I dangled my keys—"is over there."

He grabbed the keys and whisked them out of my reach.

I could barely force the words out. "The only excuse you have for taking my keys—ever—is if I've been drinking—"

"You're distraught. That's equally impairing." He dropped the keys into his inner jacket pocket.

I headed for a cab idling in front of the prison and climbed inside. Gabriel opened the other rear door, folded himself into the backseat, and gave the driver his address.

"Get the hell out," I said. "Now."

"I think you should both get out," the driver said.

Gabriel handed him a hundred-dollar bill. The man pocketed it and put the car in drive.

Gabriel turned to me. "Earlier, I apologized for treating you poorly. While I know apologies are the normal way of expressing regret, I've never seen the point. In the rare instance that I do regret my actions, it would seem that the proper way to show it is through action. I behaved badly earlier. I am now making amends."

"By stealing my keys and kidnapping me?"

He handed back my keys. I glowered at him.

"If you agree to return to my apartment with me, I'll tell the driver to go back and we'll take your car."

"Oh, sorry, not kidnapping. Just coercion."

"It's a lesser charge."

"Would stabbing you with my switchblade be a defensible action against that lesser charge?"

"No. However, as your lawyer, while I'm not supposed to advise you on how to commit a crime, I might suggest that if one wanted to stab a second party with one's switchblade, one should wait until both parties have relocated to her car. That avoids witnesses"—he nodded at the driver—"and would allow her to claim defense against kidnapping, if the second party is driving."

"I hate you."

"So you've said. It's situational. I don't take it personally."

"You should. I realize interpersonal relationships aren't your forte, but a word of advice? You don't fix problems by forcing people to do what you want."

"Then I've been doing it wrong for a very long time. At immense profit and professional success." He looked at me over his shades. "Perhaps *you're* doing it wrong."

"Gabriel . . ."

He removed his sunglasses. "While I cannot imagine otherwise wanting to force someone to spend time with me, I would concede that it's probably not prudent—and certainly not legal—to do so. However, given that you are armed with both a knife and a gun, the choice is, ultimately, yours."

"So you'll understand if I stab or shoot you to escape?"

"Hypothetically, yes."

The cabdriver cleared his throat. "I think I would like—"

"Take us back to the prison." Gabriel turned to me. "It's settled, then? You'll come to my apartment?"

"Is that actually a request?"

He put his shades back on. "It's beginning to seem prudent. May we take my car? I feel yours would be safer overnight in the parking lot."

"Overnight?"

"Hypothetically."

Back at the condo, we talked. Gabriel wasn't convinced that I was right about my parents' guilt. But that was his job, wasn't it? Could he properly defend Pamela if he knew she'd committed the crimes?

"Most of the clients I defend are guilty," he said. "They pay me to introduce reasonable doubt to the contrary. Which I do."

"But if Pamela did it, how can I help you with her appeal?"

"I don't believe that's your decision to make."

He was right, of course. Pamela was his client. I was his employee.

After a moment of silence, he said, "Your job is to investigate a case thoroughly and completely, and to bring me all evidence arguing for and *against* acquittal. What I do with that information is not your concern."

"In general, I don't have a problem with that," I said. "Everyone is entitled to a defense, and it's up to the prosecution to prove their case. But if you ask me to help free a sociopath or a rapist—"

"I don't take those cases. Too many complications. But there are cases with ethical quandaries, even for me. You will always have the choice of refusing."

"But with Pamela . . . This is different."

"Remember that your birth parents have spent twenty-two years in prison. Whatever they did, one might argue that they've paid their debt. And pose no danger to society."

Which they don't if they killed to protect me. If, in some twisted way, that was their motive—

I got up and walked to the window.

"If you need to use the bathroom . . ." he began.

I turned a hard look on him. "I'm not going to puke on your floor, Gabriel. I just need—" I glanced at the door.

"If you want fresh air or a brisk walk, then I will gladly accompany you, but if your goal is to escape me and react in private, the answer is no." He headed for his wall cabinet. "This is a difficult subject, and we are going to abandon it immediately in favor of . . ." He pulled out a bottle.

"I don't need—"

"Stop." His gaze met mine. "You don't like me attempting to control a situation, but it works both ways. If you are upset, and you don't allow me to stay with you or offer you a drink, then where do you leave me? Sitting and staring awkwardly as you suffer, which is exactly the reaction that will bother you the most."

"I'm sorry."

He poured two drinks. "I'm not asking you to be sorry, Olivia. I'm asking you to allow me to give you this"—he handed me a glass—"and not to argue about it."

I took the drink and sat on the floor in front of the window.

He turned down the lights until they were barely a glow on the ceiling, the room lit by the city outside, the sun fallen, endless lights lifting the darkness. Then he lowered himself, somewhat awkwardly, beside me and began to talk. Gradually, between the drink and the dark and the low and steady rumble of his voice, I relaxed and stretched out on the floor, until, finally, exhaustion won out, and I drifted off to sleep.

CHAPTER FORTY-ONE

I woke in Gabriel's bed, and there was a moment in the confusion of sleep, when I smelled something that reminded me of
him—his soap or his shampoo or his own faint smell—that I
smiled and reached out, expecting to find him there. Of course
he wasn't, and as soon as I realized what I was doing—and
what I was thinking—I jumped up, guilt slapping me as hard as
if he'd actually been in bed with me.

I stayed propped up on one arm, breathing hard, pushing aside
the fog of sleep, until my heart rate slowed and I could tell
myself I'd done nothing wrong, *thought* nothing wrong. Waking confusion, that was all.

I dropped back onto the pillow, pulled up the sheets, and fell
back to sleep.

When the dream came, it was harmless enough. I was wandering through dark and empty halls, searching for Ricky, more
annoyed than worried. Something had happened—I couldn't remember what—and we'd been separated, and I needed to get back
to him, which should have been much easier than it seemed. I
kept walking and calling and walking and calling . . .

That's when I fell in the hole. Or it seemed to be a hole, and
I seemed to have fallen in, but with the illogic of dreams, I

couldn't quite be sure. One moment I was wandering and the next I was in the dark, and in a full-out panic, the air thinning with each breath as I raced around the room, one hand on the walls, searching for an exit, for a ladder, for a hatch, anything, knowing I wouldn't find it because I'd been searching for hours and I was trapped here in this box. A huge wooden box. When I realized that's what it was, I screamed until my throat was raw. I was running around the perimeter of the room one more time when I kicked something. I crouched, feeling around in the pitch-dark. My fingers closed on a thin metal rectangle.

My phone! I fumbled to turn it on, holding my breath until . . .

Yes, it switched on. It had barely any power, but I had a signal. My fingers flew to the keypad, speed-dialing, and I thought I was calling Ricky, but when the name popped up, it was Gabriel's.

The call nearly went to voice mail before he answered.

"Oh God, thank God." The words rushed out. "I'm trapped. There's not much air, and I've lost Ricky, and I need your help. I really need your help."

Silence.

"Gabriel?"

"Yes?"

I gripped the phone tighter and raised my voice. "Can you hear me? I'll text if you can't. I don't have much battery left."

"I can hear you, Olivia." His voice was cool, almost icy.

"I need your help. I really, really need your help. I'm trapped—"

"Yes, I heard that."

"Good. Thank you. I can send you the coordinates—"

"No need."

"You have them?" I exhaled. "So you're on your way?"

"No. I'm not."

The line went dead. I thought I'd lost the battery, but when I looked, I still had a little. I called back, and the line rang and rang and rang, and then he picked up . . . and disconnected. And my phone turned off, plunging me into darkness.

"Gabriel!" I bolted up, his name on my lips. The room was pitch-black, and I couldn't remember where I was, still half lost in that dream—

The door opened, moonlight flooding around a dark figure.

"Olivia?"

Gabriel started through the doorway, then pulled himself up short and flipped on the light instead.

"Sorry," I said. "Sorry, sorry." I ran my hands over my face, trying to banish the dream.

"A vision?"

I shook my head. "Garden-variety nightmare."

I kept struggling to push the dream away, but it wouldn't go, alarm and dread swirling in my gut.

"Are we okay?" I asked.

"What?"

I wanted to say, never mind, I was being silly, go on back to sleep, but the words came out anyway. "Is everything okay? With us?"

His brow furrowed, and he said, "Of course," but there was something in the way he said it, something in his eyes, still too close to sleep, that wall not yet up, letting me catch a flicker that said we weren't okay, not really.

"Have I done something?"

"What?" He seemed ready to step into the room but again stopped short, his hand on the doorframe now. Keeping his distance.

Something's wrong . . .

No, it's not. You're in his bed. He's doing the right thing, the proper thing. Staying out.

I'm in Gabriel's bed.

Oh God, what am I doing? I shouldn't be here. Not in his apartment. Not in his bed. It doesn't matter if he's over there. It doesn't matter if there hasn't been a word, a touch, even a look between us. I've crossed a line. I know I have, and that's what counts. Not what I've done. What I feel.

"Olivia?" He took a half step in, his hand still firmly on the doorframe. "What did you see?"

"You left."

Did I just say that? Stop talking. Please stop talking.

Only it was as if I were still trapped in the dream, no more able to halt the words than plug a dam with my finger.

"You left, and I didn't know why. I was trapped in the dark, and I couldn't get out, and I called and you wouldn't come."

He frowned, head tilting as if confused, that sleepy look still in his eyes, not yet fully awake, not yet fully aware. "I wouldn't do that."

"I know." I took a deep breath. "I'm sorry. It was a nightmare, and now I'm babbling—"

"It *was* a nightmare," he said. "Not a vision. I wouldn't do that."

"I know."

"Anytime you need me, I'm here. If you call, I'll come."

"I know."

A surreal moment of silence followed, both of us still dazed with sleep, the barriers down as we looked at each other.

I shouldn't be here. I shouldn't.

I pushed up, swinging my legs out of the bed. "I'm going to take the couch."

His frown deepened. "Why?"

"I think I should."

"Why?"

He kept looking at me, confusion in his eyes. Innocent confusion. He seemed so young then. A boy who didn't understand what was going on, why he was in trouble, what he'd done wrong.

He put me here to be thoughtful. Because I fell asleep on his floor, and I've had a difficult day, so he's being kind. That's all it is. All it's ever going to be. Kind and thoughtful, which is as close as I'll ever get to him, and it's closer than anyone else gets, so I need to take it and be grateful and say, "It's enough."

And if I can't?

Then that's my problem, and I need to do something about it—starting with stepping back over that line, with getting the hell out of his bed.

I set my feet on the floor and stood. "I shouldn't take your room."

"But I put you here."

"It's yours. I'll take the couch."

"Why?"

He kept giving me that look, the confusion deepening to something like disappointment, like hurt, as if he'd tried to be kind and thoughtful, and I was rejecting it, and he didn't know why. That little boy, reaching out and being pushed away.

Goddamn it, Gabriel. Don't look at me like that. Wake up. Snap out of it, pull that wall back up and retreat behind it. For once, that's what I want, because when you look at me like that, it makes me think that there could be more, that I could—

I swallowed hard and stepped toward him. "I need to leave."

"What?" He blinked. "Why? Did I do something?"

Snap out of it, Gabriel. Please, please, please, snap out of it.

"I just want to go for a walk," I said. "I need some air."

He rubbed his hands over his face, harder now, raking his fingers through his hair, and when he spoke again, his voice was more his own, though still younger, less formal. "Okay. Can I go with you?" Another rub over his face, his shoulders straightening, voice deepening another octave. "I should go with you."

"I . . ."

I looked at him. The boy was gone, the man back, but the wall stayed down, the confusion lingering, not sure why I needed to leave, still feeling as if he'd done something wrong, like me in the dream, rejected and lost and not understanding why.

"I'll walk behind you, Olivia. I would simply prefer you weren't out alone at this hour." His voice dropped. "Whatever you saw, it was only a nightmare. I'm not going anywhere."

I nodded.

"Could it have been connected to the vision?" he asked. "From the park? We still haven't discussed that. I know you were going to talk to Rose first, but I would prefer . . ." He raked back his hair again, rolling his shoulders, as if still searching for equilibrium. "It might help if you talked about it. Perhaps that is upsetting you."

I'm so lost right now. My parents . . . I think they . . . I'm sure they . . . And you and Ricky . . . So lost and so confused. Except I'm not confused at all. I know what I feel—for you— and I want to blame it on the visions, to tell myself I'm just reliving a role. But I'm not. What I feel for you . . .

Oh God, what I feel for you. I don't want that. I want Ricky, and only Ricky, and no confusion, because he doesn't deserve confusion. Neither of you do.

I want to run. Get the hell out of here and run to Ricky, and tell myself I never felt like this—that I was upset about my parents and half asleep and caught in that nightmare, and I got mixed up. I just got mixed up.

But I look at you, and I know I can't run. Because you won't understand. You let yourself reach out, and I cannot reject that. I cannot let you feel rejected. You need someone, now more than ever, and I desperately want to be that someone, even if it's never going to be more than talking in front of your window and falling asleep and waking in your bed—alone.

"I'd like to talk about it," I said. "I know it's the middle of the night . . ."

"I'll make coffee."

CHAPTER FORTY-TWO

I t wasn't the middle of the night after all. It was nearly five in the morning. After I explained the vision, I tried to get him to go back to bed, but he wouldn't listen, so I curled up on his sofa, and we drank coffee and talked and watched the sun come up, and whatever I'd felt earlier passed.

No, I'm lying. It didn't pass. What I felt for Gabriel wasn't a chimera of anxiety and exhaustion. What passed was that panic, that sense of needing to escape.

I had breakfast with Ricky. Actually, I picked up breakfast— by cab—and surprised him at his place. He'd been in bed. Which led to a cold breakfast. But it also did an excellent job of banishing any traces of last night's mood and fears. It wasn't just the sex. Okay, yes, sex with Ricky was pretty much guaranteed to banish anything. But more than that, it was just being with him; alone with him, I was happy, and any other longings seemed like madness.

"I haven't quit the diner yet," I said. I was nibbling my toast, thinking how much I missed Larry's rye bread.

"Yep. You need to make a decision there. Which I think you already have, but you should let Larry know what it is."

"I know." I sighed. "I'm not going back, which I should have told him a week ago."

"I'm sure he figured it out. It's just tough to cut that tie. Throwing yourself financially at Gabriel's mercy."

I spread extra jam on my toast. "It's more than that. I don't think I can even wait on the elders again."

"I get that, and I'd agree." He rolled out of bed and headed for the front room. I watched him go. I watched him come back. Both views were equally fine.

He saw me watching and chuckled. "I'd be a lot more flattered by that look if I didn't suspect you were hoping to distract me from insisting you make this call." He waggled my phone. "If you still want to jump me afterward, I'll be here. And if you don't? That's fine, too, but just remember that every time I see that look in future, I'll think you're only trying to avoid something. It'll do irreparable damage to my ego."

"I wouldn't want that."

"No, you would not. My ego is a fragile thing." He handed me the phone. "Now call Larry, tell him you'll come by later to talk, and then you can have me."

"Should I hang up first?"

"Larry would probably prefer that."

I laughed, took the phone, and flipped onto my stomach. As I dialed, Ricky hopped back in bed, sending crumbs and plates jumping. He settled in, his head resting on the small of my back as he checked messages on his own phone.

After we talked, Larry said, "Doc Webster would like to speak to you, as well. She came by asking if I'd seen you. I know the Clarks said you'd been having fevers. Not to pry, but I'm guessing that's related to why you needed some time off?"

"In a way."

"You should call Doc Webster. I think she's concerned, but

she probably doesn't want to seem pushy and follow up if you're seeing a doctor in the city."

"I'll call her." We talked for another minute before I hung up.

"Better get that call to the doc over with, too," Ricky said. "I wasn't trying to eavesdrop, but Larry's one of those guys who thinks he's talking on a tin can instead of a shining example of modern technology."

I chuckled. "True."

"Call the doctor. Tell her you're fine so she doesn't worry."

He was right. I also had a niggling feeling I shouldn't put it off. Just to get it over with, I suppose. So I phoned and I told her I was doing all right, no ill effects after the fever.

"Are you seeing someone in Chicago?" she asked. "A doctor, I mean."

"No, I'm not sure what my plans are right now, but if I decide to stay in Cainsville, I'll be transferring to you, if that's all right."

"It is. I'll just need your medical files." When I hesitated, she said, "No rush, of course. If you decide to transfer, you can provide me with your doctor's information and I'll arrange everything. We'll need your express permission, but I can handle the rest."

I said yes, that would be fine, thanked her, and hung up. Then I lay there, staring at the phone, deep in thought.

After my first "breakup" with Gabriel, he'd apologized by obtaining my pre-adoption medical files for me. Except there had been a mix-up, and the files my former doctor sent had belonged to a girl with spina bifida. His office was still hunting for my proper records.

"Everything okay?" Ricky asked.

As he sat up, he set his phone on the bed. On the screen, I saw what looked like an artist's rendition of the sun and moon from my boar's tusk.

I reached for his phone. "Is that the tattoo—?"

He plucked it from my hand and turned the screen off. "Later. What happened with the doctor?"

"It's not important. Let's see that art."

He held the phone behind his back. "It's not going to help you forget whatever's bugging you. And whatever's bugging you *is* important. So we're going to talk about that."

I looked at him. "You always do the right thing, don't you?"

"I'm pretty sure I spend most of my life *not* doing the right thing."

"That isn't what I mean." I shifted onto my knees, my face rising to his. "With me. You know the right thing to do. Always."

"That's because I know you. Always."

I leaned forward and kissed him, and when our lips met, I smelled forest and rain, I felt the delicious chill of a night wind and heard the pounding of hooves. I felt a boy lifting me onto a horse, swinging me up behind him, me huddling against his back, basking in the warmth of him, hearing his laugh and grinning in return, holding him tight, never wanting to let go. Feeling loved and understood and at peace, that perfect bond with someone who knew me, always.

I kissed Ricky, and I whispered, "I love you," and he said, "That's all I want," and in my mind I heard *All I ever wanted* as he lowered me onto the bed.

Afterward, lying in bed, catching our breath, I told Ricky about the medical records mix-up.

"Okay," he said. "Excuse my ignorance, because it's not a condition I'm familiar with, but there's no way you *could* have been this girl, right? That you got adopted by your parents and, with their money, they were able to get it fixed? Maybe quietly, so no one knew you ever had it?"

"According to the doctor, no. I'm not familiar with spina bifida, either, so . . ."

He already had his phone in hand, searching on a browser.

"So, I could have done *that*," I said.

"No reason to at the time," he said. "But now it seems like you want to know more."

He skimmed the page, then passed it to me. It said that spina bifida is a congenital defect in which the neural tube covering the spinal cord doesn't fully form in utero. The girl with my alleged medical records had a severe form, which would have led to life-long mobility issues. If I were that girl, I'd be in a wheelchair.

Something twigged in the back of my brain, something someone had said a few weeks ago, but the thought wouldn't take form.

"No amount of money would have cured it," I said. "Not today, and definitely not twenty years ago."

"Okay, so you're thinking—" He stopped short and rolled from the bed. "Time for a field trip."

"Um, no, pretty sure that wasn't what I was thinking."

"But it's what we're doing." He went into the next room, scooping up my clothing. "You know what you're thinking. I know it, too—and I know to keep my mouth shut until we have proof."

"Uh-huh. Well, while this mind-reading thing is very sweet—and hot—most of the time, there are times when it could become . . ."

"Creepy and annoying? Yep. Which is why I'm not doing it now. I know my limits, and I'd like to stick to the sweet and hot side." He tossed me my clothing. "Although, if you can work in badass, I'd appreciate it."

I grinned. "Mad, bad, and dangerous to know?"

"Exactly. I'm the Lord Byron of bikers. Except, being a biker, naturally I don't write poetry. Or read it. In fact, for the record, I have no idea who this Byron guy is."

"Gotcha." I pulled on my shirt. "So where exactly is this field trip taking us?"

"The doctor's office. Which I know you hate, on principle, but I'll be there for moral support. And to make sure you get all the answers to your questions, whether you'll admit you have questions or not."

"Okay, but Gabriel is expecting me to work—"

Ricky was already on the phone. "Hey, Gabriel. It's Ricky. I'm stealing Liv for a couple of hours to follow up on some questions regarding the Larsen case. In other words, completely job-related." He paused, and I heard the faint rumble of a reply. "No, we've got this. I don't have classes until this afternoon. I'll make sure she gets her car back and send her your way after lunch. Sound good?"

I could swear I didn't hear an answer, but it may have just been too low to pick up.

"We're off, then," Ricky said. "Talk to you later." He hung up and turned to me. "Your absenteeism note has been delivered. Let me get dressed and we'll go."

CHAPTER FORTY-THREE

I hated doctors. Let me rephrase that. I didn't hate them—I hated the places where they practice, like offices and hospitals. Admittedly, even the sight of a white coat and stethoscope was enough to send me running the other way. I refused to date three otherwise great guys because one was a med student, one an intern, and one a lab worker. So, yes, I may have had a problem with the profession, but it wasn't personal. I thought doctors were lovely people. I just didn't want to make out with one.

Why did I have such a problem with hospitals and doctors? I had spent my life wondering that. I was so damned healthy I rarely got a cold. I had never stayed in a hospital. Or so I thought, until I discovered there were two and a half years of my life unaccounted for.

Naturally, I'd asked Pamela. She said I'd spent one night in a hospital, for a fever, actually. Todd wasn't allowed to stay in my room, so he'd slept in the waiting area and woken to me screaming, alone and terrified. That could explain my phobia, but I felt like there should have been more.

Dr. Escoda was the daughter of my former physician, who'd passed away a few years ago. Her office was packed. It didn't matter. Give Ricky two minutes with the middle-aged receptionist and we didn't just get a promise that we could see the doctor between appointments, we were shown into an exam room immediately to "protect my privacy."

Dr. Escoda showed up less than five minutes later, and as she scurried in, I smelled terror wafting from her body like bad cologne. She shook my hand, her damp fingers enveloping mine.

"Ms. Taylor-Jones," she said. "I'm so glad you stopped by."

The sweat trickling down her hairline called her a liar.

Back when we first discovered my file had been lost, Gabriel had mentioned the possibility of pursuing it as a legal matter. I hadn't ruled it out.

"We're still looking for your file," she said. "I deeply apologize for the distress it must cause you. I doubt there's anything important in those records—"

"That's not the point, is it?"

Ricky's voice was low and steady, but there was a note in it that I hadn't heard since James's funeral. Charming Ricky had disappeared in the waiting room. The guy beside me held his face impassive, his lips tight, not a hint of a smile in his eyes. His leather jacket lay over his knee, the patch clear. He leaned toward the doctor, forearms on his thighs, tattooed biceps straining his T-shirt sleeves, as he watched her like a hawk. No, more like a raven. Zero predatory interest, but a cold, calculating appraisal.

Ricky continued. "The point is not whether Olivia is healthy now, but whether there is anything in her past she should be aware of. Has she ever had chicken pox? Broken a bone? Minor issues, yes, but she has the right to know them."

"Of course." Dr. Escoda looked at me. "Your friend here—"

"Boyfriend," Ricky corrected.

"Your boyfriend is right. Getting those records is important—"

"How often does this happen?" Ricky asked, controlling the

conversation, intentionally cutting her short. "How many records mix-ups have you had in your own career?"

"None, but—"

"And your father's? How many others have you discovered since he passed?"

"None, which is why—"

"So this appears to be an anomaly. An unprecedented situation."

She hesitated before answering. "I will admit that mix-ups do happen, when records are misfiled or the wrong one is picked up, but that is both rare and temporary. We discover the mistake quickly, and it is rectified and—"

"Temporary mix-ups aren't our concern. We mean situations like this. You're saying there have been none at all."

She straightened like a witness on the stand. "Yes. None."

"And you have been unable to find Olivia's records? Despite a thorough search?"

"Yes, Olivia's—"

"Ms. Taylor-Jones."

She bristled but didn't wrest back control of the conversation. She didn't seem to know how.

Ricky continued. "So you've searched—thoroughly—and been unable to find them. Have you turned up any records of children that could have been her? I'm presuming you've looked at that angle—other girls Olivia's age?"

"My father had two other female patients within a year of Ms. Taylor-Jones's age. Both continued with him throughout their childhoods, and there is no chance that their records are hers— or that their records are the ones mislabeled as hers."

"Because of the spina bifida? It's a rare-enough condition that it would be remembered, correct? Likely by anyone who worked with the child in those records."

She didn't answer.

"Dr. Escoda?" Ricky said. "Am I right? Anyone employed at that time would recall the girl with that condition."

"It—it's been twenty years. My father wasn't a young man even then, and his employees weren't young, either, and—"

"You've spoken to them. You've asked about the girl in the file."

"My father ran a very small practice. He believed in absolute patient-doctor confidentiality, so—"

"So he would not have discussed the case with outsiders. But his nurses would know."

"He only employed three during that time, and two have passed on—"

"But you've spoken to the third."

Dr. Escoda glanced my way. I met her gaze expectantly.

"Dr. Escoda," Ricky said. "If you have not spoken to this former nurse, then we will, whether you provide us with her name or not."

"I have, but . . . she's seventy and not in the best of health."

"Alzheimer's? Dementia?"

"No, but—"

"Any mental impairment related to her health issues?"

"No apparent ones, but—"

"What did she say?"

Now the doctor snuck a look my way, pleading with me to get her out of this, only to realize I was the last person who'd spare her.

"She said . . ." Dr. Escoda swallowed. "She remembered when the Larsens were arrested. She called my father, to make sure she was hearing right—she was certain she couldn't be. When my father found out, he immediately contacted child services."

"Child services?" I said.

"To be . . ." She swallowed again and cast another anxious look my way. "To be certain they knew how to care for you.

Because of your condition. Because the Eden Larsen he had treated six months earlier had severe spina bifida."

Ricky did not back down once he got his answer. If anything, it snapped off the leash, and he went after poor Dr. Escoda with everything he had. There was no shouting, no threatening, no intimidation. But that was all implied in his voice, in his expression, in the very way he held himself on that chair. *You want us gone? Answer my questions.*

He asked whether there was any way the damage could have been repaired. She said no, and he pursued every loophole there. Could the condition have been less serious than her father thought? What were the medical procedures at the time? What about experimental procedures? Even now, twenty years later, could it have been cured? She was adamant it could not. He had her check my back. There wasn't even a pucker. My spine was perfect, my skin unblemished.

Was it possible that somehow, after the Larsens left her father's care, something happened to their daughter and I replaced her? Dr. Escoda stared at Ricky as if he was crazy. He made her answer the question. No, it was not possible. Her father and his nurse had seen my photo following the arrest. I was the child they'd treated. To be sure, Ricky had her bring the file of the girl with spina bifida and compare every identifying factor in it. Hair color, eye color, blood type . . . it matched down to a tiny scar on the back of my elbow that had needed two stitches.

I was the girl in that file. The girl who couldn't walk. Who'd been sentenced to life in a wheelchair. Who'd spent two years of her life in and out of doctors' offices and hospitals and then been taken out of her doctor's care. Who reappeared, six months later, running and jumping and playing like any other toddler . . . after her parents murdered six people.

CHAPTER FORTY-FOUR

I needed to speak to Todd. Except, apparently, I couldn't.

"Bullshit," I said to the prison clerk, my temper flaring as he smirked. "I don't know what's going on, but there is no way in hell my father is refusing to see me."

He shrugged, and kept that satisfied little smirk still playing on his lips. Ricky stood behind me. When I looked back, his expression agreed this was complete and total bullshit, but he had no more idea what to do about it than I did.

"I'm going to contact my lawyer," I said. "See if he can straighten this out."

"No need," the man said. "He's already here."

"What?"

The man threw open the door of the tiny room where we'd been brought to "discuss" the matter. As it opened, I heard Gabriel arguing with a guard. He caught sight of me and strode our way.

Gabriel came in and argued the matter, but he got no further than I had. Finally the clerk walked out.

"I came after receiving your text," Gabriel said after the man was gone. "I'll pursue this, of course. While it *is* possible that Todd himself is blocking us, perhaps unable to face you after yesterday, that doesn't seem likely. Unfortunately, with no way to contact Todd and ask . . ."

"We can't prove it."

"So our next move—" Ricky began as we walked out the front doors.

Gabriel flourished his wristwatch. "Don't you have class?"

I swore Ricky bit his tongue before saying, calmly, "If Liv needs me, I'm not worried about classes."

"Perhaps, but your father will expect—"

"Gabriel? I'm not a child."

He snapped on his shades. "You misunderstood—"

"Nope, don't think I did." Ricky said it casually, almost cheerfully, but there was a warning note there. He turned to me. "I'm guessing your next move involves Cainsville?"

"It does."

"In that case, since I'm not supposed to know their secrets, that *is* something you'll want to do with Gabriel. If there's anything I can pursue in the meantime . . ."

"Go to class. Take a break while you can."

He gave me a faint smile. "I don't need a break. Ever."

"I know. But you did more than enough this morning. Thank you."

"Anytime."

He headed off to his bike, leaving Gabriel and me walking deeper into the lot, where my car was still parked from yesterday.

As we walked toward the VW, Gabriel slowed. "Might I suggest that we take my car to Cainsville so we can talk? Your text message was hardly voluble."

"Such being the nature of text messages."

"That wasn't an accusation." He paused, as if mentally adding *not exactly*. "But clearly your inquiries with Ricky proved . . . I'm loath to say *fruitful*, as your mood inside suggests the information was not what you wanted to hear. You learned something that upset you, and it made you want to talk to Todd."

"We went to see Dr. Escoda," I said.

"The daughter of your former family physician. Yes. You should not have gone to see her after I've notified her of a possible intention to sue. If you hoped to speed up recovery of your files—"

"They *were* my files."

He stopped. Took off his shades. Looked at me. Waited.

"The girl in that file?" I said. "The one with spina bifida? That was me. Which means we finally know my parents' motivation. The purpose of whatever ritual they were enacting. They did kill those people. For me. Now we need to find out who helped them do it."

We took Gabriel's car and I explained.

"Ricky covered all the contingencies," I said as I finished. "Eyewitness accounts. Medical proof." I lifted my elbow. "And a teeny, tiny scar that I never knew I had, which rules out even the crazy 'twin sister' explanation. Someone—Cŵn Annwn or Tylwyth Teg—told my parents that I would be cured if I did what they said. A ritual or a bargain. Magical intervention. Now here I am, walking around, good as new, while my parents have spent my life in prison."

Another mile passed. He adjusted his grip on the steering wheel, took off his shades, and gave me a sidelong look, not making direct eye contact. "How are you doing? With that? The possibility?"

"Trying very hard not to think about the implications. Right now, my focus is on proving it. On finding out who did this. Who healed me . . . and destroyed my family."

———

There was little question of whom I needed to speak to in Cainsville. The person I was most angry with . . . who also happened to be the one most likely to give me a straight answer.

Gabriel fetched Patrick from the diner so I wouldn't have to face the elders.

I met Gabriel at the corner of Rowan and Main, and he told me Patrick would speak to us at his place.

"Do you know where he lives?" I asked.

"He provided the address." Gabriel waved for us to cross the road.

"But you didn't know before that?"

His brows rose above his shades. "Why would I?"

Why indeed.

As I expected, Patrick's house was neither large nor ostentatious. While he had a flair for the dramatic, it wasn't in his best interests to call attention to himself. The other elders affected the personae of senior citizens to take advantage of ageism—we pay less attention to the elderly and lose the ability to judge their true age. In choosing to stay young, Patrick lost that advantage. So he wasn't going to own the biggest house on the block.

It was Gothic Revival. Larger than Rose's Victorian dollhouse, but not by much. One and a half stories done in a classic design—a rectangular structure, steep roof with cross gables and gingerbread, a porch that stretched along the full front of the house, and an arched window under the front gable. No garden. No porch furniture. No car in the drive, either. I'd seen the Clarks in Chicago, so obviously the fae could leave town, but I got the feeling they preferred not to. Cainsville was both their sanctuary and their source of power.

Patrick had the door open before we reached the porch. He

didn't say a word, just stepped back to let us in. Once we got past the front hall, that quiet simplicity of the house's exterior vanished. Obviously, Patrick had money, and this was where he spent it.

The style was designer contemporary, with no attempt to preserve the look or feel of the house's original era. I caught a glimpse of a kitchen with granite counters, gleaming copper pots, and stainless steel appliances. Patrick took us into the living room, where he'd obviously had a wall removed to make one big high-tech bachelor pad plus library. He took us to the library side. The couch was white leather with dark wood trim. I resisted the urge to brush off my rear before I sat.

When Patrick offered tea or coffee, Gabriel's refusal came without hesitation. When Patrick asked me, Gabriel said no again, so fast and so sharp that Patrick chuckled.

"No food and no drink," I said. "I don't know if the old stories are true, but we aren't taking that chance."

Patrick settled in at the other end of the sofa. "As with everything else, what humans believe is adjacent to the truth. What's the lore? Accept food or drink, and you'll be trapped in a fairy party forever?" He leaned forward, voice lowering conspiratorially. "There's no party. Or, if there is, I've never been invited. Instead, it allows me to trigger a mental state of hallucinations. Permanent hallucinations, if I wish. In short, it drives humans mad. But neither of you is human, so it wouldn't work."

"Like the charms and compulsions don't work on us?" I said, giving him a withering look.

"They do, but only to a degree. Otherwise, you'd never have asked questions, would you? Once you understood what was happening, your fae blood overruled the compulsions, to the deep and abiding regret of the elders right now. But other fae powers will work not at all. Like the trigger of the food and drink. So if you'd like a coffee or an iced tea . . . ?"

"Shockingly, I'm not going to take your word for it."

He only smiled and settled in. "You're right to be cautious. Now, what secret business brings you here?"

"Spina bifida."

As soon as I saw the look on his face, I knew I'd come to the wrong place. He stared at me, as if replaying my words, wondering what else I might have said instead, because those ones made no sense in any context he knew.

Gabriel prodded with, "What do you know about spina bifida?"

Patrick tried to hide his confusion. "It's a medical condition, affecting the spine, I believe, and—"

"Thank you for your time," I said, getting to my feet.

Gabriel rose. When Patrick did, too, Gabriel sidestepped closer to me, his hand going to my back. As I headed to the door, Patrick intercepted me. Gabriel tensed, his fingers wrapping around my upper arm.

"I'm no threat to her, Gabriel. None of us are." Patrick's voice was low, odd, and unfamiliar without that jaunty, devil-may-care note.

"Perhaps not a physical threat," Gabriel said. "But not all threats are physical."

"Agreed, but I'm not *any* sort of threat to her." He met Gabriel's gaze. "I never will be."

Gabriel shifted behind me, his hand still on my arm. "If you can't help, then we're going to leave."

"I'd like to lie and say I know exactly why you're asking, but I've lost my chance at that. Whatever is making you ask the question, though, clearly you believe the answer is connected to Cainsville. Tell me what's going on. I can help."

He was still speaking in that other voice, the soothing and serious one, but he wasn't offering out of some sudden surge of altruism. He hated to be left in the dark as much as his son, and he always expected something in return. Quid pro quo. And I was all right with it. A fair exchange of services. That's how a *bòcan* operates.

"Spina bifida is a severe congenital condition," I said. "At least, the form I had was."

"The form you had . . ."

"Up until the age of two. Then my parents murdered six people. And, miraculously, I was cured—of an incurable condition."

"You were—?" he began, slowly.

"Olivia?" Gabriel cut in. "We should leave."

"No, hold on." Patrick walked to his bookshelf. He ran his fingers along a row of books, the spines so old the leather seemed to flake at his touch.

"Olivia?" Gabriel said. "I really would like—"

"No." Patrick's tone was sharp and the look in his eyes made Gabriel blink. "Please. I'm not trying to trick you. I don't have a solution, but I can provide one answer."

He pulled out a book, and as he did, the worn leather mended under his fingers, becoming whole and smooth. He set the book on the desk and flipped through it, too fast to see what was written, and when he did slow, the ink seemed to shift and slide, the words illegible. He skimmed back two pages and stopped. His forefinger zoomed down the page, and the words stopped moving, but that didn't help—they were in Welsh.

He straightened and tapped a line. "There. It doesn't say the name of the condition, but I'm sure it's the right one. Spina bifida is a failure of embryonic completion, correct?" When I wasn't fast enough answering, he said, with some impatience, "The fetus doesn't fully form."

"Right." I moved up beside him and looked down at the page. It was handwriting, neat and precise. While the ink no longer moved, it seemed to shimmer, a kaleidoscope of color that drew me closer still, gaze fixed on the words.

"Which makes it one of a small host of conditions—" he began.

The words parted, ink flying from the page, sailing up around me as the blank hole on the page collapsed in on itself, pulling me with it. A flash of white, as if I'd fallen through the book itself. I hit the ground, my hands outstretched, grass beneath my fingers.

CHAPTER FORTY-FIVE

expected to see the meadow again. Instead, I stared at a chimera head. I lifted my head. I was sitting outside the park behind the diner.

"Please. Please, just listen."

A woman leaned on the park railing. She wasn't more than fifty but looked older, wearing a shapeless housedress, her hair streaked with gray, the style as formless as her outfit. A white-haired couple was walking past the park. Though they had their backs to me, I only needed to see their stance to recognize them. Ida and Walter. They were dressed smartly in a style only found in vintage shops these days. The seventies would be my guess, and a glance down the walkway, at a huge boat of a car passing along Main, seemed to confirm it.

Ida and Walter turned to the woman.

"You can help him," the woman said. "I know you can."

Ida's voice was kind but firm. "No, dear. There's nothing—"

"I won't tell anyone," the woman cut in quickly. "I'll say it was a miracle from God. I won't even know what you do. I'll walk away and leave him with you."

Ida moved to the fence, her hands resting on the woman's. "You are mistaken. Whatever you think you know—"

"Nothing. I know nothing. But I sense . . . I can tell . . . You're special. You can fix him. Please."

"Special? Perhaps. But can you imagine that if we knew how to heal a child, we would not readily do it?"

"Can you do anything? If he could just walk. Please. With a limp or with a cane. My grandson has no other impairment— no mental or physical defect. If you could just ease his—"

"We cannot," Ida said. "Or we would."

The woman staggered back, her face crumpling, and I saw a boy in the swing, one of those meant for infants, though he was at least five. His rail-thin legs were bare and I could see the white of a diaper. Our eyes met, and the ground opened again, and I tumbled through.

I saw others as I fell. Other children. Other times. Other places. A toddler with half-formed arms. A teenage girl on crutches. A young boy with some form of hydrocephalus. And then, again, I hit the ground. Only it wasn't grass this time, but rough-hewn wood. I faced a small window without glass. The wall looked odd—like wood lattice, the spaces between filled with a clay-like substance. Wattle and daub. The phrase jumped from the back of my mind.

Behind me, a man spoke in a language I didn't recognize. As I turned, though, his words started coming clear, first one or two in a sea of babble, then fully English, heavily accented, forcing me to struggle to understand him, my mind latching on to words like a swimmer catching hold of a pool ladder, pulling herself up from the water.

"—changeling child."

I looked around a wattle-and-daub house that was little more than a shack. The voices came from a second room.

"Your true daughter was stolen by the fair folk," the same voice continued. "This twisted monstrosity—"

"—is my child," a woman said. "My *child*. Ask the midwife. There was something amiss from the start. A lump on her back. She is afflicted, to be sure, but she's not a changeling. She came from me. From my womb."

"I understand your distress," the man said. "But this is no human child."

"She's my *daughter*," the woman said.

"She's not mine." Another man. His voice raw and bitter. "She looks nothing like me."

I pushed up and walked to the door. Three people stood around a wooden cradle. The woman wasn't much more than a child herself, maybe seventeen. The younger man was at least a decade older, dressed in rough-spun cloth streaked with dirt, his boots and calloused hands caked with it. The older man was clean and more finely dressed, in a dark gown with a beaded chain around his neck. A wooden crucifix hung from the chain.

"Have you had any contact with the fair folk?" the clergyman asked.

"No, none."

"Are you certain?" he said. "I have heard reports that you were seen dancing in the forest on Midsummer's Eve, shortly before you realized you were with child."

"What?" the young woman said. "Dancing—? I can barely dance at all with my twisted foot. I walk in the forest when I can, gathering herbs for my grandmother, and if the summer's day is hot, I'll go out in the evening instead, but . . ."

She trailed off as the clergyman shook his head.

"No," the young woman said. "No, it's not true. William, tell him. Please, tell him."

Her husband looked away. The baby let out a wail, and the floor opened up beneath me again.

CHAPTER FORTY-SIX

I crashed back into my body. I felt the smack of it, like a belly flop, pain slamming through me. Yet I didn't make a sound, didn't move a muscle. My eyes were closed, and I was lying on Patrick's couch. I could hear Gabriel's voice, feel his iron grip on my arm, and I tried to open my eyes, but I could only lie there, limp and still.

"She's snapped out of it." Patrick's voice.

"Then she should wake up. She always wakes up."

A cool hand resting gently on my forehead. Not Gabriel's. Patrick's, then.

"She's feverish, but not dangerously so. The vision exhausted her. She's learning to cope with them."

"Cope with them?" Gabriel's grip on my arm vanished, and his knees cracked as he stood. "I don't want her to cope with them. I want them gone."

"She's fine—"

"No, she's not. Goddamn it, how many times do I need to say this? Ida, Walter, you . . . all of you tell me how important she is, how you'd never hurt her, but *this* is hurting her. The fevers and the visions. They're dangerous, and the fact that none of you give a damn—"

"We give a damn, Gabriel. But there's nothing we can do except assure you that this is a normal part of the process."

"Then stop the process. Stop whatever the hell is happening to her."

"We can't."

Gabriel's voice moved, as if he'd stepped closer to Patrick. "You don't mean *can't*. You mean *won't*. Whatever is happening to her, you need it to happen, and you won't do anything to interfere with it. You like bargains, Patrick. How about this one: find a way to stop the visions or I will make sure Olivia leaves Cainsville and never comes back."

"Mmm, I don't think she'd appreciate that."

"I don't care."

"If you tricked her into leaving Cainsville and she found out what you'd done, I think you'd care very much."

"Then you'd be mistaken. The visions are tied to Cainsville. If you can't cure her, maybe taking her away will."

"I don't think Olivia is the sort of woman who'd stand for that. If you think she is—"

"Then I'd be a fool. I make my choices, and I accept the consequences. Now, can you cure her?"

"What if I offered you an alternative? If I could tell you something that would force the police to drop the charges against you? All charges."

"Then I would appreciate that. Later. Right now, my concern—"

"It isn't two separate deals, Gabriel. It's one. A choice."

No. Goddamn him, no. Patrick and his games. His endless games. I struggled to leap up, open my eyes, but I was still trapped there, as if asleep.

Patrick continued, "So what will it be? Free yourself from the prospect of a life in prison or Olivia from the fevers and the visions?"

Did Patrick know I was awake and listening? Was that the game? Force Gabriel to choose himself over me, after I'd proven I'd do the opposite? I knew which Gabriel would pick. I didn't care. I could live with the visions. I could not live with myself if he went to jail because he got mixed up with me.

"Exoneration or a cure," Gabriel said. "That is my choice?"

"It is."

"And my decision will remain between us?"

"Of course."

"I mean that, Patrick. I will demand your word on it. Whatever I choose, Olivia will never know that I had a choice. Correct?"

"You have my word."

"Then cure her."

No! The word echoed in my head, but I couldn't move, no matter how hard I struggled, fighting against the prison of my body.

You son of a bitch, Patrick. You goddamned—

"I wish I could," Patrick said. "Sadly, I cannot. Nor do I know anything that would set you free. It was a hypothetical."

A thud. A gasp and a hard thump, and then Patrick, wheezing as if struggling for breath. "While I applaud your reflexes, Gabriel, I might suggest that it's unwise to target me with them."

Gabriel's voice came low, razor-edged. "As it is unwise to target me with your games, Patrick. Particularly if they involve Olivia."

"I see that." A grunt, as if Patrick was pulling himself up off the floor. "I apologize for the trick. I believe I did pose it as a hypothetical, and if you misunderstood—"

I shot upright so fast I started falling. Gabriel's reflexes saved me from that ignoble fate, though I might wish he'd caught me by the arm or the shoulders instead of grabbing me by the collar, leaving me dangling like a kitten. A choking kitten. He released me fast enough, letting me settle upright onto the sofa.

"Are you all right?" he asked.

"Fine." I looked around, getting my bearings. Seeing Patrick watching, I got to my feet. "I think we should leave now."

"I would agree."

Gabriel stood between me and Patrick, as if blocking him, while I rose and started for the door.

"Wait," Patrick said. "We need to discuss—"

"Nothing," I said. "We need to discuss nothing."

"I can explain the spina bifida. It's—"

"One of the side effects of fae blood. One of many, apparently. Now, if you'll excuse us . . ."

"I believe I can shed more light on the subject and what may have happened with your parents."

"No, thank you," I said. "I'll find my answers elsewhere."

"I can help with Gabriel's case."

That slowed my steps, and even when Gabriel murmured, "Keep going," and I knew he was right, I couldn't help myself. I turned to Patrick.

"That's what Gabriel and I were discussing when you were recuperating," he said. "While I don't have any answers, I do have a few ideas. Leads, as you'd say. I could pursue them, if you'd like."

As he said the words, perhaps he realized how they sounded— he'd only help free Gabriel if I agreed to talk. More likely it was the sudden surge of blood pressure turning my face an unhealthy shade of red that made him quickly retract with, "I will help either way, of course. But I'd like to discuss this as well."

"No," Gabriel said. "We don't need your help. Olivia?"

Patrick kept his gaze fixed on me. "As for the fevers, while I'm sure they concern you, Liv, they shouldn't. Am I correct that none have been as serious as that first one?" When I didn't reply, Patrick took that as agreement and continued, "Your body is learning to cope with them. As it must. They are a vital part of the process." A quick look at Gabriel. "The process of you coming into your powers, which benefits you as much as any of us. The visions are a protective mechanism, though they probably don't seem like it right now."

"What do they protect me against?"

"Us."

He waved me to the couch. I hesitated, but if Patrick had won me over with the promise of help with Gabriel's case, this is how he won Gabriel. He used us against each other, and I could rage at that, but deep down, part of me had to say, *Well played, sir.*

Gabriel headed into the living room and I followed.

Patrick continued. "The visions are hereditary memories, as you may have figured out. Think of it as a massive repository of knowledge from countless generations. My collection would be a mere shelf in your mental library. The problem is that there are too many books for one person to ever read. Too many memories for you to ever absorb. So you are thrown from one to the next, as you require them."

"You said they protect me from the Tylwyth Teg."

"Tylwyth Teg. Cŵn Annwn. And every other type and sub-type of fae out there, because there are many, and you are valu-able to all of them. You can keep Cainsville alive. Or you can let it burn. There are many who would be overjoyed by either option."

"How do the visions protect me?"

"By showing you truth. Without them, you're left relying on us for answers. Which we'll withhold until it suits us. Then we'll twist answers to our purposes and outright lie if that serves us better."

"What I saw, about the children . . ."

"A failure of completion. You are correct that it is one of the side effects of fae mingling with human. *This* form"—he gestured at himself—"is not *our* form. So procreation with humans can result in a body that is not entirely complete. Even when it happens, which is rare, the effect is usually not even noticeable. Shortened finger joints, missing wisdom teeth, one fewer rib than there ought to be. On occasion, though, it is more serious. In spina bifida, the spinal column fails to form completely, therefore fails to properly enclose the spinal cord. Which isn't to say that every child born with spina bifida has fae blood. But it is one of the most serious manifestations of the problem."

Manifestations of the problem. He said it so formally, so abstractly. A child is born unable to walk because a fae chose to impregnate a human woman. That child's condition is nothing more than a somewhat regrettable side effect. Like breeding cattle experimentally. Eventually, you're going to get one with a fifth leg, but the risk won't stop you from breeding them.

I hated their attitude. But did I hate *them* for it? No. They interbred to survive.

"We've confirmed Olivia had this condition," Gabriel said. "It has been verified beyond any doubt. But you knew nothing of it."

"We knew nothing of Liv," Patrick said. "Not until the Larsens were arrested. Then we realized that the girl was our Mallt-y-Dos. Which is why the elders facilitated her adoption. Hiding her until she was old enough to bring home to Cainsville."

"The leak," I said. "My identity. The Tylwyth Teg leaked—"

"Certainly not." Patrick looked affronted. He might hold himself separate from the others, but he was still one of them. "We would not orchestrate such a debacle. It was careless and thoughtless, and could as easily have driven you to Peru as to Cainsville.

I'm sure the elders would point fingers at the Cŵn Annwn, but if pressed, they would admit it was too clumsy and dangerous for them as well. I don't doubt that whoever leaked it wasn't entirely human, but it was not one of us. Back to your condition, though. We had no knowledge of that. You were a healthy, happy child when we found you, and we had no reason to think you'd ever been otherwise. If it's true, though, that this condition cannot be reversed by medical means, then you have almost certainly answered what was one of our biggest questions: why your parents did it."

"You knew they were guilty."

"We knew only what we read in the papers. We thought perhaps the mingling of blood, and the coming together of Tylwyth Teg and Cŵn Annwn, produced . . . an unsatisfactory result."

Turned my parents into killers, he meant. That their darker fae natures had played off each other and stripped away their humanity.

"This is a more satisfactory answer." He caught my look and quickly added, without much conviction, "Though not as satisfactory as discovering they were innocent."

"It was not the Tylwyth Teg who offered the Larsens this deal, then," Gabriel said. "You are certain of that."

"I am. We don't have the power to reverse the condition, no more than we can alleviate the fevers better than modern medicine. At one time, that was different. Our knowledge of plants and herbal medicines helped. But these days, you can pick up something better on the shelf of any drugstore."

Gabriel seemed ready to pursue it, but I shook my head at him. What I'd seen in the visions confirmed they could not fix the children their blood had damaged.

"Who has healing powers?" I asked. "Or *what* does? Which fae?"

"None."

When I gave him a hard look, he threw up his hands. "We don't. What you are looking at is a ritual. Presumably your parents killed in that specific manner for a reason, and that reason is tied to your cure."

"If you tell me it was a satanic rite . . ."

He made a face. "Nothing so pedestrian. Or ludicrous. Demons are a very human creation. You look for ways to explain evil, and instead of seeing it in yourselves, you offload the responsibility onto monsters. The monstrous exists in the mirror, not in the sulfurous depths of some fantasy world."

"Or in the fantastical world of fae."

"It's not that fantastical, as you can see. We don't live in another realm. We're here sharing yours. There's no such thing as an evil race of fae. No more than there is an evil race of humans. Individuals, yes. But for the rest of us, we are like you—neither wholly good nor wholly bad. We simply don't feel as compelled to hide the bad."

"And as fascinating as this philosophical discussion could be, it doesn't help me solve the problem."

"True. Another time, then."

"Or not . . ."

Patrick only smiled. "You should at least humor me, Liv."

"You wouldn't respect me if I did."

"Also true. Back on topic. Fae may not have innate healing abilities or a direct line to the imaginary world of demon sacrifices, but there are . . . powers."

"Like healing?"

"No, I mean . . ." He made a vague gesture. "Powers. Higher powers, you might say, though I'm not inclined to put it that way."

"Gods?"

He made the face he had when he'd talked about *demons*. "That's why I didn't put it that way. I wouldn't call them gods or deities. Just . . . powers."

"Uh-huh. Are we talking about the Druids again?"

"Not really."

"That isn't an answer."

He sighed. "There are powers. Those powers have greater abilities. It is possible to invoke their favor."

"Like demons."

He made a noise in his throat that sounded remarkably like Gabriel's soft growl of frustration. "This is the problem with talking to *boinne-fala*. You have your boxes and everything has to fit into them or you'll damn well cram them in. God, demons, saints, monsters . . . There are powers. They have powers. Those powers can be invoked."

"By us?"

"No. Only fae. However, we could do so on behalf of a human."

"How is that different from having the actual power to heal?"

"It's vastly different," he said.

"It still comes down to the same thing. Any of you could have made the deal with my parents."

"I suppose that's true," he mused. He caught my darkening look. "But we didn't. It wasn't the Tylwyth Teg. At least, not the Tylwyth Teg of Cainsville."

I heard Gabriel sigh. This was going to be a long conversation.

CHAPTER FORTY-SEVEN

We didn't get anything more from Patrick. Nothing useful, at least. He suggested I begin with the Cŵn Annwn. Not that he had any reason to actually suspect them, but it was a place to start. Except, you know, I shouldn't actually attempt to contact them, because that wouldn't be wise.

"We *will* have to speak to one of the Huntsmen," I said to Gabriel as we left Patrick's.

"I would agree."

"They've invited me to make contact, but they haven't exactly left a cell number." I took the boar's tusk from my pocket, rubbed it, and squeezed my eyes shut. "I'd like to speak to the guy in charge." I opened my eyes and looked around. "Nope, that's not it."

Gabriel's lips twitched in a smile. "We'll figure it out."

"I hope so."

After that, I talked to Larry. He hoped I'd "work out whatever I needed to work out" and come back to Cainsville. I didn't say much to that. I couldn't.

Gabriel and I detoured to the prison to get my car. We also

tried again to see Todd. Nothing had changed. If some branch of the fae Mafia was blocking me, it was doing so at a level high enough that I couldn't dodge around it.

I'd just made it to my car when Ricky called. I put him on speaker and followed Gabriel's car from the lot.

"I want to see you tonight," he said as I drove.

"Um, good, considering that's what we had planned."

Two seconds of silence told me those plans had changed.

"Club business?" I asked.

"Yeah. Just a private meeting with my dad. Stuff we can't discuss on the phone. He needs me to come by at nine, which is going to totally fuck up our evening. Unless I can convince you to come with."

"To the clubhouse?"

A shuffle in the background. I could hear the distant murmur of voices. Still at school, then, taking a moment between classes.

He continued. "We discussed you making an appearance at the club, just coming by, hanging out, showing the guys . . . you know."

"That I don't think I'm too good for them."

"Mmm, yeah."

What I'd just learned from Patrick was huge. Overwhelming, too. I needed time to clear my head so I could work it through. Spending the evening in a biker clubhouse was pretty much guaranteed to be all the distraction I needed.

"I'll come tonight."

"Thank you."

The Saints aren't your typical biker gang. Ricky downplays the differences, because he doesn't want them to seem like justifications. Running a successful criminal operation means you do make choices, and some the Saints make may seem ethical, but it's more about profit and self-protection. If you stick within certain lines of the law, you can skirt the notice of the law.

Within the club, the rules are equally strict, but again each one has a purpose. A biker gang is not a democracy. There's a guy in charge, and he owns your ass, and that's okay, because it's a way of life that the guys in a gang understand. Give them democracy and they'd smell weakness, toss your ass overboard, and seize control for themselves.

Yet as progressive as Don was, equality for women didn't rank high on his reform list, because the gang wanted it about as much as they wanted democracy, which was to say, not at all. This was one reason Ricky hadn't been rushing me out for an evening at the clubhouse. If there was a drop of sexism in Ricky, I hadn't seen it. He didn't go out of his way to treat me as an equal, because to him, I just was. Now he had to ask me, for an evening, to accept an inferior role. I'd never seen Ricky so uncomfortable as when he had to lay out those expectations before our visit.

"It's okay," I said as we talked at his place. "I get it. You're not asking me to dress in micro shorts and serve them beer before the wet T-shirt contest. The rules are simple enough. One, treat you with respect, which I hope I always do."

"You do."

"Two, don't pay too much attention to other guys, because it could be taken the wrong way. Wallace and CJ will be there, and when you're gone, they're in charge of me, so I'm to focus on them. No one will misinterpret, because you put them in charge of me."

He exhaled. "That sounds so bad."

"Let me rephrase, then. In your absence, they will be my genteel hosts. So those are the rules. Respect you. Don't pay too much attention to other men. Act like I think you're brilliant, gorgeous, charming, and I'm crazy about you. All of which is easy to do because it's true. And you're especially gorgeous when you blush."

He chuckled. "Thank you."

"What matters is how *you* treat *me*, and there are no issues there. As for putting up with culturally ingrained sexism, you do remember where I grew up, right? You want equal rights? Don't go to the biker club *or* the country club. Now, if you can excuse me for twenty minutes . . ." I lifted a shopping bag. "I brought wardrobe."

He grinned. "Micro shorts and a white T-shirt?"

"Sadly, no, but if you'd like that for a private evening at home, we can talk."

Styling my hair didn't take more than a few minutes. I'd cut it shoulder length when I was trying to hide from the media. It was growing, but it was taking its time. The fake color had long since washed out, leaving me my usual ash-blond.

Next came the outfit. I could say my jeans were snugger than I usually wear, but that'd be a lie. For a shirt, I'd gone uptown. Button-down, classic oxford. Designer label. It seemed more insulting to Ricky's friends if I dressed in Walmart fashion, as if that's what I expected would fit in.

I will say that I got the shirt on sale. I can't claim the same for the Louboutin boots. They were my first real indulgence since leaving my parents' home, and I wasn't going to regret it. Besides, they looked killer with the jeans.

When I walked into the living room, Ricky's look agreed one hundred percent. He checked his watch.

"No time," I said.

He laughed and kissed my cheek. "I'm that transparent, huh?"

"Yep. I'll claim my bouquet later."

328 • KELLEY ARMSTRONG

"Bouquet?"

"In recognition of an acting job well done, delivered *after* the performance. Now let's go so I can earn it."

I started to walk away. He caught my hand. When I looked at him, the smile had vanished and he looked as nervous as a boy about to meet his girlfriend's parents.

"Speaking of bouquets," he said. "I mentioned before that I'm not very good at romantic gifts."

"You got me a switchblade. I think that was very romantic."

"Yeah, I'm much better at giving weapons than . . ." He took a box from his pocket and opened it. Inside was a silver chain. He swore. "See? I can't even manage the presentation properly. Damn thing slid . . ." He fished the chain out, pendant popping from inside the box. He caught it, hand closing around the necklace before I could see what it was. "I wanted to say thanks for tonight."

He held out the necklace. It was white gold. The pendant was a crescent moon, filigreed and inlaid with clear, sparkling gemstones that I was damn sure weren't cubic zirconia.

As I stared, he pulled his hand back. "I overdid it, didn't I? Shit, shit, shit—"

My arms went around his neck, kissing away that doubt; then I disentangled myself and opened his hand to look at the necklace.

"It's gorgeous. If you think you don't have great taste in jewelry, you could not be more wrong."

I turned around and lifted my hair. He put the chain on and kissed the back of my neck.

"I'll model it properly for you later," I said. "With less clothing in the way."

"And by moonlight?"

"Of course." I fingered the pendant. "That's only fitting."

CHAPTER FORTY-EIGHT

The clubhouse was a half mile down a dirt road and sur-rounded by woods. That might look as if the Saints are hiding. They aren't, because the clubhouse is exactly what it purports to be—a private social club for motorcycle enthusi-asts. They might talk business in the back room, but they aren't stupid enough to keep drugs, guns, or any other product on the property.

The secluded location is an aspect of being a good neighbor, and not the only one they try to fulfill. If one of their neighbors is putting up a fence or hauling a tractor out of the mud, Don sends a few guys to help out. An elderly couple lives down the road, the old woman caring for her Alzheimer's-stricken hus-band. Don has someone check in with them twice a week to bring hot food and see if they need anything done around the house. That's not because he's a misunderstood nice guy—it's because he knows the wisdom of being a good neighbor.

At eight on a Tuesday evening, the place wasn't exactly hop-ping. Don, Wallace, and a few others were drinking beer, talk-ing "shop"—for the auto shops they run, that is. Ricky joined in as I nursed my beer and listened.

As the clock closed in on nine, more guys began trickling in.

330 • KELLEY ARMSTRONG

Some girls, too. Well, women more than girls. The only one under thirty was Lily, whom I'd met the first time I was here.

The women, including Lily's mother, were hard, passed from guy to guy, desperate for attention or protection or something life hadn't otherwise given them. I wanted to take nineteen-year-old Lily aside and have a chat about life choices. But I've worked long enough in shelters to know that impulse was wasted on someone like her. At least it was if it came from someone like me.

The fact she had the hots for Ricky really didn't help. He knew it and had made it very, very clear that she didn't have a hope in hell of climbing on his bike. It was the same attitude he extended to all the women: respectful and polite but distant. Don was that way, too, and Wallace from the interactions I saw. It was a subtle hint for the women to take their hopes and dreams elsewhere, with the knowledge that "elsewhere" probably only meant a gang that wouldn't treat them as well, and in light of that, maybe it was best not to make them feel too unwelcome.

CJ showed up right before nine. When Ricky had said he'd be leaving me with CJ and Wallace, I'd thought he meant informally. But no, there was an actual handoff. He made it as casual as possible—"You guys keep Liv entertained while I'm gone?"— but it was a clear message for everyone to hear. Then Ricky took my beer can and murmured to CJ, "Get her something from the cabinet, and don't let her tell you she's fine with beer."

"What'll you have?" CJ asked when Ricky was gone.

"Tequila?"

"Got it. How about entertainment? You're not going to want to spend the next hour talking to two old coots, so pick your poison. Darts, poker, pool . . ."

"I'm okay at poker. Better at darts. I think I've played pool twice in my life, and both times I was drunk. It didn't help my aim. I would love to learn someday, but I won't make you give lessons."

"Happy to. Your choice, then." He motioned at the dartboard. "Play to your strengths. Or learn something new and risk making a fool of yourself."

"Well, if you put it that way . . ." I walked over and picked up a pool cue.

CJ grinned. Wallace only shook his head.

"You rack them up. I'll get the drinks." CJ glanced at me. "You know how to rack them up?"

"Nine balls and a convenient triangle to place them in."

"Good girl." He walked to the bar and held up two bottles for me to choose from. When I did, he said, "You like power over price tag, huh, Livy?"

"It's Liv," Wallace rumbled, his first words since Ricky had left.

I shrugged. "Liv, Livy, Olivia . . . whatever works."

"How about Eden?" said a voice from across the room.

We all turned. The guy who'd spoken sat at one of the tables, with Lily on his knee. He wasn't anyone I'd noticed before— maybe late twenties, making him one of the younger guys in the room. Dark-haired. Smirking.

"What'd you say?" CJ delivered my tequila shot and kept walking, advancing on the guy.

"I asked if she ever goes by Eden. Valid question."

Lily snickered. She stopped at dual looks—one from CJ and one from her mother—and she slid off the guy's lap.

"Yeah?" CJ said. "Here's a *valid question*. What the fuck is *your* name? 'Cause I don't think you've been here long enough for me to remember it. Which means you haven't been here long enough to open your mouth. Especially if you're going to ask stupid, *invalid* questions."

The guy lifted his hands. "Sorry. I was just teasing the girl."

"The girl?" CJ stopped behind the guy, who had the sense to

rise and face him, his posture submissive—shoulders down, gaze lowered, a dumbass smile on his face. "Who is *the girl*? And be very, very careful how you answer that."

"She's, um, Ricky's old lady."

"And who is Ricky?"

The guy paused, and I sensed disrespect in that pause. After a moment he said, "He's the road captain, right?" A self-deprecating laugh. "Sorry, I guess I'm not ready for the membership exam, huh? I'm still getting used to the titles."

He babbled on for another few minutes, until CJ silenced him with, "You ever want to have a chance of becoming a prospect, boy? You'll learn to keep your mouth shut. It's not one of the official rules, but for some people, it ought to be."

To join the Saints, you first had to get to know guys from the club. If they approved, you could hang around while they vetted you. If they liked what they saw, you became a prospect and got to wear part of the colors while the club put you through your paces—a process that could last years. Only then did you become a patched member.

While Ricky was old enough to have his patch, he was young for road captain. But it was a message from Don. *My kid is on the succession track. He's going to prove to you that he can handle it, but if you don't like the idea, the door is over there.*

CJ left the guy alone after that and gave me a pool lesson as he downed two beers. Wallace watched and drank nothing. When we started a game, CJ invited Wallace to join in, but he only grunted, arms crossed, looking as if he could think up a hundred and one better ways to spend his evening.

"We'll play," someone called.

It was the guy from earlier, sauntering over with his arm around Lily.

"Sit the fuck back down," CJ said.

"No," Wallace said. "That's up to Ms. Jones."

I snuck a look at Wallace. Did he expect me to stand firm and refuse to play with people who'd mocked me? Or rise above the insults?

"It's fine," I said.

Wallace's expression didn't change, and I got the feeling there was no right answer. He just wanted to see which I'd pick.

The game went fine for about fifteen minutes. I'll flatter myself and say that I did reasonably well, considering my inexperience, but that didn't keep Lily and her new beau—conveniently named Beau—from smirking and sharing eye rolls every time I missed a shot.

Finally, Lily said, "You don't belong here, you know."

CJ started to answer, but a look from Wallace stopped him.

"I know," I said. "I'm going to need a lot more practice."

"I mean *here*," she said. "In the club. With Ricky."

"He seems to think otherwise."

I said it calmly, but as I reached to line up for my shot, Lily suddenly took hers, the ball cracking hard against my hand.

"Whoops," she said.

"Lily . . ." CJ warned under his breath.

I turned to her. "I'm not in your way."

"Huh?"

I met her gaze. "It wasn't happening, even without me here."

I was trying to convey the message as obliquely as possible, but when I went to line up my shot again, another ball smacked into my knuckles.

"Let me put that more bluntly," I said, setting down my cue. "I'm not stopping you from getting Ricky."

Her cheeks reddened. "I don't know what you're talking about."

"My mistake. If you'll just play pool, then so will I."

"What's that supposed to mean?"

CJ cut in. "That if you don't shut your mouth, neither will she, and I don't think you're going to like what she has to say, Lily-girl."

I lined up my shot. She brought her cue down hard on my hand. CJ grabbed it from her, but a look from Wallace warned him to stay out of it.

"Okay, let's clear the air," I said. "The day I walked in here, you were no closer to having Ricky than the first time you laid eyes on him. That's no insult to you. You just aren't his type. You could dance naked on the table and pour tequila down his throat, and you still wouldn't—"

She flew across the table at me. Or she tried to. It isn't a maneuver to be attempted by anyone without gymnastics training. So it was more of a "scramble onto the table and crawl over" at me.

I grabbed her by the arm and threw her down. Then I planted one boot on her stomach and leaned in. "Maybe it would make you feel better to knock me around, but you don't seem to be very good at it. So I'm going to take my foot off you, and we'll retreat to our respective corners and call it a draw."

This seemed a perfectly reasonable solution. But as soon as I stepped off, she went for me again. CJ grabbed her from behind and looked at Beau, who backed away, hands up.

"Meribeth?" CJ called to Lily's mother. "Take your girl out of here. I don't want to see her back for a month."

Lily howled. Meribeth tried to wheedle the suspension down to a week. I glanced at Wallace, but he shook his head, telling me not to interfere. Then he picked up a pool cue and motioned for the game to resume.

CHAPTER FORTY-NINE

We played two more games. Beau backed out after the first and left the room, presumably going after Lily, playing his choices down the middle—don't piss off the senior club guys by supporting her, but don't spoil his chance of getting lucky, either. Another guy took his place. When that game finished, I excused myself to use the restroom. I came out to find Beau waiting.

"All yours," I said.

His gaze slid over me and he grinned. "Really? Well, I appreciate the invitation, but I'm not sure Ricky would approve."

He said it as "Rick-ee," drawing out the diminutive with a sneering falsetto. I hadn't seen him drink much in the clubhouse, but the stink of booze rolled off his breath. I resisted the urge to retort, and brushed past with a simple, "Excuse me." His arm shot out to stop me.

"You handled yourself well in there," he said. "It sure got me all hot and bothered. Is that what Ricky likes? A girl who can stand up for herself?" He smirked. "No, I bet Ricky likes to be the one on the floor with your heel digging into his chest. Am I close?"

"Not by half. Now move—"

"Oh, come on, tell the truth. We all know which one of you wears the pants."

"Ricky prefers me in skirts. Easier access."

He choked on a chortling laugh. "No, sweetie. If anyone's wearing skirts, it's the pretty boy. Everyone knows he's soft. They just don't know *how* soft. But now that he's got himself a ball-busting, smart-mouthed girlfriend, his secret's out."

"Move. Now."

"Did I mention the tough-girl act turns me on?"

"Yep, and if that's a threat, may I remind you that you're in the middle of a clubhouse full of bikers? The only one you need to worry about, though, is Ricky. Lay a finger on me and he'll want you all to himself. And if you think that's nothing to worry about, you're even more clueless than you seem, which is damned clueless, having spent the last couple of minutes yapping without noticing the switchblade at your gut."

He looked down and saw the knife.

"A present from Ricky," I said. "Yes, he does like a girl who knows how to take care of herself, because he can't be there all the time. Very sweet, don't you think?"

"No, very stupid. You know the problem with giving a girl a knife? The second someone takes it—"

He grabbed for it. I slashed, and he fell back with a yelp.

"Did I mention he showed me how to use it?" I said.

He dove at me, snarling, "You bitch."

Before I could react, someone grabbed him from behind and yanked him off his feet. It was Wallace. He put Beau up against the wall. He didn't say a word, just held him there. Then he dropped him, stepped back, and waited. Beau struggled to his feet. He stood with his fists at his sides, one hand dripping blood. When Wallace made no move, Beau hightailed it down the hall.

"You need to tell Ricky," Wallace said.

"I know."

He eyed me. "I mean it, Liv. If that boy went after you, Ricky needs to handle it, even if that's not how you normally do things."

"It isn't. I am going to tell him, though. Not because the guy cornered me, but because he insulted Ricky, who needs to know a potential prospect doesn't respect him."

Wallace grunted. He seemed marginally impressed.

"Beau wasn't really hitting on me," I continued. "He was taking a shot at Ricky. That seems a stupid thing for a potential prospect to do."

Wallace shrugged. "With some of these guys, testosterone runs higher than IQ. I'm just glad I saw that side before we started seriously considering him. Guys like that are not welcome."

"Guys like what?" Ricky rounded the corner and stopped beside me. He slid an arm around my waist. "Something up?"

"Beau," Wallace said, and gave me a look to say he'd handle this.

"Beau?" Ricky said. "Oh, right. New guy."

"He was drunk," Wallace said. "Too damned drunk for ten o'clock on a weeknight. First, there was a dustup with Lily. Olivia handled it. Lily's earned herself a month's suspension. Beau seems to have hooked up with her, and I don't know if that's what made him go after Olivia or—"

"He went after—?" Ricky saw blood on the floor. "Did he hurt—?"

"No," Wallace said. "That's his. Apparently, you gave Liv a knife."

Ricky's arm tightened around me as he leaned in to whisper, "You okay?"

"I am."

Wallace said I'd handled it fine, that it was just one asshole being an asshole and Beau had better never step on the property

again, but Ricky strode to the door and opened it with a hard
kick. We followed him outside, and he surveyed the lot.

"He's got a Super Glide, right?"

"Yeah." Wallace stepped out behind us. "He's long gone."

Ricky's gaze fixed on the road. My hand tightened on his. He
murmured, "I want to go after him."

*I agree. I want you to show him why he should respect you.
And yet . . .*

"And yet . . ." Ricky murmured, the echo sending another
shiver through me. "I need to start reining in my temper. It
doesn't lead me anywhere good." He raised his voice for Wallace. "We know where he lives, right?"

"Where he's staying, yeah."

"Then I'll pay him a visit tomorrow. Better to do it once I've
cooled off and he thinks he's gotten away with it. If he shows up
at the clubhouse before then, I want a call. Good?"

Technically, being sergeant-at-arms, Wallace was in charge
of enforcement and discipline, so it made sense for Ricky to run
this past him. But more than that, he was wisely asking advice
of someone older and more experienced. Wallace nodded, and
even if he only grunted, "Yeah, that works," there was a glow
in his eyes, his star pupil proving, yet again, why he deserved
the extra attention.

Ricky rolled his shoulders, his gaze swinging to the forest
behind the clubhouse as he leaned toward me. "If I walk it off,
will you come with me?"

"Of course."

This wasn't an amble through the woods. Ricky was pissed,
temper rolling off him. Finally, he stopped and peered into the
forest, his shoulders tight, as if expecting attack from all sides.
Then he took my other hand and tugged me in front of him. He

met my gaze, his dark eyes like a tumultuous night sky, clouds roiling through, no hint of that moonlit glimmer I'd seen before. He blinked and the clouds dissipated, but only for a second before gathering again.

"I'm okay," he said.

"I know."

"It should be easier. Shaking this. I did the right thing, letting him go for now."

"You did."

"So why—" He bit off the word and made a noise in his throat.

I stepped closer. I didn't try to kiss him, even to touch him, but as soon as I made a move his way, those clouds shifted and twisted, lust flaring behind them. He blinked hard and shuddered.

"You don't want to do that," he said.

I moved closer. "Why not?"

"Because I'm still . . ." He rolled his shoulders, trying to shake it off again, but it held fast, and when he met my gaze, his breathing came harder. "You don't want me like this."

"You need to shake it. I'm offering to help."

He tugged me to him, just close enough for me to feel his chest brushing mine as he took deep breaths.

"I want to shake it," he said. "Not vent it on you."

"How about a compromise?" I disengaged my hands from his and unbuttoned the top of my shirt. "We'll get a little more fresh air first . . ." I backed up and undid the next button, flicking open my front bra clasp with it. "A little more exercise . . ." I opened two more buttons. "Work off the edge . . ." The last button. "But just the edge. I'll take the rest." I let my shirt hang open. "Or I will . . . if you can catch me." At last I saw that glitter in his eyes, moonlight behind the clouds. "Is that a yes?"

He lunged. I wheeled, laughing, and raced off into the forest.

GONE

icky was dreaming of the Hunt. He was in the forest, chasing Liv, adrenaline pounding, the snap and jab of branches only making his breath come harder, lust and excitement tingeing the forest red.

He could see her ahead, naked, the chain around her neck glittering in the moonlight. Hell, he swore he could smell her, her own excitement and adrenaline pulsing from her like threads that threatened to break each time she rounded a tree and disappeared from sight, and he'd barrel forward, fear licking through him, fear that he'd lose her, and when he spotted her again, that relief mingled with a fresh surge of resolve, and he'd find a little extra speed, determined to catch her before she . . .

Disappeared.

He slowed. Liv had darted around a big oak ahead, and when she hadn't reappeared, he thought it was his line of sight, but now he'd come around the tree and found himself staring into empty forest.

He weaved one way and then the other. She had to be there. She never went far. This was a chase, not hide-and-seek. That's what he hungered for and she knew it, as she always knew, absolutely and instinctively. So if she was gone . . .

His heart jolted so hard pain shot through his chest.

No, it's a mistake. She misjudged and thought I was closer. She'll realize it any second now, as she looks back to laugh, to grin, to tease . . .

But the forest stayed silent. No questioning cry. Not even the thump of running feet.

"Liv?" he called.

His heart thudded again, and he gritted his teeth against it. Unreasonable fear. Ungrounded fear. Yet he couldn't help it. If he woke in the night and saw her side of the bed empty, he'd scramble up, dread filling him, a black wave of it that stole his breath, until he'd hear the flush of the toilet or the pad of her footsteps, and he'd sink down again, closing his eyes so she wouldn't see the lingering fear. He'd wait until she crawled back into bed and move against her, as if in sleep, his heart slowing only when he felt her there, nestled against him.

"Liv?" he called. Then, "Olivia!"

His voice thundered through the forest, and even after it died away, he swore he could hear the four syllables of her name, pounding like hoofbeats. Then it was actual hooves. The ground shook with them, seeming to come from every direction.

The hoofbeats stopped. Ricky stood there, watching the forest shift as the moon slid between cloud cover, the trees going light and then dark, the branches above and all around rolling like waves. A horse snorted. He turned fast but saw only trees. Even when the moon snuck out, one patch of forest stayed night-dark. He strode toward it, one hand clenched in a fist and the other holding his switchblade, the weight comfortable and reassuring. He flicked the blade then shut it again, never looking down, no need to look, the move reflexive.

A horse whinnied and stamped. Still the patch of forest stayed dark. Ricky pushed aside branches and stepped into a clearing to see a man astride a stallion. The horse was as black as the surrounding night, and it towered above Ricky. Its eyes glowed a faint red. The man wore a cloak so dark it looked black until Ricky's eyes adjusted enough to see it was black and green, decorated in a swirling Celtic design.

I know that design.

The connection wouldn't quite close, and he turned his attention to the man instead. He was dark-haired, dark-eyed, dark beard stubble obscuring the bottom half of his face, but even at a glance Ricky knew it was no one he recognized.

And yet it was . . .

Again, the connection wouldn't form, like a smashed bridge over rapids, no way across, the thunder of water drowning out thought. The thunder of one question drowning out all others.

"Where is she?" Ricky said.

"Gone." The man looked down at him. "He couldn't stand to lose her and neither could I, so in the end, we both did." Pain darkened the man's eyes to black pits of grief and guilt. "But no one lost more than she did. No one."

"I don't under—"

"Find her."

Ricky jolted from the dream. He pushed up so fast one hand buckled under him and his foot slid in the dew-damp leaves. He patted the ground beside him, not trusting his eyes despite the moonlight flooding through the trees. He reached and he looked, but he knew what he'd see: an empty spot where Liv had been sleeping.

He scrambled to his feet.

"Lose something?" a voice asked.

Ricky spun as Beau sauntered out of the forest. His gaze slid down Ricky. "I'll give you a moment to get dressed."

"Where is she?" Ricky advanced on Beau.

"You sure you don't want to put some clothing on?"

He grabbed Beau by the throat. Fingers closed on warm skin, and he felt the throb of a jugular, and then his hand snapped shut on air. He blinked and stared at the empty space in front of him.

"We do have time for you to get dressed," Beau said, now ten feet away to his left.

I'm still dreaming.

Except he wasn't. Everything was as it should be—the forest lit by moonlight, the distant glow of the clubhouse, the smell of burnt rubber from someone tearing out, the whistle of wind in the treetops, even the fact that he was naked. All normal . . . except for a man who could disappear.

Not a man. Not human, at least. When he looked at Beau, he knew everything Liv had told him was true. He hadn't doubted it, not really. If she believed it and Gabriel believed it, then it must be true, because they were two of the most sensible and grounded people he knew. Yet he had still felt, if not doubt, then confusion, a sense that maybe, just maybe, there was another explanation. Now he knew there was not.

"I really feel we could do this better if you were dressed," Beau said.

"No," a woman's voice whispered from the trees. "That would be such a shame."

"He's so pretty," another giggled.

A third echoed with a lilting, "So very pretty."

Fingers grazed his ass. He wheeled, but no one was there. He could hear more voices, whispers, and giggles, and feel tickling touches and strokes, fingers running down his cheeks, his thighs, his biceps . . . and elsewhere. He resisted the urge to shove them away. There was no one to shove.

Beau came close—too close. Smirking, as if expecting Ricky

to back away. He stood his ground and let Beau step up until his hand brushed Ricky's hip.

"Where is Olivia?" Ricky said.

"You *are* pretty." Beau stroked his cheek. "Such a shame, really. There are so many powers. So many skills and abilities. And this is all your kind get. A pretty face and charming ways. That's how you won her, you know. Fae charm." His gaze slid down Ricky, lingering as it went. "As for the rest, if you're going to fuck it, it helps if it looks deliciously fuckable. But mostly, it's the charm. That really is all you have."

"It's served me well so far."

"True. You're very good at what you do. And what is that, again? Right, you're a biker. The bar isn't set too high there, is it? A pretty face and false charm. It's not enough. Not nearly enough."

"But he's Arawn," one of the women whispered. "He doesn't need power. He *is* power."

Fingers slid across his thigh and stroked him. He held his ground and met Beau's gaze. "Tell me where she is."

"Mmm, what's the rush? She's safe. I promise you that. Relax." Beau grinned. "Enjoy yourself."

More fingers touched him. More hands fondled him. Beau leaned in, lips coming to Ricky's, chuckling when Ricky tensed. Beau kissed him. Ricky let him. He parted his lips, and when Beau's tongue slid in, he chomped down. Beau screamed. It wasn't a man's scream—not even a human scream. It sounded like the wail of some creature flying overhead.

Beau fell back, but Ricky didn't let him go, just kept biting down. Beau flailed and shrieked, his eyes rounding and bugging. Blood filled Ricky's mouth and he kept biting down until, at last, Beau pulled free, and Ricky spat out the bit of flesh in his mouth.

"Arawn," one of the women whispered. "He is Arawn."

"Lord of the Underworld?" Beau snarled, his face barely human now, barely bothering to keep it human, blood dripping from his mouth, spattering as he spoke. "No. This is a boy. A foolish, stupid boy. Not a king. Not even a prince. Page of the Underworld. A pretty page boy, suited only for getting on his knees and wrapping his pretty lips—"

Ricky grabbed Beau, again by the throat. There was no rage in it. No surprise. Just cold resolve. His fingers wrapped around Beau's throat, and he concentrated on holding on to him, willing him to stay where he was, not to disappear. And he did. Beau hung there, suspended by the throat, eyes rolling. Then whatever held him broke, and he flashed away, gasping and growling like a wounded animal.

Beau railed at Ricky, his insults tinged with fear now, coming fast and hard. The women cooed and flattered him, whispering in his ears, stroking him, fingers everywhere.

Distracting me. Whatever works. Insults or fawning. Threats or come-ons. Distracting me from finding Liv. From ...

He tensed and looked around.

Distracting me from figuring out what the hell is going on. From realizing she's not gone—I am.

He looked around the clearing. He couldn't tell whether it was where they'd fallen asleep. When he'd caught Liv, he'd been so intent on claiming his reward that they could have been in an ice-cold stream and he wouldn't have noticed. Not before. Certainly not during. And even afterward, when he'd collapsed beside her, thinking of nothing but her and them, and how good it felt being with her.

He hadn't even taken a look around before dropping into sleep. But one thing was certain: when he'd caught her, he'd still been dressed. In his jeans, at least, the jacket and shirt coming off as he'd gotten close, not wanting to waste a second once he had her. But his jeans and boxers should be here. And they were not. Which meant he hadn't woken up to find her gone. He'd sleepwalked away from her, lost in his dream.

Lured away.

"Liv!" he shouted, as loud as he could. "Olivia!"

"Calling for your girlfriend's help? That's very sweet in a modern-guy kind of way. Not exactly manly, though."

"Liv! Stay where you are."

"Oh, you were warning her. My mistake. If you honestly think she won't come to your rescue—"

Ricky pounced. He caught Beau around the neck again and concentrated as he squeezed. His fingers dug in, blood flecking him as Beau coughed and sputtered.

Can I choke him? Do they breathe?

It was only a momentary thought, but the doubt was enough to break whatever mental hold he had. Beau vanished. This time, he reappeared behind Ricky, leaping on his back. Teeth dug into Ricky's neck. Ricky bit off his howl mid-note and flipped Beau. Blood sprayed. *His* blood. Streaming down his neck.

Don't worry about that.

Beau sprang at him. Ricky slammed him in the gut, but it seemed to have no more effect than if he'd hit him in the ribs, and he jumped on Ricky again. Ricky caught him by the hair and wrenched him off. He was throwing him down when Liv came at a run, dressed only in her shirt, half on and unbuttoned. She skidded to a stop as she saw Beau. Her hand flew out and light seemed to flash from it. It was the switchblade, moonlight striking the blade as it flicked out.

She ran at Beau. He disappeared.

"Not human," Ricky said, clamping a hand to the side of his neck.

"So I see." Her eyes widened when she saw the blood. "You're—"

"Watch—!"

He didn't have time to say more. She was already spinning.

Beau rushed her and Ricky was too far away. Liv's hand swung back. The blade flashed as she drove it into Beau's gut. Then Ricky was on him, Beau screaming that nightmare scream as he fell, the blade stuck in his gut. Ricky grabbed the handle and wrenched it up, blood spraying, Beau screaming. Around them, the forest seemed to erupt. Dark shapes poured out, shadowy wraiths, flying at them, shrieking.

Ricky knocked Liv down and fell overtop her. The things struck him, battered him, claws ripping into his back. He tried to grab one, but his fingers passed through it.

Then hooves thundered. A dozen hooves, pounding the dirt, coming so fast the horses were almost upon them as soon as Ricky heard the sound. Then the forest erupted from the other side, huge black dogs barreling out of the trees, charging at the wraiths as the creatures screamed in terror and the hounds snarled. There was one moment of sheer deafening sound, driving into Ricky's skull, the shrieks and the growls crescendoing and then . . .

Silence. So sudden it was almost as disorienting. He squeezed his eyes shut until he felt a hand against his neck, Liv wriggling out from under him.

He opened his eyes as she pressed her shirt hard to the wound.

"I'm okay," he said. "If he hit anything vital, I'd have bled out by now."

"Comforting."

She scowled, but she swung the look away and directed it at the figure climbing off a horse. It was not the man he'd seen in his dream. While he wore a similar cloak and rode a similar horse, this man was older, maybe his father's age, similar in size and even in looks. As Ricky watched him, he heard his grand-mother's stories about the Wild Hunt, and he had no doubt what he was seeing, no more than he'd doubted Beau was not human.

Liv strode toward the man. "What the hell is that?" She pointed at Beau, who lay on the grass, not moving.

I've killed a man.

No, not a man. Not really.

Does it matter?

It didn't, but when Ricky looked at Beau's corpse, only a pang of intellectual horror darted through him. He'd done what he'd had to. Beau attacked him, attacked Liv, and there was no doubt his intentions had been lethal. The response had to be equally strong.

"*Dökkálfar,*" the man said.

Ricky looked up sharply, then realized he was answering Liv's question about Beau.

"Which is . . . ?" she said.

"A dark elf."

"Elf?"

"Not from the North Pole." The man's lips tweaked in a smile. "Before you ask."

"I was thinking Middle Earth, but both come from the same place. Norse, Germanic . . ." She looked at Beau. "I'm guessing he does, too?"

"Originally. Another immigrant, from centuries past."

"And those other creatures?"

"*Disir.* Also known as wights. Norse as well. They're usually protective spirits, guarding land or water. Here, being dispos-sessed, they often protect a being, such as a dark elf."

"Fascinating." Liv's tone ought to have warned the man, but he only nodded, pleased at her attentiveness. She stepped in front of him. "That elf tried to kill Ricky. It lured him away from me and tried to *kill* him."

"Yes, it does seem—"

"*Does seem?* You never gave me a word of warning. Never told me he could be a target. Never. Said. One. Word."

Liv shook with fury, her voice barely above a whisper. She stood there, wearing only the open shirt, the necklace glittering in the moonlight, furious and fearless and magnificent, and the man smiled, pleased again. Ricky strode to them, his hackles rising. The man nodded, and Ricky had no idea what that nod meant, but he relaxed.

The man took off his cloak and held it out to Liv.

"No, thank you," she said. "If you're offended, turn around. I don't usually wander around the forest naked, but then I'm not usually ambushed and forced to fight for my life quite so soon after waking."

"You weren't in danger." He glanced at Ricky. "Their target was clear, and I apologize for that. If I'd thought there was a serious risk that anything would attack—"

"Serious risk?" Liv said. "How about *any* risk? Better yet, how about admitting why there would *be* a risk? And, yes, I know why. No thanks to you. I had to figure it out for myself."

The man tilted his head, his gaze meeting hers. "Is that not the best way? The way you'd prefer? Because it seems to me—"

"I should have been told." She clasped Ricky's hand. "*We* should have been told."

The man looked at Ricky. "So you also know . . ."

"Not yet," Liv said. "I was working up to it. There's a weekly limit of weird shit you can dump on anyone, and explaining you guys and the fae was quite enough to start."

"All right, then." He turned to Ricky. "You—"

"Uh-uh." Liv's hand tightened on his. "You don't get to do

that. You don't have the right. I'll explain—in private. You'll stay here until I'm done."

The man's eyes wrinkled, amused. "Will I?"

"Yes."

As they turned to go, the man said, "Wait. You'll need this." He held out his hand to Liv. She took whatever was in it and he said, "For him. He should have it."

"He should have always had it," Liv said.

The man nodded. "Yes. But he will now, and you shouldn't be so careless with yours. If you'd had it on you, you wouldn't have needed our help."

Liv said nothing, and they headed back to where they'd left their clothing.

CHAPTER FIFTY

As furious as I was with the Cŵn Annwn, they were just a convenient target. Patrick had talked about outside fae and other creatures that would have a stake in this power play between the local Tylwyth Teg and Cŵn Annwn. I should have extrapolated that to mean Ricky could be targeted. I hadn't.

Now I had to tell him what he was. I cleaned his neck wound as I did. Was I purposely keeping busy? Avoiding looking him in the face while I explained that he had Cŵn Annwn blood and I'd kept that from him? Yes. But as soon as I said it, he tugged me in front of him.

"So I'm descended from them?" he said. "The Wild Hunt?"

I nodded.

"Well . . ." He paused, looking pensive. "I suppose that explains a few things. The motorcycles, for one. Substitute horses. The thrill of the ride. And earlier."

"Earlier?"

His eyes glinted. "The thrill of the chase."

I laughed.

He caught me in an embrace, squeezing hard and whispering

in my ear, "I don't blame you for not telling me. You're right. There's a weekly limit of weird shit anyone can take."

"Have you passed yours?"

"Not yet, but I have a feeling there's more to come." He settled me on his lap. "Want to tell me who Arawn is?"

I stiffened.

"You do know, then. Can I ask? Or have you reached your weekly limit of weird shit you care to explain?"

I exhaled. "It's a long story."

"I'd like to hear it."

I nodded and told him everything. About Matilda and Gwynn and Arawn. Then about the three of us—the roles we played in that old drama.

When I finished, he said, "Huh." Then, "Well, that explains even more."

"Like why you stick with a girl who causes you so much trouble?"

He said nothing, just sat there and looked at me until I squirmed and said, "Sorry."

Ricky shifted closer, our legs brushing. "Like you said, this isn't reincarnation. We aren't them. Thank God for that, because the guys both sound like self-centered pricks." He paused. "Does Gabriel know?"

I choked out a laugh. "The phrase 'self-centered prick' prompted that question?"

"Not entirely. But I don't know what's tougher to swallow—me as King of the Underworld or Gabriel as King of the Fairies."

I laughed, then sobered and looked at him. "I've told him the story. His role? No. I . . . I suppose I should. I'm just . . ." I took a deep breath. "My gut tells me he won't handle it nearly as well as you did."

"Because he's playing the role of the guy who won you?

Betrayed his best friend? Lied, lied, and lied some more until the woman he loved died horribly, because he couldn't stand to share her—even in friendship—with another guy?"

"All of the above."

Ricky went quiet. After a minute, he said, "I'd like to say you're wrong, and he can handle it. You and I both know how he is, though. My advice? Don't tell him now, but if there's any chance he'll find out, you need to get the jump on that. I wouldn't have cared who told me. Gabriel will—especially if I already know. I don't want to cause trouble. I know how much he means to you."

"I—"

"I know he does, and now I understand why, and that doesn't change anything, because I always knew not to interfere, that the worst thing I could do would be to come between you two. You're with me. That's all that matters. Gwynn and Arawn might have claimed they were best friends, that they both loved Matilda, but they didn't seem to give a shit about her or about each other. I'm not that guy. I'm never going to be that guy. Gabriel is my friend. But even more, he's *your* friend. *More* your friend than mine. I will not interfere with that. Ever."

I kissed him. As I did, I pulled something from my pocket and pressed it into his hand. "For you."

He looked down at the boar's tusk.

"It's not mine," I said. "That's for you from what's-his-name."

"They don't have names?"

"I haven't asked. That would imply that I care."

He laughed. "Okay. So this is what I'm supposed to keep on me to avoid elves and wights?"

"Apparently, though he wasn't clear on that when he gave me mine. They aren't clear on anything."

He lifted the tusk and turned it over in his fingers. Then he stopped. "If this is from them, then these symbols . . ." He touched the moon. "That's the Wild Hunt. The night and the moon."

I nodded.

"Then that's you." He pointed at the intertwined moon and sun. "Sun for the fae, moon for the Hunt. You're both. Blood from both. And the moon is mine." He touched my necklace. "That's why you hesitated when I gave it to you."

"Guilt," I said. "You sensed what you are, and I wasn't telling you. I meant to—"

He kissed me to silence. "I'm not accusing you of anything, Liv. I'm just making connections. You knew what this was"— he pointed to the moon on the tusk—"when you said you wanted it for your tattoo. You knew what it symbolized. Me. The Hunt. Arawn. All of it—how it fits together, what it means."

"I still want to get it, if that's okay with you."

He paused and I held my breath.

"I'm not sure how to answer that," he said. "If I'm honest, and I say yes, then you'll feel obligated to go through with it. Which I *don't* want. So I'll just say that the fact you considered putting that on your body, permanently, is enough. It means enough."

When we returned, the Cŵn Annwn had disposed of Beau. The Huntsman assured us that no one from the clubhouse would have heard the commotion.

I told the Huntsman what I'd learned about my parents and their crimes, finishing with, "Meaning they did it because someone promised them the cure for me."

"And delivered."

"So it was you. Or your kind."

"Yes."

I'd expected a denial, and when I didn't get one, my questions dried up.

Ricky took over. "You made the deal with the Larsens?"

"Yes."

"You specifically?"

"Yes."

"You cured Liv?"

"I orchestrated the events that led to her cure. I cannot heal or I'd fix that bite on your neck. I'd strongly suggest washing it well, with antiseptic. I'm not well versed in the exact nature of elf-to-human transformations, but I wouldn't discount the possibility of bacterial transfer."

"I know how to treat a fight bite."

He smiled at Ricky. "I'm sure you do."

"But you made the deal. You instructed her parents to kill six people."

"Yes."

"And you didn't see fit to tell Liv this? Before she started investigating?"

"Why? It would have stopped her. It was the answer she wanted before she met them: proof they were the murderers that society thought they were, and they deserved to spend their lives in jail, so she could forget them." He turned to me. "That is what you wanted, wasn't it? A tidy answer? Black and white?"

I saw no point in admitting it.

"But now it's not so black and white," he said.

"Because they murdered six people for me?" I shook my head. "I was *two*. I didn't ask for spina bifida. I didn't bring it on myself. In fact, if I'm right, you guys 'did' it to me—your blood. A failure of completion."

"Fae."

"What?"

"The condition is caused by fae blood."

"You *are* fae. You might go by another name, but that's what you are."

He pursed his lips, as if ready to pursue it. Instead, he said, "You are not to blame. Nor your parents. However, we could not fix this for them. We could not take the lives ourselves or we would have. For you. To make you whole. To protect Mallt-y-Nos and leave her in a good, loving family. But that could not be."

"So you offered a way to fix it, if they murdered six innocent—"

"Do you know what we do, Olivia? The Cŵn Annwn? Our purpose?"

"I know versions of the story."

"And you?" he asked Ricky.

"Same."

"Then tell me."

Ricky checked with me, but when I nodded, he proceeded. "In some, you're just hunting and anyone who sees you dies later. In others, you come to fetch the living and take them to the underworld. Sometimes, you're randomly hunting people whose time is up. In other versions, you target the wicked."

"Which is correct?"

Ricky rocked back, shrugging. "I have no—"

"In your gut, which is correct?"

"I've always liked the last, but that's only because it makes the best story. Killing randomly is more frightening as a concept, but killing for cause is more interesting."

"It's also the version that makes sense. That suggests a purpose. A reason for the Hunt."

"That's it, then?" I said. "You're executioners?"

"Not quite the word I'd—"

"Vigilantes, then."

"We exact justice where the human world cannot. Our purview is crimes against those from the Old World. All manner of fae. Them and their descendants."

"What does this have to do with my parents?"

"What indeed."

I looked up at him. "You aren't going to tell me, are you?"

"No, I am not, because as much as you complain about not getting answers, you don't trust any we give. You need to find them for yourself. I will say only that your parents are not as guilty as you fear. Nor as innocent as you hope. Do you want a hint? To start you on your way?"

"Will it cost me?"

He smiled. "I rest my case. You are too suspicious. It will serve you well."

"Uh-huh."

"Here's the hint, freely given. Focus less on your parents. Look at the victims. Connect the first pair to the second, and keep an open mind. The connection will not be what you expect. Forget the third for now. Focus on the first two pairs."

"More," Ricky said.

The Huntsman looked at him.

"She needs more," Ricky said.

"She needs to find answers for herself—"

"Agreed. *We* need to find answers for *ourselves*. But Liv needs a concrete place to start. Gabriel has been charged with murder, which puts us on a tighter timetable."

A twist of the man's lips. "I'm not particularly concerned with Gabriel Walsh."

"Because you were involved with that, too?" I said. "Getting Gabriel framed for James's murder?"

He frowned. "What would I have to do with that?"

"Someone visited Pamela and told her Gabriel did it. I think it was you."

"I haven't seen your mother in many years. Nor have any of the Cŵn Annwn. We have helped ease her situation, but only from a distance. We had nothing to do with either James Morgan's murder or Gabriel Walsh being implicated."

"But I do," Ricky said. "Because I'm the one who attacked James Morgan and beat the shit out of him."

"You didn't kill—"

"I'm also Gabriel's alibi. At the time, I was with him getting legal advice, which he can't admit without the police thinking it's awfully suspicious I was asking for legal advice the night my girlfriend's stalker ex was murdered. If there's any chance he'll be convicted, I'll turn *myself* in. Does *that* concern you?"

"You should not involve yourself—"

"Yeah, actually, I'm pretty sure I should. It may not be in your best interests, but I get the feeling it's in mine—in *ours*. We'll stick together. Me, Liv, and Gabriel. Arawn, Matilda, and Gwynn. You can deal with that later. What I want now is a starting point. Don't tell us what the connection is. You're right—we won't trust you. But where do we look first?"

"Marty Tyson's girlfriend."

"The second pair of victims. Tyson and his girl— Wait, no. It was his wife, wasn't it?" Ricky glanced at me. "Tyson was killed with his wife."

I nodded.

"But he had a girlfriend?" Ricky said.

"Yes," the Huntsman replied. "The police saw no reason to make that public knowledge, as it did not affect the case and would only embarrass the families of the victims. It's in a file somewhere."

"All right, then," Ricky said. "We have our breadcrumbs."

We turned to leave. The Huntsman made a noise, getting our attention. When we looked back, his gaze was on Ricky.

"Do you have questions?" he asked. "About what else you've discovered tonight? What you are?"

"That depends. Is there anything that'll get me into unexpected trouble? Sudden appearance of strange powers, maybe?"

A faint smile. "It doesn't work like that."

"So, nothing I *need* to know, then?"

"No, but I'm sure you're curious—"

"Nope. I'm good." Ricky put his arm around my waist and led me away.

CHAPTER FIFTY-ONE

When we left the Huntsman, I texted Gabriel a quick *You still up?*, which got an immediate *Of course*. I called and told him we had information and a lead. Gabriel didn't even let me finish that sentence before naming a coffee shop halfway between his place and the clubhouse.

The coffee shop was surprisingly funky—surprising in that Gabriel knew of it. At one in the morning, most patrons were sitting alone, headphones on, chugging coffee, catching their second wind as they chased some deadline or other. Gabriel had taken a table and comfy chairs in a corner nook.

Three cups waited on the table. Gabriel's coffee, of course. Black. A mocha for me, with slowly melting whipped cream. Black coffee for Ricky, too, with cream and sugar on the side. Apparently, buying him a coffee and knowing how he took it demonstrated the proper degree of consideration—fixing it for him would cross a line.

"Eventful evening?" Gabriel said as we sat down.

"I killed an elf," Ricky said.

"A *dökkálfar*," I said. "If I'm saying that right."

"Which is why I'm sticking with elf." He looked at Gabriel.

"It was self-defense. It attacked." He pointed to the bandage on his neck. "Elf bite."

"Vampire elf?" Gabriel said.

"There is no such thing as vampires." I turned to Ricky. "He keeps hoping for them, and he's always disappointed."

"I am not—" Gabriel began.

"Are too."

He opened his mouth to retort and settled for, "You're serious, then. About the . . . *dökkálfar?*"

"I wouldn't lie about elves," Ricky said.

"We were in the forest outside the clubhouse," I said. "We got separated. Ricky was attacked by a dark elf who'd been posing as a hanger-on in the club. There were also *disir.*"

"Wights," Ricky said.

"I like the foreign names. It makes these conversations mildly less ridiculous."

"We're still talking about being attacked by an elf."

"True."

"So I killed it," Ricky said. "Killed *him.* I shouldn't call him an it. Makes it sound better, less culpability, but yeah, it was still a guy, of some sort."

"Who tried to murder us," I said.

"True. Then the Cŵn Annwn showed up," Ricky said. "They've looked after the evidence. The remains, the knife. I'll get Liv a new one as soon as possible."

"You said this *dökkálfar* was passing as human? Is that a concern?"

"I doubt it," Ricky said. "There was an incident at the clubhouse earlier. No one will expect him back. The Huntsman said he'd take care of the rest."

"We should be fine," I said. "I don't think Illinois law covers elf-icide."

Ricky found a smile for me. I knew it bothered him more than he let on. I'd pointed out earlier that I'd been the one who put the knife in Beau, but we both know that wasn't what killed him.

"So why exactly did this *dökkálfar* attack *you*?" Gabriel asked.

"Taking out Liv's bodyguard." Ricky lied as smoothly as Gabriel, then redirected the flow. "I found out about myself, too. My heritage. I'm up to speed on all counts."

Gabriel glanced at me.

"I told him the Matilda connection, too," I said. "He needed to know why they all want me. Which leads back to the original purpose for this meeting. I know who offered my parents the deal, but that doesn't tie things up as neatly as we might have hoped."

As we talked, I e-mailed Detective Pemberton to see if he'd give me the name of Marty's girlfriend. I gave him a story adjacent to the truth—that we had a good lead on someone who said she'd been involved.

Even without the name, Gabriel wanted to start digging, and I was fine with that. There's no way I could have slept. Ricky had a presentation in the morning, so he took off.

Gabriel drove and we were halfway across the city before he said, "About what the Huntsman said . . . Your parents . . ."

"Hmm?" I said.

He fell silent, shaking his head.

I looked over. "I know you said it doesn't matter if they're guilty or innocent, you'll still defend Pamela. This doesn't change anything, then? Knowing she's guilty?"

He drove another block, streetlights flickering through the car. "Under the circumstances, you might prefer I dropped the case. I would consider it if you did. But . . ." He rubbed his thumb on the steering wheel. "I don't know what my decision would be."

"Okay," I said. "Thanks for saying you'd consider it. And thanks for being honest."

We spent the next few hours at the office combing through the first two pairs of murders again, hunting for a connection and finding none. When my yawning got too loud, Gabriel promised we'd leave soon, and suggested I rest in the chaise longue in the meantime. I did . . . and woke four hours later to find him still in his office chair, laptop shoved aside, arms folded on a stack of papers, his head on them. Sound asleep. He looked adorable. I considered taking a cell phone picture for future blackmail. I may even have done it, but I'll admit nothing.

I went out and returned a half hour later. Gabriel woke when I placed a steaming coffee beside his head. He groaned as he opened his eyes. Groaned louder, pairing it with a wince, when he lifted his head.

"Yep, that's going to hurt," I said. "You should have taken the longue."

"It was occupied." He winced again as he pushed himself into a relatively upright position. "Even if it wasn't, I don't fit on it."

Which was true. It looked as if it had never been used. He was too tall to sleep on it, but I'd bet he'd never even sat there. So why buy it? Another Gabriel mystery.

"Coffee," I said, pushing it toward him. "Extra large."

"Thank you."

"And this." I fished a vial of Tylenol from my bag. "For your neck. But don't take it until you've eaten. Luckily, food is also provided." I set down a box of four still-warm muffins. "Blueberry, banana nut, lemon poppyseed, and double chocolate. Your pick."

He took the banana nut and set the double chocolate down by my coffee cup. I smiled. "Thank you."

He leaned back with the muffin and coffee as I settled into

the other chair. He eyed the painkillers but didn't open them. I reached over, popped the lid, and shook out two.

"Your neck is hurting from sleeping like that. It's only going to get worse. We may have a full day ahead. Take."

He did.

"Thank you," I said. "Now, when you're feeling better, Detective Pemberton got back to me with a name."

He looked up so fast he winced, pulling his neck again.

"Relax," I said. "Let the meds kick in. It can wait."

"You realize, as your employer, I legally have access to your e-mail."

"I didn't use my office one." I smiled and let him simmer for a minute, just for fun. Then I said, "Imogen Seale," and he was on his laptop in five seconds flat.

I waited until he said, "All right. I have—" Then I passed over my notebook, with Imogen's current address and a page of notes.

"Early bird gets the scoop," I said. "Eat, drink, let those pain meds do their work, and we'll get out of here."

We were heading out as Lydia arrived. I left the two remaining muffins on her desk. She said, "Good morning," and refrained from comment on the early hour or the fact I wore an oversized Iron Maiden concert shirt, grabbed from the Saints clubhouse because mine had been stained with blood.

"It's too early to buy a shirt, isn't it?" I said to Gabriel as we walked down the front steps.

"At this hour, if you hope for business wear, yes. There are a few options, though. Nothing fashionable, but perhaps a little less . . ."

"Like I slept with an aging roadie, and he ripped my shirt off?"

A quirk of a smile. "Yes."

"Lead on, then. I won't ask how you know where to buy clean clothes at eight in the morning."

CHAPTER FIFTY-TWO

T he shirt came from a diner, a tee that advertised their business. Whch was better than what the other one seemed to "advertise."

By ten, we were at Imogen's house. Or the house where she lived, which actually belonged to her mother. At twenty-four, *I'd* felt too old to still live at home. Imogen was forty-three.

When we arrived, I was certain we'd made a mistake. We were looking for a house. This was a street of walk-ups and apartments. And, as it turned out, one house, wedged between two towering buildings, like a recalcitrant dwarf squatting between giants, refusing to give ground. Which is, I suspect, exactly what happened. Imogen's family had refused to sell, so they were left there, in the shade of those apartments, with only a house and a strip of grass.

Gabriel knocked. When a stooped, elderly woman answered, he still did the "foot in the doorjamb" trick. Rightly, as it turned out. She took one look at me and tried to slam the door.

"Get your damned foot out of there," she said. "Or I swear I'll crush it—" She yanked feebly on the door, her face reddening. Then she peered up at Gabriel. "I'll call the police."

"We'd like to speak to Imogen Seale. She's your daughter, I presume?"

"Get the hell off my property."

"We believe Ms. Seale has information vital to a case—"

"What case? Setting two psychos loose?"

She turned on me, her wizened face threatening to fold into its own creases. Our research said she was in her early seventies, but she looked more like ninety, her wrinkled skin yellowed by tobacco, the stink of the cigarettes blasting on her breath.

"I don't know why you're here to see my girl, but you're not going to. She's barely been out of her room since you turned up in the news, reminding her of all that mess. Do you know how long it took to get her right again? After what you people did?"

"You people?" I said.

"Your parents, murdering the man she loved. After that, she wasn't right for years. *Years.* And now you pop up in the news, upsetting her again. The apple doesn't fall far from the tree, does it?"

I could have pointed out the logical inconsistencies in that. Sometimes, though, it's clear you aren't dealing with a logical person. Or even a particularly bright one. So I let her rant and nudged Gabriel to silence when he seemed ready to jump in.

"She can speak to Mr. Walsh alone, then," I said when she paused for breath.

"How's that supposed to help? It still dredges up . . ." She continued talking.

I counted to three, then cut in with, "Gabriel? I'm going to let you handle this. I don't want to cause trouble. I'll wait in the car."

As soon as I started down the stoop steps, he eased over, blocking Mrs. Seale's view of me before resuming his requests to speak to Imogen.

I made certain the old woman's attention was on Gabriel.

Then I scooted between the house and a neighboring apartment. Ahead, a shadow scurried behind that next-door building. Imogen, making her escape. I jogged along the wall until I could peek around it.

A middle-aged, painfully thin woman with badly bleached hair stood midway between the apartment and the adjacent parking garage. Her gaze darted about, dark eyes too big for her gaunt face. She reminded me of a bird. Not a raven or an owl, but an undernourished sparrow that's had one too many run-ins with the big guys. She was breathing hard, fluttering in place as she watched for trouble.

I evaluated my position. Five feet from a window in the Seale house. Ten from the back door. In other words, too close to where I could be spotted by a pissed-off momma bird. But Imogen just stood there, catching her breath after the short dash and watching her house, as if expecting us to come after her.

I picked up a fist-sized rock and sent it rolling her way. Hardly a sign of descending enemies, but Imogen was skittish enough to flee. I followed. Again she didn't go far, stopping in the mouth of the parking garage.

I texted instructions to Gabriel. Then I settled in to wait. A few times Imogen peeked from her shadowy spot, as if contemplating a return to the nest, only to decide it was too soon.

When I got a text from Gabriel, I set out. I made it halfway to the garage before Imogen did one of her peek-checks. She saw me and retreated fast. I heard a shriek, and I burst into the garage as she was wheeling to run back out, a large shadow blocking her other escape options.

I lifted my hands. "We just want to speak to you."

"I don't have anything to say." Her voice was girlish. Everything about her was, now that I closed in and got a better look. A pink blouse, white jeans, bare feet with hot-pink nails. She even had pink barrettes in her hair. Cute on a seventeen-year-old. Sad at forty-three.

"Your mother says you're having a rough time," I said. "With me popping up in the news. Bringing back memories, is it?"

Her sharp chin bobbed.

"Memories or guilt?" I asked.

"Wh-what?" Then she glanced quickly at Gabriel, her look pleading. A woman accustomed to turning to men. When Gabriel only stood there, silent and impassive, she inched toward him and directed her answer his way. "I don't have anything to feel guilty for," she said.

"No?" I stepped toward her. "That's not what I've heard."

She flinched.

I continued. "Marty knew the first victims: Amanda and Ken. Their connection is very intriguing. One that would be of great interest to others. The police, the press, my parents . . ."

She dove to the side. I had no idea where she thought she was going. We were in an enclosed parking garage. Cars lined either side of the narrow lane. One exit was behind me, another behind Gabriel. But she chose to race sideways, smacking into the rear bumper of a pickup. Then she dropped and scuttled under it.

I looked at Gabriel. He shook his head and took up position on the other side of the truck. It didn't seem as if she planned to escape that way—or any way at all. She was just hiding.

"All right," I said. "I take it that means you'd rather speak to the police."

"I'm not talking to anyone," her breathy voice whispered.

"I don't think you'll have much choice in that. It's a murder investigation. You did hear that it's reopened, didn't you? I proved my parents didn't kill Jan Gunderson and Peter Evans. All the murders are being reexamined. As soon as I tell the police about that very interesting link I found—"

"It was her fault."

I paused. "Amanda's?"

"No, Lisa. Marty's bitch wife. It was her fault. Her idea."

I glanced at Gabriel. He was thinking fast, his gaze gone distant, but no answer seemed to be forthcoming quickly enough.

"Is that what Marty told you?" I said.

"It's the truth. He always told me the truth. She tricked him into marrying her, and then she threatened to hurt him if he left. She tricked him into the other thing, too, and threatened him if he told anyone."

"He was ex-military and twice her size."

"That doesn't matter. She knew stuff—satanic stuff. She was evil."

Gabriel's eyes snapped wide, as close to a genuine *Holy shit* look as he could manage. Luckily, being under the truck, Imogen couldn't see us staring dumbfounded at each other.

In fishing for a connection, I'd been throwing my hook wide and blind, having no idea what could connect the two couples. *This* hadn't occurred to me.

"That's why they did it," I said. "Witchcraft."

"Satanism," Imogen said. "It's not the same thing." A two-second pause. Then, belatedly, "I mean, that's what the bitch was into. I don't know what you mean about *why they did it*. Did what? I never said anything."

"Um, yes, you said she made him do it. We both know what we're talking about, Imogen."

"I never said—"

"Marty and Lisa killed Amanda Mays and Ken Perkins."

Another two seconds, during which I heard her breathing. Then a weak, "What? You're crazy. I never said that."

"You didn't need to," I said, and walked away.

CHAPTER FIFTY-THREE

W̶as it possible that the Tysons had killed the first two victims? While my gut embraced it, my brain threw up a stop sign. It was like saying . . . well, it was like saying Cainsville had been settled by fairies. Seemingly preposterous.

"I don't know," Gabriel said as we slid into his car. I hadn't asked a question. I didn't have to. "We need to break it down."

He started the car. When I said nothing by the first turn, he glanced at me and jerked his chin. I knew what he meant. Work this out aloud for him.

"There are a bunch of questions we'd need answered before we could seriously consider it," I said. "Questions that we can't get answers to, because the suspects are dead. Long dead. Where were Lisa and Marty on the night of the Mays and Perkins murders? Do they have an alibi? Any chance we can put them in the vicinity? Any chance of finding the murder weapon? That's all gone, washed away by time. They were never suspects, so there's no way to answer those questions now."

A quick look. I understood that one, too. *Don't dwell on what we can't answer.*

"The big connection, then, is the so-called satanism," I said as I took out my notebook and started writing. "We might be able to dig up something. Getting details from Imogen would help. Once we've come up with a list of questions for her, we can use her mother to our advantage. The woman doesn't want anyone messing with her baby. We can convince her that there's no way to avoid that, and compared to the police, we're the lesser evil. Obviously, the police would still speak to her after we made our case, but I don't think Imogen or her momma are bright enough to realize that."

"Agreed." Gabriel paused. "We can convince her to talk. The fact she withheld evidence and watched your parents be convicted of the murders would be important leverage."

"Blackmail."

"*Persuasion.* With an implied penalty for failure to be persuaded."

"I'll let you handle that," I said. "Back to the witchcraft or whatever. That could explain why we never connected the ritual to anything else. There are elements of Druidism, but nothing that more strongly suggested an actual fae influence. If it was the Tysons who devised the ritual, it would be exactly what your experts concluded: a mishmash of elements taken from God-knows-where. If the Tysons killed the first victims, then they established the pattern, meaning the pattern itself would be meaningless. The ritual elements. The method. The locations. Even the day of the week." I stopped writing. "But that *was* significant. It was my parents' date night."

"I would suspect Friday is a popular date night. Meaning a good time for the Tysons to find a couple."

I nodded and made a note of that. "Wait—what about the eyewitness who ID'd my parents as the people fleeing the first crime scene? She picked them out of a lineup, right?"

"Yes, but if I recall correctly, the Tysons were roughly the same age, body type, and coloring. They didn't resemble one another in any significant way, but if the witness spotted them from a distance, it would be close enough, particularly if the lineup was skewed. I'll look into that further."

"If the Tysons killed Mays and Perkins, then my parents were following their pattern. Trying to hide the crime by emulating the victims' own crimes. Which would throw a serious wrench into any investigation."

"It would have been an even bigger wrench if there had been any forensic evidence with the first couple. Fingerprints. DNA. I could have gotten your parents off with that. It's reasonable doubt."

"Just their bad luck, then, that the Tysons were good. Or lucky. Which may also explain why the Cŵn Annwn took an interest. If they needed my parents to commit murders and their purview is killing killers, the Tysons would have been an ideal case. They left no clues, so they stood little chance of being caught and convicted." I paused, thinking it through. "Chandler and Evans copycatted their murders with Jan and Pete— after my parents copied the Tysons. So the chances that someone else murdered the third pair, in yet another act of copying . . ."

". . . is infinitesimally small." He drove another half block before saying, "Still, does this help?"

"Does it make it easier, you mean?" I closed the notebook, my forefinger still marking the page. "Little steps, you know? Along a continuum. At one end, my parents are sadistic monsters who deserve to rot in jail. At the other, they're innocent victims of a cruel miscarriage of justice. Finding out that they didn't kill Jan and Peter took them a step away from the monster end. Learning they killed only four people, who were likely murderers themselves? Short of innocence, it's the best I could have hoped for. The Huntsman was right—I wanted simple. Black or white. This isn't anywhere *near* either."

"No, it isn't."

I flipped open the notebook. "Still, it's only a theory. As you've told me many times, I can't get too attached to it. We have work to do."

"True. But . . ." He idled at the light. "It's a solid theory. Very solid. I think you should prepare yourself to accept that this is the answer. Of all the ones you could find, there's only one better," he said. "And we knew innocence was unlikely. This is good."

"I know."

"If I can prove the Tysons killed the first victims, it will throw the case wide open. With that, I should be able to set your parents free." He met my gaze. "Is that what you want?"

"It is."

We needed answers, and the quickest way to get them was to go straight to the source: my parents. Yes, that's what they were to me. My parents. They had been for a while, even if I hadn't realized the shift. That didn't change what I felt for my adoptive parents. They were still Mum and Dad. But those were names for a child, and I was no longer a child. The Larsens were Todd and Pamela. My father and my mother.

My first choice was Todd. It had been when I was a child, whether I'd skinned my knee or drawn a picture—he was the one I went to. Gabriel called the prison and bullied some poor desk clerk, but Todd was still off limits. That left Pamela. Which meant this would be tougher.

I asked Gabriel to stay out this time. He agreed without hesitation. I needed to win her confidence, and I wouldn't do that with Gabriel in tow.

In the past, when I've wanted something from Pamela—which is, admittedly, every time I've visited—I've gotten straight down to business. Stick before carrot. *Be straight with me and then we can be mother and daughter for a while.* Now I reversed the process. I talked about my life. I had a new job as a research assistant. A crappy but comfortable apartment. A cat. And a boyfriend. I was most honest about Ricky, because that's where I could light up, let her see how happy I was, and even if "biker MBA student" wasn't her idea of son-in-law material, she focused on the student part of that, proof that the biker half was a young man trapped in his family business, working his way out.

In my openness, I manipulated her. I accept responsibility for that.

"I know about the spina bifida," I said finally.

She jerked back as if I'd slapped her, and I wish I could say I felt guilty. But I only leaned across the table and lowered my voice. "I know about the deal with the Cŵn Annwn, and if you deny it, I'm going to walk out."

She went very still.

"I need to ask something I *don't* know. Something I only suspect. Please listen until I'm done, okay? I know this isn't easy for you." I locked gazes with her. "But it's not easy for me, either."

She pressed her lips together, as if to ensure she wouldn't interrupt.

"I think you didn't kill Amanda Mays and Ken Perkins. I think it was the Tysons. The Cŵn Annwn needed lives as part of the deal they offered you. They chose the Tysons. They also chose Stacey Pasolini and Eddie Hilton—I don't know why, but I'm presuming it was a similar reason. The Cŵn Annwn could justify their deaths, and so *you* could justify their deaths. Am I correct in those assumptions?"

She said nothing. I inched forward, close enough to earn the attention of a guard before I eased back.

"I know you aren't innocent. The fact I'm not in a wheelchair proves that. So either you stopped killers, or you murdered innocents. Which would you have me believe?"

I could see the struggle in her eyes, the muscles in her cheeks twitching. I pushed my chair back.

"Then I'll speak to my father."

She shot up so fast I jumped. So did the guard. Pamela froze. Then she sank back into her chair. After a deep breath, she reached out, her hand going over mine.

"Have you seen him?" she asked.

"Yes, but he doesn't have anything to do with what I discovered. I hit the medical lead when I went searching for my records. Things kept piling up until I made the connection. Someone from the Tylwyth Teg confirmed that spina bifida is a common condition among those with their blood. Someone from the Cŵn Annwn confirmed the deal they made, and then they set me on the Tysons' trail. My father had nothing to do with any of that."

A lie, but I could tell I pulled it off.

"He would admit to it. He wants—" She looked up. "He *needs* you to believe in him, Eden. He needs you to believe he's not a killer. At heart, he isn't. He's just a man who would have done anything to help his little girl. Those two things collided— the gentle man and the devoted father—and one had to give. It was never going to be the father. Never."

And there it was. The confession. I sat there, processing it, accepting it. That came more easily than I might have expected. There'd been such a slow build to this moment, so many possible answers, so many times I'd been certain the answer would be "my parents are sociopaths." Gabriel was right—this was a good answer. Imperfect but acceptable.

"Okay," I said. "I understand why you did it—"

I was going to say I understood even if I didn't agree, but as soon as I said "you did it," she flinched, and I stopped.

"It *was* both of you," I said slowly. "Wasn't it?"

A shot in the dark. But when I took it, the look on her face, guilt and more, so much more . . .

"It was him," I whispered. "All him."

Her head snapped up. "No. Never. It was a joint decision and a joint action. We both—"

"No, you didn't," I said. "He did. Only him."

"I . . ." Her mouth worked, panic filling her face as if she was trying to get the words out and couldn't. "I . . ."

"Why are you in prison, then?" I said. "If it was my father, and only my father—"

"I couldn't do it," she blurted. "My nerve failed and *I* failed. I failed you. I wasn't strong enough. He told me the deal, and I refused to consider it. So he did it without me knowing."

"But you were together on those nights."

"We . . . we didn't have a lot of money. We wanted a house for you, and it all went into that, so on our date nights we'd just go for walks. In the forest. Your father always liked the wilderness." Not surprising, given his bloodline. "We'd walk and then . . . we'd take some time alone." Uh-huh. Pretty sure I knew what that meant, but I sure as hell wasn't asking for confirmation. "Afterward, we'd fall asleep for a couple of hours, with his watch alarm set. All I remember from those nights is that I slept very well. I presume there was something in the wine. We never discussed it."

"But you went to jail. For something you didn't do."

Her eyes flashed. "For something I *should* have done. *We* should have done, together. The DNA evidence was mine, Eden. I'm presuming someone planted it there. Maybe the Cŵn Annwn—I never trusted them. Or maybe one of their enemies. After that, how could I claim innocence without turning him in? Turning *on* him? As long as we both proclaimed our innocence, there was a chance we'd both be freed. I was willing to take that chance. I still am, and I always will be."

CHAPTER FIFTY-FOUR

Y ou should celebrate," Gabriel said as he pulled out of the prison parking lot.

"Um . . ."

"When we first met, you were trying to reconcile yourself to the fact that your parents were cold-blooded serial killers. You know now that they are not. Your father killed four people, all of whom, I suspect, deserved it, and he did it out of love for you. Your mother is completely innocent. That's a long way to come, Olivia." He looked at me. "It is."

"I know, but . . ."

"Yes, perhaps 'celebration' is the wrong word. But you deserve an evening to appreciate what you've accomplished, and to relax. So that is what you're going to do. I insist. We're going to . . . not celebrate."

I managed a laugh.

"You know what I mean," he said. "We're taking the night off, and you're going to enjoy it."

"Yes, sir."

His fingers tapped the wheel. There'd been an electricity in the car, an excitement after I'd explained. I could be brutally prag-matic and say Gabriel was happy at learning his client really was innocent. He was also happy that resolving this would free us to investigate James's death and clear Gabriel's own name. But I'd like to think he was also happy for me, for *us*, having gone through all this together and finally finding an answer, the second-best possible solution.

He'd made his offer of a celebration in a surge of ebullience. Now, when my reaction wasn't what he'd hoped, that wave crashed and the energy seemed to suck back into him, like a black hole.

"That sounds good," I said. "Really good."

His hands relaxed on the wheel. "Does it?"

"A moment to lift our heads from the cesspool and recognize how far we've *both* come before we dive back in again."

A soft chuckle. "That doesn't exactly invoke the mood I was aiming for . . ."

"You know what I mean. Yes, I'd like a not-celebratory evening, please."

My phone buzzed, and he tensed. "Ricky?"

"Mmm. Hold on." I texted back. "He's just checking in."

He kept his gaze on the road. "If you would rather spend the evening . . ."

"He has homework to catch up on."

He drove two blocks in silence. Then, "I *would* understand if you wanted to spend the evening with Ricky. A lot has happened today, and he's . . . better with that sort of thing. We could do this another time. I mean that. I would understand."

"You're the one who had to put up with me through this whole mess. So you're the one who has to not-celebrate with me, too."

A flicker of a smile. "All right, then. We will do something special. Not dinner. Something different. Something fun." He paused, and I could smell smoke as his brain whirred, furiously

searching for a *fun* activity. The longer he struggled, the harder
I had to bite my cheek to keep from laughing.

"Can I make a suggestion?" I said. "Since it's my noncelebra-
tion?"

He exhaled in relief. "Yes. Please."

We went to the beach. I'd remembered being at Villa Tuscana
with Gabriel, before everything went wrong, how we'd walked
down the steps and I'd talked about sitting out by the lake with
a bottle of wine. That's what I wanted to do. Not there, of course.
But I wanted that feeling again.

We spent the afternoon in the office, working on James's
murder, so we wouldn't feel guilty about the evening off. Then
we bought wine and drove up to my spot. It was a wild place,
all driftwood and long grass and thin stretches of sand mingled
with eroded, treacherous paths. No one came here—there were
better, safer, more scenic places.

I took off my shoes and socks before I even climbed out of the
car, and I rolled up my pant legs. Gabriel got out, still in his suit
and his loafers.

"Uh, gotta at least take off your shoes," I said.

"I'll be fine."

I didn't argue. Gabriel had to experience an obstacle for himself, which he did, as soon as we'd walked fifty feet and hit a
patch where the path vanished, and water swelled over the sand.
Gabriel eyed the lake as if he could intimidate it into retreating.
It refused to yield.

As I waded in, Gabriel headed farther up the shore, only to
curse as he stepped on boggy ground.

"You're stubborn, you know that?" I called.

He grumbled under his breath.

"This is a beach, Gabriel," I said. "No Ferragamos allowed."

He looked down at his shoes.

I sighed. "All right. Fine. There's a boardwalk a few miles up. We'll drive—"

"No, I can do this."

He started back toward the car. Then he lifted a finger, as if I might think he was making his escape. I walked to a small embankment and perched on the edge, my toes in the water, sinking into the mud below.

"Better?" he said when he returned a few minutes later.

I turned. He hadn't just taken off his shoes and socks. He'd rolled his trousers and lost the coat and tie, even if the top button on his shirt was still fastened.

"Much better. Now let's walk. By the way, I want a house right there." I pointed at the windswept plateau above the lake's edge. "A tiny house with a huge porch. I'll come out every morning, with my coffee and my newspaper, and I'll watch the sun rise."

"I don't think you can get newspaper delivery here."

"You and your practicality."

He chuckled as I climbed the incline to the grassy rise. I stood on the edge, face lifted as the wind whipped my hair back.

"My porch will be here. And if you mention the high probability of erosion, I will throw this bottle of wine in your general direction."

"It's a magical spot. There's no erosion."

"Thank you. I'll sit on my porch with my coffee and my *book* every morning. I might even, on occasion, bring work. You will not, however, be able to check that I'm doing it, because I will have no cell service."

He looked at his phone. "Actually, there is—"

"I will find a provider that doesn't cover this spot, except on

Tuesdays, if the wind is blowing north and I hold my phone just right. Otherwise, I am out of contact."

"That might not be safe."

"It'd be safer for everyone else. I can't call for help and get you guys killed by a roving pack of evil elves."

I moved to the edge of the bank and lowered myself to the ground. "Come and sit on my porch. It's time to open the wine."

He climbed up, then looked at the spot beside me.

"Yes," I said. "There is dirt. The earth is made of it."

"I was actually checking for bird droppings."

"There are those, too, in the dirt."

He sat beside me and pulled the corkscrew out of a pocket. "I thought you wanted a house of ruins?"

"I do. And a pretty little cottage on the beach. And a ramshackle cabin in the woods. Also, a Victorian with English gardens. Oh, and a condo with a view."

He pulled the cork. "Which are you going to get first, once your trust fund comes in?"

When I didn't reply, he said, "Wrong subject?"

"I want the freedom money gives me, but I'd rather have earned my own."

"It is your own."

"You know what I mean. If anything, it should go to the Tylwyth Teg, for finding me rich parents. Which brings up a whole other category of subjects I'd rather ignore tonight."

"I always wanted a Victorian house," he said.

"Like Rose's?"

"No, I want a haunted one."

I laughed. "You want pet ghosts?"

"Not haunted by *ghosts*. Just haunted." He passed me the wine. "We forgot glasses."

I drank from the bottle. "Mine now. I have cooties. Little guys, with wings."

He retrieved the bottle. "I believe I have the same ones."

"So, your haunted house," I prompted.

He drank deeply, his eyes tearing at the corners, as if he were slugging hundred-proof moonshine instead of Bordeaux.

"There was this house," he said. "When I was a boy. We moved a few times, but it was often within walking distance. It was condemned and boarded up. An old Victorian on a street of slums. I thought it was the fanciest house I'd ever seen. It probably reminded me of Rose's, but it was this big, run-down, rambling place. Inside, though, you could see hints of what it had been. The flooring. The plasterwork. Even some antique furniture. It felt haunted, but in a good way. Memories and history. I would find things inside and imagine the families that had owned them. I used to tell myself that one day, when I was financially well off, I'd go back and fix it up."

"Is it still there?"

He shook his head. "Long gone. Demolished. I'd never have bought it. Practicalities." He snuck a look my way. "I can't avoid them."

"No one can, not if they have a drop of sense. You'd go back, and you'd see that it'd be a money pit in a bad neighborhood, and you'd feel like you'd lost that dream. Better it was removed due to circumstances beyond your control."

"Yes, that's it exactly." He sipped from the bottle this time. "I would have felt guilty choosing, too. I'd want the condo, and I'd feel like I abandoned the house. Which sounds silly."

"It's not about the house. It's about the dream."

"Yes." Another gulp of wine before he passed it back. "The condo was a dream, too. When I was in college, I had to do a joint project. Normally, I could wriggle out of them or do all the work myself, but this guy insisted on working together. We'd go to his father's, an apartment in the building where I live now. I'd see that view and . . ."

"You wanted it."

"I did. Part of it was just setting the goal. *This is what I'll have someday.* A status symbol. But really, I wanted the view."

"It's a million-dollar one."

"It is." A crooked smile. "Luckily, when the housing market crashed, I got it for less. But it was nice to achieve that goal earlier than I expected." He undid the top button on his shirt and leaned back, his hands braced behind him. "I wouldn't mind a secondary residence. As an investment, of course. That's the only way I could justify it. But . . ." He took off his shades, the sun having dropped almost below the horizon. "Someplace quieter. The condo is quiet, in its way . . ."

"But it's still in the heart of a very big city."

"It is."

I took a hit from the wine bottle. "So tell me what you'd want. Perfect world. No practicalities."

"There are always practicalities."

"Pretend there aren't."

When he said, "I don't think I can," there was a look in his eyes almost like panic.

"Allow for them, then," I said. "Just don't dwell on them. What would you want? Forest, lake, mountain, ocean . . ."

"Meadow," he said. "Not the most exciting landscape—"

"Doesn't matter. It's whatever you want."

"Meadow, then," he said. "Grass as far as the eye can see. A stream running through it. Forest around it, blocking everything else. I'd build a house . . ."

CHAPTER FIFTY-FIVE

We talked about our dream homes. Then we talked about whatever came to mind, chasing tangents as we emptied the bottle and evening turned to night, the moon reflecting off the water, lighting the dark shore to twilight.

It wasn't just the alcohol. We'd hit a milestone, a huge one, and though it didn't solve Gabriel's problem—he was still charged with murder—that didn't seem to matter tonight. It was a start, and that false charge was connected to my parents' crimes, which meant it was still progress.

Tonight, we had wine and we had solitude. And I had him. For one night, I had Gabriel—really had him, the secret him, the hidden one, lazing on the bank, shirtsleeves rolled up, those light blue eyes like faded jeans, warm and comfortable. I had him talking. I had him smiling. I even had him laughing. And as I lay on my side, watching him tell me a story, I knew I loved him. I couldn't brush it off as "not that way," as platonic love, as intellectual love. It *was* that way.

I loved Gabriel. And I loved Ricky. It wasn't the same, but it wasn't different enough, either, not as different as it should have been, not as different as I wanted it to be. That twisted and burned. I wasn't this person. I'd never been this person. I gave myself to one man at a time, and I never so much as looked in another direction—and now that one acknowledged truth had been warped. I was still fiercely loyal—to two men. Two men I loved. Two men I'd do anything for. Give anything to protect.

That was fickle. It was selfish. It was wrong. And it wasn't fair to the guy who thought he had all of me, committed and faithful in every way.

I would never cheat on Ricky. If Gabriel had given some sign that he wanted more, had leaned over and kissed me, I'd have pulled back and said no. What mattered was that I wouldn't *want* to say no.

Even if a romantic relationship with Gabriel wasn't an option, I had to choose: break it off with Ricky or commit myself to him. Work with Gabriel, yes. Be his friend, yes. Sit on a beach, drinking and talking, for half the night? No. That was where I went too far.

The realization that I had to make that choice should have been like falling into the cold water of Lake Michigan. I should have staggered to my feet, blurted some excuse, and escaped, fleeing this perfect evening as fast as I could.

I didn't. The realization came hard and painful but bitter-sweet, too, as if I'd been mentally picking my way across the rocks for weeks now, this destination in view, getting ever closer until I reached it, dreading it a little, but knowing I had to get there. I had Gabriel—really had him—for those few hours, and maybe after tonight I'd choose to step back and I'd never have this again, and if that was the case, then I was grabbing it with both hands and hanging on while I could.

When I started yawning, I stifled it, but eventually Gabriel noticed.

"We should think about getting back," he said.

I nodded, and we did nothing more about it for at least an

hour, talking instead about college, which subjects we'd liked and those we'd gritted our teeth through. Finally, yawning wasn't enough. My eyelids were flagging.

"Let's get you back," he said. "You spent last night in my office. You shouldn't spend this one on the beach."

I wanted to say I'd be fine with that, but as the alcohol slid from my bloodstream, I knew I shouldn't. If I'd come to the realization that something needed to change, I couldn't start by spending the night with Gabriel, however innocently.

We started out, still light-headed, joking about who was in better condition to drive, making each other walk straight lines and recite Sherlock Holmes quotes.

"The fact that you're admitting you can recite Holmes quotes proves you're in no shape to drive," I said as we crested the last rise.

"I've read the comics."

I laughed. "And *that's* better than admitting you read novels? How—?"

Gabriel grabbed my arm, and the next thing I knew I was staring at his back.

"Take three steps backward," he said.

It took a second to realize he was talking to someone else. I peeked around him to see a thin man, brown-haired, not much older than me. Or *looking* not much older than me, though I suspected he was many times my age.

Tristan raised a hand. "I come in peace."

"Bullshit." I sidestepped around Gabriel. "The last time we had contact with you, it was through your flunky, Macy Shaw, when she tried to *kill* us."

"In opposition to my explicit directions. I made it very clear you weren't to be harmed. Either of you. That's the problem dealing with humans. Petty grievances and jealousies flare, and they ignore orders. Logic, too, as it seems. If one has to deal with them, one is better choosing *siol*. They're usually able to rise above that."

"*Siol?*" I tried to move closer, but Gabriel gripped my arm, and he was right. Maintain distance.

"Descendants," Tristan said. "For us, it means those descended from our kind. *Disgynyddion* in Welsh, but that's a mouthful. In my language, it's *diyskynnyas*, which is just as bad, so we'll stick to Gaelic. I'm not Gaelic. Or Welsh. But you are. Both of you. Part Tylwyth Teg, part human, part . . . other things. Cŵn Annwn among them for you, Eden. That's the thing about *siol*. They're terribly attractive to fae, at least as breeding stock. Keep hitting the same lineage over and over, and eventually you get quite an interesting mix."

I glanced at Gabriel. "So that's where we get it from. The hyperverbal gene. Fae do love to talk."

"True . . ." Tristan said. "But in this case, I believe you're the one who wanted to talk to me. You left an invitation." He held out a scrap of notepaper. On it I could see my phone number . . . in my own handwriting.

"You're Jon Childs," I said.

"Among others. But you've invited me to talk, so I'm taking you up on the offer, though this might be a somewhat one-sided conversation. It appears you have a problem I may have caused."

"Besides the fact that your psycho assistant tried to murder us?"

"Yes, besides that."

Gabriel's hand moved to my shoulder. "We have nothing to say to you, whatever you are."

"*Spriggan*," Tristan said. "I'll give that information freely as a token of my goodwill. As for what a *spriggan* is—"

"You murdered Ciara Conway," I said.

"Mmm, no. Macy did, attempting to restrain her. I will

admit, however, that I did utilize her corpse in ways you might have found disturbing."

"You left her *head* in my *bed*."

"Her spirit had long fled. I was simply using the shell to encourage you to discover your own heritage. I was being helpful. If you look at it in the right light."

I couldn't even respond to that.

"Why did Edgar Chandler ask me to kill you?" Gabriel said.

"That's . . . complicated."

"You have one minute to find an uncomplicated answer. If you do so, you will earn five minutes of our time."

"You're very cute," Tristan said. "Both of you. You act as if you have a say in the matter. As if you could, indeed, just push me out of the way and go about your evening."

"Is that an invitation to try?" Gabriel said.

"Not particularly. I lack your fondness for confrontations."

"Chandler," I said. "He wanted us to kill you."

"No, I don't think he did. He wanted you to find me. I'd gone to him once before, when he was working on his brainwashing techniques with the merry Huntsman. I'd made him an offer. He refused. I believe he was reconsidering, namely because he realized he was in deep trouble. He sent you after me. He thought I would use my abilities to overpower you and learn who sent you, and then I'd go and speak to him. He was overcomplicating things, as usual. I wouldn't have bothered with him. He was damaged goods by that point. There's your answer, so I'll take my five minutes." He gave us no time to object. "I'm the one who started the business with James Morgan. Making him think Eden was in danger from you, Mr. Walsh."

"What?" I said.

"I had a plan," he said, with a combination of nonchalance and smugness that left me staring.

They aren't human. You need to remember that. Don't expect them to think, to act like humans.

Tristan continued, "I want peace, Eden, and you could start a war that will make this entire corner of the world a very uncomfortable place for those like me. So I'm going to help you make the right choices. If you don't . . ." He shrugged. "I'll have to kill you. Which would be regrettable."

"All right," Gabriel said. "We've heard enough—"

"I still have four minutes. The point is that I ruffled Mr. Morgan's feathers for the same reason I toyed with Ciara Conway's unfortunate shell. All part of my plan. Mr. Morgan was a pest. Pests need to be eradicated."

I lunged forward. "You killed—?"

His hands shot up. "An unfortunate choice of words. Please allow me to finish. He was a nuisance because he was distracting you from discovering your identity and your role. I expected Mr. Walsh would stomp him, and in the process the bond between you and Mr. Walsh would strengthen. That bond is important, as I'm sure you know by now."

I glanced uneasily at Gabriel, but he only watched Tristan with the same wary look he'd had since we'd been waylaid.

I answered quickly. "So you made James think Gabriel was a danger to me. You compelled him—"

"Which was only possible because he was quite willing to be persuaded," Tristan cut in, as if that made a difference.

"You got Gabriel arrested for assault and trespassing—"

"*That* I didn't expect. Morgan was more committed to you than I anticipated. The situation escalated."

"No shit it escalated." I stepped toward him. "*You* escalated it. You sent cult deprogrammers after me, in James's name."

"No, I presume Morgan was behind that. And now our Mr. Walsh has been falsely charged with his murder."

"Do you know who did it?"

"Well, no. Not yet. I believe if we pool our resources—"

I laughed.

"I realize you haven't seen me as an ally," Tristan said. "Though I'd argue I am. In fact, I'm the only one who doesn't seek the destruction of either side. I want peace."

"Is that an option?" I said. "Because according to everything I've heard, I have three choices: I choose to align myself with one side and let the other die out. Or I choose neither and both die. I'm not hearing an alternative."

"I haven't exactly worked out the logistics—"

I groaned and turned to Gabriel. "Can we go now?"

"The Cŵn Annwn," Tristan said. "They're the most likely suspects. They want to get rid of Gwynn so Arawn controls the playing field."

"We need to go," I said, reaching for Gabriel's arm. He lifted it out of my reach without even looking over.

"Gwynn?" Gabriel said. "Arawn?"

"You do know who they are, I presume?" Tristan said.

"Of course," I broke in. "Matilda, Gwynn, Arawn. The myth or history or whatever it is. Gabriel, can we—?"

"In a moment. This could be important." He turned to Tristan. "Explain what you mean—"

"Gabriel, please." I gripped his elbow.

He seemed to catch the growing desperation in my voice. He nodded. "All right." Then, to Tristan, "We'll speak—"

"Investigate the Cŵn Annwn. I haven't been able to prove they're behind Morgan's murder, but it's the solution that makes sense. If you're arrested, that removes Gwynn from the equation, and leaves the biker boy, Arawn."

"Gabriel," I said loudly, trying to distract him from Tristan's last sentence, but it did no good. Gabriel stared at him so intently he could have read his lips.

"Biker boy?" he said.

"Richard Gallagher."

"You're saying Ricky is Arawn? And I'm . . ."

"Gwynn, of course. Gwynn ap Nudd. King of the Tylwyth Teg."

Gabriel pivoted on his heel, so slowly I swear it took ten seconds before he was facing me, and still it wasn't enough time to plaster on a look of confusion.

"Olivia," he said. "You knew . . . ?"

"We aren't them," I blurted. "Not reincarnations. It's a role. You have Tylwyth Teg blood and Ricky has Cŵn Annwn, and I have both, and we know one another, so we've been thrust into these roles—"

"Not exactly," Tristan said. "True, it isn't reincarnation, but it's not happenstance. There couldn't be another Gwynn to your Matilda. It's all preordained. He is *the* Gwynn—"

"Enough." Gabriel's voice was so low we both turned, as if uncertain we'd heard it. "That's enough," he said, articulating each syllable. "We are going to leave now. If you wish to speak to us, you know where we are."

Tristan thrust business cards at both of us. "Or you can call me. Anytime. I really do think we can solve—"

Gabriel had already walked away, leaving the card in Tristan's outstretched hand. Tristan tucked mine into my pocket.

"It's not the Cŵn Annwn," I said to Tristan. "Unless James has murdered someone with fae blood, they can't kill him."

"That's the general idea, but I'm not convinced it's a rule."

"It is," I said.

"That makes it more complicated," he said, sighing. "Why don't we—?"

Now I was the one walking away—jogging, actually—to catch up with Gabriel.

"I can help you," Tristan called after us.

"That's what everybody says," I muttered, and raced after Gabriel.

I've had quiet drives with Gabriel. Sometimes it's a comfortable, worn-in kind of silence, both of us relaxed and burrowed deep in our thoughts. Sometimes it's like being stuck in an empty chamber, painfully and uncomfortably aware of the lack of communication. That night, the silence was a living thing, a rat gnawing at me as I sat bound to my chair, unable to throw the beast off and escape. Gabriel's silence forbade discussion and told me that if I opened my mouth, said a single word, it would only make the situation worse.

We were nearly at the city before he spoke.

"It isn't true," he said. "I'm not Gwynn."

"I know. It's just a role—"

"No, Olivia. I'm sorry. You seem to believe this, but it isn't true. In fact, I'm beginning to suspect none of it is true. I understand that you've been in a difficult place, your world turned upside down, and it's easy to get confused—"

"Are you suggesting I'm imagining the visions?"

"Not entirely. I think you've been in a susceptible state, and these creatures—fae, what have you—are taking advantage of that."

I struggled for words, for breath. "Don't do this, Gabriel."

"If you're being manipulated—"

"The only one manipulating me here is you."

His hands gripped the wheel. "That's not fair and—"

"In everything that's happened, who's been the believer? The one who won't let me be skeptical, won't let me make up excuses, forces me to face the truth, however harsh—"

"Exactly. *However harsh.* That's what I'm doing now. This isn't true, Olivia. You know it isn't. You dream of some fairy prince and say I'm him?" A brusque laugh. "I didn't expect you to fall for romantic nonsense like that—"

"You aren't my fairy prince, Gabriel," I said, barely forcing the words through gritted teeth. "Not by any stretch of the imagination. You aren't him, and I'm not her. In the original, Matilda chose Gwynn. I chose Ricky. Arawn. That alone should prove—"

"—should prove it's nonsense. All of it. You didn't choose Ricky over me, Olivia. I wasn't an option. I hope you realize that. If you didn't, and I somehow conveyed the impression—"

"You conveyed no such impression." I managed to get the words out, my chest frozen, my gut on fire, brain numb. "That is exactly what I meant. Gwynn and Matilda were lovers. Arawn and Matilda were only friends. That's how things have changed. I'm with Ricky. You and I are friends."

He snorted. And of everything he'd said, that was the flaming arrow that cut deepest, scorched hottest. The snort that said we weren't friends. Not even that.

The Jag slowed at the first stoplight we'd hit. As soon as the tires stopped rolling, I opened the door.

"I can get myself back from here," I said, and climbed out.

Did I pause a second, giving him a chance to protest? Yes. He said nothing. I slammed the door, and when the light changed, he sped away, leaving me on the street corner.

CHAPTER FIFTY-SIX

I expected Gabriel to come back. I really did. It was 1 A.M. and a look around told me I was more likely to hail a rapist here than a taxi. Empty streets. Dark buildings. Two guys on the corner, locked in a drunken exchange, me moving my gun from my purse into a pocket.

Gabriel would realize what kind of neighborhood he'd left me in, come screeching back, put down the window and say, "Get in." He wouldn't be happy about it, but even if he'd all but said *We aren't friends*, that thread of basic human decency would bring Gabriel back.

Gabriel did not come back.

I called a cab company and gave them the intersection. They said it would be "hours." In other words, they weren't coming here. I started to walk. I headed toward the two drunk guys, only because I didn't dare turn my back on them. They stopped arguing and fixed me with assessing stares. I stared back. One grumbled and resumed the argument. The other gave in after a pause, and they went back at it, ignoring me.

I called Ricky. "I hate to do this," I said when he answered. "But could you pick me up?"

"Sure." The *thud-thud* of his feet hitting the floor, followed by a stifled yawn.

"I woke you, didn't I?"

"Nope. Just finishing a very boring reading, waiting for my good-night text. What happened? Where's Gabriel?"

I paused and then said, "You were right."

"And from the sound of you, I'd rather I wasn't. What was I right about?"

"He found out about Gwynn and Arawn. That he's Gwynn. He . . ." I inhaled. "It went badly. Really badly. We argued. I got out of the car. He took off. I waited in case he came back, and I did phone a cab, so I wouldn't bother you—"

"Call me first. Always. Where are you?" The click of the door and the scrape of the key as he locked the deadbolt.

I told him.

"He left you *there*? God-fucking-damn him. What do you see? We need to get you someplace safe until I arrive. Restaurant, coffee shop, corner store—hell, even a twenty-four-hour laundry. I'll stay on the line until you're there."

Ricky picked me up and took me back to his apartment, where we made love. It really was making love, not having sex. It was my apology, even if he'd never know I had something to apologize for.

I remembered everything Gabriel had said in that car, lashing out in the way guaranteed to hurt the most. Telling me what, in my gut, I feared most—that I'd been tricked, that this was all a ruse, and I was steering my life based on hallucinations. Telling me that I was also hallucinating anything between us, that if I thought we were friends, then I was a silly little fool.

That's the guy I'd considered leaving Ricky for. Just so I'd be free to be with him, however he'd have me. Exactly how pathetic was that?

I really had been a silly little fool, and now I made it up to Ricky. Afterward, we lay there, Ricky on his back, me curled up against him, my hand on his chest, feeling his heart slowing as I traced the edges of his triskele tattoo.

"Can I see the designs for ours yet?" I asked.

"They're on my phone," he mumbled sleepily. "You get it, and we'll look. If I can open my eyes."

I smiled. "It can wait until morning. Go to sleep."

"No, get it. I'm just resting for round two."

"It's almost four A.M."

"Which is why there probably won't be a round three. However, if you insist, I'll try to accommodate, because I'm selfless like that."

I laughed, fetched his phone, and held it out.

"Go ahead," he said. "Nothing on there you can't see."

He directed me to a project management app.

"You've got a lot of projects," I said as I skimmed the files.

"I'm organized."

"Trip list? Don't tell me you make packing lists, too."

"Yes, I do, but that's not one of them."

"Can I open it?"

He flipped onto his side. "Did I say there's nothing on my phone you can't see?"

I opened the file. It was a list of places. The Three Sisters, Texas. Tail of the Dragon, North Carolina . . .

"Top ten motorcycle roads in North America," he said.

"How many have you done?"

"Zip." He looked at me. "You want to change that?"

His fingers rested on my thigh. His tone was confident, but his gaze was slightly lowered, in that way he had when he suspected he might be pushing into territory that could send me backpedaling. I've never backpedaled, but Ricky intuits better than anyone I know, and I couldn't help wondering if he'd picked up on my confusion with Gabriel.

"Are you offering to take me away from all this?" I said.

"More like take you away when *all this* is over."

"Let's do that." I held up the list. "Pick a spot."

"Nope." He turned the phone around. "You."

"I'd have to research—"

"Uh-uh." He scooched me over against him and covered my eyes. "Pick one."

I did and opened my eyes. "Cabot Trail, Nova Scotia?"

"Hope you have a passport."

"I do. But if you want someplace closer—"

"Nope, I do want to take you away from all this. As far from it as we can get." He rolled onto his back and pulled me down with him. "At least for a little while."

"God, I love you."

"You'd better. 'Cause you're about to spend two weeks alone with me in the middle of nowhere."

"Perfect," I said, and leaned down to kiss him.

I awoke to a text from Gabriel, telling me not to come in to work.

"I think I just got fired," I said.

Ricky got out of bed fast. "He sure as hell better not." He peered at my phone. "Bastard. It's a temporary overreaction, but still, that's your job. Your only source of income after he convinced you to quit the diner. He'd better not fuck with it because he's feeling pissy."

Ricky grabbed his jeans. "I'm going to go chat with him." Before I could protest, he cut me off with a lifted hand. "No, not to give him shit for that text. He's freaking out about the

Gwynn shit, and he's pissed that you didn't tell him, and I'm part of both those things. I just want to talk about that." A half smile. "I promise not to hit him, however tempted I might be."

"Maybe I should try first and . . ." And if I did and Gabriel failed to reply and then Ricky showed up, it really would look like he was taking a message from me. "Okay, go on. After breakfast."

Ricky returned an hour after leaving, barely time for him to have made it to Gabriel's office and back.

"He won't see you?" I said.

"Oh, he did. For five minutes, during which he said exactly seven words, though admittedly he did repeat them a few times."

"What'd he say?"

"I don't know what you're talking about."

"So he's playing it like that?"

"Yep." Ricky headed for the bathroom. "Try texting him later. See if anything changes."

I texted Gabriel three times that day. On the third, I said, *Can you answer please? So I know you're getting these?* He replied with *I am.* I stopped texting.

I spent the day investigating my parents'—my *father's*—victims. Ricky helped.

I heard from Tristan twice. The first time, he left a message hinting that he was onto something. I ignored him. The guy had left a girl's *head* in my *bed*. He'd lured me to an abandoned psych hospital in the middle of the night, pretending to have kidnapped the young woman who ultimately tried to kill us. He'd turned James from a sweet former fiancé into a crazed stalker ex. Call me a grudge-holder, but I was having some trouble getting past all that.

And yet . . . Well, as I'd been told—and shown—many times

in the last few months, the fae didn't think like us and couldn't be expected to act like us. To them, the psych hospital and the James manipulation and even the surprise body parts were cattle prods, guiding this reluctant human in the direction they wanted her to go. We *were* cattle to them. Useful. Perhaps even necessary for survival. But not terribly clever.

Tristan texted later that afternoon.

Solid lead. Need GW 2 chk P Larsen visitor logs. OK?

I showed the message to Ricky.

"I find fairies with cell phones disconcerting enough. Do they really need to use text talk?" He shook his head. "You going to answer?"

"I am curious—what the hell would he need those logs for? But one, I can't trust Tristan. Two, I don't dare ask Gabriel to do anything right now. And three, I don't trust Tristan." I put the phone away. "I'll ask Lydia tomorrow if she can get the logs. I don't like going behind Gabriel's back, but . . ."

"One, he's being a dick. Two, you're doing this to help him avoid jail time. Three, he's being a dick."

I smiled at him. "Exactly."

Four hours later, we'd just returned from a late dinner when I got another text from Tristan.

Must talk. Big problem. Need privacy. Come 2 place we met 2nd time. Trust no one.

"Seriously?" I said, showing the text to Ricky. "*Trust no one.* Now fairies are watching *X-Files?*"

"He just wants you to believe."

"No shit. Well, he's officially piqued my curiosity. I'm calling back."

I did, as we walked up the stairs to Ricky's apartment. I called twice. Tristan didn't answer. The first time, it went to voice mail, and I hung up to try again. That time, I got a "number not in service" message. I called a third time, in case my redial had screwed up somehow. It hadn't. The number was no longer in service.

"Okay. Apparently, his number doesn't work anymore."

"So we're still going?" he said.

"To an abandoned psych hospital? Once was enough. I'm not playing his game again."

Inside the apartment, I slowly took off my shoes, so lost in thought that I didn't realize Ricky was gone until I looked up and saw him coming out of the bedroom.

"Okay," I said. "I know this will sound crazy, but—"

He handed me a new switchblade. "You're going to need this."

CHAPTER FIFTY-SEVEN

Yes, heading to that psych hospital suggested I might belong in one. I'd like to think I'm not the dumb blonde in a B horror movie, saying, "You're a supernatural being with an agenda that might involve killing me, and you want me to come to an abandoned psych hospital at night? Well, okay, then!" It was almost certainly a trap, but I couldn't sit at home, playing it safe, when taking a risk meant answering the question: What was Tristan really up to? Proceed with extreme caution and take what I could from the situation, because if I refused, then maybe next time he tried to trap me, I'd stumble in without realizing it.

I called Gabriel on the walk to Ricky's bike. That was part of exercising extreme caution. Yes, he'd made it clear he didn't want to hear from me, but this wasn't *Hey, I'd like to talk.* For this, he would answer. I was sure of it.

I called and got his voice mail.

"I need your help," I said. "Just hear me out, please. Tristan wants me to meet him at the psych hospital. I'm sure it's a trap, but you know that won't stop me from going. Ricky and I are on our way. I could really use your advice, though. You're probably too busy to talk"—*meaning that you don't want to, but I'll give you an escape route here*—"so I'll e-mail the details. If you *can* talk, for a minute, I'd appreciate that, but even an e-mail reply will do. Hell, I'll take a text, Gabriel. Am I making a really dumbass move here? Is there anything I should know? Any advice you can give? Thanks."

I hung up.

"He'll answer that," Ricky said, handing me my helmet. "Guaranteed."

For once, Ricky was not right.

When I started to worry, Ricky pulled over at a gas station with a graffiti-covered pay phone. I called Gabriel from it. He answered, which took away every possible explanation except the one that hurt the most: I needed him, and he didn't give a damn. I hung up without a word.

The psych hospital. It had a name, I was sure, but I'd never looked it up. I would have preferred never to think of it again.

There was an unconnected local cemetery beside the hospital grounds. The first time we visited, we'd walked through it and I'd reflected that, as creepy as graveyards are supposed to be, it didn't bother me at all. But the abandoned hospital? It was the most frightening place I'd ever seen—in real life, in movies, even in nightmares.

The hospital buildings sat on at least ten acres of overgrown decay. I should have been fascinated, as I was by Villa Tuscana. I was not fascinated, except perhaps in the most basic definition of the word, where you can't look away in spite of yourself. The visions I'd had there were enough to make me not want to go back. Yet it was more than that. It was the pervasive sense of the place, a dread and terror that crept under my skin and nestled in the marrow of my bones. Whatever one's faith, death means the end of life on this earth. The prospect is unpleasant, but I figure once it happens, it happens, over and done. The hospital represented a very different kind of death.

There is no escape from the prison of the mind. I'd seen those words there. Phantom words left imprinted on my brain. Madness was inescapable. The hospital wasn't an old-fashioned lunatic asylum, with chains welded to the floors, but you'd be imprisoned there nonetheless. In my visions, I'd seen people trapped there. Women. The little girl said that I was tapping into hereditary memories. Were those women like me? Tainted by fae blood? Driven mad by it?

Could I be driven mad by it?

Like before, the chained gates had appeared locked until we got close enough to see that the lock itself was undone. The gate gave an ominous whine as Ricky swung it open.

"A word of warning," I said as we walked in. "The last time I was here, I saw visions."

"When you were with me?"

"Yes."

His gaze settled on me, not angry that I'd kept that from him. Only concerned. "Well, if it happens this time, tell me. Please. That might make it easier."

"It will. Thanks."

We headed up the overgrown road, picking our way past chunks of pavement, the grass and weeds breaking through, leaving a cobblestone of old asphalt. Trees stretched over us, the branches reaching out to one another but not quite meeting. I could imagine this road fifty years ago, in the bright summer sun, a cool and dark passage with a wind whispering through the leaves. A pretty sight, I'm sure, but I'm equally sure that no one was thinking of beauty when they planted these trees. They were a landscape transition, hiding the buildings beyond from the outside world. You'd turn in from the country road, pass through this leafy tunnel, and come out in the stark, cold reality of the hospital grounds.

After a quarter mile, squat industrial buildings replaced the trees lining the road. In their day, they'd have held little architectural interest, and even as ruins they weren't any more enticing. Ugly cinder blocks with boarded-up and broken-out windows.

"Eden . . ."

The voice came as a whisper on the breeze. I turned.

"Hear something?" Ricky asked.

"You didn't?"

He made a noise that sounded like a no, as if reluctant to admit to it, reaching over at the same time to touch my hand, his closed switchblade refreshingly cool against my fingers.

"We'll go that way, then," he said, nodding in the direction I'd turned. "Whatever happens, stay close. No splitting up this time, okay?"

I nodded, and we headed along a narrow passage between two buildings. There was no path there, not even a worn strip of dirt, but we walked through and found ourselves at a gate so ivy-choked that, from the road, it had looked like a bush.

"Where's the path?" I said. "If there's a gate, there should be something leading to it. More than a gap between buildings."

"Yeah."

I took a closer look at the ivy. "I'm no gardener, but I helped ours enough to know this isn't native to Illinois. It was planted here." I eased back and looked at the thin wrought iron, completely engulfed in flora. "It's almost like they tried to hide the gate. Or is my imagination just running away with me?"

"Then we've got the same imagination." He cleared enough ivy to peer through the gate. "Okay, that's weird. We have a fenced yard of nothing."

He took hold of the gate and yanked. The ivy fell away easily. Too easily.

"Someone's opened this for us," he said.

"Yep." I took the gun from my pocket. "I think we've found our trap."

"Then it's a very strange one." He threw open the gate. "Because if someone's hiding, I don't know where."

It really was a "yard of nothing"—unless you counted weeds. The wrought-iron fence encircled a patch about two hundred feet square. And there was nothing inside except grass and weeds.

Before he let the gate swing shut behind us, Ricky examined the fence. He knocked his boot into a space between the slats and heaved himself up.

"Yep," I said. "Even if the gate mysteriously locks behind us, it's a six-foot, climbable fence. At worst, you could boost me up and over."

"Weird."

"Uh-huh. So maybe not a trap?"

He grunted, meaning he wasn't going to be so quick to dismiss the possibility. "We'll have a look around, in case there's something we're supposed to see here, but don't take a step without clearing it first."

"In case we walk into a literal trap."

He nodded. We each moved forward, testing the way as we went. I got about three paces before my sneaker nudged something unyielding. I started to bend.

"Hold up." Ricky came over and prodded it with his boot. "Go stand by the gate."

"Um, so if it blows up, you'll be the one who loses fingers? Very chivalrous, but I found it. You go stand by the gate."

He rubbed his mouth. "Sorry. This place . . . I didn't like it the last time and it's worse now. There's something that makes me want to sling you over my shoulder and carry you out, and it's bad enough that I'd almost be tempted if I didn't know you'd kick the hell out of me."

I moved closer and rubbed between his shoulders. The tension there was rock-hard. His face was just as tight, pupils constricted despite the darkness.

"What do you want to do?" I asked.

"Honestly? Leave."

"If you feel strongly about that—"

"Nah. I'm not the one with psychic powers. I'm just . . ." Another look around. "Uneasy."

"Check whatever I found, then. I'll stand by the gate."

A light kiss, and some of that tension fell from his face. "Thank you. Next time, the dangerous part is yours. I promise."

"You're so sweet."

I backed up to the gate. Ricky knelt and prodded whatever was buried. His brows pinched. He grabbed a handful of undergrowth and ripped it off. Then he kept going, clearing it and sweeping away the dirt.

"Not a bomb, I'm guessing," I said as I came close.

"Death-related but not death-causing."

It was a grave, its marker set so deeply into the ground that it was almost as if whoever planted it there hoped it would soon be covered.

I looked around. "That's what this is. A cemetery."

"For those who didn't have family willing to claim them. A necessary part of the hospital, but obviously not one they cared to advertise to the other patients."

That's why it was hidden away back here. No path to the gate, tucked behind buildings, without standing stones to advertise its purpose.

Interesting, but did it mean anything? I'd heard someone call my name. Was that to get me here?

Gabriel always told me to follow my instincts. Well, he did before he decided that my instincts were all in my head.

I eased back on my haunches and looked around.

"Want me to start clearing the stones so you can read them?" Ricky asked.

"And you say you're not psychic." I forced a smile, but my heart wasn't in it. The same sense of foreboding that niggled at him pressed down on me, the darkness closing in despite the bright moon.

I searched for an omen. Even a raven or an owl gliding overhead would have been a sign that everything was all right, that I was under someone's protection.

"Do you have your tusk?" Ricky asked. "As much as I can't believe I just said that."

He got a real smile for that. "Yes, I have my handy-dandy evil-repelling tusk, which has never actually been proven to work, but since I didn't have it when we were attacked by elves, I'll presume it does. You have yours?"

"Yep."

"Then let's start clearing."

CHAPTER FIFTY-EIGHT

There were eleven graves in the small cemetery.

The first six names meant nothing to me. I noted them, in case they turned up in our investigations. Then I hit number seven.

Given the date, it was actually the last stone set in the cemetery: 1970. The date of birth was 1901. And the name? Isolde Carew.

The Carew house. My great-great-grandmother's house. Her first name had been Glenys. Welsh, like her granddaughter, Daere. I didn't need to look up Isolde to be pretty sure it came from Wales, too.

"Liv?"

"I think . . ." I brushed my hands over the stone. "This one might have been a relative of—"

The gravestone dropped into the earth, and I tumbled head-first, falling through darkness. I hit something hard and sharp that cut into my knees. Hands scooped me up.

"Ouch," a man's voice said. "That must have hurt."

"Are you all right, baby?" A woman's voice now.

I looked to see them towering above me. A dark-haired man and a woman with lighter hair, somewhere between brown and blond, her bright red lips pursed with concern as she squeezed my bare leg.

I know that face. I've seen it. Or some version of it. Older, much older . . .

"Better put her down, John. She's getting too big to carry."

The man lowered me to the ground and patted my head, telling me to watch my step. As I turned, the first thing I saw were stairs. Concrete stairs leading up to a massive door.

I know that door.

The mental hospital. I looked down the street and saw hulking sedans from the sixties. The buildings were in ill repair, some of the doors boarded over. The grounds were halfheartedly kept, with weeds already poking through the pavement. Mother Nature starting a tentative takeover, seeing if anyone cared to oppose her.

"It doesn't look very nice, does it, baby?" the woman said. "It used to have flowers and pretty lawns. I hate the thought of Aunt Isolde living here."

Isolde. The gravestone.

"It won't be much longer," the man said.

A deep sigh from the woman. "I know."

They led me up the stairs. I looked down at myself. Long dark hair lay straight over a miniskirted dress. Tiny, gleaming shoes. From what I could see, I wasn't more than four.

The man reached for my hand and pushed open the door. When he did, my legs locked. I seemed to waver there, in control of the body and the mind. Then it was like falling into that grave. I stumbled and pitched forward, and this time, when I recovered, I was still there, still standing, but my thoughts had been pushed to a small corner of my brain, and hers had taken over, and all I could feel was absolute terror.

"Come on, baby," the woman said. "I know you don't like it here, but your aunt Isolde will be so happy to see you."

"She doesn't know me," the girl whispered. "She doesn't know anyone."

A firm hand gripped my shoulder. "Of course she does. Now, none of that." The man bent and whispered in my ear. "This is important to Mommy, Pams. Do it for her. Please."

Pams.

I could no longer move the girl of my own volition, but I could see the woman out of the corner of my eye. See her face, soft and pretty and worried.

I know that face.

Grandma.

A stream of memories shot back, of a kind, quiet woman in a long skirt. Grandma Jean. She'd called the man John. That was my grandfather's name, though he'd died before I was born. John Bowen. Daere Jean Carew. Which made me . . .

Pams.

Pamela.

My mother.

They led me into the hospital, and it felt as if I was me again, that gut reaction when I caught those antiseptic medical smells. But the smell was faint and the feeling was more terror than hatred, and I knew it wasn't my reaction, it was hers, Pamela's. Her shoes felt made of lead and her legs ached, but she forced them to move.

Do it for Mommy. Do it for Mommy.

But I hate it. Hate, hate, hate it!

My grandfather checked in at the front desk. Pamela stood at his side, clutching his hand. She couldn't see over the counter, but I could imagine it, having seen the ruins. After a few words to the nurse, he led Pamela down equally familiar corridors, so dingy and worn they didn't seem far removed from the ones I remembered in the abandoned version.

We climbed the stairs and walked into a huge ward. I remembered this, too. Even the beds were as I recalled them, two rows of metal cots. Only a few were in use, the rest exactly as I'd seen them, bare and rusting.

"It's so terrible," my grandmother whispered. "I can't believe they've let it go like this."

"Funding cutbacks," my grandfather said. "I hear it'll close soon. They haven't taken new patients in over a year."

He led Pamela to the last occupied bed. A young nurse stood beside it, holding a wrinkled hand. When the nurse turned and smiled, her face seemed to ripple. Beneath her eyes, light poured, bright light. Her skin glowed with it. Her doughy features sharpened, pocked skin smoothing, teeth straightening, and inside Pamela, I stared, thinking how beautiful she was, but the thought formed only in that corner of my mind that was still my own, and the overwhelming thought instead was hate.

Get away from Aunt Isolde. Don't smile at me. Don't pretend you care. It's your fault. All your fault. I hate you. Hate you all so much.

Pamela gripped her father's hand tighter, as if to keep from launching herself at the woman, and the hate roiling through her was unlike anything I'd felt before. Black fire, consuming everything it touched.

"How's she doing today?" my grandfather asked.

At the side of the high bed, Pamela couldn't see more than that wizened hand, and I mentally swallowed, remembering a hand just like it, on another hospital bed, when I'd gone to visit Pamela after her attack. My first vision.

"She's comfortable," the young nurse said. "That's all we can hope for at this point."

"Is it . . . ?" my grandmother asked.

"She'll be free soon," the nurse murmured. "Her passing will be comfortable. I'm sure of it." The nurse squeezed the old woman's hand. "She's had such a hard life. It'll be better soon."

As I listened to her voice, I heard only genuine compassion. I saw it in her eyes, too. But Pamela didn't. The hatred scorched through her.

Your fault. It's your fault. You did this to her.

The nurse was fae—I was certain of that. Whether Pamela knew it or not, she could see though the mask and knew it as a mask, and it filled her not with fear but with a loathing I wouldn't have thought possible for a girl her age. One that chilled me to my core.

"Come see your aunt," my grandfather said.

His hands went around Pamela, and she squirmed, her hate liquefying into fear, making her protest and her father whisper, "Please, Pamela. For Mommy."

He lifted her up, and I saw the figure in the bed, and I recoiled, a scream exploding in the corner of Pamela's mind that was still mine, a scream that mirrored her own, the one screeching through her head as we both saw the figure.

It was the old woman from the hospital. So thin she seemed a skeleton wearing skin and a nightgown. Her eyes were covered with a thick bandage, but I knew what I'd see if that bandage was removed. Empty sockets.

Hair fanned out over the bed. Gray hair streaked with dark, and when I saw it, I saw another woman here, in the hospital. A woman rising from the murky water of a deep tub. A woman straitjacketed in a chair. A woman with bloodied bandages over her eyes and a mouth with no tongue . . .

The nurse squeezed Isolde's bird-thin arm and the old woman's chin jerked, as if she was waking.

"Daere is here to see you," the nurse said. "With John and little Pamela."

Isolde's mouth opened, and she made a sound. A garbled sound, like speech but not, and from where Pamela hung, in her father's arms, I could see into her mouth, the stump of her tongue—

Pamela shrieked, her scream joining the one echoing through my head. She fought, and I seemed to fight with her, clawing and scratching, then hitting the floor and scrambling up and running as fast as Pamela's small legs would take us, that scream still resounding in her head, all but drowning out the cries of her parents behind her.

Pamela turned down one corridor after another, zigging and zagging as the footfalls behind her grew distant, her parents missing her turns. Finally, she threw open a closet and flew in, slamming the door behind her and huddling in the dark, knees drawn up, gasping for breath as she shook uncontrollably.

Footsteps passed but kept going. Then the door creaked open and the nurse stood there, her body shimmering with light, features morphing. Pamela shrunk into the shadows, but the nurse only smiled and bent to the girl's level.

"Scary, isn't it?" she said in her soft voice. "Your poor auntie. She's had a hard life, Pamela, but it will be over soon. She'll be at peace, and, I hope, happy."

"Liar." Pamela spat the word, small body quaking with rage.

The woman backed up. "What—?"

"I know what you are. I see it. Behind your face. The glow."

A pause, and the nurse gave a slow, sad smile. "Ah. So you see me, do you?"

Pamela nodded, and in a blink the nurse disappeared. In her place was something my brain couldn't quite latch on to, the form ethereal, more glow than substance. I could make out a face, beautiful with sharp features and golden hair.

"Is that better, then?" the fae nurse said. "No disguises?"

She smiled, but the rage still whipped through Pamela.

"It's your fault," Pamela whispered. "What happened to her. She was tainted."

"Tainted?" The nurse tilted her head. "That's a big word for a little girl. Who told you that?"

"No one. I know. I just know."

"I see." The nurse crouched lower. "Then I won't deny it, *bychan*. The fault was ours. In her blood. I wouldn't call it a taint, but sometimes, when you're different, your mind can't quite manage it. Have you ever tried to hold a raw egg?"

Pamela squeezed herself tight, as if trying to block the words.

"It's like that," the nurse continued. "You can see us. You have memories. You know things you shouldn't. And as little as you are, your mind is strong. It can hold those ideas tight, like a hard-boiled egg. But for some, like your poor auntie, it's like trying to hold a raw egg. It slips and slides and oozes, and they try harder and harder to hold on, until they just can't. Do you understand, *bychan*?"

"I understand that it's your fault."

The nurse sighed. "It was not me, specifically, and we did try to help—"

"Liar!"

Pamela flew at the nurse. She hit her and I kept going, tumbling out, falling into darkness again, and then . . .

I bolted upright, the vision gone.

CHAPTER FIFTY-NINE

A s I struggled to my feet, I felt a familiar weight in my pocket. I reached in and touched my gun and switchblade. I patted my other pockets. Cell phone and tusk, right where I'd left them.

"Liv!" It was Ricky, shouting, his voice distant. "Olivia!"

At first, I thought I was in the grave, that I really had fallen in. But when I reached out, I touched only air. I pulled out my switchblade and flicked on the light.

I was inside the hospital. In a room I didn't recognize, one without windows.

"Liv!"

"I'm here!" I shouted. "In here!"

He kept calling my name, obviously unable to hear me. I took out my phone, speed-dialed his number, and got a "customer unavailable" message. I hung up. Tried again. Same thing.

I looked around. The sequence of events that had brought me from the graveyard to there should have been of some concern, but really, all that worried me was the possibility that I was still trapped in a vision, and only because that would mean it was futile to keep shouting and phoning. Yes, that's what my world was reduced to: zap from location A to location B, only wondering, *Is it live or is it memory?*

The fact that I was dressed as I had been, with my phone, suggested this was live.

I set about finding my way back to Ricky. I could hear him, and the building wasn't that big.

I walked into the next room, the one with creepy human-sized cribs for patients. Ricky and I had found Macy locked in one. I could even see our old footprints in the dust.

As I turned to the door, something scraped behind me. I glanced back. Fingers poked out from the crib slats. I froze. Swallowed. Stared at those fingers.

"Is someone there?"

A muffled response, as if from behind a gag. I walked over carefully, gun in hand. More fingers appeared between the slats. Then more. I stopped short and looked at the third hand. There wasn't enough room in that crib for two people, not unless they were crushed together—

More fingers appeared, and more, and more, reaching through the slats, beckoning me, that muffled cry turning to grunts and squeaks and snarls, the fingers clawing, one hand slashing at another, catching it in the wrist, blood spurting—

I raced out of the room and leaned against the corridor wall, panting and rubbing my eyes, the cold gun stock knocking against my cheek. Then I peeked in again. No fingers. No blood. Just our old footprints.

"Liv!" Ricky's voice.

I shouted back, as loud as I could, but he just kept calling. I pulled up the map from memory and walked. Turn here and then here and I should be in the—

I was back in the room with the cribs. And one was rocking,

back and forth, on its stand. Then a baby started to wail, and I could see it inside the crib, waving pale arms in the darkness.

I walked over, my feet moving as if of their own volition, and pulled the cover off the crib. It came away easily. Inside was a little girl, blond-haired and green-eyed, maybe almost a year, ready to crawl and walk, but lying on her back, waving her fists in the air, her cries howls now, enraged and frustrated howls, her face beet-red. There was a brace on her back.

"Shhh," whispered a voice somewhere beside me. "Daddy's here. Come on, sweetheart. Let's take you out of there."

I knew the voice. Todd.

"She gets so angry," he said.

"Do you blame her?" Pamela's voice. I turned, but they weren't there, only their voices.

"No." His voice broke on the word. "I keep hoping the brace will help—"

"It's not helping."

"God, why doesn't something *work*? All that medicine, and they can't fix her?"

"What if we could fix her?"

"Don't," he said, his voice low. "We've been to more doctors than we can afford, and I'd work three jobs if it would help, but they all say the same thing."

"I mean us, Todd. What would you do to fix her?"

"Anything." Anger in his voice. "You know that."

"Anything?"

"Of course."

"Would you kill for it?"

"What?" Voice sharp, as if he'd misheard.

"Would you kill someone to fix her?"

"God, Pam, don't even talk like that."

"So the answer's no? Not even if it was someone who deserved it?"

He didn't answer, only scooped the baby up, and my infant self disappeared from sight, my howls turning to soft sobs as he cooed and whispered to me.

"You said you'd do—" Pamela began.

"You've been working too hard. Go take a nap, and I'm going to pretend we never had this conversation. If you want me, I'll be at the park with Eden. *That's* what she needs from her parents."

The baby stopped whimpering, and the voices disappeared. I looked down at the cradle.

Not Todd. It was never Todd.

Of course it wasn't. No matter how much he loved me, he wasn't that kind of person. He just wasn't.

And Pamela . . . ?

"Olivia? Are you up here?" Ricky sounded closer now.

I dashed out of the room. "Here!"

"Where are you?"

I raced toward the sound of his voice, cutting through one room after another until . . .

I swung through the door of the crib room again.

I'm going in circles.

No, I wasn't.

I must be.

A figure stepped from behind the door.

Fingers closed around my arm. I twisted to see a woman holding me.

"You aren't real," I said.

"I wish I wasn't," she said. "So many times I've wished it. Please let me be a figment of my imagination. But I'm not."

She clutched my arm in a cold iron grip. I looked at her. She was a little older than me, with snarled dark hair and dark eyes. I knew the face, but the eyes threw me, because every time I'd seen her, there'd been deep pits there, bloody holes.

"Isolde?" I whispered.

"You know me?" A faint, sad smile. "I wish you didn't. I wish you'd never seen me, not like that. Not you and not her, poor little duckie."

"Pamela."

"They're wrong, you know. When they say you can control it. You can't. When it goes bad, it goes so bad, and there is no control. Only madness. You'll see that soon enough."

I tugged again, but she held me fast.

"There is a way out. One I could never find. Or perhaps they were right—I wasn't strong enough. But you are." She gestured at my gun.

"Wh-what?"

Her dark eyes met mine. "Set yourself free."

"Like hell."

A sad chuckle. "You sound like your mother." She lifted her gaze again. "Soon you'll be like her. That's your madness. The rage can go in or it can go out. Mine went in; hers went out. As will yours."

"I'm not like—"

Isolde's grip tightened. "You're *exactly* like her. Fierce in your passions, fierce in your loyalties. That will become rage, and it will explode." She lifted my hand, gun rising with it. "Fight back, child. Tell them you won't play their game. End it now. You'll save so many."

I dropped the gun. It hit the floor with a clang. I looked at her straight on and said, simply, "No."

"Then you are lost. The only question is, which will be your imprisonment? Here? Bound to a bed, screaming? Or like your mother, pacing her cell for a lifetime? One will come. You cannot fight it. Remember that I tried to help."

She thrust me away, and I stumbled. When I looked up, she was gone. I reached for my gun, and my fingers shook so badly I barely dared lift it.

I'm not like them. Not like either of them.

I staggered from the room. As I ran down the hall, words followed me, bloodred words on the wall, on either side of me.

There is no escape from the prison of the mind.

"Ricky!" I shouted. "Can you hear me?"

No answer. I caught the distant thump of footsteps, seemingly right below me. I ran down a hall, into the tub room and through to the room with the straitjacket rocking chair. Isolde was there, bound and moaning, blood dripping from her mouth and eye sockets. I ran right past her to the hatch in the floor, and when I reached it, I didn't bother with the ladder. I crouched, grabbed the sides, and swung through. My arm jerked, pain ripping through. I let go and hit the floor. My ankle twisted, but I forced myself up onto my feet, and as I did, I looked up to see . . .

A solid ceiling. The hatch was gone. I blinked and looked down and there, to my left, were the damned cribs again. Fingers poked out between the slats.

I tore from the room and stopped in the hallway. I stood there, eyes squeezed shut, struggling against panic.

There is no escape from the prison of the mind.

Oh hell, yes, there was. And if one way didn't work, I'd find another.

I took out my cell and speed-dialed. I'd meant to try Ricky again, but when I heard the line ringing, I knew that wasn't who I'd called.

"This is Gabriel Walsh. Please leave a message . . ."

I rocked on my toes as I waited for the beep.

"Gabriel? It's Olivia. I know you're pissed off with me, but listen. Please listen. I need you. You promised—" I sucked in breath. *No, don't remind him of that. Don't whine and accuse.* "I need you. Not to come here. Not to do anything but pick up the phone and talk to me. I'm at the psych hospital and I'm . . . I'm lost." A short laugh, laced with panic. "I'm lost in so many ways. Ricky's here, and I can't find him, and it's some kind of magic. I'm trapped with these visions, and if this keeps up, I . . . I feel like I'm going crazy, Gabriel. Maybe I am. You seemed to think so, and . . . Hell, tell me that. Just pick up the phone and tell me it's all in my head. Talk me through it or snap me out of it. I don't care. Just pick up or call back. Please." I paused, then shut my eyes and let the words out, not caring how desperate and sad they sounded. "I need you."

I hung up, and I waited. And Gabriel did not call back.

TOO LITTLE, TOO LATE

Gabriel was not dreaming, but it was perhaps the closest he'd ever come. The images spooling through his sleeping mind were still memories, yet bits and pieces of them, strung together like a clumsily tied rope of mismatched cloth.

He started in the car, the night before, telling Olivia she was imagining things, as a voice in his head yelled at him to stop, just stop, what the *fuck* was he doing, but he kept saying it, and when he saw the shock and pain in her eyes, he was glad of it. Satisfaction and shame, roiling together. Then they were back in Evans's basement, his leg bleeding as he told her to get out, escape while she could, that he wouldn't stay for her. She said she didn't care. And she didn't. It wasn't about tit for tat, helping him because he'd do the same for her. She'd believed he would have left her, and yet she'd stayed for him.

At the car now, the burning car, the girl—Macy—ordering Olivia to climb into it or she'd shoot him. Later, standing by his window, sharing a drink, he'd had to make sure Olivia crawled into that burning car only because she knew Gabriel would get the jump on Macy.

"Mmm, not exactly. But I had a plan."

"Good. Don't put yourself at risk for anyone, Olivia. Ever. It isn't worth it."

In his car again, telling her she was imagining things, saying exactly the words that would hurt her the most. *You're delusional.* Laughing when she said they were friends. That voice in his head screaming for him to stop, but a louder, more determined one prodding him on. *You have to do this. Disillusion her. Teach her not to trust anyone, especially you. Hurt her a little now, and you'll save her that pain later.*

He wasn't her fairy prince. The idea was ludicrous. If she expected him to ride in and rescue her . . .

Except she didn't expect that. She never had. And that wasn't what Gwynn had done anyway, was it? No knight-in-shining-armor there, but a selfish bastard who didn't even have the guts to try to win Matilda from Arawn. He'd betrayed his friend. Betrayed his lover. Forced Matilda to choose when she already had. Gwynn refused to share her time or attention. He'd lied and manipulated and betrayed everyone he supposedly cared about, because he didn't really care about anyone except himself.

And Gabriel said he *wasn't* Gwynn?

But that was their choice, wasn't it? That's what Olivia meant—they weren't really Matilda and Gwynn and Arawn. Olivia was no flighty girl, believing Gabriel's lies, accepting his betrayals. Ricky wasn't simply her friend, and he wasn't the arrogant Lord of the Underworld, either—he cared about Olivia and he respected her, and if Gabriel ever suggested the kind of pact Gwynn had with Arawn, Ricky would tell him to go to hell.

Ricky and Olivia had broken from their roles. And Gabriel . . . ?

The memory changed. He was standing in his bedroom doorway, Olivia sitting up in his bed, her eyes wide from whatever she'd been dreaming. No, not *whatever*.

"You left," she said, *"and I didn't know why. I was trapped in the dark, and I couldn't get out, and I called and you wouldn't come."*

"I wouldn't do that."

The memory shifted. He was eating dinner tonight. He couldn't even remember what it was—takeout bought at a drive-thru, mechanically eaten as he'd sat at the table, staring at a pile of papers and pretending to read. Then his phone rang.

Olivia's ring tone. She'd set it up a week ago. They'd been talking when a client called, and he'd gotten annoyed because he'd had to pause the conversation long enough to check his call display.

"You need ring tones," she said. "So you'll know if it's important without needing to take two entire seconds to check."

"Do you really think I know how to set a ring tone?"

She'd put out her hand. A few minutes of tapping and she handed his phone back. "One for Rose and one for Lydia. One for Don, too, as your premier client. One for Ricky, because he'd feel left out otherwise. And, of course, one for me, so you'll know I'm bugging you, and you can ignore it."

Which would never happen. That's what he'd thought, with an oddly warm feeling. *I'll know it's you, and I'll always answer.*

Now the phone rang, her ring tone, a jaunty little tune that reminded him of Olivia in a good mood, chipper and bouncy. It rang and it rang, and he did not answer.

Back to the bedroom.

"Anytime you need me, I'm here," he said. *"If you call, I'll come."*

"I know."

She'd called once more after that. Late, as he was in bed, trying to sleep. He'd heard it ring, and he'd rolled over and waited for it to go to voice mail. He didn't check the message. Nor had he checked the last one. Ignoring voice mail, texts, and e-mail. Getting his distance. That was best for both of them.

Because I am Gwynn, and I can't escape it. He destroyed her, and he loved her. I'll destroy you and . . .

He fell into the memory again, Olivia sitting up in bed, eyes wide as he assured her he'd never fail her. He'd always be there for her. Always, always, always.

"Gabriel!"

He shot upright, as if he'd been only dozing. He blinked and peered around the room. The dark and empty room.

I was trapped in the dark, and I couldn't get out, and I kept calling and you wouldn't answer.

His phone started to ring. It wasn't her ring tone, but he'd gotten another call, not long after the first one this evening, from a number he hadn't recognized, and he'd answered and heard nothing, and known it was her.

But this time, call display showed a client's name. He hit Ignore and flipped to his voice messages. He was going to listen. He should have listened, damn it. Just in case.

As the first message played, his heart picked up speed with every word. Tristan? The hospital? Goddamn it, yes, that was a trap, and she shouldn't have gone without him.

And how the hell was she supposed to know that when you wouldn't answer your fucking telephone? Besides, she has Ricky.

That didn't matter. Yes, Ricky would look after her, but no matter how much he knew, he didn't really understand. He couldn't.

How many times over the last week had Gabriel felt that kernel of jealousy grow, felt that Ricky was taking everything, leaving nothing that was his alone? This was. Ricky didn't understand the magnitude of the situation, of the danger, the threat, because if he did, he'd be on that phone himself, telling Gabriel to quit his sulking and get the hell down there to help her.

Gabriel rolled out of bed and grabbed his trousers from the chair.

Now you're going to help her? Three hours after she called? Much too little, much too late, and you know it.

That's when he remembered the second message. Calling to tell him it was all right? Situation resolved?

He played the message, and when he finished listening, he pounded in her number, punching the keys so hard that he kept striking two at once.

It's been an hour. A goddamn hour. She needed you, and you rolled over and went back to sleep.

The phone rang once. He exhaled, eyes closed, waiting to hear her voice telling him it was fine, she was fine, they were fine. *And by the way, Gabriel? Get the fuck out of my life and stay there.*

The line clicked.

"I'm sor—" he began.

A computerized voice intoned, "The customer you are trying to reach is not available. Please—"

He grabbed his shirt and raced out the door.

Gabriel strode down the corridor of the main hospital building. That seemed to be where Olivia had called from, if he was inferring correctly. No, not inferring. Not deducing, either. He was worried enough to strip away those logical explanations and admit the truth to himself.

I know she's here. I just know it.

As for "where" here, well, that was the problem. He'd tried

calling on the drive. Tried Ricky, too, only to get the same "customer unavailable" message.

He climbed to the second floor, and when he walked along the main corridor, a board creaked overhead. A footstep sounded, then another.

So where the hell were the stairs? He continued down the hall and found them. Broken steps, half the treads rotted, but footprints on the remaining ones. As he climbed, he saw someone passing in the hall above. The figure stopped.

"Gabriel. Thank God. I— Whoa! Stop!" Ricky's hand shot out, palm up. "That whole stair is rotted. I already put my foot through it. Step over it to the next one."

Gabriel grunted and did that. "Where's Olivia?"

"I was hoping you'd tell me. She's here. I *know* she's here."

That knot of jealousy tightened. *Of course he knows, too.*

"What happened?"

"We were talking outside, in this little graveyard, and the next thing I know, she's walking toward this building. I go to grab her and it's like grabbing air, and all of a sudden she's ten feet ahead of me, and when I get in here, she's gone completely. I know something like that happened with you, so I went back out and waited, figuring I hadn't really seen her leave. When she didn't reappear, I came in. Only I can't find her, and it's been two damned hours. I've scoured every inch of this place."

Gabriel nodded. "We'll do it again. Systematically, room by room."

"That's what I did." That flash of annoyance Gabriel knew well. Ricky's don't-treat-me-like-a-child look. Which was never what Gabriel intended—he simply didn't trust anyone else's intelligence, which was perhaps equally insulting. Ricky's intelligence, like his maturity, was just fine. Unfortunately.

"Never mind," Ricky said. "You're right. We'll do it again. Reverse order this time. Starting up here. You search rooms while I stand in the hall. That way there's no chance she'll get past us accidentally."

While there was a niggle in Gabriel's gut that wanted to amend the plan, simply for the sake of amending it, he did as Ricky suggested, searching room by room, checking behind every item that could hide Olivia, unconscious. He didn't hear so much as a rat scuttling until he reached the belfry. That's when he caught a moan, half stifled, as if it had escaped unbidden, Olivia injured and gritting her teeth, trying not to cry out. Which is exactly what he'd expect of her, so much so that he didn't pause. He loped straight for the ladder and climbed up, ignoring Ricky's "Hey!" below.

Ricky's boots pounded as he ran into the room below the belfry. Gabriel was already at the top. The room was bigger than he'd expected, perhaps eight feet square. And empty. Completely empty.

He heard the moan again. Coming through a hole in the opposite wall. He started toward it.

"Whoa!" Ricky said. "Stop!"

Gabriel rocked there, shooting a look back at Ricky.

"Hey, don't glower at me, big guy. I'm not trying to stop you from finding her. I'm saving your ass *again*. Look down."

Gabriel did. Like the stairs, the floor was rotted, boards missing or half broken.

"I heard—" Gabriel began.

"Yeah, so did I. But you're a good thirty pounds heavier than me. Which means I'll be the one crossing the rotting floor and hoping I don't plummet to my doom."

He wants to rescue her. He wants to be the first face she sees.

Which was ridiculous. The floor was clearly rotted. Ricky was smaller. He'd stopped Gabriel from hurtling into danger twice and now offered to take the risk. Any competition existed only in Gabriel's mind, and he was ashamed of that.

He's doing it on purpose. Showing you up.

Gabriel growled softly and shook his head.

That was Gwynn. The part of him that was Gwynn ap Nudd. As Gabriel, he could look at Ricky and see someone he respected, trusted. An ally who could even be considered a friend. Then he'd think of Olivia, and jealousy would surge, sometimes more than jealousy, something bitter and hard, almost like hate.

That's not me.

Or is that just an excuse?

"You got my back?" Ricky asked.

"Of course."

Ricky started picking his way across the floor. The boards groaned and creaked with each step. One gave way, but he jumped off it fast enough. Then, as Ricky was still leaping over the broken board, something flew from the hole in the wall. Something bright and fast, flying toward Ricky, his switchblade rising with a "What the hell?" The thing hit him in the neck. Blood spurted. Ricky fell.

No, Ricky was *pushed*. Shoved hard toward the front railing. He hit it and it shattered, wood exploding as he fell through.

Gabriel lunged toward him, but the first plank he hit gave way, his foot falling into the hole, enough for him to stumble, and when he recovered, he could see Ricky's hands, grasping the edge of the floor.

"Gabriel!"

"Hold on. My foot . . ." He wrenched his leg. His foot was wedged into the hole. He bent and pulled at his shoe.

Are you sure you want to help him? This time the voice came, not from his head, but as a whisper, right at his ear. He turned and saw no one there.

Look at him. He's barely hanging on. He's bleeding badly. It's a four-story drop. The fall would likely kill him, and if it didn't, he'd bleed out before help came. All you need to do is stay right where you are. Or better yet, walk away. No one knows you were up here.

Gabriel managed to get his foot free. He took one careful step, calling, "Just hold on."

Is that really what you want? You're right. You aren't Gwynn. You don't have the balls to be Gwynn. You pride yourself on being a man of resolve. You see what you want and you go after it, everyone else be damned. This is what you want. Ricky, dead. Olivia, yours. And all you need to do is turn around and walk out.

He took another careful step forward.

Don't pretend you aren't thinking about it.

Gabriel tested the next board with his toe.

It's not safe. You should just stop. Stop and think about it. Imagine it. Ricky, dead. Olivia, yours.

He stopped. He imagined it. Ricky called for him, confused, but Gabriel stood there, lost in his thoughts.

Then he made his decision.

CHAPTER SIXTY

abriel never called back. I tried Ricky again but continued getting the "customer unavailable" message. In desperation, I dialed Gabriel's number forty minutes later,
only to find that I had no reception.

Maybe he tried to call.

That wasn't it. I'd checked for messages every few minutes as
I'd wandered the hospital, the endless halls and sequences of
rooms that only ever brought me back to the cribs. My phone
worked fine then.

When I realized he wasn't calling, I'd thought of dialing someone else. Anyone else. Hell, 911 if it would help.

Nine-one-one, what's your emergency?

I'm lost.

Where are you?

*In an abandoned hospital. I can give you directions, but I
don't think you could find me even if I did.*

I had to get myself out of this. Only I couldn't. Walk in any
direction and I ended up back with the cribs. I'd tried staying
there, in case there was more for me to see, trapped in a performance where the exit doors wouldn't open until the final cur-
tain call. But the same scenes had repeated over and over.

"Okay!" I finally shouted. "It was Pamela. Todd was the innocent one. I get it. And also, you'd like me to kill myself. I get that, too. Not happening!"

No one answered, of course. Ricky had long since stopped shouting for me, if it ever had been Ricky at all, and not just a phantom voice. If it hadn't been Ricky, where was he? Was he all right?

Those were just the kind of thoughts that sent my brain flapping madly, like a bird in a too-small cage. I'd told Gabriel that I felt as if I might go mad in here. I'd been trying to joke—hey, if it gets any worse, I'll *belong* here, *permanently*, heh-heh—but it was no joke. I kept thinking about Isolde and seeing those words, feeling the truth of them, along with the very possible truth that I wasn't in the hospital at all but had already gone mad, and that's why Ricky wouldn't answer and Gabriel wouldn't call back. I was trapped in the prison of my mind, and there was, indeed, no escape.

Finally, I did what I would have sworn I'd never do.

I gave up.

I stayed in that crib room as long as I could bear it, until I was certain there was no more to see. I walked in every direction, only to end up where I'd started. Then I walked into the hall and sat. Just sat, because for the first time in my life there was honestly nothing I could do, no action that would fix this, and that was, perhaps, the surest sign that I was, in fact, losing my mind.

My surrender didn't last for long. I'm not sure if that's a sign of sanity or sheer bullheaded insanity, banging my head against a brick wall and expecting it to crumble before I dashed out my brains. I redid the circuit, taking every possible route out of the crib room, only to end up back there. On my fourth return visit, I stepped inside to see a figure with his back to me.

I knew who it was. There was no disguising that back. God

knows, I'd stood behind it often enough. The white shirt was rumpled. The shoes were brown . . . under black trousers. But there was still no denying who it was. Or who it was *supposed* to be.

Gabriel turned as my sneaker squeaked. When he saw me, his shoulders sagged, as if he'd been holding his breath. Then, "There you are," with a note of impatience, as if I'd waltzed off five minutes ago. Maybe that should have told me it was really him, but I'd been in this place too long, seen too much that wasn't there.

"What's the first Sherlock quote you said to me?"

"What?" His brow furrowed. Then, "You've been having visions, and you think I'm one of them."

No shit, I wanted to say, but I waited until he said, "*The game's afoot.*" A twist of a smile. "Although, if I admit to it, that might seem proof it can't really be me."

"I'll take it. Okay, so you're here." I glanced around. "You know the way out, I hope."

From the look I got, this wasn't the reaction he expected. And what *did* he expect? That I'd break down sobbing in gratitude that he'd finally come looking for me? Maybe that's unfair. I *was* grateful, but I couldn't forget that he'd taken almost two hours to reply to my frantic call for help.

Gabriel used to be very clear that I couldn't rely on him. If we'd stuck with that, then I *would* be grateful right now. But I'd blurted that nightmare to him, one that now seemed more premonition than dream, and three times he'd told me it was wrong. Three times he'd said he would never ever ignore me if I needed help. That was why I blamed him—not for failing to run to my rescue, but for telling me that he would.

"You haven't seen Ricky, have you?" I said. "I lost him when all this started and . . ."

I trailed off as I saw his expression.

"Something happened," he said. "Ricky . . ."

"Is he hurt?"

I hung there, waiting for that expression to disappear in a blink as he saw I was freaking out, for him to say, *No, nothing like that.*

But the look did not change.

"Gabriel?"

"There was . . . an accident."

"But he's all right?"

"He was when I left, but . . ."

"*Left?*" I strode into the hall. "You left him?"

"To get help, Olivia. We should go and phone for—"

"You go. After you tell me where the hell Ricky is."

"The belfry."

I started to run. Every other time I'd gone that way, I'd never found the stairs. But now the hall kept going, exactly as it should, the stairs ahead. Gabriel thundered after me, saying, "Hold on."

I swung onto the stairs.

"They're rotted!" he called after me.

I ran up, moving fast enough that when one gave way, it broke after my weight was on the next. Gabriel kept calling after me, telling me to stop or at least slow the hell down. He actually said "hell," which was probably code for *I'm serious.* I did exactly what he'd spent the day doing to me: I ignored him.

I found the belfry ladder. When I reached the top, the first thing I saw was blood. It arced across the wall and dripped onto the floor. The belfry railing was broken. A hole in it, just the size for someone to have fallen through, with fresh jagged splinters on both sides.

"Ricky!" I started running toward the hole.

"Olivia! Stop!" It was Gabriel. "The floor—"

My foot hit a hole, and I stumbled. As I did, I saw Ricky, unconscious, propped against the wall, his neck bound with strips from his shirt, the rest discarded beside him. His chest rose and fell with steady breathing.

I took a step in that direction.

"Careful!" Gabriel said, his voice harsh as he crested the steps.

I picked my way toward Ricky.

"We thought we heard you up here, and something attacked him," Gabriel said. "It cut his neck and knocked him through the railing. Luckily, he caught the edge. I hauled him back in and bound his neck. When I left, he was conscious but weak from loss of blood. Is his breathing—?"

"It's all strong," I said, putting my hands to his chest.

Gabriel exhaled. "Good."

As he crossed the floor, I saw why he'd been slow coming after me. He was limping—badly.

"You're hurt," I said.

He gestured at the hole in the floor. "It's the same leg I injured before. It's just acting up. I'm fine."

It was doing more than *acting up*. Pain flashed in his eyes with each step.

"I'll go for help," I said.

He shook his head. "I don't want you getting trapped again."

"I think that's over," I said. "And from the looks of it, if you take another flight of stairs, you'll end up at the bottom. Keys."

"I can handle—"

"Give me your damn keys, Gabriel. Someone's blocking cell service in here, and I may need to drive to get a signal. The longer you argue, the worse Ricky is going to get, and—"

He handed over the keys.

"Now sit," I said. "There. And don't move."

At a pained quirk of his lips, I hesitated, and then said, "I'm glad you're here. I'm sorry if I didn't say—"

"You don't need to. I'm the one who's sorry, Olivia." He met my gaze. "For everything."

I nodded. He looked away then, lowering himself to the floor beside Ricky and saying, "There, I'm sitting. Now go on."

CHAPTER SIXTY-ONE

At the bottom of the steps, I hesitated. I fingered my gun and switchblade. I should have given one to Gabriel. At the very least, I should have told him to take out Ricky's knife. He'd said something attacked Ricky, which meant we weren't alone here.

I was considering going back up when I heard Gabriel's voice, so distant I had to strain to pick it up.

"I know you're there," he said.

I slowly climbed three steps.

"Stop hiding in the shadows," he said. "I'm not the one who sees visions and hears voices. I know you're there. Come out."

I quietly picked my way past the rotted steps.

"Are you sure that was me, Gabriel?" a man's voice said. "I suspect it sounded a lot like that little inner devil you humans seem to have, the one that sits on your shoulder and whispers all the things you want to do and know you shouldn't."

"That's called a conscience," Gabriel said. "Mine might be underdeveloped, but I recognize its voice perfectly well."

The man laughed. "No, boy. That's not conscience. It's cowardice. Which is much the same with your kind. You tell yourself you should not, when in truth you only dare not."

I knew that voice. It was exactly who I expected to find here: Tristan.

I continued down the hall, painfully slowly, testing each step first, for the rotted boards and to keep silent.

"I'm not going to kill Ricky," Gabriel said, and I stopped dead, my heart pounding. "You can whisper all you like. I'm not Gwynn."

"No, boy. You don't have the balls."

"If you think that will provoke me, then you understand me much less than you believe. I might be Gwynn's representative in this drama. I'll accept that. I'll even accept that there's more to it than that, that part of me *is* Gwynn. But the whole is not, and that's a choice I am free to make."

"Pretty speech, but you aren't in front of a judge here, Gabriel. I've already rendered my judgment and delivered my verdict."

"Arawn dies at Gwynn's hands. Something tells me you don't want peace after all. What a surprise."

"My, you are cynical. Your darling Matilda bought it quite handily." Tristan's voice took on that earnest tone from the lake. "*I just want everyone to get along. Give peace a chance.*" His voice reverted to normal. "You didn't believe me for a second. Too bad you didn't tell her that. So, Mr. Walsh, attorney-at-law, tell me, what's my real plan? Let's see that illustrious mind at work."

"Chaos. That is your plan. Your only plan. You set James against me to separate me from Olivia. When that failed, you decided to remove me from the picture. But you can't kill me. You don't dare provoke the Tylwyth Teg like that. So you murdered James and framed me. I did consider the possibility you were working for the Cŵn Annwn, since all your plans involved removing me. But the fact that you're now ordering me to kill Ricky proves the Cŵn Annwn are innocent in this scheme. Which means your plan is, as I said, chaos. War, to be precise. The Tylwyth Teg already blame the Cŵn Annwn for my arrest. Then the Cŵn Annwn would blame them for Ricky's death. You take both of us away from Olivia, and you set the two local fae factions at war, with their so-called champions both lost."

Gabriel had been raising his voice for each of his speeches. Nothing obvious, just enough that, if I was still in earshot, I might pick it up. It also helped to muffle my footsteps as I returned, picking up speed as he talked, then slowing when he stopped.

"Would you like to know your next step, too?" Gabriel continued, in that same unhurried way, as if he were indeed in front of a judge, and the case wasn't really all that important.

"Please."

"Your attempt to play on my sense of competition failed, so you will now appeal to a stronger motivation: my sense of self-preservation. You're holding a gun on me. You'll threaten to pull that trigger unless I reach over and . . . strangle him? Yes, I suppose that would work best, though I'd need to remove the bandages first, so my fingerprints will be on his neck, leaving no doubt that I killed him."

A short laugh. "If you really expect me to believe you'll give in that easily, you think me a fool, boy. You would kill him to save yourself, but the prospect of life in jail is going to give you pause. No, you're stalling, waiting for . . ."

Tristan swung on me, poised at the top of the ladder. He pointed the gun. "You both think you're clever, but you're still human. There are limits and—"

Gabriel sprang—his leg obviously not as bad as he'd pretended. He snatched the gun from Tristan's hand. "No, I don't believe there are limits. Not to fae arrogance, that is."

Tristan laughed. "Do you think that will hurt me? Go ahead. Shoot. See what happens."

"Nothing," Gabriel said. "My goal was simply to stop you from pointing it at her."

I lunged and buried my blade between Tristan's shoulders. We both went down, me on him.

"That won't kill you, either," I said. "But it will slow you down. Particularly with this." I rammed a nail into the hole. He snarled and bucked.

"Iron," I said. "Again, it won't kill you. But there is a grain of truth in the lore." I leaned over to his ear. "I had a little chat with someone about *spriggans* today. He wouldn't tell me how to kill fae—probably afraid I'd use it on him—but he did tell me how to incapacitate one. Cold-forged iron. Or regular iron inserted under the skin. Seems to work quite well."

"You two do love to talk, don't you?" Tristan snarled under me.

"It's genetic. So let's keep talking. Yes, the Tylwyth Teg would suspect the Cŵn Annwn killed James and framed Gabriel, but that's complicated. Having Gabriel kill Ricky is a much better guarantee of chaos. So why start with James?"

"I'm sure I had a reason," Tristan said. "Or perhaps someone else did. Someone with a slightly different agenda. Someone whose allegiance I could use."

"Pamela."

I didn't think before I said her name. It just came out, and as soon as I heard it, I expected him to laugh. Which he did. But it was not the laugh I wanted to hear.

"Pamela?" He feigned shock. "Your sweet, wrongly accused, deeply devoted mother? Whatever would make you say that?"

Yes, Pamela was the one responsible for the Valentine Killer murders. In my gut, I knew that was true. The pain of that was alleviated by the conviction that she'd done what she thought best. She'd done it for me. But this? This was like a right hook to the gut, leaving me gasping inside, screaming I was wrong, even as I knew I was not.

Pamela hated Gabriel. Even the fact that he represented her best chance of freedom didn't help. She hated fae, too, and recognized that blood in Gabriel. Moreover, he was their champion. She wanted to hurt the Tylwyth Teg and to wrest me from their clutches. Framing Gabriel would do both.

What had Tristan told me in his message? Check Pamela's visitor log. Tipping his hand in arrogance, delighting in pointing me in the right direction, knowing I wouldn't find him there because he'd used an alias.

"Pamela conspired with you to kill James and frame Gabriel," I said. "I don't know if you had anything to do with Ricky beating James, but if not, I'm sure it was an added bonus, throwing extra confusion in the mix. Mutilating James to match Pamela's victims threw a little confusion in there, too."

"Bravo," Tristan said. "Guilty as charged—on all counts, though I suspect dear Pamela won't appreciate my saying so. There's very little of your father in you, Eden. Poor Todd, always trying to do the right thing, a coward hiding behind the cloak of conscience. Like your mother, you'll do whatever it takes to protect those you love. I think you and I can come to an agreement, as long as I promise not to harm your darling boys."

"I don't need your promise. You're right, I'll protect them— by myself, as my mother did for me. I'm my father, too, though. I can worry that my voice of conscience is too soft, but it's loud enough that I want nothing to do with you and your plans. Here's mine. Once I get help for Ricky, you're coming with us— to the Tylwyth Teg or the Cŵn Annwn or whoever wants to deal with you. So—"

"Actually, I believe I can simplify this next step," said a voice from the ladder. Patrick pulled himself up, fastidiously wiping his hands on his trousers as he stepped into the room. "Tristan, good to see you—particularly in that position. You've caused a lot of trouble, and I'm going to win a heap of gratitude turning you over to the elders." He looked at me. "Don't worry. I know you don't trust me enough to turn him over so easily. Gabriel will accompany me back to Cainsville with Tristan, while you take care of the boy."

Patrick walked over and looked down at Tristan. "Nicely done, Liv. You took my instruction well. After both you and Gabriel called today, asking about *spriggan*, I knew something was up. Fortunately, Gabriel was more forthcoming with a name. Tristan's associate, Alis, supplied the rest after some effort. She told me where to find you. I arrived just in the nick of time, before anyone got hurt." He looked at Ricky. "Well, close enough."

Patrick smiled at me, very pleased with himself. It wasn't only the elders he wanted to win gratitude from.

I pretended not to be impressed, and said only, "Gabriel's hurt, too. He'll be fine to accompany you, but he can't carry Ricky. That'll be your job."

His brows shot up. I hauled Tristan to his feet and led him out.

CHAPTER SIXTY-TWO

After Patrick finished with Tristan, "Jon Childs" turned himself in and confessed, and Patrick promised that Tristan would give the police evidence they needed to be certain he murdered James.

The next day, I went to the jail to confront Pamela.

Pamela now. Not my mother. Maybe never again my mother.

I didn't know how to process what Tristan said she'd done. I wanted to say it wasn't true. He was fae—he couldn't be trusted. But I knew it was true. In my gut, I knew.

Gabriel drove me to the jail, but I left him outside. This I had to do alone.

I don't remember walking into that room. Don't remember sitting. I do remember Pamela coming out, that moment when a two-year-old girl in my soul screamed, *How could you?* and I had to squeeze my eyes shut, clench my fists, banish that girl, and remember I was not Eden Larsen. I was Olivia Taylor-Jones. My mother was Lena Taylor. My ex-fiancé was James Morgan, deceased. My boss—and, yes, friend—was Gabriel Walsh, framed for a murder he did not commit. Framed by the woman sitting in front of me.

"I know everything," I said as she sat.

444 • KELLEY ARMSTRONG

She sighed. That was her reaction. A sigh, and a shake of her head, as if I were a child coming to her with some vicious rumor. "I don't know what you mean, Olivia, but whatever it is—"

"It was you. Not Todd. Pamela Larsen. Not my dad."

And that, perhaps, was the second-worst thing I could have said to her, the way I phrased that, and she flinched, and then I added the worst, a lie I needed to tell: "Dad confessed . . . after I told him how you tried to blame him."

Pamela reeled then, and all I could think was, *Good. I'm glad I hurt you, for all the ways you hurt them: my father, James, Gabriel. And me. Yes, for all the ways you've hurt me.*

"You think you did it for me," I said. "But you know what wasn't about me? James."

"Wh-what?"

I lowered my voice so the guard across the room wouldn't hear. "You conspired with Tristan to kill James and frame Gabriel."

It took her a moment to say, "I don't know what you mean," and that moment's hesitation answered any remaining question I had.

"Gabriel was your best shot at freedom," I said, struggling against the rage that swirled through me. "He would have gotten you out. *We* would have—Gabriel and I, together. You screwed yourself over. You get that, don't you?"

She shook her head, and I understood then. I understood that it didn't matter. That her hatred of fae was pathological, and it wasn't so much because Gabriel was part fae—so was she—but that his role, as Gwynn, was to bring me to the Tylwyth Teg, and she could not allow that. As for freeing her, she didn't believe that would happen, not really. After all, she was guilty. I suspected she'd only rehired him to keep him close enough to watch and to have some control over him, as leverage to separate him from me, which had failed. Step two, then, was more permanent.

"Why James?" I said, forcing as much calm into my voice as I could muster. "What did he do?"

"He was obsessed with you. I saw that when he came to speak to me. I didn't mean for that *spriggan* to kill him. I only wanted him hurt enough to scare him off."

"And then frame Gabriel for the assault."

"Yes. Assault, not murder."

"Then Tristan did kill James. You were horrified. You confessed to me what happened, told me he planned to frame Gabriel and you couldn't let that happen because it went too far, much too far. Oh, wait. No. That's not how it happened."

"I . . ."

"I don't know if you planned for James to die or not, but you knew it was a possibility, and when he did, you continued as planned. One innocent man died and another was due to spend his life in prison for the crime."

"Gabriel is not an innocent man, Olivia. Far from it. The sooner you realize that, the better off you will be." She leaned in. "He wouldn't have gone to prison anyway. He's too good a lawyer for that."

"James is still dead."

"Yes, and that is a tragedy, but I had nothing—"

"James is still dead!" I spat, leaning across the table, Pamela falling back, the guard across the room shooting forward. I moved back and the guard stopped.

"James was innocent," I said, my voice barely above a whisper now, the pain too great. "And he is dead, and as far as I am concerned, you are responsible for that, as much as if you'd put your hands around his neck yourself."

I stood and I turned away, and as I did, she got to her feet. "Olivia, no. Please. I can explain."

I walked to the door. "Olivia," she called. "Please."

I opened the door, and as it closed behind me, I heard her shout, "Eden!" and I kept walking.

I was now permitted to see Todd. The prison officials explained it had been an "administrative miscommunication," which I interpreted to mean there'd been some magic at work, likely Tristan's.

On my way into the waiting room, I'd grabbed a tissue, but if I did cry, it wasn't going to do me much good, because by the time that door opened, it was shredded on my lap, my fingers still pulling apart every scrap big enough to shred.

Todd walked over, that tentative *I'm not sure of my welcome* smile playing on his lips. When I smiled, he returned it and slid into his seat.

"Hey, there," he said.

"Hey."

He glanced at Gabriel, standing over by the wall. "Tell him to grab a chair."

"He'd rather stand."

"Loom, you mean."

I smiled again. "Exactly. More intimidating." I took a deep breath. "I know the truth. I know who did it, and I know why, and I know it wasn't you." I met his gaze. "It was Pamela. All Pamela."

Todd jerked back. "What? No. Whoever told you that—"

"She did. I figured it out, and she admitted it."

"Then she's lying."

"She's not, though I'll admit she's very good at it. You, on the other hand? You need to work on your technique, Dad."

He'd opened his mouth to protest. Then, realizing what I'd called him, he froze. His mouth worked and then stopped as his eyes glistened and he shook his head. "Shit."

"Yep," I said.

"Whatever she said, I'm sure she exaggerated to protect me."

"She blamed you."

"She—?"

"She told me you were the one who did it. That she was the guilt-stricken conscientious objector who went to prison to protect you and support your actions."

He stared, and I almost wished I could pull the words back. He didn't deserve that. But he hadn't deserved any of it, and that was why I had to plow on, however much it hurt him.

"She . . . she must have had a reason. A plan." He gave a twisted smile. "Your mother always has a plan."

"I know," I said. "And sometimes, as much as she thinks she's protecting the ones she loves, she hurts them. Hurts them so much."

"She doesn't mean it."

"Maybe, but we need to stop making excuses for her. It's time for you to tell the truth."

"What?" He blinked hard. "No. We have an appeal. Gabriel will—"

"No, Gabriel won't. Not for her. Even if he did, freedom is far from a guarantee. I want a guarantee. For *you*."

"Your mother . . ."

"There's more." I told him what she'd done: ordering James's death and framing Gabriel.

When I finished, he seemed to have aged ten years, his face sagging, his eyes dark with pain.

"I know that in some twisted way she was trying to protect me," I said. "But she killed someone I loved and tried to destroy someone else I care about very much. There is no justifying that."

He dipped his head in a slow nod.

"I know you feel you owe her, for what she did for me, but I think you've repaid that. You've repaid it and repaid it, and even if you still love her, you don't owe her a thing." I crumpled the remains of the tissue in my hand. "And I want you back. I really want you back."

He tore his gaze from mine. "I will tell the truth," he said. "But first, I need to let Gabriel work his magic, try to free me without turning on her."

"What? No. Gabriel's good, but I want guarantees, Dad. I need a guarantee."

"Even my telling the truth doesn't guarantee anything, sweetheart. If the appeal fails, I'll do it. But you need to give me this chance, Liv. Whatever she's done, I need to try it this way first."

CHAPTER SIXTY-THREE

Gabriel never told me why he'd taken so long to answer my calls for help. He had come, eventually, and I guess to him that was enough. Which told me what I needed to know. That he was there for me, in his way and on his time. I needed to come to terms with that.

I was there for him, no matter what. He did not need to reciprocate. Those were our choices, and I wasn't going to change mine because it didn't match his. He *had* come for me. He'd come in the middle of the night, with a wrinkled and misbuttoned shirt and the wrong shoes. The commitment was there, even if it didn't match my own.

I did bring it up once, in the few days that followed. We were at lunch, and I said, "About that night, on the beach, with Tristan," and Gabriel tensed fast. I said, "I'm sorry I didn't tell you about Gwynn sooner," and he relaxed, brushing it off with, "That's fine."

"No, it's not," I said. "But I wasn't sure how to broach it. Ricky found out by accident, and then we discussed it, and he agreed with me that you might not take it well."

"Which I did not."

"We weren't going to hide it forever. Just until we figured out how to handle it. We agreed that if there was a chance you'd find out, though, we'd tell you. With Tristan, I tried to get you out of there to explain. It didn't work. So I apologize."

He stuck his fork into a piece of sausage and pushed it across his plate before answering. "I would have liked to hear it from you, but I understand your reasoning, and I believe my reaction showed that your presumptions were correct. I handled it poorly." He cleared his throat. "What I said about the visions, that you were hallucinating. I didn't mean that. I—"

"I know."

He nodded. More sausage pushing. Another throat clearing. "The rest. When you said we were friends, and I laughed. I was angry. We are. I hope you know that."

He didn't say *We are friends*. Just "We are," as if the word itself was too difficult. But it was enough, and I nodded, and he changed the subject quickly, as if relieved to push past and move on.

We *were* friends. I've always said that being more than friends with Gabriel would be a very bad idea. That I was certain other women had hoped to break through his wall, and I wouldn't fall into that trap. That I'd be happy with friendship. But there's a difference between knowing a thing and accepting it. Now I accepted it.

The police dropped the charges against Gabriel. They'd lost Jon Childs when he vanished from jail a few days after being arrested. He hadn't escaped. He'd been "dealt with," as the Cŵn Annwn promised. But his incarceration, however brief, had been enough for the police to decide Gabriel wasn't responsible. They'd even dropped James's assault charges—a little hard to pursue now that their chief witness was dead. So Gabriel was free *and* on his way to overturning Todd's life sentence, which meant business was booming, with a dozen new client hopefuls for every one he'd lost.

Two weeks later, I was getting ready to leave work early. I wore jeans, an old T-shirt, and an equally old denim jacket. Even my new ankle boots, while gorgeous, did not make the outfit business-friendly, or even business-casual. I'd only popped in for some job-tidying before Ricky picked me up for our trip.

Gabriel and I had come up with a "schedule of availability"— times when he could contact me on my vacation. Telling him *not* to wouldn't work. As I waited for Ricky's arrival text, I showed off my tattoo to Lydia, having just removed the bandage that morning. I had my foot up on her desk as she inspected it.

"Hurt?" she asked.

"Like a son of a bitch."

She laughed.

"Apparently, the closer you ink to bone, the more it hurts, but the less likely it is to look like crap in twenty years. Above the ankle seemed a good choice. Easily hidden, but not always hidden."

She took a closer look. "Ricky has the same one?"

"Matching tattoos would be a bit much. His is similar but different."

"In my day, we just exchanged class rings. This would have been so much more fun. Of course, considering the rate I went through boys, I don't think I'd have an inch of skin left."

I laughed and she looked up at me, voice softening. "Was he happy?"

I nodded.

"I bet he was." She settled back into her seat. "Normally, a couple of weeks alone on the road in the wilderness wouldn't be what I'd suggest for a young couple, but I think you'll do just fine."

I smiled as I tugged down my pant leg. "We'll survive."

"I hope so," Gabriel said behind us. "I'll have work waiting when you get back."

He headed to the coffee machine. As I put on my boot, he looked toward my ankle.

"Yes, I was showing off my tattoo," I said.

He selected a pod from the carousel and popped it into the brewer. "It's relatively discreet, I hope."

"Yes, sir, though I would point out that since I'm getting my private investigator license, it would be perfectly acceptable for me to have tats. I'm also thinking of a piercing or two."

He snorted and waited for his coffee. My phone chirped.

"That would be my ride," I said. "So long, and don't work too hard."

Lydia said goodbye. Gabriel apparently considered it redundant, having said it in his office, but he came out after me, murmuring, "Wait a moment."

He shut the door behind him and checked down the hall, making sure we were alone.

"Before you go," he said. "I wanted to assure you that Todd's appeal is my top priority."

"I know. Thank you."

He glanced toward the outer door, then adjusted his tie. "So everything is . . . all right?" The last word rose, question rather than statement.

"Everything's fine."

"And you and I? We're . . . fine?"

I smiled for him. "We are. I know this isn't the best time for a vacation, but—" It wasn't as if I was leaving for good. This was my job now, and we had plenty to do still, between setting my father free and figuring out how to handle the Matilda legend. Two weeks, and we'd be back at it. Together. That hadn't changed.

"No, no. You could use a break. I just . . ." He trailed off. Another phone chirp. Ricky telling me he was parked in the lane, not rushing me, but Gabriel said, "You should go."

"I'll see you in two weeks."

I got as far as the front door, my hand on it, when he said, "Olivia?"

I turned. He stood there, hands in his pockets.

"I . . ." he began. His gaze dropped to my ankle. Then he cleared his throat and straightened, pulling out his hands. He reached over and squeezed my upper arm, awkwardly but lingering as he said, "Take care of yourself and have a good vacation. You deserve it." He released my arm, gave a quarter smile, and headed back for his office.

I opened the front door. As I stepped out, I thought I felt Gabriel watching. I looked back, but he was already disappearing into the office. I paused, feeling the impulse to run after him, to ask if he'd wanted to say something more, to say anything, to hope that—

No, I'd made my decision. I couldn't keep questioning it. I just couldn't.

I took a deep breath and continued out to where Ricky waited.